STARLIGHT and STORM

Books by Rachel Greenlaw

For young adult readers:
Compass and Blade
Shadow and Tide
Starlight and Storm

For adult readers:
One Christmas Morning
The Woodsmoke Women's Book of Spells
The Ordeals

STARLIGHT *and* STORM

RACHEL GREENLAW

HARPER FIRE

First published in the United Kingdom by Harper Fire,
an imprint of HarperCollins *Children's Books*, in 2026
HarperCollins *Children's Books* is a division of HarperCollins*Publishers* Ltd
1 London Bridge Street
London SE1 9GF

www.harpercollins.co.uk

HarperCollins*Publishers*
Macken House, 39/40 Mayor Street Upper
Dublin 1, D01 C9W8, Ireland

1

Text copyright © Rachel Greenlaw 2026
Map and illustrations copyright © Daisy Davis 2024
Cover illustrations copyright © Nico Delort 2026
Cover design copyright © HarperCollins*Publishers* Ltd 2026
All rights reserved

ISBN: 978–0–00–866477–0
PB ISBN: 978–0–00–864264–8

Rachel Greenlaw asserts the moral right to be identified as the author of the work.

A CIP catalogue record for this title is available from the British Library.

Set in Berling LT Std by HarperCollins*Publishers* India

Printed and bound in the UK using 100% Renewable
Electricity at CPI Group (UK) Ltd

Conditions of Sale
This book is sold subject to the condition that it shall not, by way of trade
or otherwise, be lent, re-sold, hired out or otherwise circulated without the
publisher's prior consent in any form, binding or cover other than that in which
it is published and without a similar condition including this condition being
imposed on the subsequent purchaser. No part of this publication may be
reproduced, stored in a retrieval system or transmitted in any form or by any
means, electronic, mechanical, photocopying, recording or otherwise, without
the prior written permission of HarperCollins*Publishers* Ltd.

Without limiting the exclusive rights of any author, contributor or the
publisher of this publication, any unauthorised use of this publication
to train generative artificial intelligence (AI) technologies is expressly
prohibited. HarperCollins also exercise their rights under Article 4(3)
of the Digital Single Market Directive 2019/790 and expressly reserve
this publication from the text and data mining exception.

*For Rosie and Izzy, always.
And for Amelie, who read this first.*

Wild North
Arnhem
Highborn
Hail Harbour
Port Graine
Port Trenn
The Fortunate Isles
Finnikins Way
Ennor
Penscalo
The Far Isles
Rosevear
Penvith
Morgana
Leice

The Spines
THE CONTINENT
Innish Tar
Mines of Valstra
The Straits
Stanvard
Hafenged
Skylan
FIVE PRINCIPALITIES OF THE MIDDENWILDS
Nestra
Bergstat
Kir
Hindelmach
Lorra
Gelve
Mavena
The Southern Ocean

Chapter 1

Mira

MY WORLD IS A ROARING furnace. We were so close to freedom – *real* freedom. As the watch's stronghold on Penscalo went up in smoke, the captives who were set to hang were released. And it felt like an ending. A beginning. The watch couldn't hurt us any more. We had rid them from the sea and the land of the Fortunate Isles. We would rebuild on Rosevear. Ennor would be safe, all the Fortunate Isles would at last be safe. Eli would take his cousin Lowri, a witch, to his father's world, traverse between here and there, save her from burnout and finally meet his father. He would get the answers – the *closure* – he craved. And then he would return to me, and we would be together. The isles would prosper.

We would all be free.

But as we sailed away from Penscalo aboard *Phantom*, the witches appeared, too many of them, and that man with the pale hair and cruel features twisted with something akin to hunger spoke those chilling words . . .

You're mine.

I piece all of it together, our victory on Penscalo, then all of us sailing for Rosevear, for home. Eli leaving to cross to another world, then suddenly Seth . . . dead. Blood blooming from a bullet wound in his stomach. The boy who had betrayed me, who was shipwrecked on Rosevear's shores, who I saved . . . and who maybe, in time, I might have forgiven. Merryam, his cousin, screaming. They had only just reconciled. Mer, one of Eli's most trusted, had promised to vouch for him. Then a witch pressed a blade to Agnes's throat, my best friend, my sister in all but blood, her cries of pain slicing through me . . . but before I could reach for her, to save her, that witch with ice-blue eyes clamped a hand round my wrist. She whispered a witch word, *Inferna*.

Then all I knew was fire.

I had been taken by those witches, stolen away from aboard *Phantom* – I knew that much – and taken to the very heart of my enemy's stronghold.

'Mira? Mira, wake up!'

I burned all night, my mind trapped in flame and agony. But now, I blink my eyes open.

'The Trials begin in three days, Mira,' the boy says, eyeing me carefully. 'They captured us both.'

My breathing grows shallow and fast as the words beat in my temples, darkness nudging at the corners of my vision. I leap to my feet and take in my surroundings, go to the window. This room, with its view on to a courtyard far below, the patrolling guards in scarlet jackets, the rifles slung across their shoulders . . . it's the royal court.

I'm a captive in the ruling council's court in Highborn. Gripping the window ledge, I sweep my gaze over the room, taking it all in with swift blinks. Whitewashed walls, the sparsest of furnishings, a single bed. More a cell than a bedroom, but high in a tower, rather than in a basement. The boy stands a few feet away, watching me. I can't be here. I was aboard *Phantom*.

I was with my friends . . . We won. We had *won* . . .

'Did you say the Trials?' I ask, my voice coming out scratchy and wrong.

The boy nods. 'They must think you're special, like me. That you'll do well in the Trials, and that Arnhem will triumph and make the other rulers of the continent quake.' He shrugs, his words echoing around my skull, drawing me back to this room, to this place in which I'm trapped. 'We have no other choice but to do our best.'

The Trials are something for which no one on the isles ever ventured to Highborn to be put forward – not since the first call went out years back, and none of the hopeful contenders returned home. The rumours and whispers I've heard are that this is a series of challenges for which every territory on the continent puts forward contenders to represent them. It's all political. If a territory does well, they will get more favourable trade contracts or perhaps new alliances will form. The rulers and merchants meet while the Trials are happening, all gathering at court to watch the challenges along with the crowd. I shiver, head still thumping and tender from the witch's curse. But now the realisation of what lies ahead slowly creeps in.

'Or what?' I ask the boy, turning away from the window to face him. As the words draw up my throat, I taste ash on my tongue, as though I was indeed consumed by real flame.

'Or we could die.'

I haul in a breath, needing it to fill my lungs. Swallowing down that lingering taste of ash and magic, I sink to the cold floor and push the heels of my hands into my eyes. I need to think. My chest is too tight, thoughts flashing and fracturing. How did they get me here? How long have I been here? And the others . . . Agnes, Kai, Merryam, my crew aboard *Phantom* . . . my friends. What of them?

'My name is Kell,' the boy continues. 'They found me on the Far Isles. I was trying to leave with my guardian, Helene. It was becoming too hard to run our inn; we had no customers. We were trying to get to Leicena, where Helene is from, but we didn't have travel permits. The watch found us and then . . .' Kell looks away. 'Brielle told me not to show anyone what I could do, but when they put their hands on Helene I couldn't help it. They were going to hurt her.'

'Did you say Brielle? Brielle Tresillian?' I ask quickly, getting to my feet again.

Kell nods. 'Yes. Do you know her? She's a hunter from a coven in Highborn. I always cook for her. She visited recently, stayed at our inn and—'

Before he can finish his sentence, footsteps sound outside the room and the door bursts inwards, guards in scarlet jackets pouring in. I scramble backwards, spine jarring against the wall before two guards grab me.

'Just bring the girl. Escort the boy back to his room – he's not needed for this,' one of them says, and my gaze darts between them: a sea of scarlet coats, gold buttons blazing down their fronts, the Arnhem lion roaring from each and every one.

'Get your hands *off* me,' I grit out as hands clamp on my shoulders, shoving me towards the door. But it's no use – they're not listening, their features set in stern lines – and I'm pushed along the marble corridor, separated from Kell as the drumming of their boots rings in my ears.

A huge set of double doors comes into sight at the end of a hallway, swinging open ominously before I'm marched inside. The room is dazzlingly bright, all pale marble and white walls, with three gleaming silver thrones on a dais. A map of Arnhem and the continent blazes behind those thrones . . . behind the three men sitting on them. I realise with a jolt that the one on the left is the man I saw before that ice-eyed witch burned my mind with her magic.

You're mine . . .

As his gaze meets my own, I notice his eyes still have the same twist of feral hunger. I wonder if he's the man Agnes, Seth and I overheard speaking with Captain Leggan in the watch's stronghold on Penscalo before we were ambushed. If he's the one who toasted our downfall with Captain Leggan and spoke of a law to control all magic . . .

The ruling council.

I force down the panic suffusing my veins as the guards shove me to the ground, my knees barking in pain. The three men regard me, not saying a word, two of them propping up their chins on a fist, elbows resting on the arms of their thrones, like this is just an everyday occurrence, kidnapping a girl and forcing her to kneel before them. The panic in my blood turns like the tide and I see red.

'How utterly wonderful to have not one, but *two* champions from the isles,' the man in the middle says, breaking the silence, 'the Far Isles and the Fortunate Isles represented at the Trials. What a proud moment.' He's dressed in pale cream with gold thread embroidered over his jacket and breeches, just like the other two. They all look so similar; there isn't much to tell them apart. Then I realise, of course, that they're related. They have to be brothers. The ruling council, the rulers of our country, are brothers. 'We truly have excellent champions this year for the Trials—'

'I will *never* be your champion.'

'Now, now, Mira, dear, let's not talk in absolutes,' the man to the left says, tutting. That voice, it has to be him. He *was* the person toasting in the office with Captain Leggan, discussing that law, right before we left Penscalo. They're all smiling now, as if I'm being chided for a mishap, delighted with themselves. 'It is an honour to compete in the Trials, an honour to represent Arnhem. You should be proud—'

'I am *not* proud,' I say, raising my chin. 'I refuse to represent you.'

'Such strong words for a little monster . . .' the man on the right says with a smirk. 'Tiberius, shall we?'

Tiberius, in the middle, nods and signals to the guards surrounding me. 'Bring her in.'

There's a scuffling at my back, then a stifled shriek and my blood runs cold. I try to turn and see who it is, but the guards force me to stay facing the ruling council on their thrones. The sound of a body forced to its knees and a soft whimper prick my ears. I look to my left.

My heart stops.

Those eyes, smudged with tears. A deep bruise blossoming on her forehead. Her red, wild hair. A slip of fabric secured round her mouth.

Agnes.

I lunge for her, fighting the guards' grip. I take three steps before I'm tackled to the floor, the marble coming up to meet me, smacking me in the face. I lie there, bellowing, threats and curses curdling on my tongue, eyes on Agnes as she cries quietly, trying to struggle away from her own guards, trying to reach for me.

'That's quite enough,' Tiberius booms, voice shaking the hall.

I whip my head up to meet his gaze, narrowing my eyes, marking him as the man I will kill first. 'Release her. If you want me as your champion, you'll *let her go.*'

'Why would we do that when it's so clear how much she means to you?' the man on the right remarks calmly.

'Quite right, Otho,' Tiberius agrees. 'Allow her to kneel again. Come now, we're not brutes.'

The guards haul me back up, keeping their hands on my shoulders, and I face the ruling council once more on my knees. Every part of me is aware of Agnes, only a few feet away – a distance that right now seems insurmountable. I cool the fire in my heart, thinking fast. 'You have no need for her here. It's me you want to control.'

'On the contrary, my dear. We need you both very much for the Trials to fall in our favour,' the man on the left says.

I snap my gaze to the man in the middle as his features quirk into a vicious smile. Out of the three of them, he seems to be the one in charge, the one to whom the others defer. 'If you resist us, if you plot against us, Mira, if you do anything to erode our victory in the Trials, there will be consequences. For you, and for Agnes.'

He lifts his hand and a shadow lengthens across the room. It comes from his hand, crawling faster and faster, devouring the light in the hall, reaching out—

A scream rips from my throat as it lashes Agnes, and she begins to choke.

I struggle against the guards, desperate to save her, to stop those shadows from clawing down her throat, into her lungs.

She turns towards me, wide eyes brimming with fear, her throat constricting as she begins to thrash wildly.

'Stop!' I shout, my voice guttering into a sob. 'Please! Please stop! Please . . .'

All at once, the shadow dissolves and Agnes collapses to the floor, panting.

'You will find that the shadows your friend Elijah Tresillian commands are nothing compared to the ones at *our* fingertips,' Tiberius says, his voice cold and cruel and, I suddenly realise . . . old.

I turn slowly towards him, to the ruling council and really look at them. Their faces are as smooth as stone. Their eyes are cold, as though they've never known emotion or love or warmth . . . as though they are almost eternal. They wield the same magic as Eli. The same shadows curl around their fingertips.

It's impossible, it can't be real.

'How?' I manage.

'Elijah's father was not the first to discover this world.'

A roaring begins in my ears.

'Consider this a friendly reminder, Mira Boscawen,' Otho continues. 'Agnes will remain at court as our guest for the duration of the Trials. And if you are unsuccessful in securing glory for Arnhem, or try something so reckless as an escape . . .'

'We will not hesitate to crush all you love, beginning with her,' Tiberius booms. 'You and Kell will compete in the Trials as our champions. You will win and prove Arnhem's dominance against the territories of the continent. You will show that we are the superior nation, and they will bow before us. There is no room for failure. We *will* be victorious.' His features relax into something almost akin to a smile. 'Do you agree to our terms? Or shall we score them into your skin with a bargain mark?'

I bite my lip, even as my entire being trembles with barely contained rage. There is no room for negotiation, not with Agnes as their captive. Not without knowing what happened to the others aboard *Phantom* that day we were captured. For all I know, those witches stole them away too and I cannot risk a single one of them.

But when I work out how to escape, how to free Agnes from their grasp, and I will, there will be a reckoning. They will pay for this.

'Well?'

'Agreed,' I say, raising my chin, even as everything within me thrashes with defiance. 'I will be your champion.'

'Excellent,' Tiberius says. 'Now you must be thinking, why me? Why am I the fortunate chosen one?'

I remain silent, bracing myself.

'A girl of your talent, half siren, half human, and just like your mother.'

'A storm bringer,' Otho says quietly.

The man on the left smiles ravenously, leaning forward. 'The power to control and wield storms. Quite the ability.'

'Indeed, Nero,' Tiberius says, the smile dropping at once. 'Show us now, Mira, and Agnes will not suffer.'

I swallow, thinking quickly. It's no use denying it, not with Agnes here, an easy target for any form of punishment. 'I'm weak from the witch magic. I have not eaten . . .'

'Show us.'

'You will have to unhand me.'

Tiberius nods to the guards and their hands drop away from my shoulders. I roll them back and get to my feet, tilting my head to one side, then the other, calculating how far I'd get if I ran at the brothers. Could I take out all three? Just one, or maybe two of them before the guards tackled me?

'We're waiting, Mira,' Nero says softly.

I close my eyes and release a breath. It's no use. This isn't the time. So, instead, I lean into my fury. I curl around it, nurture it, then feel the trickle of magic as it suffuses me. As I call upon it. There's a dim rumble in the distance, but I cut it off. I don't want to reach that far. I cannot risk the people of Highborn, not when I'm so unsure of my strength and how much I can control.

'It appears she is not quite as powerful as we believed,' Otho says wearily.

I snap my eyes open, levelling them on him. Then I unfurl my fingers and will all my rage towards the dais. Lightning streaks from my palms, cutting grooves in the walls, in the marble floor, and I aim directly for Tiberius in the centre. He chuckles and then a shadow opens like a gaping wound, my lightning pouring into it, diverted through the opening he's made. I gasp, instantly closing my hands to fists, pouring cool on my anger, snuffing out my siren side.

But it's too late. Lightning cracks through the opening he's formed with his magic, and I see a glimpse of a village beyond. Farmland. People working the fields, a barn, homes . . .

The fork of lightning strikes the tallest building.

I drop to my knees, the horror of what I've done, what I've destroyed, instantly consuming me. The home begins to smoke, flames leaping and a woman rushes out, a child in her arms. Then the opening closes, the shadow disappears. And I'm left staring at Tiberius. For a moment, there is only silence, thick and weighted, and all I can hear is the thrum of my pulse in my ears.

Then Tiberius clears his throat. 'I believe, Otho, Nero, that she is *exactly* what we need. Our weapon to wield.'

I'm escorted back to my room in a daze. All I can see in my mind is Agnes sobbing and broken as she was shoved out of that lifeless marble hall, taken from me. And what I did, those people, the smoking home I unleashed my lightning on through that portal . . . I shudder. As the guards shove me over the threshold of this cell room, I find that Kell has left and I am alone. I wait until I hear the click of the lock before collapsing to the floor, shaking as that roar of rage and defiance turns into a distant tinny ring.

I can't save her. *I can't save her.* It's all I can think, all I know, as the shock of what I've witnessed sinks into my very bones.

A member of the ruling council of Arnhem . . . used

shadow magic. And, not only that, he made it clear where they're from. Another world. The very world Eli and Lowri crossed into in search of Eli's father. My breathing comes shallow, too fast and quick, as panic takes over once more. What if they're not safe in that other world? What if, even now, they're trapped there by people like Tiberius? What if they're never able to return?

I get up off the floor, draw in a breath and *scream*.

I scream for all that the ruling council has done to us. Done to me. And when there's nothing left I curl up on the small bed, drawing my knees into my chest. For now, there is no escape. All I can do is compete in the Trials as they bid me and just hope their attention doesn't turn on the isles while I am gone. With every fibre of my being, I hope that my people will stay safe. Stay alive. I hope that everyone else aboard *Phantom* managed to escape.

Somehow, in the space of one night, we've come untethered, all of us. We've sunk beneath the waves, and with no hope of rescue, of safe harbour. We're drowning.

But my heart is still beating, and if I'm still alive then I can still fight. I draw my hands into tight fists, relishing the huge mistake they've made in capturing me, in bending me to their will.

I may be a girl made of storms.

But I am no one's weapon to wield.

Chapter 2
Brielle

TEN DAYS AND THREE TERRITORIES of overland travel leaves Brielle cramp-legged and short-tempered. Leicena wasn't so terrible. The post carriage ran like clockwork, the roads were quiet and well maintained and every few hours they would stop at an inn for refreshments. But Skylan, with its sprawl of mountainous tracks and lack of reliable coaches, never failed to dampen her mood.

She's questioned agreeing to Nova's idea more than once since they left the isle of Ennor, but thoughts of Lowri always brought her back to the plan. To create a true Tresillian coven, one unlike the coven in which they both grew up, something to which Lowri could return home, a new future for them both, on their terms. A purpose, a plan, to rescue as many wraiths as they can, turning them into the witches they should have become. Idealistic, perhaps foolish, but she wants to try. She has to know if what Nova – Lowri's familiar – and Tanith – Ennor Castle's resident librarian – believe is possible can actually be done.

Now, two days deep in the thick southern forests of Stanvard, Brielle has to remind herself hourly why she agreed to this assignment. She is very ready for a warm bath, a roaring fire, a decent meal and to no longer be sitting in a box on wheels.

If you offered a bribe to the driver, we would be there by now, Hunter.

She glares at Nova, who gives a suspiciously un-catlike meow and begins licking her paws. Nova chose Lowri as her witch when Lowri was just a young witchling, and ever since she's accepted Brielle, though Brielle is not convinced the familiar altogether likes her. It's a mutual acceptance, if anything, balanced on the fact that they are both fiercely loyal to Lowri. And while she is gone with Eli in another world they need a purpose, a distraction from dwelling too much on whether Lowri, the burned-out witch they both love, will make it back to them, whole and well. They need to give her something to return to, a new coven, renewed hope. A future.

Their shared anxiety does not soften one to the other, though, especially now the journey is dragging on. And Brielle, usually so measured and calm, cannot help but show her irritation more frequently. 'I'll offer *you* as a bribe, shall I?'

Nova yawns, slouching on the seat across from her. *Give it a try. I'm sure Lowri would love to hear how you frittered her beloved familiar away for a bit of comfort and faster travel.*

'Oh, shut up,' Brielle snaps, crossing her arms and turning pointedly to face the window. The trees flash by the carriage in a sea of dark green, and she ponders how Lowri is, *where* she is. Has Eli managed to get her to his father's world and has he found someone to help her? Burnout in a witch can be fatal. And the way her sister was the last time she saw her, listless and ink-veined, her grip on the world around her tenuous at best . . . Brielle swallows, blinking quickly to shift the image away. No use dwelling on what she cannot control. All she can do now is keep moving forward, and trust in Elijah Tresillian and his strange, otherworldly magic.

What *is* in her control, though, is proving more frustrating by the hour. They should have crossed the border by now and be well on their way to a tavern of which she is particularly fond in the northern region of the principality of Lorva. In fact, they should have left this stretch of the forest behind some time ago.

'Driver,' she calls, knocking on the ceiling of the carriage. 'Driver, a word!'

Three hours later, with a considerably lighter purse, Brielle and Nova arrive at Tavern Lomask as night falls. Much like the Inn Melusine on the Far Isles, Tavern Lomask has slumped and sagged since her last visit, as though weary of the world. The plaster no longer gleams white, a beacon along this stretch of road for tired travellers, but instead sports a greyish hue, the colour of thin, autumnal rain. The windows appear dingy, with only the faintest light shining through them, stiff curtains mostly drawn against the encroaching dark.

Looks friendly, Nova comments. *I'll be catching mice.* Then she stalks off towards the back of the building before disappearing into the gloom beyond.

'Friendly as a witches' tea party . . .' Brielle murmurs, reminding herself that she's here for a rest and to gather any local gossip. The five principalities of the Middenwilds are always rife with tales of wraiths, so when Nova suggested the idea, this seemed like the best place to begin. She tries the dark wood front door and the hinges give with a groan. She stumbles inside, finding a scattering of locals from the village a mile or so away, hidden off the main road through the forest, and the tavern owner with a polishing cloth slung over his shoulder.

Recognition softens his features, shoulders dipping in apparent relief as he makes his way behind the bar. 'Hunter Tresillian. If I'd known you were coming . . .' He scratches his grey-streaked beard, sunken eyes swivelling to hers. ''Tisn't safe at night. Not alone. Your driver should have known better.'

Brielle smiles, leaning her forearms on the bar. 'I paid him handsomely to get me here before midnight.'

'The main road is rough between Valstra and Lorva now. No money for repairs, or so they say, and many avoid the nights and what lurks beyond the treeline.'

Now *this* sounded interesting. 'You've had some trouble?'

'Trouble is a polite way of putting it,' the owner says as Brielle manages at last to fish his name out of her memory. Gregor Kain. Kindly widower with two daughters. The last time she visited, though, he was quicker to smile. She could hear the music and merriment now, spilling from every corner. Or, at least, the ghosts of them.

'How are the family?' she asks.

Gregor stiffens and blinks. 'My oldest girl, she turned seventeen a month ago and . . .' He sighs then reaches for a bottle half full of a thick mauve drink, pours himself a tiny glass and downs it. 'She changed. Became agitated, fearful. Had these outbursts she couldn't control and then . . .'

'The forest took her,' a voice says. Brielle turns to find a girl with wild black curls, scrunched fists and gleaming eyes. 'My sister, Liska, hasn't returned since.'

'Sad times indeed,' Brielle says softly, eyeing the slightly younger sister. 'Dreska, isn't it?'

The girl bobs her head, not taking her eyes from Brielle. 'She's been gone two weeks.'

Brielle asks for a room to be prepared, orders a plate of pie and mash, which tastes of the woodsy herbs grown in the loamy, rich soil thereabouts, and washes it down with a glass of ruby blackcurrant wine. She watches Gregor as he polishes glasses, grumbles with the other patrons about the trees being felled to make way for a new landowner's plans a few miles away and sends Dreska off to bed. In everything, he seems absent. As though his mind wanders, deep into the thickening night.

Pudding is a sweetened milk and bread dish, filling but burned at the edges. Brielle chews it mechanically, listening to a group in the corner murmuring about the woods, the mist and the recent cries heard in the night. She takes her leave as they do, all of them moving together in a pack, glancing behind their backs with chalky faces, lanterns held aloft. Brielle walks slowly to the room prepared for her up the creaking staircase, just as Gregor bars the front door with a sturdy dark wood bar laced with metal after the last patron bids him goodnight.

She finds Nova waiting for her, curled up on the windowsill, eyes pale moons, flashing in the gloaming. 'Told you the Middenwilds were our best bet. I believe we've found our first wraith.'

It appears so.

When she's sure the innkeeper and his daughter are asleep, Brielle leaves the inn through the window, Nova like a shadow at her heels. With a full set of blades in the sash across her chest and magic at her fingertips, ready to be released with a pinch of words, she walks into the foreboding forest. It seems to close in their wake, the moonlight soon extinguished, as though a great door made of leaf and bark has swung shut, trapping them within.

Brielle tightens her jaw, attuning her senses. Places like this, moorland and river and thick tumbles of woodland, are where she feels most at home. There is a different set of rules to follow here; this is not a place governed by manners and laws and skin-deep civility like the courts of the continent. It's raw and wild and real. If she missteps, ignores an instinctive tug, it could lead to her death. And something lurks in this forest. She can feel it.

Something is hunting *her*.

She isn't afraid, exactly. She hadn't felt true fear on any assignment after she stalked the vile wyvern that killed her mother and left their carcasses scattered across the snowclad heights of the Spines. Nothing, except Lowri's pale features, a shade too close to death, has caused real fear in her since then. But, still, she never ignores that tug in her middle. Tonight, she is wary. A twig snaps under her left boot as she prowls through the trees towering tall as giants, branches crowning their tops as if they have formed a new night sky. She listens, and she waits.

There wouldn't be another hunter here in these woods, of that she is sure. Not enough coin in these parts to tempt a coven away from the assignments in Valstra – ridding fire sprites from the rich merchant mines, or the creatures infesting the courts across the continent, searching for jewels and shiny trinkets. No coven would have sent a hunter to a lone tavern owner who might not pay more than a couple of coins and a hearty meal. Certainly not her coven, or, rather, her *old* coven. Brielle licks her lips, listening intently as the forest at night awakens. So strange to think of Coven Septern that way, so absolute and final. But Brielle does not dwell, moving onwards, even in her thoughts. No, she is the only witch here tonight.

A huff, like a trembling exhale, sounds a little way to

the east, accompanied by the thuds of a creature and then a thin, warbling wail. It shakes the damp air around her, the noises of the forest fading to silence. Brielle swallows, keen senses homing in on the creature that has made those sounds. Whatever it is, it's large, lumbering and sad. She quirks an eyebrow at Nova just ahead of her.

A creature, but it feels . . . odd.

'You're a lot of help,' Brielle murmurs, moving towards the warbling and the shifting trees. She emerges into a clearing and quickly retreats under the cover of the branches. In the centre is a creature, slumped against a single tree with bone-pale bark and long, curved limbs, stripped of leaves. Brielle bites her lip, calculating its size and heft, the witch words needed to incapacitate it and whether she could still just slink away, unseen.

It's a wither beast, round and covered in silver fur, with the features of a bear, huge catlike eyes and paws with claws several inches long. Her heart drums in her ears as she calculates, blinking quickly. To disturb a wither beast, particularly a female . . . She takes another step back and winces as a twig cracks beneath her boot.

The wither beast's eyes snap to hers.

Brielle holds her breath as the great creature rises, swaying as it stands, and she walks forward to greet it. There is no use in bolting now. It would only give chase and, given its size and those claws, she doesn't fancy her chances of getting away completely unscathed. She draws a blade, taking up a stance, eyeing it as it pulls in a breath . . . and sobs.

'What in skies?' Brielle says softly as the wither beast slumps back sadly against the tree. It has a human voice. The cry of a girl, the same wailing cadence. 'But, if you're not a wraith—'

'She's not.'

Brielle whips round as a figure steps into the clearing wearing a ruby-red cloak, drawn low over their forehead to cover their face and hair. 'Show yourself.'

The figure draws back their hood just as the wither beast sobs again softly. 'My sister isn't a wraith, nor is she a wither beast.'

Brielle's eyes widen as she takes in the wild black curls, the gleaming eyes. The daughter from the inn. Dreska.

'It's you!' she says, shaking her head. How did she not realise? 'You're the wraith.'

'Not quite yet, but I fear it won't be long until I disintegrate. Until I can no longer control what is inside me, what is bleeding out,' Dreska says, the first hint of fear creeping into her words.

This other daughter of Gregor, the younger one, who must be around sixteen, turns her gaze on the wither beast, sorrow and desperation changing her features completely as she holds out her hand. Brielle notes her nails, ebony black, smoke ghosting around them. The sign of a witch whose power is leaking out of her, who may be using too much of that power, or who is not fully in control of it.

'I didn't mean to do this to Liska,' Dreska says. 'Please help us. Save her. Change my sister back.'

Chapter 3

Lowri

'SHE'S FADING.'

Strong arms circle Lowri, lifting her up. All her choices have brought her to this, a bed in a castle, a lonely path in the dark, moving further from herself. Burnout is fatal in a witch and she used far too much of her power. She delved too deep; she knows that now. But she would do it all again. For herself, for her home, for her family. If only it hadn't cost her so much.

She opens her eyes just enough to know it's Eli who lifts her, and finds her cousin's calm, capable eyes staring back at her. He's always protected her, is as much a brother to her as Caden, and as she senses the thrum of his heart pressed to her ear she remembers a shell he gave her on one of his visits to the coven house, so she could listen to the ocean surrounding Ennor and feel as if she was there with him and Caden. She clings to that memory now as Eli steps towards a threshold that didn't exist before. One forged of darkness and silence and power.

They slip out of Ennor Castle, out of her entire known world and into a shadow that is not a shadow at all, but a doorway. And on the other side is forest. It warps as Eli steps, then steps again, twisting into shadow, then snow, then a mountain range. So many places, but never the right one. Never the right doorway.

'Eli,' Lowri whispers, but her voice is a thread. She clings to him, fighting to keep her eyes open. This is not like traversing between shadows. This is not a spell.

This is something else.

'Hold on, Lowri. I just have to find the right doorway.'

They step into a library, then through trees on the side of a mountain. She catches a glimpse of people on broomsticks, towering buildings set on top of sheer cliffs. They see people from other places, other worlds. And still Eli keeps stepping.

Then the sky blanches to grey, a steady drizzle misting a garden surrounded by trees, that forest she first saw. No, not a forest, not with these carved marble stones, these flowers neatly arranged, already picked.

A graveyard.

Lowri can feel Eli's heart pounding inside his chest. He's holding the necklace, the eight-pointed star tight in his fist, the chain draped over his fingers, glowing softly. His link to this world. She raises her eyes to his and finds he's staring over her head, to where a single black-clad figure stands before a grave. The drizzle thickens to rain that slips down her cheeks, but she forces her eyes to stay open. Fights to stay awake. Eli carries her to this figure by a gleaming black gravestone, flecked with white and carved with a name.

Isaiah Kellinick

'Excuse me?' Eli says, and the figure turns towards them. Lowri's breath catches. She's staring into Eli's mirror image. Black-brown hair, the same deep, soulful eyes – but green rather than blue – set under thick brows, the same set to her shoulders. But this girl is slightly younger, Lowri's age. The girl blinks away her shock, seeing what Lowri sees, similarities that outweigh the differences between them.

'I'm afraid you just missed him. He's been waiting. He always hoped . . .' The girl's gaze drifts to the necklace in Eli's hand, then to Lowri's obsidian eyes, before she jerks up her chin, lower lip trembling. 'You're too late by five days. Your father is dead. You . . . you shouldn't have crossed over.'

A sudden breeze ruffles the girl's collar, casting the scent of ink and parchment towards Lowri as she feels Eli's arms tense round her. She burrows deeper against the chill, regarding the world surrounding them in swift blinks. A stone garden of death, grave after grave, all painted in bleak, colourless lines. She tries to remember where they were, all the places they stepped through to reach here. The side of a mountain, a library and perhaps somewhere else, but she cannot think right now, can't quite grasp the details. She is not just burned out.

She is dying.

'I had no choice,' Eli says, voice thick, glancing down at Lowri. She meets his eyes for a moment, catching them fray at the corners with worry before he looks back up at this unknown girl that seems so much like him. 'She needs . . . Lowri needed him. *I* needed him.'

'We all did.' The girl shrugs helplessly. 'Come with me. I'll see if I can do anything to help your friend.'

'Who are you?' Eli asks hesitantly, and Lowri's heart expands, wanting to comfort him, wanting him to know that he's not alone in this moment, as it hits him that his father is dead. He's too late by only a handful of days. 'Were you related to my father?'

'I'm Isaiah's niece,' she says, nodding. Lowri notices that the uncanny similarities between this girl and Eli extend even to the way she dips her chin. 'And his apprentice. Come on. We really should leave, get your friend inside. She seems unwell.'

The world around Lowri stutters in and out of focus as the rain drips down her cheekbones, until, like a flickering candle flame, it's finally snuffed out. Lowri hears nothing more as she slips further away into the beckoning pool of cold, dark nothing.

When Lowri wakes, it's seemingly full night. A fireplace flickers with black flames. As her awareness trails over her surroundings, she finds she's huddled under a heap of blankets, dark wooden floorboards just below her, a small crooked window looking out on to a night sky without stars. There is a collection of books scattered on a small table next to her, one with a pen tucked in to mark a place, and a ring from a mug that's tattooed its past contents on to the wood.

She's still so tired. Her thoughts are fragmented, twisting away when she tries to grasp them, a headache prickling at her temples. They stepped into Eli's father's world – that's all she knows. But that was in a graveyard. She cannot remember reaching this house.

Eli sits across the room, eyes closed. He seems to have slumped into his clothes, as though he has tried very hard to stay awake, and perhaps only drifted off momentarily. A door to Lowri's left clicks open, light rushing through from a hallway.

In stalks a creature.

Entirely made of shadow, but in a cat sort of shape, the creature leaps on to the books piled up on the table beside her. Balanced precariously, it sniffs Lowri, whiskers quivering as it emits a delighted sound that could almost be a purr.

Oh, you'll do nicely, the creature says.

Lowri blinks, then quickly reaches out, swatting at the creature. But her hand moves through the space where there should be fur and bones, meeting only something that feels like a thunder cloud. Damp sparks crackle over her fingers and she flinches, eyeing the creature warily.

The creature leaps again, this time on to Lowri, pattering across her hip to drape itself over her chest.

She has the peculiar sensation of being wrapped in shadow, storm and strange magic.

You won't get rid of me that easily, witch.

'He's called Gracious,' a voice says from the doorway. Lowri cranes to look and finds the girl from the graveyard standing there, a silhouette against the light spilling over the threshold. The girl crosses to the fireplace and heaps on more coal from a scuttle, ebony flames enveloping them hungrily. 'He won't hurt you. He belonged to my uncle and now, I suppose, he just belongs here.'

'You suppose?' Lowri asks faintly as the girl tuts at Gracious, shooing him off Lowri's chest. She crosses back to the doorway before disappearing for a moment, then returns holding a tray.

'He's a grimalkin,' the girl says by way of explanation, as though Lowri should understand what that means. Setting the tray down on the floor, she passes Lowri a plate of buttered bread that looks more like a wedge of cake. Lowri shuffles up against the cushions, feeling the prickling headache become a stubborn thump as she accepts the plate, then a mug of steaming tea. The girl smiles. 'The tea will help restore you a little, temporarily. It's Fallow Fog.'

Ignoring the mention of the grimalkin, which looks and moves suspiciously like Nova, a creature *assuming* the form of a cat, rather than being an *actual* cat, she drinks the tea and finds it tastes like sugared fruit and cream, yet slips down her throat like warm smoke. 'Why is this tea called Fallow Fog?'

'It's named after our city – Fallow. And it has a few drops of the fog in it.'

'The fog?' Eli asks quietly from the armchair by the fireplace. Lowri's attention slips to her cousin, who stretches and rubs his eyes.

'You're awake! Good,' the girl says, hurriedly passing him a plate of the cake bread too. 'And to answer your question, the fog is above us, covering everything.'

Eli frowns. 'I thought that was just because it was night time when we reached the city?' His gaze fixes on Lowri, concern marring his features. 'You'd passed out by that point.'

The girl shakes her head, eyes wide. 'No. The fog is eternal. It lingers over the entire city of Fallow, has done since long before I was born. A remnant of the war that no one can shift.' Then she turns to Lowri. 'I'm Ethlet, by the way. You were out before we even left the graveyard. Sorry if this all feels a bit unsettling.'

'She helped carry you here, Lor,' Eli adds, getting up to stretch his limbs even further, then putting his hands in his pockets. He regards Lowri. 'How are you feeling? Traversing, let alone world walking, can take a toll.'

Lowri frowns at the girl, then at the grimalkin, who appears to be licking his paws. 'Are you sure you got the right world, Eli?'

Ethlet and Eli exchange glances. 'Ethlet here is my cousin. Do you remember her saying that in the graveyard? She was also my father's apprentice. This,' he indicates the small, cosy lounge, and the roof over their heads, 'is – *was* – his home. His and Ethlet's.'

'So you're a . . . what kind of apprentice are you?' Lowri asks Ethlet.

'I'm not actually very much of anything yet. It was Eli's father who was good at shadow and light magic.' She swallows. 'I hadn't really thought about what I am now that he's gone. Untrained, I suppose.'

There's a stretch of silence before Eli speaks. 'Is that why you told us we shouldn't have come? Because there are no answers here?'

Ethlet shakes her head, swiftly gathering up the used mugs and plates and placing them back on the tray. 'No, it's not that. The fog? It's an overuse of magic. It drips over everything, like ink, and no one can rid the city of it. The fog is everywhere; there are few patches of sky left that haven't been consumed. Your father, my uncle, was trying to find a way to remove the fog. He discovered a way to create a portal and crossed into your world, back before I was born. But when he returned with his research, ready to show to the society, he found that he couldn't return to your world. He couldn't find a doorway to you.' She bites her lip. 'I'm afraid that you may not be able to get to your world either now. You might be stuck here in Fallow.'

Eli and Lowri exchange a hurried glance before Eli clears his throat. 'Forever?'

'I'm afraid so.'

Lowri's heart misses a beat.

Forever.

For a moment, there is only the sound of Gracious as he yowls softly, curling up by the fireplace.

'But can anyone else do what Eli can do? What his father did?' Lowri asks desperately. 'Create a portal, step through it?'

'Only the brothers,' Ethlet says quietly. 'The Rexilium brothers. They are the ones who are responsible for the fog. They created it with the overuse of shadow magic and it grew and grew, consuming light magic. They started and then lost the war and made their escape into your world. Now we are left with the fog, and they have never returned.'

Chapter 4

Mira

THE GUARDS BRING ME FOOD and fresh clothes, escort me to a bathroom and ignore every one of my questions. It's only when the day wanes to evening that Kell knocks on my door, accompanied by a witch. A hunter. I jump to my feet and back away, but she doesn't cross the threshold.

'She's assigned to us for the Trials,' Kell says, jerking a thumb at the hunter. 'To train us so we win. To ensure we survive and don't do anything reckless.'

'*She* is called Hira,' the hunter says, scowling at us both as she folds her arms. I purse my lips, regarding her. She has hair so black it has a sheen of deepest navy, eyes like piercing pools and deep brown skin. 'And though this is better than the assignment I was previously given, to fish out fire sprites in the mines of Valstra, it's not better by much. If Brielle hadn't defected, I wouldn't be here at all. I'm not on their side, I'm not on yours and I'd appreciate it if you'd just let me carry out my assignment.'

I frown. 'You know Brielle?'

Hira nods. 'We were both at Coven Septern, before—'

'Have you heard from her? Is she well?' I blurt. 'Could you get a message to her?'

'And disobey my Malefant?' Hira shakes her head. 'I think not, creature. Brielle may have betrayed us, but I remain loyal to my coven. My task is to ensure you two don't mess up. We will begin training tomorrow morning, and I will find out what I have to work with. Then, in the evening, it's the grand ball for the competitors and the visiting courts, and you will both attend. Ensure they can all get a good look at you, keep to yourselves and return to your rooms without incident. Yes?'

Kell and I both stare at her stonily.

'I take that as acquiescence. A guard will collect each of you after breakfast tomorrow, and we will begin.'

'What kind of training?' I ask, narrowing my eyes. The horror of the lightning I unleashed on that farm building is haunting me. If the ruling council want me to do that again, to be that kind of weapon . . . how will I get through this?

Hira smiles. 'Apparently you both have some command of magic, enough that the ruling council believes you will be victorious. And I must ensure you can use whatever gifts are at your disposal, and that you avoid dying in the first Trial. I told my Malefant it was an impossible task, and yet here we are. Don't ask me any questions like, but why Hira, but what do the ruling council *want*, Hira . . . because I don't know and, frankly, I don't care.'

'Because you're just carrying out your assignment,' I say through gritted teeth, beginning to understand why Brielle and Lowri walked away from their coven. If all the witches and hunters are like this . . . well.

'Exactly. Glad we understand each other.' She nods to a guard behind her, who nudges Kell to move along. 'Now, both of you, stay in your rooms and don't cause any trouble. The faster we get through this, the faster I can return to my coven and leave this soulless palace.'

Hira's training seems to consist of snarling at us in a disused hall as we work through a series of jabs and kicks, then she's summoned elsewhere before we can move on to a demonstration of our *gifts*, as she calls them.

A few hours later, as the sky turns to dusk, Kell and I are escorted to another part of the vast court, along silent corridors and wide staircases, to the only room that seems to hold any life.

The music and merriment spilling out are like the scrape of foul claws in my mind. I enter the grand ballroom in an outfit that was chosen for me: a fancy gown woven in gold and cream, symbolising Arnhem. It reminds me too much of the one Renshaw put me in on board her ship and anger coils within me. The first thing I do is scan the crowd for Agnes's red hair, hoping against hope that she's somehow in here too, that I can speak to her, make sure she's all right . . . but after discarding every glint of red I find my heart deflates. She's not at this party.

'At least the guards aren't going to tail us in here,' Kell mutters, tugging at the hem of a tunic they've chosen for him, also woven in threads of gold and cream. 'They're barring every exit.'

I couldn't escape now, even if I had the chance. Not without Agnes, and I've yet to think of a way to save us both. There's still too little information. I have no knowledge of the court, its layout or where they're holding her. For now, I have to learn more about the Trials, and what I need to do to survive. This ball, to welcome the competitors and members of their courts from across the continent, seems like a fine way to glean vital details.

'There's food, and it's better than the rubbish they've been feeding us,' I say with a shrug, tamping down my frustration. 'Keep your wits about you, though. We don't know how competitive these other champions will be.'

Kell narrows his gaze as he casts it over the ballroom, a sudden peal of high-pitched laughter spearing the air like an arrow. 'Agreed. Although they'd be pretty foolish to poison someone in another court . . .'

'Depends how desperate they are,' I say gruffly. Picturing Agnes, I know how desperate *I* am. And, although we both know the rules of the Trials, we have little knowledge of this side of them. Perhaps the moments in between are just as important as the challenges themselves. I learned long ago that where there is money, there is purpose. And the ruling council have not scrimped on this spread, which means there is a reason for this assembly. Perhaps it is just to display the wealth and superiority of Arnhem, but maybe the members of these other courts will use this gathering to their advantage. I wish we had an ally here.

The tables along one wall are laden with food and drinks, platters piled high with produce from across the continent. The extravagance leaves me cold as I step over to the tables, loading up a plate and picking my way through it. There's fish, meat, vegetables in pickled slivers, delicate piles of leaf and sauce, and the puddings are all towering confections in bright colours. It's a disgusting display of greed and wealth, a feast that would feed the whole of Rosevear for a week. The ruling council is wasting no time or resources in showing their might. But is it a display to unnerve the visiting members of the other courts, or are they trying to impress?

When we reach the drinks table, Kell makes a snort of disgust. 'Frost-flower syrup. Subtle.'

'What do you mean?' I pick up one of the pearlescent coupe glasses, swirling the pink, fizzing drink within.

'Frost flowers grow in the north. It's the first place the ruling council conquered, or so I've heard tell from people passing through. They were a symbol of freedom, of the mountains and the wilds.' He sniffs at the drink and frowns. 'The ruling council has tamed the wild north, and they want everyone here to bear that in mind.'

I shudder, placing the glass back down, and reach for a goblet of honey-hued wine instead, knocking it back. 'You never told me why they brought you here. What are you able to do?' I ask Kell quietly.

He scrunches up his nose, then checks to see there are no eyes lingering on us. He holds out his right palm, and a pale smouldering flame uncoils from his skin. I whistle, skimming my fingertips over it, and quickly snatch them back. It's real. This boy can create actual fire. 'But you're human. You're a boy . . .'

'Magic is changing,' Kell says, closing his fingers into a fist and snuffing out the flame. 'Evolving. I don't know if there are others like me, but I'm hoping that here, maybe another competitor . . .' He trails off, swallows. 'And what the guards say about you is true? You are half human, half creature?'

I nod. 'And though the ruling council believe me to be some huge threat, or a weapon they can use, I'm only just uncovering what it means. What I can do. And . . . how to control my powers.'

He tosses back his drink and wipes his mouth. 'We'll figure it out. Together. But right now keep your secrets close. There's someone over there taking a keen interest in you.'

When I look round, I find a pair of eyes watching me with a sneer I know all too well. Captain Spencer Leggan. He saunters over, bedecked in his watch uniform, and my fingers stiffen round the glass I'm holding. The man who was going to hang my father and would have happily seen me swing from his gallows as well. I plant my feet, the anger coiling inside me even tighter, and I wonder if I can get away with murdering him right here and now.

'Mira Boscawen of Rosevear,' he says, that sneer threaded through each syllable. 'I hear you've gone up in the world. Subservience suits you.'

'And you remain down with the dregs,' I snap.

He chuckles. 'Now, now. We're all on the same side here. Both representing Arnhem, both with skin in the game, so to speak.'

'What?'

'Well, the Trials aren't easy, are they? Not only do you have to stay alive, you also have to beat all the other contenders to the top spot and impress the right people,' he says, then leans closer. 'If you want your little island-wrecker friend to make it out of this court alive.'

Impress the right people?

I grit my teeth, exhaling slowly, then I smile sweetly up at him. 'If there weren't so many witnesses, I'd ram this glass into your throat.'

He takes a step back, the sneer dropping from his features. 'Murderous little thing, aren't you? Shame you'll probably die in the Trials. I'd have taken great joy in hanging you myself.'

Gripping the stem of the glass, I squeeze too tight, snapping it in two. His eyes trail to it then lift back to meet mine as I murmur. 'Even a splinter, or as you put it, a *thorn in your side* can end a life, captain.'

He blinks quickly, fear plain on his features before he can hide it, then walks away. I watch his back grimly as he greets people as he goes, before he's swallowed by the crowd.

'Who was that?' Kell hisses.

I shove the broken glass on the table and turn to appraise the ballroom. 'A man I would very much like to drown.' Then I turn to Kell and smile. 'But he made a good point. We need an edge, and we don't know who the other contenders are yet. We need more information.'

'True.'

'How's your footwork?'

Within minutes, we're clumsily spinning across the ballroom dance floor, eyeing the crowd. It works, because as soon as the song has finished, we're both approached by other partners who want to rub shoulders with a competitor. The young man who asks me to dance has a shock of ginger hair that sticks straight up from his forehead, and wolfish teeth. He takes the lead, and all I have to do is try not to step on his feet as the band strikes up.

'Are you a contender?' I ask as we step sideways to the left, swaying to the side before continuing the same pattern to the right.

He laughs. 'No, my territory wouldn't send *me*. I've no special talent, cunning or brute strength. I'm an ambassador.'

'And which is your territory?' I ask as he spins me round, then pulls me back in.

'Stanvard,' he says. 'You represent Arnhem, don't you? And your friend too.'

'How can you tell?'

His bark of laughter is harsh in my ear. 'They want to show you off. Everyone taking part in the Trials. You all look like trophies.'

My eyes widen and I sweep my gaze across the near crowd, then the other dancers. He's right. There's one other dressed like Kell and I, a young man with a shaved head, wearing a deep green and purple tunic in the same style as ours, thick set with grey eyes and ruddy skin. 'Trophies?'

'There'll be bets placed after tonight. But don't be fooled: this isn't just some spectacle to delight and entertain the masses,' he says as we step gingerly in a huge circle, all round the dance floor. 'Strategies will be formed, alliances made, trade deals struck – all based on your performance. Everyone is watching you. Seeing who they believe will fail the first Trial, who will triumph. Who the *real* competition will be. The continent is changing, alliances breaking and reforming. This is about power and control.'

I suppress a shudder. 'And who's your money on?'

He blinks at me in surprise. 'Stanvard's competitors, of course. You'll see them tonight, wearing our colours: ruby red and rich brown. The earth, the mines of Valstra, the bloodshed to bring prosperity to Stanvard. What we bring to the continent is immeasurable wealth, and our competitors will remind everyone of our value.'

'What a charming sentiment.'

He stops as the music ends and nods his head. 'A word of advice? Steer clear of the Skylan contenders. A territory defending that many borders whose only worth is the sea route they control? That's a dangerous territory to cross. They produce nothing and the mine owners are tired of their levies. Not to mention the other territories that have their eye on that route . . .'

I frown. 'Which territories?'

But he's gone before I can ask any more and I realise I didn't even get his name. Pinpricks of unease spread over my skin and I feel as if I've had my first brush with the true reason for the Trials. If that man is an ambassador for Stanvard, his interests lie in securing deals and favourable trading terms for the metals mined in Valstra. And it sounds as though he does not consider Skylan an ally. Interesting. If anything, it makes me more keen to meet the contenders from that territory.

'What did you learn?' Kell asks, and we slink to the edge of the ballroom. 'Mine was a dowager from Leicena. She said her territory's representatives will win.'

'Hmm.' I brush a finger back and forth across my lips as I pick out the individuals dressed like Kell and I, just in different colours. Before realising I'm doing it, I begin scanning for Agnes again, then blink quickly to hide my disappointment and fear over her not being here tonight. 'Mine said he'd bet on Stanvard winning, his own territory. Stanvardian contenders are dressed in brown and red.'

'I see them.' Kell points as two tall girls with long dark hair, huge eyes and brown skin, who appear to be sisters, amble up to the food, sniffing each dish. 'Mine said to watch out for Skylan.'

'Interesting,' I murmur. 'So did mine. Do you think—'

But my words are cut off by a roar that shakes the entire room. Glasses shatter and cries of surprise echo through the ballroom as a sound like beaten air comes from outside, growing louder. I look at Kell and we move to the nearest window, peering into the dark. The guards cannot contain everyone as they spill out on to the terrace, and Kell and I slip in among the moving crowd. I gasp.

Above us, two huge winged shapes soar down, aiming straight for the court. My heart lodges in my throat as the majestic creatures land effortlessly on the lawns beneath the terrace, shaking the ground. The scent of ash wafts over us.

'Drakes,' we hear a man say. 'Firedrakes from the Spines.'

I swallow, watching as a girl jumps down from the back of one, the drake's midnight scales glinting. She's wearing fur, hair braided like mine but white-blonde like Pearl's, the girl I first met aboard *Phantom*, a member of Merryam's crew and her partner. For a moment, I picture Pearl, my friend, and it jolts me. But this girl is taller, her hair almost fading into the icy pallor of her skin, and she carries an axe across her back. The boy who jumps down from the other, a dark-green-scaled drake is dressed similarly, with the same coloured hair, which is shaved on both sides, strands running up over his skull and tied at the back. When they both step forward, it's clear they're even wearing scales under the fur, like armour. They're at least a foot taller than Kell and I, armed to the teeth with knives slung across their chests and, as they gaze around, the girl bares her teeth. Several of the guests stumble back, a wave of gossip gushing over us.

'. . . won the last Trials.'

'Lost her brother recently . . .'

'Fire breathers, have to be. What a power play.'

I'm suddenly aware of a girl standing by my side, eyeing the competitors and their drakes with apparent delight. Then she looks over at me and raises one eyebrow. 'Do you think they actually rode drakeback *all* the way from the Spines,' she says, 'or is it so we all quake in our little boots?'

'You think they mean to intimidate us?' I ask her, intrigued. She shrugs, throwing a berry up high in the air before catching it in her mouth. She's unremarkable in every way, snub-nosed with a dusting of freckles, brown hair that's too plain to be considered pretty and eyes that are neither brown nor green but somewhere in the middle. It's the crooked twist in her lips, the dart of her gaze, that has me marking her as more than she first appears.

Or *wishes* to appear.

'I think this is turning out to be far more diverting than Heath let on, quite honestly. The contenders from the Spines have revealed their hand a tad early, though, in my opinion.' She turns to look at me squarely, thrusting out her hand. 'Sember Lockswift.'

I smile despite myself, holding out my own to shake hers. 'Mira Boscawen.'

'Excellent. Now, don't take offence, but I believe we are rivals. And Heath gets *very* gloomy if he doesn't come in first. Not even second will do. It's the royal in him. He can't help it.'

'Skylan,' Kell hisses in my ear, eyeing her warily.

Sember shrugs one shoulder and it's only then I realise what she's wearing. A deep, leaf-green gown, the colour symbolising the green mountains and forests of the central territory. The one bordered on all sides but one. 'Afraid so. I promise not every rumour about us is true, though. Only the very worst ones. The rest you can ignore. We spread them ourselves.'

She's off before I can reply, whisking so deftly through the crowd that she's gone between blinks. And yet, before she disappears, she looks back over her shoulder at us both, and it almost seems like an invitation to follow.

Kell sighs. 'Well, at least we know who is representing Skylan. Prince Heath himself, the second son, not the heir to the Skylan throne. Not at all intimidating.'

'The spare. Interesting,' I murmur, turning my gaze back to the drakes and the contenders from the Spines, a plan unfurling in my mind. These Trials are about more than the events themselves. And, if I am to free Agnes and myself, we need more information from the most unlikely sources. We also need allies in this court. Fleetingly, I imagine having Eli by my side. His purposeful swagger would cut through this sea of people and I wish, keenly, that he was here with me. He would know how to navigate these waters; he would know who to trust and who to avoid. But he's not, and if I ever want to see him again . . . I swallow. I will need to play a dangerous game indeed. 'For now, Kell, I think we keep what we are both able to do a secret. Let's learn all we can before revealing anything. Unless we make allies, it may be the only advantage we have.'

The ground rumbles ominously. The drake on the right, the green-scaled beauty, is eyeing the crowd in agitation, a growl reverberating deep in its throat, sending shockwaves down into the ground. The guards surge forward, a guest nearby gasping as she's shoved aside, her wine glass shattering on the terrace. The other drake scrapes at the lawn, baring fangs, and that's when I notice what the Skylan contender is doing.

Sember Lockswift is baiting the drakes.

CHAPTER 5
Brielle

LEAVING LISKA IN THE WOODS wrenches Brielle's heart. As she follows Dreska back to the tavern, the moonlight casting a river of silver for them to follow, all she can hear is the quiet whimpering of Liska in her witherbeast form as she lumbers behind them at a distance.

Once they reach the very edge of the forest, Dreska says a quiet goodbye to her sister before they walk the winding road back to the tavern, and Brielle turns away, giving them a moment. All she can think of is that no coven would touch this, not at this time of year when assignments from more affluent clients abound in the courts and mines, not with so little benefit to them. Certainty fills her like a smouldering flame. No other hunter would, but *she* can help. *She* can fix this.

'I accept the assignment,' she says formally to Dreska as they trudge along the packed mud and stones of the road. 'I will help you free your sister from the form she is trapped in. But . . .'

'But?' Dreska says, eyeing her.

'You are a witch, Dreska. You are not a human girl, even if you were born to human parents. 'You are a witch, and right now you cannot control your magic. It is beginning to control *you*.'

Dreska exhales slowly. 'I know. Maybe I've always known that I'm different. That I'm not like Liska. I'm not good like her.'

Brielle stops, turning to her. 'Being a witch does not make you bad,' she says gently. 'You can still be good, still be true to yourself and be a witch. It's what we do with our power that shapes who we are.'

Dreska bites her lip, bowing her head. 'But I will become a wraith in time, won't I? If I have no control. I've heard the whispers, the stories. I will become a creature of anguish and sorrow, and feed off my family, draining their spirits and forever darkening their days.'

'No. It doesn't have to be that way,' Brielle says, shaking her head slowly. Nova suddenly appears beside them and Dreska starts as the familiar purrs, brushing up against Brielle's leg.

'Is this your familiar?'

'Not mine,' Brielle says. 'My sister's. But Nova is with me for now.'

'You have a sister?'

'I do.' Brielle nods, her voice softening. 'And I would do anything for her too. Anything to keep her safe.'

'It's odd – I feel calm around Nova. Like she's taken

the edge off.' Dreska exhales, finally looking up at Brielle, desperation tinged with steel in her eyes. 'Tell me what I must do.'

Brielle hesitates, weighing her words as an unseen creature shrieks like a cut through the woods. 'You must survive the night of Clarus, out here in the darkest depths of the forest. You must face the very heart of yourself – your fears, your worries, your strengths, your magic – and you must gain absolute control over them all.'

'And if I don't? If I lose control?'

Brielle blinks steadily, taking in the girl's slim frame, her knitted brows, the jut of her bottom lip, quivering slightly, despite how brave she is trying to be. 'Then by morning you will have become a wraith, your own power consuming you whole, or you will have died. And you will no longer be able to reverse the curse you placed on Liska.'

When the clock strikes midnight the following night, Brielle meets Dreska at the tree line. A cool mist has rolled in, and it envelops them, turning nothing but thin air into wisps and the ghostly shapes of false wraiths.

'Are you ready?' she asks.

Dreska looks fearfully to the woods, then nods to Brielle, clutching her sleeves. 'I don't want to ever hurt my family again. Or anyone else. I must change Liska back, reverse the curse I placed on her. And I want more. I want to understand what I can feel, what I can't quite grasp.'

Brielle briefly closes her eyes and sighs. Dreska's words are almost identical to what Lowri had said to her just before their Clarus. For a moment, she can feel the ghost of Lowri here beside her, and her heart squeezes. 'Then step into the trees. Keep walking for about an hour, until you find a clearing, somewhere far from humans. I'll be nearby to make sure you are undisturbed.'

'How will I know when it's begun?'

'You'll know,' Brielle says thickly. 'You always know. Witch or wraith, it's down to you tonight. When dawn wakes, the rest of the world will know too.'

She waits as Dreska squares her shoulders and steps over the threshold of the forest. Then she counts to thirty, until she's sure the trees have swallowed her whole. Brielle releases a charged breath before glancing down at Nova, staring far too intently at the trees. 'After you, creature.'

Nova licks a paw and stalks into the undergrowth. Brielle takes her time, aware of everything, the crackle of twig, the bristle of thorn and leaf, the birds watching her with gleaming eyes from the knots and whorls of ancient bark. The mist coats her like a second skin, dew and the scent of moss clinging to the back of her throat as she follows the sounds of Dreska and her descent into Clarus. She had to simulate it. It is not the night marked as Clarus on the witch calendar. That night is when day and night are of equal length, so instead she ensured Dreska had a couple of drops of wyvern blood mingled with the hot berry juice she drank at supper. This would draw her true nature to the surface, and with a few witch words, a spell cast over her in the clearing and a drop of Brielle's own blood to thread a warding around her, Dreska would tip either way over the next few hours.

Witch or wraith.

Or death.

Finally, Brielle settles into the undergrowth, whispering the words *umbra tuttela* then, as she nicks the side of her palm with a small blade, allowing a couple of drops to hiss on the edge of the clearing, *Clarus inquisitio*. The mist clears to the edges, as though the clearing is now a wide, pale marble, and in its centre stands Dreska. The whole world seems to tremor, then hold its breath.

Dreska's spine suddenly snaps straight, her head tipped to the sky, light and dark pouring from her like ethereal smoke. The light and dark whirl as a storm, tearing though the clearing, raking up leaves as Dreska's mouth opens in a silent scream.

Then the storm takes the form of a wither beast, crying with her sister's voice. It grows huge and substantial, lumbering round her in a circle, and Brielle watches with gritted teeth as Dreska's shoulders drop and a sob escapes her throat. *Keep it together*, she wills her silently. *Put yourself aside and figure it out.*

As Dreska and the wither beast circle each other, Dreska wiping at her eyes with her sleeve, Brielle is dragged back to memories of her own Clarus, to the beast freed from the enclosure of her own mind, her own flesh.

A wyvern.

One of the murderous monsters that killed her mother, that split such a mighty hunter in half, merely for sport, when Brielle was far too young. Brielle remembers how she shook with rage as the wyvern circled her on Clarus, how she used her cunning and her might to drag it down to the ground, then staked its wings to the cold earth. She cried over it, she remembers that, cried for her birth mother, for the lack of warmth, lack of love in her life, all except for Lowri's. Then she bled the wyvern dry, the light and dark pouring back into her as she claimed the kill, and she knew what she would do, what she had to do.

That was the night the plan hatched in her mind to hunt down those wyvern in the Spines, the entire pack, and slaughter them all. It was only when Lowri shrieked in pain and sorrow that she jolted back into herself, to see what it was that her sister faced. Wraiths. Many, many wraiths, all swooping to claim her, their eyes shaped like the Malefant's. She couldn't interfere, but she stood with Lowri as her sister swept them all away. All her fears and sorrows, all her unworthy, poisoned thoughts were crippling her, but, in the end, Brielle and Lowri were together as dawn crested the land in the wild north of Arnhem. They conquered Clarus together.

She smiles at the memory now, how they grinned at each other, clothes torn and filthy, how they both knew at the same moment that they were witch and hunter.

Brielle, so lost in memories of her own Clarus, in monitoring Dreska's, does not hear the soft pad of footsteps behind her, nor the sigh of brushed leaves as someone approaches.

Not until there is steel at her throat.

'And what have we here?' a voice rumbles in her ear.

Chapter 6

Lowri

'THE REXILIUM BROTHERS?' LOWRI ASKS, foreboding blooming inside her as she looks to Eli. 'Have you ever met anyone that can do what you can do?'

Eli frowns and shakes his head. 'No one. It's why I wanted, why I was so interested in finding my father.'

'I know,' Lowri says quietly. 'But perhaps it's best you didn't find these brothers if they started a war here and caused such damage.'

'More than damage,' Ethlet says. 'Devastation. They tried to conquer our world and were beaten back, but at great cost. Come outside. I think it's time you see Fallow with your own eyes.'

Lowri gathers her temporary strength from the Fallow Fog brew to step outside, into the world beyond Eli's father's house. What she finds is an abomination. Magic – overused and twisted in such an unnatural, vicious way – has left a legacy of darkness that drips over Fallow. She watches as a drop falls from the dense fog above, descending like tendrils of onyx smoke.

Where it meets the paved street it splashes like ink, before dissipating. She licks her lips, cowering away, all too aware of the repercussions of twisted magic from the experiments in the lower levels of Coven Septern. If these Rexilium brothers did this, if they are capable of this level of destruction that cannot be undone . . . she watches as another droplet falls, then another. She cannot see the sun or moon or stars. The fog obscures it all. Ethlet sighs, stepping out beside her, and opens an umbrella with a *pop*, covering them both.

'You probably don't have long before you weaken again, but let's take a walk. Traversing is disorientating, from what I've been told. Isaiah said Fallow is like walking through a fractured mirror of Highborn. You may find it . . . strange.'

Eli declines an umbrella, holding out his hand for a drop of fog to land on his fingertips. It wreaths his skin in shadow for a heartbeat, then disappears. He rubs his fingertips together, regarding them impassively, then turns to Ethlet. 'Lead the way.'

They follow Ethlet past rows of crooked homes, all three or four storeys tall that don't just go up, but sometimes across, a room borrowed from one side or the other in jagged lines. It's not until they cross a street that two things occur to Lowri: there are no carriages, no horses or carts using the roads, and the houses all look as if they're falling over, as though suspended before the very brink of collapse.

People hurry past, clutching umbrellas that hide

their faces, and Lowri makes a point of observing their shoes instead. It's the only part of them not painted in black or grey like the streets of Fallow surrounding them. Ruby-red heels, burgundy flats, cerulean boots, even shoes that sharpen to a point, glistening and gold. She searches in vain for any other hint of colour in this city, but even the shop windows are bereft. They hold garments in shades ranging from shale to granite, umbrellas that all look the same to her untrained eye, and one shop holds cage after cage of mice, all pale grey with black beads for eyes.

'Why the shoes?' she murmurs to Ethlet as they round a corner on to a square with a gated garden at the centre, complete with muted grey rose bushes and stygian trees. 'And why is everything else grey?'

'It's another after-effect of the war. All the colour, all the light, was absorbed into the fog. Well, most of it. A few glints remained. If you had a little colour left, a little light magic, what would you use it on?' she asks. 'It's a glimmer of hope, and it's also just the fashion. I've got a pair of blush-pink boots I'm rather fond of.'

'So the shadow magic has been overused, whereas the light magic has all but vanished?' Eli asks, reaching out to pluck a rose petal through the black bars surrounding the garden. 'And it's light magic that brings colour to your world?'

'Pretty much,' Ethlet says with a small shrug. 'A world in balance has every shade of light and shadow, but when the Rexilium brothers were through with

Fallow, they had blotted out most of the light and left too much shadow behind. Now we are in the after, and even the Society cannot fix it.'

'You've mentioned the Society before. Who are they?' Lowri asks, stepping round a puddle that could just be rain, or, she realises, could be fog.

'Oh, careless of me,' Ethlet tuts. 'They're a collective of the very best and brightest minds, stretching across the land. Shadow and light magic wielders, they experiment, theorise, revolutionise. They use magic for the betterment and advancement of our world. Only now, of course, they have just shadow magic left.'

'And my father?' Eli says, glancing at her. 'Where did he fit into all this?'

Ethlet pivots down a side alley, bringing them back to a wider street. 'He was a member of the Society. He'd been trying to restore the balance of magic for a lifetime. But, in the end, it all comes down to a singular thing.'

'What's that?' Lowri asks.

'Our world is almost completely drained of light magic,' she says, eyeing them both. 'Isaiah believed that if we could only find a source, even just one person, we could reintroduce colour and light to the world. Then, the shadow magic would reduce, and magicians would replenish, having both light and shadow to draw from, the two twisted strands of magic reinforced. The cycle would begin again, and the world would heal itself over time. The fog would disappear.'

Lowri bites her lip. 'Just one source?'

'But there is no source, and there are no magicians left with that kind of power. Only scraps. So the people of Fallow weave any found glimmers into their footwear, and when we walk around Fallow, we recognise our neighbours, even if we cannot see their faces concealed under their umbrellas.' She smiles. 'Life finds a way, even in a world turned over to shadow.'

Ethlet's words echo through Lowri's mind with each step as she contemplates them. They stop outside an imposing building with pillars set beside huge doors thrust open on to the street. A few people mill in and out, putting up umbrellas to step back on to the street, or shaking them out, before walking inside.

'This is our museum. It tells the story of the war, if you'd like to take a look.'

'Yes,' Lowri agrees, ignoring the way her vision already sways, the effects of the Fallow Fog brew already wearing thin. She must have answers.

They wander through rooms filled with artefacts and paintings, telling the story of the history of Fallow. Eli moves slowly, examining each one with wonder, but Lowri strides ahead, to the room named *War*. And there, in a framed painting, maybe once in vivid colours but now depicted in shades of grey, are the Rexilium brothers. She gasps, the floor beneath her tilting sickeningly as she stumbles back. For they may be the Rexilium brothers in this world, but in hers . . .

They are the ruling council of Arnhem.

'Eli!' she calls, a dull thump beginning once more behind her eyes.

He hurries in, looking first at her, then to the painting she points out to him. He stills, taking in the cruel twist of the brothers' mouths, their pale skin, their eyes. Then he swears softly. 'My father was right, in that letter he left. He was right about them.'

'They're monsters,' Lowri says, lowering her arm. 'What they've done to this world . . .'

'We have to go back,' Eli says. 'If they have magic like mine, if they can wreak havoc like this, then the Fortunate Isles are in danger. Mira, Caden, Brielle . . .'

'None of them are safe,' Lowri whispers. 'Our *entire world* is not safe.' Then the last drop of strength leaves her, and she collapses.

Lowri wakes again on the sofa, the ebony flames crackling from the fireplace across the sitting room.

'Lor? Thank *everything*. Ethlet, she's awake. She's awake.'

Lowri blinks slowly, finding a figure hovering over her, quickly joined by another. Her whole body seems so heavy, and her mind is like cloud, her thoughts drifting too slowly, too hard to grasp.

'At last,' Ethlet says, but she's already moving away. 'I'll brew more Fallow Fog. If a slip of shadow magic gives her even a little strength, she needs to keep drinking until we find a more permanent solution for her.'

Eli takes Lowri's hand, and he thanks Ethlet before

turning troubled eyes on her. 'You're cold, Lor. Too cold.' He frowns. 'I have to find some way to help you. My father's work, it's all in the attic, in his office. I'll be back. Now you're awake, now that I know you're not . . .' He shudders, releasing her hand. 'Ethlet will bring the brew in a moment. We will fix this, Lor. I'll find a way.'

He leaves her too, the door snicking closed behind him, and she breathes into the silence. But before she can follow her thoughts into sleep, she's aware of another presence. A creature.

You know, I could probably help you, witch.

Lowri's eyelids peel back, and she finds Gracious peering up at her. More shadow than cat, she notes the way he moves, like the fog in the sky above Fallow. Like he's a physical, breathing embodiment of it. 'In what way, creature?'

Can you sense what I am?

'You are shadow itself.' Lowri scrunches her nose, tiredness weighing on her, staring at the grimalkin, parsing back its form, finding what appears to be beneath. 'Magic made almost flesh, aren't you? You feel a little like another creature I know. My familiar, Nova.'

Gracious purrs. *Clever, you witches. I have not met a creature like you before. If only you had brought more with you. Stronger ones filled with light magic.*

'You were too greedy, weren't you?' Lowri murmurs, beginning to understand what a grimalkin is as she fights to stay awake. 'You absorbed too much shadow magic. You were almost consumed by the fog. I can – I can sense it.'

Clever, clever witch.

Lowri squints at the grimalkin. 'You have no light magic left?'

Gracious licks his not-quite paws. *Yes. In another world, perhaps I would be a cat. But there was so much shadow, an abundance, and we grimalkin did not realise the true cost of our hunger.*

'And how do you think you can help me?'

A deal of sorts. I help you, and you in turn help me.

Lowri blinks heavily, knowing what it is to make a deal with a creature. Knowing it may have a greater cost than it first appears. 'Go on.'

If I give you some of the shadow magic I consumed, it will lessen my burden and it will help you too, witch. You're on the brink of death. I can feel it. But if you take some shadow magic, if you can twine it round the little light you have left, then maybe you'll live. Maybe you'll be able to regenerate your light magic, as Isaiah believed to be true of the nature of magic.

Lowri considers this offer, watching the cat that is not really a cat. 'You have not told Ethlet what you are? What you can do?'

She is but a child. Gracious twitches his tail. *Isaiah did not want her to be afraid of me. He wanted to ensure I stayed with her. That I protected her.*

'Keeping secrets never helps. In the end, the truth may be harder, but it's always better than a lie.'

Perhaps. Do you agree to the deal?

'I . . .' Lowri begins. Footsteps sound outside the door and she turns to see Ethlet framed in the doorway and holding a mug of Fallow Fog. When she looks back to the grimalkin, he has gone.

Chapter 7

Mira

I NUDGE KELL, POINTING TO the far end of the lawn, beyond the terrace where we are standing in the crowd, to where the darkness spills over clipped grass. Sember tosses down a huge joint, raw and bloody, and the drakes scent the air, growing even more restless. My jaw drops. Where in skies has she got that from? Just as quickly, she's gone, moving from shadow to shadow, and I realise none of the guards are looking at me. They're too focused on the drakes, on their riders snapping viciously at anyone getting too close.

'Keep to the edges of the crowd and don't run until I do,' I murmur, and Kell nods, understanding tightening his features.

Slowly, we make our way through the crowd as I clock Sember again, pausing for a moment, as though making sure we've spotted her before whisking round the corner of the terrace. When I reach the last smattering of guests, I bolt as one of the drakes roars.

Kell and I race across the lawn, sticking close to the

palace walls, and when we leave the crowd behind I duck down beneath a window. 'You know, I wouldn't blame you if you chose to escape,' I say. 'If it weren't for Agnes, I'd do the same.'

He shakes his head. 'Wouldn't even make it through the city. Wards everywhere, or so Brielle told me once. Whole place is riddled, like a string of invisible bells.'

Eli said this too, the first time we traversed in for our visit to Coven Septern, and for a moment my chest grows heavy at the thought of him, at being so far apart. He is on the edge of my thoughts always, a constant ache in the corner of my heart. 'I guess we're stuck in this together, then.'

'Looks like it.' He shrugs. 'Doesn't mean we can't get the lay of the land, though. And work out what that Skylan contender is up to.'

I grin. 'My thoughts exactly.'

Shuffling round the corner, I catch a flash of light, then hear a click as a door is opened. There's no time to ponder what it was or what Sember did to create that flash before we're both up, moving through the folds of shadow. On silent feet, I dart towards the door, catching it before it fully shuts. A door that leads back inside the palace . . . but one almost concealed in the wall, small and hidden behind a hedgerow from the lawns. I tilt my chin to the darkness beyond and Kell nods, flexing his fists.

On the other side we find a narrow hallway leading to a spiral staircase with uneven treads winding up. Wishing I had a blade, I move upwards, inwardly cursing every time a step groans all too audibly from my weight. At the top we find a web of storerooms and, further down the hallway, light and heat emanate from the kitchens along with the chatter of many voices.

A hand pinches my arm, jerking me into a storeroom. Sember holds a finger to her lips as Kell follows, fists raised. The door shuts at my back, and I whip round to find a boy leaning up against it, arms and ankles crossed with an amused smirk.

'The Skylan spare, I take it,' I say, shrugging out of Sember's grip. 'Were you planning to get those drakes so riled up that they'd torch *all* your competition?'

The boy sniffs, gaze travelling past me to Sember. 'I thought you said they were interesting.'

'Heath, for goodness' sake, you can't turn your nose up at everyone.'

'Yes, I can. I don't see why—'

'We need them!' Sember says in exasperation, folding her arms as she glares at him. Then her eyes land on me. 'And, to answer your question, no. The poor things just looked hungry after their long flight, and I needed a distraction. You caught on fast at least. I didn't fancy finding another huge steak in the cold store and lugging it down all those stairs.'

'What? He wouldn't have done it?' Kell asks, pointing at Heath.

'*He* is a prince and shall be addressed as such,' Heath says haughtily.

Sember snorts, covering it with a cough. 'You'll have to excuse him. He's a little grumpy about missing out on all the fun. I couldn't risk him being targeted by some overzealous courtier that hates Skylan.'

'Drakes are exceptional creatures, and I'm missing an opportunity to study them up close.'

'You wouldn't want to get too close to these ones,' I mutter. 'So why do you need us? Why draw us away?'

Sember looks at us both and shrugs. 'Because, somehow, I have to keep His Majesty here alive, and you're the only two contenders who I think can help me with that.'

'How so?' Kell asks.

'Rumour has it neither of you entered the Trials of your own free will,' she says quietly. 'And you're, shall we say, a bit different?'

I cross my arms, matching her stance, and watch her closely.

Sember sighs, casting her eyes to the ceiling. 'Look, we need allies and we want to team up with you.'

'What about the final Trial?' I ask, not giving an inch just yet. 'What about winning? Because, if you've heard a rumour about us, you should also know that I have a vested interest in victory that has nothing to do with status or glory. I couldn't care less about Arnhem's standing in the continent, or the trade deals and advantages the ruling council would garner from us winning.'

'We're aware,' Heath drawls. I look at him, and his expression softens under my gaze, the haughty air dropping away. 'We might be able to help with what you are interested in.'

'We haven't located your friend yet, but if she were to disappear unexpectedly . . .' Sember chips in.

'Disappear out of the reach of the watch and the ruling council?' I ask quickly, raising an eyebrow.

Sember nods. 'Exactly. Safely, unharmed, all in one piece with not a single gorgeous red hair out of place.' She glances at Heath. 'I must say, I rather think I could pull off being a redhead . . .'

'Stick to the point,' Kell says.

'We want you to work with us, to help us win this thing for Skylan so that Heath's father has no reason to shunt Heath off to marry some hideous person in another court to form an alliance to benefit Skylan. If Skylan prospers, Heath will be left alone to study creatures and their magic to his heart's content, far away from the courts and his father's schemes. And, in return for your help, we will ensure you survive, and escape. Including Agnes. All three of you,' Sember says impatiently. 'Well? Do we have a deal?'

Something niggles at me about what they're offering, and as I regard Sember I note the edge of desperation in her eyes. There's something they're omitting – I'm sure of it. But right now, with Agnes's life on the line, I'll take any deal that secures her safety. I look to Kell and raise my chin. He nods briefly, gaze sliding to Heath. 'As long as the spare here doesn't need too much babysitting.'

Before Heath can explode in indignation, I thrust my hand out to Sember. 'Deal.'

We return to the grand ball, careful not to be seen with Sember again, and glean every detail we can. By midnight, we have a list of names of all the other contenders. And when, the next day, we're taken to the same disused, dusty hall where we trained the day before, Hira is waiting for us, arms folded and sour-faced. I glance at Kell and he nods in agreement. If we're going to survive this and ensure that our end of the deal with the Skylan contenders holds up, we need Hira on our side. We need all the allies we can get, because, once we break out of this court with Agnes, there's no guarantee that Sember and Heath can get us beyond the city unnoticed. Not with all the witch wards. Which is where Hira comes in.

'There's something you should know,' I say, as soon as the guards leave us.

Hira sighs heavily, as though she'd rather be anywhere but with the two of us. 'This should be good.'

I plough on, ignoring her tone. 'The night I was captured, I overheard something. A conversation between Captain Spencer Leggan and one of the ruling council.'

Hira's eyes narrow, pinned to mine. 'Go on.'

'Before she tells you, we want something in return,' Kell pipes up. 'A favour for a favour.'

'You dare to bargain with me, boy?'

I shrug neutrally. 'Call it that if you like, but, so far, you've done very little to prepare us for the first Trial, and that is quite literally your *entire* assignment. Isn't it best you have some leverage in case this all goes wrong for you?'

She snorts. 'You're really going about this the wrong way. When someone wants a favour, usually—'

'The ruling council are planning to declare a new law,' I blurt out. 'It'll affect you and your coven. It'll affect every witch in Arnhem.'

'Or we can do it that way . . .' Kell mutters.

Hira blinks quickly, her arms dropping to her sides. 'What kind of *law*?'

'First, the favour,' I counter, thrusting up my chin. 'I need you to deliver two messages. One to the woman Kell worked for at the Inn Melusine on the Isle of Egan, and one to Caden Tresillian. On the Isle of Ennor.'

Silence hangs thick in the air between us.

'Perhaps you should let me do the talking next time?' Kell says out of the corner of his mouth.

'No,' Hira says, looking at him, then at me. 'Better to cut straight to the heart of it.'

'So you'll help us?' I ask.

'Depends on what you're planning to write in these messages, really,' Hira says. 'And why I'd help you. What information about a law would my Mal be interested in?'

'Look at it this way. You want us to live, right? That's half your assignment here. Little room for failure at

Coven Septern, I'll wager,' I say evenly. 'And, trust me, you want to be able to go back to your Malefant with the information we have. You want to be the first witch to bring it to her. Because, if you do, it won't matter if you fail this assignment. You'll still win her favour.'

A smile spreads slowly across her face. 'I'm listening.'

'Two messages. Just saying we're alive, and that we're competitors in the Trials. Nothing more, no elaborations,' I say, then swallow. 'We just want them to know we're alive.'

Hira runs a hand down her face, staring at every point in the hall except us. Then she folds her arms again, gaze fixed to mine, then Kell's. 'I'll think about it. In the meantime, you show me what you can do. What we have to work with.'

By lunchtime, it's clear that Kell has the most control. He can summon those pale flames at will, coaxing them from one palm to the other, then stoke them until they're a towering column of fire. But all I've managed to do, or all I've *wanted* to show Hira I can do, is call a blanket of clouds to hang moodily over the court. After the incident with the lightning, I refuse to push it any further. The thought of hurting someone, even accidentally, churns my stomach. Hira calls time and Kell exhales in relief. We go inside and Hira runs through what to expect in the coming days.

The guards bring our lunch – meaty broth, bread and water – and I gulp thirstily before digging into the food. I barely taste it, but Kell scowls before shovelling it in.

'You both got a good look at the other competitors last night?' Hira asks before tearing off a chunk of bread.

I nod. 'We saw some of them.'

'And you understand what you're facing?'

'We know we have to get through the Trials if we want to live,' Kell says stonily.

'Good,' Hira says, sweeping the crumbs from the table, then points at me. 'Unless you've got some trick up your sleeve, you need to find a weapon as soon as it begins. And you –' she jabs a finger at Kell – 'cover her and stick by her side. She'll protect you; she's far more vicious than you. Try not to die. It'll reflect poorly on me. And, if you're victorious, it will make things easier for your friend.'

'Is that all?' I ask her, ignoring the stab of fear at the lingering threat hanging over Agnes.

'No. I'll deliver your messages.' She grins at us. 'My Malefant is going to be intrigued indeed by what you have told me about this law. She'll want to investigate and I hope for your sakes that you've told the truth.'

'Why would I lie about that?' I ask.

Hira sighs, sitting back in her chair. 'To discredit me at my coven? I haven't exactly put a lot into your training, I know. Truth is, I wasn't given much time. I do wonder if this is as much a test for our coven as it is for the two of you. If you die, the ruling council can blame my Malefant and favour another coven. If you live, they reward our coven. Seems to me they're playing us against each other. So if this information about a law to control magic is true . . .'

'Which it is.'

'Then there's more going on here than I realised. Games upon games.' Hira shivers. 'I never did like court politics. But training you isn't that bad. And I suppose I see no harm in these messages. Now, to strategy . . .'

Hira crosses the room, pulling a folder from a bag and bringing it back to the table. 'What's this?' I ask, peering at the scrawled handwriting, littered with dates and names of past contenders.

'An analysis I pulled together of previous Trials both here and hosted by other territories.' She leafs through the pages and taps on a list. 'Trial types. Water-based, land-based, sky-based. In the past, there have been battlefields, monster hunts, mazes and traps . . . anything that will delight and engage a crowd of spectators.'

'Any idea which type the first Trial might be?' Kell asks, raising his eyebrows. 'Capture the flag — that doesn't sound so bad—'

'The flag was a drake egg and the mother was set loose to hunt down the team who captured her unborn young,' Hira says darkly. 'That was long, long ago and none survived.'

I shiver, running my eyes down the rest of the list. 'Do they often repeat Trials?'

'Occasionally,' Hira says. 'You should view this analysis as a set of examples, not absolutes. Be prepared for anything. Play to your strengths, keep each other alive. And try not to piss off the other contenders, or they could turn on you.'

I finish my food, listening as Hira and Kell discuss past Trials and hide the flush of triumph blooming in my middle. All I need is that one message to reach Ennor, and when Eli returns he will come for me. I want to believe that Sember and Heath will keep their deal with us and ensure our survival, but I am done trusting others. I cannot sit idly by and pour my hope and Agnes's very life into a stranger's hands.

And, in the meantime, I will make the most of being here, in the ruling council's court. I will find out what they intend to use me for. I will be a weapon, but not one wielded by *them*.

Chapter 8
Brielle

BRIELLE STILLS, EVERY INCH OF her focused on the cold touch of the blade against her throat. A thousand thoughts chase each other across her mind as she calculates her own odds, and that of Dreska's.

'A strange way to greet a hunter,' she says softly, chancing a glance to her side, taking in as much detail as she can. The hand holding the blade is covered with a rough brown glove, the kind worn by foot soldiers. His jacket sleeve is deep green, almost black, equally rough spun and designed to blend with the forest. A ranger, perhaps? Or a man from one of the nearby Lorvan towns, bent on slaughtering the beast casting fear in these parts. 'You're fortunate it's only me that you've found out here tonight.'

'Fortunate?' He chuckles softly before retracting the blade. 'Brielle Tresillian, I am counting my blessings.'

Brielle inhales sharply and spins, a dagger from the sash at her chest pressing into this stranger's own throat in less than a heartbeat. She blinks in surprise, finding a young man she recognises. Rue, who she met at the court in Highborn. His hair is a little longer than when she saw him there, blond streaks telling a tale of time spent outside the marble halls of the court over the past few weeks. Yet there is that same quiet gentleness about him, so at odds with the people for whom he works and the sense of unease they elicit. 'An ambassador for the ruling council of Arnhem, now this *is* unexpected. You are alone?'

He holds up his hands, showing his palms. 'I always travel alone.'

Brielle weighs how much danger he presents, how much Dreska faces, and decides that, right now, it's minimal. She could disarm Rue if it came to it. His lips twitch into a smile as she replaces the dagger in her sash. 'What are you doing here, in a northern forest of Lorva?'

'I could ask you the same,' he says, leaning against a tree trunk, crossing his arms. 'Unlikely place for an assignment. Your coven usually favours requests from Leicena or the mining region of Valstra at this time of year. Can't be much advantage to accepting anything from these parts. Not enough coin. Unless Coven Septern have fallen on hard times?'

'An unusual assignment, shall we say. One no hunter would usually wish to handle.' Brielle realises he may not yet know that she has broken ties with her coven. Which means he believes she is still an ally to the ruling council, a fact that she can most definitely turn to her advantage. 'I am out of favour at my coven since, well . . .

I must prove myself.' She coughs discreetly, hoping he catches her meaning, that she failed to capture and bring in Mira. He nods, as though in understanding. 'When we met, you didn't mention where your work takes you.'

'I did not,' Rue agrees, and she is struck, like the first time they met, that his accent and manner seem unplaceable. He's someone who can blend quite seamlessly. Someone with a canny knack for observing. But, in all her travels, she likes to be able to place a person, to learn quickly what makes them tick. With Rue, she is unsure. 'My work brings me to the Middenwilds this season.'

'Developing good relations with the principalities?' Brielle asks.

'Of a sort,' Rue replies cryptically. 'The ruling council are always seeking good terms, trade deals and allies. In Lorva, Kir . . .'

'Hindelvach?'

Rue blinks as though swiftly calculating a response and smiles. 'You know, I haven't visited the court there recently.'

Brielle senses the lie, the slight stiffening of his tone, but decides not to press him. Whatever he's keeping from her regarding that principality, there are better ways to uncover the truth. She'd rather he believed her an ally. For now, anyway.

'Nice evening for a wander in the forest,' she remarks, watching him. 'A little far from the court of Lorva, though.'

He only smiles again, looking past her to the fog-laced air seeming to bounce off a curved, invisible surface. 'What are you up to, Hunter?'

Brielle shrugs. 'This and that. If I were you, I'd move back to the road, find somewhere to bed down for the night.'

A growl rakes the air, and she swears. But Rue just settles in more comfortably against the tree trunk, seemingly unaffected by the nearby cries of a wither beast. 'I can see you are unafraid. Which means you're hiding something.'

'As are you,' Brielle says softly. 'Let's play a game. One truth, one question.'

'Seems reasonable. Ask away.'

'What is the ruling council's interest in the Middenwilds?'

He chuckles, shaking his head. 'Straight for the jugular? All right. The ruling council want to establish a trade route. A way of bringing materials from Valstra through one of these territories.'

Brielle frowns in confusion. The locals at Tavern Lomask did mention the felling of trees by a landowner, as though they were being cleared. It seems Rue has been busy indeed, if Lorva has agreed to that. But why through the Middenwilds, with its border of Skylan on one side, the sea on the other? The sea that no one has dared cross for decades due to the vast monsters lurking in its inky depths. The last crossing by a merchant left a fleet torn in two, with horrifying whispers of krakens and worse feasting on human flesh. 'But the sea route through the Straits is established. It's—'

'Owned by Skylan, a territory that raises exorbitant levies to line its dwindling coffers.' He raises an eyebrow. 'My turn. Is that a witch you're hiding in that fog behind you? Or a creature?'

She crosses her arms, contemplating her response. 'I don't see why I should tell you.'

'Fair's fair, Hunter.'

'It's a girl who is nearly a witch. I am trying to save her from becoming a wraith.'

'Ah,' he says, eyes flaring wide. 'That doesn't sound like an assignment from your coven at all. I've had few dealings with Coven Septern, and this doesn't strike me as a valuable venture. Or one to earn you clemency.'

'Was that a question?'

A smile dances at the corner of his mouth, and she wonders if he's realised he's been led towards a lie. That she is not working for her old coven at all. 'Merely an observation.'

A cry, more girl than beast, ricochets around the clearing and Brielle turns to see that the mist is slowly dispersing. She steps closer, heart in her throat, searching for any sign that Clarus is over for Dreska. That the witch has survived. 'Stay back,' she says quietly to Rue over her shoulder. 'If she marks you, she may think you're a threat. She might not be in her right mind just yet and a new witch is often extremely powerful for a short burst.'

Brielle steps closer, approaching carefully, and finds Dreska standing in the centre of the clearing, hands limp at her sides. Her eyes are closed, ebony smoke snaking up her wrists. The phantom shape of a wither beast lies motionless at her feet, fading quickly to nothing but dust. Brielle exhales softly, the relief leaving her dizzy, fast replaced with something harder. Stronger.

Victory.

Dreska opens her eyes and turns to her. 'Am I a wraith?' she asks. 'Am I a danger?'

'No.' Brielle smiles, closing the distance to place a hand on her shoulder. 'You survived Clarus. You fought your very self, and won, and now I can train you. Welcome, witch, to your new life.'

A twig snaps and Brielle turns, seeing Rue walking away. He looks over his shoulder just once, raising a hand in farewell before he is swallowed up by the forest and the night.

She feels a strange kind of melancholy, an ache, as though there is suddenly an absence in her life. It's uncomfortable and odd, but Rue has somehow lodged himself inside her thoughts and she's not sure how to shake him free. It must be the mystery of why he was really here, she reasons. Her head has never been turned by a young man before, especially not one allied to an enemy. Frowning, she turns her attention back to Dreska, the witch pale and shivering. But it's not time for a warm fire and celebrations just yet. Now Dreska has embraced her true self, she must figure out how to untangle the curse she placed on Liska.

'Can you feel the shape of your power now?' she asks Dreska. 'Can you sense the form of the curse on your sister?'

She bites her lip and nods slowly. 'I think so. We were arguing, and I wanted to banish her to the woods so badly, and all I could see was my own hurt and pain. All I could feel was how out of step I was with everyone around me. I'm so sorry. It was cowardly and selfish of me.'

'I do not ask in order to judge you,' Brielle says softly. 'Only to help you figure out how to release Liska from her torment.'

'That makes sense,' Dreska says, a ridge forming in the centre of her brow. 'It . . . it was like tonight, a rush of so much energy that I could barely contain it, and I hurled it at her.' She sighs. 'Except tonight I absorbed it and confronted it all.'

'So, what is the opposite?'

She presses her lips together, eyes softening. 'Love. Acceptance.'

'And do you think you're ready? If I give you the witch words to shape your thoughts and turn it into an unravelling spell?'

'Yes,' she says fervently. 'I'll do anything to save Liska. Anything to take it back.'

'Good,' Brielle says. 'We have an hour before dawn.'

* * *

Hunting down Liska takes barely any time. When they find her in a nearby clearing, Dreska moves straight for her, embracing her. Her sister shakes, crying quietly in her wither-beast form, the sound like a continuous low huff of breath. Brielle utters the witch word for Dreska to use and, for a moment, the forest grows still and watchful, the very air sharpening and pinching with the scent of burning and metal. Then Dreska whispers the witch word, *Retexene*, over and over, as Brielle taught her, and slowly the air calms, the scent of the forest returning: rain and loam and fresh leaf.

And, as Brielle looks on, the magic takes, and there are two sisters, crying quietly together. She smiles, a contented twitch of her lips, and motions to them to follow her, leading the witch and the girl away from the woods in which they were lost, and back to their world beyond.

When they return to Tavern Lomask – Liska rushing ahead to her father – Brielle senses Dreska's hesitation as she hangs back, giving her sister and father space. 'I could have cursed her to that life forever.'

'But you didn't. You found a way to unpick it,' Brielle says.

'Only with your help.' Dreska bites her lip. 'I can't stay here. Please, take me with you. On your assignments or back to your coven. Please, Hunter.'

Brielle eyes her steadily. 'I had planned to speak to you and your father of this. You will need to join a coven anyway now. You will need to train your power.'

'Then let it be with you,' Dreska says, rounding on her. 'You have shown kindness and you haven't judged me. And no one else came to help. No one else would – I realise that now. The world is big and our corner of Lorva is small, and coin makes the world turn, but we have little to spin it in the direction we wish.'

Brielle nods. 'So be it. I'll speak to your father.'

Brielle accepts the praise of the tavern owner, Gregor, for returning his lost daughter, but refuses the coin. Instead, she bargains for something else. An apprentice.

'I have need of one such as her,' she says over a pint and a plate of wild forage pie. 'On assignment, there are often lodgings to secure, laundry, coin to change, messages to send. She would be a help.' Brielle chooses not to mention that the daughter Gregor thought he had is actually a witch. She has learned over the years that prejudice can follow shock and she wishes for Dreska to reveal who and what she is at her own pace.

Gregor scratches his beard, regarding Dreska. 'And you wish to go?'

She nods quickly, dark hair gleaming, her telltale ebony fingernails hidden inside the gloves she hasn't taken off. 'I wish to see the world. To find my place within it.'

'Then I see no reason, now that Liska is found,' he rumbles.

'And I wish to remain,' Liska adds, tucking a wisp of hair back neatly into her bun. 'And hear of Dreska's adventures when she returns.'

So, the following day, Brielle leaves Tavern Lomask with a complaining Nova (*Hunter, I'd only just discovered the mice*), a witch and a rucksack overflowing with supplies. They walk to the nearest town and from there procure a coach and driver, and head up north to the mines of Valstra. Brielle keeps a weathered eye on Dreska, but the witch seems more at home in her own skin than ever before.

'So why Valstra?' she asks as they begin their bumpy journey out of the northern forest of Lorva. 'Why not into Skylan, or another principality, or . . .'

Brielle drums her fingernails on her knee, impatient to reach the next stop. And all the while pushing away thoughts of Rue. 'Because covens send their best hunters to Valstra to work for the mine owners, but the actual folk that work the mines are all but forgotten. There are always murmurings of wraiths in those parts. Families haunted by creatures that couldn't let them go.'

Dreska swallows. 'What I could have become. You're saving them, the wraiths?'

'Trying to. Me and Nova here,' she says, glancing to the familiar at her side. 'Although *she's* yet to prove her usefulness.'

All in good time, Hunter.

'Did your coven send you to do this? I've never heard of any coven caring about anything but coin.'

'They did not,' Brielle says with a small smile. 'It's a personal assignment. I'm building a new coven, one based on a different set of values. One that does not just stand by and allow things to *happen*. One that gets involved and helps to make things better.'

'That sounds like the kind of coven I'd like to be part of,' Dreska says with a smile. 'I could still become a wraith, couldn't I? If I don't train?'

'I'll train you,' Brielle vows, trying not to think of Lowri and the last time she saw her, drained and depleted, a husk of a witch. 'I'll train all of you, as I promised.'

Chapter 9

Lowri

LOWRI GULPS THE FALLOW FOG brew. This piece of the fog, the shadow magic of Fallow, is only enough to give her the strength to eat and get up. Her veins are still ink-riddled, her eyes like chips of obsidian. Pallid and weak, she knows she cannot restore herself on these sips of magic. She needs a better solution. And perhaps the grimalkin of this world are exactly the cure she needs. Perhaps they are like familiars.

She cannot speak to Eli or Ethlet. She cannot give away the secret Nova whispered to her as a child, of that on which a familiar feeds, and how they bond with their witch. But if Gracious fed too much, too voraciously, it could follow that he ended up like this. A creature bloated with shadow magic. She did not know it was possible; Nova never spoke of this. She had only ever taken what she needed and what Lowri, her witch, could offer up.

'How do I know you won't give me too much?' Lowri whispers to Gracious when Eli and Ethlet both leave the sitting room. The grimalkin is not bonded to her. The push and pull of magic between them is not intuitive. Gracious could expel shadow magic and weigh Lowri down with far too much.

I suppose you will have to trust me.

'Trust a creature so greedy he took so much magic that it changed his form?'

Gracious hisses, tail twitching.

'You have a temper. That bodes well,' she remarks dryly.

And you're extremely stubborn. Every hour you refuse the deal, you sink further towards death.

Lowri shrugs, but her nonchalance is a front. She taps her fingertips against the empty mug, considering her options, which are all too few. If she doesn't accept this creature's help, she knows the Fallow Fog brews will only preserve her strength temporarily, but not restore her. And she will leave Eli here alone. She will never return to Nova, or Brielle or Caden . . . which to her is intolerable. She's only just left Coven Septern, only just tasted freedom. And, given what they have discovered about the ruling council, the depictions they found of the Rexilium brothers in the Fallow Museum . . . well. They have to return. They have to warn everyone.

Are you ready yet, witch? Or must you be crossing death's threshold before you agree to the deal.

Lowri closes her eyes, wanting to shut this world out. Wanting to be back at Ennor Castle when she opens them. But all she can see is her own demise. 'Is this going to hurt?'

Probably.

'Excellent.'

So, you agree?

She opens her eyes and stares at the grimalkin before finally nodding.

When the grimalkin reaches out a paw, brushing her fingertips, her mind implodes with darkness. She cannot breathe. Her thoughts turn to panic as Eli bursts into the room, as dark blots out her vision. She tries calling to him, but she cannot. And she realises she may have made the biggest mistake of all in trusting this creature from another world.

Lowri senses storm and shadow, a construct of thunder and rain, but no light. Then the darkness recedes, her vision returning, and she watches Gracious as he places a soft paw on her chest. In the stillness between heartbeats, there's a shift, deep within her. A weight, the harsh edges of burnout, begin to peel away, and she feels warmth skipping over the ice in her blood. Looking down at her arms, she gasps as the black ink of her veins fades slightly, as her magic sparks inside her.

She is suddenly aware of Eli shouting her name and she looks up at him, standing there across the room. But she is in an impenetrable storm of magic with Gracious.

I have given enough, witch. Now, it's up to you.

All at once, the heavy storm surrounding them lifts and she blinks steadily at the grimalkin. Now, Gracious is not only shadow. She can see his features, a pale twitching nose, a fleck to his fur. And, if she's not mistaken, there's an amber sheen to his eyes. Before, he seemed almost formless as he moved. Now there are bones and claws shifting within all that shadow. She realises how like Nova he is.

Thank you, witch.

'You can call me Lowri,' she says as Eli exhales in relief across the room. 'Is a grimalkin another name for a familiar? You are very like Nova.'

Not exactly, although you could say they are sisters to our kind, he says, then licks his paw delicately. *Familiars are always hungry, siphoning slowly but consistently, unless they have not bonded with a witch, whereas we absorb too much all at once. And here there is only shadow. In another world, perhaps I would be a house cat and would spend my time catching mice.*

'Always hungry?' Lowri asks, scrunching her nose, her mind catching on those words. Nova has never drained her of magic completely, but they are bonded. Now that Nova is cut off from her, has been left behind, she cannot feed at all on Lowri's excess of magic . . .

The grimalkin yawns, jumping off her lap to wander to the fireside. *It's why there are no familiars in our world. No witches for them to bond with.*

Lowri's eyes dart to Eli's. 'Where is Nova?'

'She's with Brielle. Hunting for wraiths to form a new coven,' Eli says quietly.

'Skies . . .' Lowri breathes as it suddenly hits her what Nova has planned. Wraiths are formed by too much magic, a lack of control as it vibrates, explodes out of a witch's skin and bones. They are walking calamities of magic – volatile and destructive. But perhaps to a familiar they are something else entirely. A food source, and a big one. It dawns on her why Nova chose her, why she rarely wants to be apart from her. But now she's on a quest in their world, looking for something to sate her hunger in Lowri's absence. She swallows, searching Eli's eyes, seeing the knowledge drop like a stone inside him too. 'She's gone with Brielle to feed.'

Eli pushes back his hair, features troubled, as Ethlet walks in. She pauses, eyeing Gracious then Lowri, a frown forming. 'What . . .?'

Lowri clears her throat, staring pointedly at Gracious. 'There is something this grimalkin needs to share with you about his kind.'

As Lowri walks the streets of Fallow with Eli the next morning, she feels different. No longer entirely burned-out, but not quite herself yet either. *Too much shadow*, Gracious told her. *It's overpowering the light in your blood. You need time. You need to regenerate.*

'Could Nova have healed you?' Eli asks.

'No, I don't think so. Familiars are not the same as grimalkin. I've never come across a creature that can do what Gracious can. Give magic like that, after absorbing it like a sponge.'

'But because there is not enough light magic in this world . . .'

'Shadow was all he had to share,' Lowri finishes.

'But if you hadn't brought me here I would have died. I would have burned out. That your father had the creature that could heal a witch . . .'

Eli reaches for Lowri's fingertips and squeezes them. 'No more talk of you dying. You know you're my favourite cousin.'

'What about Caden?' Lowri asks in mock shock.

Eli grins, some of his old swagger returning. 'He's my favourite almost-brother.'

They step round a woman and a small child wearing shoes with little pink cat faces and continue into a gated garden. As they walk the gravelled paths, crunching past an array of grey and black flowers and trees, Lowri considers Ethlet's words: that Isaiah believed this world just needed a source of light magic strong enough to restart it. 'So now that I'm not about to collapse every few minutes, should we discuss why we're really here?'

Eli sighs. 'My father. His work. His knowledge of this place.'

'Just so.'

'But now we know about the Rexilium brothers, and who they are in our world, it changes everything.'

'We still need to find out more about them, though. We can't just rush back, we need to understand their motives, their weaknesses. Then return, ready to expose them, to take them out.'

Eli pauses, crouching down to examine a black rose. 'I walked in a walled garden like this one in Highborn when I brought Mira to the coven. She gave such a huge piece of herself then.' He draws in a breath. 'I miss her like I miss half my soul. The thought of her in danger, of her believing she is safe when really—'

'We will return to her,' Lowri says, placing a hand on his arm. 'She will be safe again. We all will. But we need answers first. We cannot help those we love without the information that Fallow can offer. I know you miss her.'

He nods, releasing the rose, and they resume their walk. 'When did you become so wise?'

She puts her arm through his. 'When I realised my cousin and my brother really, truly listened to me.'

'Time to pay a visit to this Society Ethlet spoke of, then?'

'Yes,' Lowri agrees. 'It's time to see where your father developed his work. We'll ask Ethlet to request an audience, but . . .'

'Yes?'

'How do I phrase this?' She sighs. 'You should keep searching your father's study. Keep looking through any notes he left behind. This Society do not appear to have helped Ethlet, and they have not undone the fog. Knowing how ancient organisations work in our world, well . . .'

'I should keep my wits about me?'

'We do not know everything about this world yet. This Society may welcome us. But we have to be prepared in case they don't.'

Chapter 10

Brielle

THE TOWN OF ICHBARROW IS one unbroken line of squat buildings situated half a mile from a mine shaft. It's a cold, desolate sort of place, even in springtime, with homes made of tin and windows so small they barely let in any light at all. There's a silence here, a lack of soul that Brielle finds unnerving, and she instructs Dreska to remain close. These places, sprung from nothing but a merchant's hunt for metals in the ground are not real communities. They live to serve the greed of men, and the children grow up either compliant or with so much fire in their chests that they burn themselves from the inside out.

'Are you a hunter?' a man asks before sucking in a lungful of air and hacking into his scrunched fist. He blinks up at Brielle, the crevices of his face accentuated with the dirt from the mine, as if the clouds of it have marked him, claimed him for the unlit world below. 'We have no coin.'

Brielle glances at Dreska, then back at the man. 'I am. But if it's sprites or knockers your mine owner should pay to have them cleared—'

'No,' a woman cuts in, wiping her hands on an apron tied at her waist. ''Tis a haunting. A ghostly creature. A wraith.'

'From a local family?' Brielle asks quietly. There are eyes all around her, skimming over her blades, assessing.

'A lost daughter,' the woman says. 'My sister's girl. Things always were a little strange, a little *different* here since she was born. Doors that locked on their own, hail in the summer months, loaves of bread baked with coppers flowing from the middle when cut open.'

'Expect you all liked that,' Dreska says, squinting at her.

She shrugs. 'Some things were good, some bad. Just enough good, though, to stop anyone mentioning it to the mine owner.'

'Then what happened?' Brielle prompts.

'She turned seventeen. One day a girl, the next a phantom,' the man says. 'There was this thin wail of misery, like she was being burned alive. It shook the roofs of every home in Ichbarrow and now . . . Well, the bread is dry as dust. No coppers to be had. No more seams to follow for the prospectors, and it's cold all the while. Even now it's springtime.'

'And the family?' Brielle asks, scanning the homes surrounding them.

'My sister keeps to herself,' the woman says. 'Her

husband and eldest boy are down the mine on longer shifts. Owner working us all to death for his profits.'

A common story, Nova purrs, meowing in that strange, unconvincing way before idling towards the drabbest tin-roofed home. *I can sense a presence in this one.*

'Lead us to the inn,' Brielle says to the woman, stalling for time while Nova searches for the wraith. 'Find us food and lodgings, and I'll give you my answer.'

They're offered a room with bunk beds and a chipped basin and Brielle advises Dreska to drink only what is boiled. They have tea next to a warm fire downstairs, a local kind infused with black, bitter leaves, which the other patrons enjoy with tiny, fermented cherries. Brielle asks for two plates of whatever is good and gets out a stack of cards that she sometimes uses on assignment to loosen up a gathering. Dreska seems anxious and it occurs to Brielle that this is her first time away from home, let alone in a new territory. She and Dreska play Kill or Crown, eat potatoes and mutton, then order more black tea as Nova appears at Brielle's side, tail twitching.

It's a wraith, all right.

Brielle nods, murmuring from the corner of her mouth. 'And the family?'

They need to leave the home before we attempt a reversal. Three of them, all with eyes dipped in charcoal.

'They're tired?'

Nova gives her an un-catlike stare. *They're haunted, Hunter.*

Brielle heaves a breath and turns to Dreska. 'Ready for our first assignment?'

'I think so,' Dreska replies, piling up the cards neatly, biting her lip.

'It's a girl, already a wraith. Family suffering from it.'

Dreska winces. 'It's what could have happened to me. To my family.'

'It was not your fault,' Brielle reminds her softly.

'Thank you,' Dreska says, and raises her chin, a hint of her stubborn wilfulness shining through. 'But all I want now is to help as many as I can. I want to feel worthy of my sister when I next see her.'

Brielle's heart twists, but she says nothing, rising from her chair. She has an awful feeling that Dreska will always want to atone simply for being who she is. They follow Nova out into the gathering dark.

The family live on the outskirts of Ichbarrow, mountains rearing up in the distance behind their home, the howl of grindlewolves like some discordant chant, eddying and echoing over the plains. Brielle smells coal and ash before they step inside, but in the sitting room the fire is unlit. The temperature drops, cool air slipping over her neck, and she wonders if the family have not been able to light a fire in some time.

The mother rises, her sister – the woman from before – is sitting with her. 'Men are at the mine still,' she says, taking her sister's hand. 'The girl is upstairs. She won't . . . You might not be able to see her. She drifts in and out of focus.'

Brielle licks her lips, listening to the creak of floorboards from above. 'Her name?'

'Inesh,' the mother whispers, her cloud of dark hair bobbing as she casts her gaze down. Nova was right: she does look haunted, as if she's never learned how to sleep. 'My daughter, or what was my daughter. Her name is Inesh.'

Dreska sits down beside her, taking her other hand. 'I know what this is, the crushing weight of it, and I hope we can help you.'

The woman's head bows, as though the weight truly is pressing down on her, the knowing that her daughter may never return. That she could live out her days with her ghost. 'Thank you,' she whispers. 'Please. Please save her.'

Brielle glances at Nova then at Dreska. 'I accept the assignment. I'll do all I can for Inesh.' Then she moves to the staircase, Nova at her heels. 'Dreska, stay behind me, no sudden movements. If the wraith lunges for you, you block her, yes? Just like we talked about.'

'Yes,' Dreska says, curling her hands into trembling fists.

Brielle slips up the cramped staircase, following the scent of burning and the sound of pitiful crying. When she opens the door to the girl's bedroom, she finds the wraith, crouched on a faded rug. Inesh is a pale apparition, a shadowy form of who she once must have been. Dark hair like her mother's in a crop above her shoulders, a blue gown, thin shoulders. She glances up as Nova slinks towards her, freezing as the familiar winds her tail round her knees. Her gaze is pinched, as though hungry, and sadness leaks from her, tendrils of it latching on to Brielle, dampening her mood instantly. She falls into her training, drawing up a mental barrier between herself and Inesh. A wraith cannot help but create misery, consuming all hope like a flame devours air, suffocating all the happiness you hold in your heart.

'You're not a cat,' Inesh says, voice sharp and serrated. Then her eyes meet Brielle's, before straying to Dreska. 'You – you're all so bright. Like walking stars . . .'

Now, Hunter, you will see why I'm of use. Tell the young one to shield herself and, if I forget who I am, bring me back.

'Nova? What do you mean?'

Brielle blinks down at where the familiar was, and in her place she finds something monstrous. Fangs and claws and smoke, all in a tiny, vicious storm . . . A storm that is growing, expanding.

We familiars form a bond with a witch for a purpose, Hunter, and I'm afraid that my witch has been gone too long. I will try not to take too much.

'Nova, talk to me,' Brielle says, trying to still the shake in her voice as she steps in front of Dreska, shielding her with her own body. 'What are you doing?'

Feeding.

Inesh snaps into full focus, eyes widening in terror as her gaze meets Brielle's. 'Please,' she manages, before she's engulfed.

Brielle freezes, heart pounding like a fist. Then it hits her, what a familiar is, what it . . . what *Nova* wants from this wraith. What feeds her.

'Nova, no!' cries Brielle as she leaps for the tempest of chaos and magic. She's aware of Dreska, aware of the room, then almost at once, all there is around her is storm. Magic engulfs her, seemingly endless, depthless, a twisting swirl of night and stars and colour. She can barely see, barely breathe, as the world the wraith and familiar have made seems to expand and contract, where the rules of time and distance do not apply. 'Nova!'

I'm here, Hunter, and nowhere, Nova purrs in her mind like the scrape of teasing claws. *This wraith is a well of magic, almost depthless. Do you want to save her?*

'Do you?' Brielle thunders, turning this way and that, ribbons of light and shadow and chaos dashing across her vision. 'Did you ever intend to?'

Of course. Why do you think I suggested this assignment?

Then Nova is beside her, twice as big, all edges and sharpness, with none of the fat folds and feline fur of her usual form.

If I feed, I am no longer hungry. And the wraith no longer has an uncontrollable outpouring of magic. She'll gain some control, enough to be a witch once more. One you can train. One you can ensure doesn't become a wraith again.

Brielle narrows her gaze on Nova. 'Have you been feeding off me? Dreska?'

A little, I admit. But you don't taste right. Neither does this wraith, but food is food and hunger is hunger.

'You like the taste of Lowri's magic,' she says with a shudder.

Nova, in her true form, turns to her, revealing rows of jagged teeth and eyes like the night. *Yes. And now you know our secret. The greatest secret of our kind. What we only ever reveal to the witch we bond with, that we sustain ourselves by feeding on their excess magic. In your world, at least. Now, please . . . help me detach from this young witch. I cannot take too much.*

A sudden surge of magic knocks Brielle backwards, and Nova whips round, facing the wraith, who is now once more in the shape of a girl.

Inesh.

Nova stalks forward, tail lashing, and pounces at the witch. Brielle gasps, staggering back as waves of magic explode and pummel her, Inesh's cry a deafening roar.

Brielle blinks rapidly and throws out her hand towards Nova, speaking a word with the command of a witch.

'*Dimmita.*'

Brielle collides with the wall behind her, and suddenly there is silence. Stillness. A ringing, like tinny bells in her ears. She groans as she gets to her feet and finds the room in splinters. Dreska crouches by the door, eyes fixed on the middle of the room, furniture in pieces all around them. And Nova is unmoving, pulsing oddly, a glow to her fur that lingers for a moment. She seems to have grown, now bigger than a cat ought to be, and the figure lying next to her . . .

'Inesh?' Brielle whispers, moving towards the witch. 'Inesh, can you hear me?'

The girl uncurls, blinking into the room, and Brielle finds a witch with brown skin, a tight coiled weave of dark red hair and startlingly blue eyes. Her hand whips out to grab Nova. 'What did you take from me, creature?'

And Brielle grins, heart calming to a patter as she kneels beside her. The witch stiffens, head swivelling slowly to meet Brielle's gaze.

She's like you were. All tangled thorny magic. Fearless.

'You're right, Nova,' Brielle says quietly. 'She is like me. I believe we have found a new hunter for our coven.'

Nova flicks her tail and begins to stalk away.

'Nova?' Brielle calls after her. 'You and I are going to have a chat. Set some boundaries, expectations . . .'

Of course. A hunter managing a creature.

'That's not what I meant.'

But you are right. One not as strong as I, not so used to being a witch's familiar, may have taken too much. May have become too greedy. Those creatures are no longer familiars, and their greed can lead to death.

Brielle releases a breath. 'Just tell me next time? No more secrets. But what you did . . . You saved her.'

You're welcome, Brielle.

When they emerge from the house, it's daytime, a thin streak of grey rising up on the horizon. Brielle squints, tracking the progress of a hawktail as it soars towards the town. Hawktails, messenger birds, provide an expensive but dependable service. And she's fairly sure it's flying towards her. She braces herself as it circles, then she holds out her arm for it to land.

'Aren't you a beauty,' she murmurs, catching the jade and violet flecks in its black wings as it lands. She unfastens the message tied round one of its legs. Ripping open the letter, her tiredness from the long night dissolves, forehead pinching as she races through the news it contains. Then she bunches the message in her fist, throwing her arm up in anger. With a cry, the hawktail ascends, leaving her at once.

Turning to her three unlikely companions – a familiar, a witch in training and a hunter in training – she sizes them up, finding three sets of fierce eyes, all resting expectantly on her.

'We return to Ennor,' she says, dropping the message in her pocket, 'as swiftly as we can. Pack your things and make ready for the journey home. My friends are in danger. Clarus for Inesh, to bind you as a hunter, will have to wait.' She turns, muttering to Nova. 'And if that hawktail can find us with a message . . .'

Then we are too easy to find.

Chapter 11

Mira

I HEAR THEM LONG BEFORE I see them. The baying crowd, restless for entertainment. Crying out for blood. For a victor.

Pulse thrumming in my veins, I take step after step. With each footfall, each moment as we pass through a tunnel, towards a window of daylight, I sink deeper within myself. This is who I am, who I've always been. A girl, one of the seven who swam out on the rope from Rosevear, going into a storm.

Except today it's an arena and there is no rope to lash myself to, no safety net, no Agnes or Kai or Bryn. Just me, fierce and ready, walking out to meet the first Trial. I glance to my right, catching Kell's eye. He's walking beside me, dressed as we all are, in breeches and a fitted vest, no weapons, no artifice. He nods and I nod back. Our only aim in this first Trial is to survive. The ruling council may want us to be victorious, but we cannot win, cannot free ourselves and Agnes, if we are dead.

My hair is braided, snaking down my left shoulder, much like the female contender, Fey from the Spines, just ahead of us. Behind us are Sember and Heath, the contenders from Skylan with whom we have made a deal. We've done all we can. We protect them; they protect us. And now messages are on their way to Ennor and Egan so our people know we're alive. When we get out of this tunnel, when the Trial starts, I just need to find a weapon. And then I can ensure we all make it through the first Trial with beating hearts.

I hold up my hand to shield my eyes as we emerge from the tunnel, the sun glowing like an old god in the sky. Between the fractured rays of sunlight beaming through my fingers, I see the crowd, a wave of them surrounding us, stacked up in rows, all facing towards a sunken arena. In the centre, the huge oval-shaped space is filled with water. It tumbles, as though to imitate the sea, a ship listing on its side in the centre, rocks crowding around it. Did the ruling council engineer this as the first Trial to show me, their champion, off to the crowds? I would not put it past them. If everyone here only knew . . . It's tantamount to cheating.

For a moment, I'm sure we can do this: we can survive. This Trial is nothing compared to the storms around Rosevear, the nights I've swum out with the seven, lashed to a rope, a breath from death, into the tide. They may want to show me off as their competitor, the symbol of the lion of Arnhem, roaring in victory, but to me it only means that we will not die today.

But then . . .

There's a flash in the water – scales, like iridescent plates of armour – there for a heartbeat and gone in the next breath.

'Did you see that?' I murmur to Kell. 'In the water?'

He shakes his head, eyes darting everywhere. I notice how pale he's become. 'Mira, I have to tell you something, before—'

'Ladies and gentleman!' a voice booms across the arena, and we all fall silent. 'The day is upon us, the first of the infamous Trials!'

A roar rises up around us and I cover my ears.

'We have contenders from across the continent representing their countries and territories to win this Trial for the glory of their people. One team will be victorious, but only those that survive will pass to the next Trial. There are three Trials in total, three for the competitors to prove their worth. Who are you supporting?'

There's a cacophony of voices, cries of Skylan, Middenwilds, Arnhem, Leicena . . . all melting into one deafening note.

'Now there can only be one victor. One territory or country that will triumph over all others. The contenders will win acclaim and honour as well as a bountiful prize bestowed by the ruling council of Arnhem. Three Trials! May the best pair win. Are we ready?'

I cringe as the noise of thousands beats in my chest.

'I said, ARE WE READY?'

I glance at the other contenders, the guards at their backs, every face betraying a spectrum of emotion. It's the first time it occurs to me to wonder if they all *want* to be here? Are any of them being forced to compete, like Kell and I are? Then Sember locks gazes with mine and she winks. I wink back, then turn to face the sunken arena. I was born for this, monsters or no. I will get us through.

A hand grips my arm and in the short lull before the Trial begins, Kell whispers frantically in my ear. 'Mira, I have to tell you. I can't swim.'

My eyes dart to his, finding the panic, the terror filling them. The ruling council can't have known. I open my mouth to respond, but my voice is drowned out by the commentator once more.

'The rules are simple: contenders must find a piece of treasure in the sinking ship and bring it back to shore. At least one member from each pair must search for and secure a piece of treasure. Once the treasure has been found, each pair must return to their circle at the edge of the arena. They must both reach this to progress to the next Trial. If a pair fails to find a piece of treasure and bring it back to their circle . . .'

The voices all around us rise and fall.

'. . . then they will not go through to the next Trial, but, not only that, each contender must enter the water. Sending just one contender to retrieve the loot is not permitted. So straightforward, so simple . . . is it not?'

I look again at the churning water and catch another flash of scales.

'Of course, there are creatures of myth guarding their horde. Contenders, take your places.'

Before I can scan the water again, discern what it is that lurks in wait, we're shoved across to the right, separated into pairs, and Kell and I find ourselves in a marked circle on one side of the arena. Each pair is spread out round the edge in similar circles, the crowds at our backs and before us, all facing the arena in an oval. The drop down into the water isn't far, and I stare over the edge, finding that the sides are rough rock, perfect to climb. If it was just me, if it was just my life I held in my hands . . . I look at the other contenders, assessing them in turn. They're all focused, an air of fear about them, and I wonder what they have at stake. What they have to lose if they do not win this first Trial, or all of them. After Sember's flippant comment about Prince Heath being married off, I can see what awaits him, the endless maw of a life of unhappiness and duty. But what of Sember? What of the others?

'When you say you can't swim at all, Kell, can you get into the water?' I turn to him, breaking my gaze from the others and see that he is shaking.

'I can stay upright, but that's it. I can't swim a length.' He blows out a breath, looking at me. 'Am I going to die?'

'Not today,' I say fiercely, keeping my eyes on his. 'You are going to get into the water, then stay by the rock. They said each contender has to *enter* the water, not swim through it. A pair need to find a treasure, not each individual. We can still do this.'

Relief spreads through Kell's features. 'Thank you. I will make this up to you. I will.'

'Our only aim today is to survive, remember?' I say. 'Let me deal with the technicalities.'

As the crowds quiet, the sun still a heavy orb hanging overhead, I take a moment to scan the rows of people, searching for a cascade of red hair. I'm sure I see a flash, but it's too difficult to discern and I wrench my gaze away. Instead, I pick out where the Skylan contenders, Heath and Sember, are standing – directly across from us. I raise my hand, as though in greeting, and Heath raises his back.

Then as a mighty horn blasts through the arena, signalling that the Trial has begun, I dive.

Bubbles stream past my face, my blood igniting in the waves. I've been starved of this connection to half my very self, and, for a moment, I close my eyes and feel the water as it undulates between my fingers. Then I break through the surface and wait as Kell splashes down, before nudging him gently to the edge.

'Thank you,' he breathes, fear marking every flail of his limbs as his hands grasp the rock. It's only when he's clinging to a handhold, head and shoulders above the water, that I turn, surveying the waves, and find Sember and Heath treading water, waiting for me.

'Stay here, Kell. I'll be as fast as I can. Don't move

too much. Don't attract attention. We're not alone in this water.' Then I dive again, aiming for Sember and Heath like an arrow.

When I emerge, they eye me warily, Sember already clutching a silver spear. 'Game plan?' she asks.

'We swim to the ship, you guard, I seek treasure for us both, then we get back to our circles,' I say. 'Where did you get that?'

'She's annoyingly resourceful,' Heath drawls. 'Is Kell not joining us?'

'Can't swim,' I say, watching as the other contenders strike out like us, or edge towards rocks, where various weapons gleam temptingly. 'You're stuck with just me on this one, Prince.'

'Lead the way,' he says, and I grin at him before heading in the direction of the ship. I'd give anything for a blade right now, a weapon, in case I get too close to another contender, but they're too far off course, and I need to get back to Kell. He's too vulnerable all alone.

As I reach the ship, checking Sember and Heath are still swimming behind me, I scan for the other contenders. No one else has quite reached the ship yet, most have hauled themselves on to rocks and are now fastening weapons at their hips. But a flash of movement makes me gasp. A contender from Stanvard, one of the two girls I saw at the ball, has a rock. She moves swiftly, pouncing on to the back of a Middenwild contender, a boy named Pascha, as he swims past. He gurgles, disappearing underwater, and she raises the rock to strike.

There's a whip of scales, a cavernous mouth, and they both sink, blotted out by a wave. I scan back and forth, heart in my throat, but neither of them emerges. My hand trembles as I wave at Sember and Heath to hurry, dragging them up and out of the churn as a tail whips up, then crashes down no more than a few lengths away.

'Stay out of the water,' I say quickly, pressing them back into an opening in the ship's side. 'If any other contenders get close . . .'

Sember nods, tightening her fist round the spear. 'I'll be ready.'

I take a few halting footsteps into the near dark of the wrecked ship. It was always Agnes's role to hunt for treasure and cargo back on Rosevear, but now it must be mine. As I move deeper into the belly of the ship, the sound of cries outside snatches at my focus. But I keep moving, edging towards a doorway out of the cargo hold, and slip through.

There is a corridor on its side, and I clamber along it, listening intently for any sign that I'm not alone. But there are only the creaks of a dying ship, and my own heart thundering inside my ribs. I kick each door open, peering in, but find only a scatter of barrels or coiled rope and sack cloth. When I reach the ladder stairs, I crawl up at an angle, emerging on to the level with the captain's cabin. This door I open softly, the light catching in jewelled pools along the walls.

The first thing I spy is a blade on the floor, as though it has fallen off the wide table in the centre of the room.

The second is a small, ornate box, set with mother of pearl that glints and lures on the other side of the room. If there is treasure inside it, then that counts as two pieces, surely. I can swipe it and run. Then I look up at a stirring of movement and freeze. The creature in the corner smiles, all long dark hair, pale lidless eyes and row upon row of sharp, shiny teeth.

'You took your time,' the creature says, and lunges.

Chapter 12

Brielle

IT'S NOT UNTIL THEY REACH the Leutewild Inn, nestled in the foothills of a mountain range in Skylan that Brielle senses they are being followed. They step off the stagecoach that Brielle, Dreska and Inesh have shared with two others on the journey into Skylan so far. A governess, who will now change coaches to reach her final destination, the capital city of Bergstat and a man who peers at them quietly from under a wide-brimmed hat, muttering a farewell before setting off to his farm, a few miles east on foot.

Brielle moves through the press of pipe smokers and travellers to a table under a window by the bar, shuffling her two young charges into seats. Inesh droops in her chair, a little green still from the stuffy coach and bumpy lanes, but Dreska, keen-eyed as ever, is already signalling to a barman. She holds Inesh's hand, squeezing it gently. 'You just need to line your stomach.'

Brielle hides her smile, a flare of pride startling her.

She's never mentored anyone before, but, for the first time, she wonders if it will suit her. If this might be her calling after all.

That's when she hears it. A low hum of voices, words indistinct, the cold touch of a witch's eyes brushing the back of her neck. She freezes, then forces herself to joke with her young charges, handing out the glasses of water from the barman, as though nothing is amiss, but it's unmistakable. There are witches in this inn, hunters like her, and they're searching for Brielle.

She accepts a plate of roast meat and seasonal vegetables, cooked slowly with the local herbs grown in the loam of the fields. She pours thyme sauce over the meat, relishing how Inesh eats a full plate and asks for seconds, the colour and life returning to her after her time as a wraith and the long, arduous journey. Casually, she glances around, signalling for ale and a second helping for Inesh, sweeping a long, unhurried look over the other patrons. A flash of silver, a pair of eyes snagging on hers, and she knows for sure. There are hunters from a coven here, and they've marked the three of them.

Nova winds through the chair legs, pausing at Brielle's side and she pretends to drop her fork, bending down to scoop it up. 'At least two witches and they're watching us. Will you find our driver?'

Nova yowls. *I see them. Witches indeed and no friendly purpose, I fear. I will search for the driver so we can be on our way.*

Brielle gulps down her ale before wiping her mouth with her sleeve, and finds Dreska watching her.

'Something is amiss, isn't it?' she asks.

'Do you sense it?'

Dreska shrugs, crossing her cutlery on her plate and leaning back. 'I sense a press, or a brush of eyes. Someone, or something, studying us.'

'Good,' Brielle says with a nod. 'That's your witch sense. Some never develop it, but as a hunter it's vital.'

'Do you know who they are?' asks Inesh between mouthfuls.

'No. And as they have not approached us openly . . .'

Dreska nods in understanding. 'We should leave.'

'Quietly,' Brielle agrees. 'And swiftly.'

Inesh watches wistfully as a server carries a tray of treacle tarts to another table. 'I suppose there's no time for pudding?'

'Sadly not,' Brielle says as she spies Nova by the door. She pushes back her chair and raises her eyebrows. 'We must return to the coach at once. Be alert.'

Outside the Leutewild Inn it is eerily quiet compared to within. The ostler has taken in the horses to be fed and watered, the coach left in a row with two other carriages and a cart. Brielle eyes them thoughtfully before seeking out Nova. 'No sign of the driver?'

None, Hunter. I've searched high and low, but his scent begins and ends in our coach. As though he didn't even make it inside the inn.

'Can you sense magic? Any ill workings?'

Nova scrunches her nose. *I cannot be sure. There is an odd, cloying scent masking almost everything.*

For Brielle, that's enough of a warning. She's learned over years of assignments that when your own senses clang like discordant bells it's time to move. She flags down a passing stableboy, pressing a copper into his palm to bring the horses round. The ostler appears a few minutes later, grousing until Brielle presses more coin into his palms too. Her eyes dart everywhere as the ostler secures the horses to the coach and she checks the horses herself, inspecting the coach, the wheels.

Dreska and Inesh clamber inside and she casts a wary look back at the steamed-up inn windows, then at the two other carriages. 'Nova, I need you to stay inside the coach with Dreska and Inesh. Keep them calm.'

And what do you intend to do?

Brielle smiles. 'Our coach needs a driver.'

She runs a hand over the horses and speaks softly to them, opening up a path between her and them. She finds they are weary but well fed. She whispers a witch word to each of them, giving them strength and courage, and leaps on to the driver's seat, taking up the reins. As she urges the horses forward, rain peppers the seat beside her. She looks up, finding the grey clouds shrouding the last of the sun as it dips down, near the horizon. She doesn't want to make this journey now. If anything, they should hunker down, allow the horses some rest, take a room and set off at dawn. Slick roads, poor daylight and the chance of witches on their heels is a poor recipe for success. But they have little choice.

Brielle clicks her tongue and the horses pull forward, away from the inn. She peers over her shoulder through the steadily increasing rain and, just before they round the corner, she sees the door fly open, two figures emerging. She was right. They are being watched. She whispers again to the horses and they launch into a trot, needing to put distance between them and the hunters. If they can just reach the mountain pass, they can find a place to hide. There's a village where she has friends, where she rid them of a ghoul a year ago . . .

It's dangerous, this pass, and at this time of the year, if the rain has swelled the river, if the horses baulk . . . but she has to try. She sets her sights on the road, determination steeling her as the rain trickles down inside her jacket. She clicks her tongue again, picturing those witches already in pursuit. 'Faster, beauties. Faster!'

Then she hears it, between the sounds of this coach's wheels and the horses' hooves as she attunes her senses. Another coach. No, two coaches, the clatter of many hooves, of wheels clashing against the stone and ground as they pull away from the inn.

She swears softly, calculating the time to the pass, hoping that this coach doesn't throw a wheel. The horses can canter, but only over a short distance while attached to the coach and there's no time to unhook them now. She clicks her tongue again, her entire being tensing, fizzing with the possibility of a skirmish with these hunters.

As the rain falls around them, the wind whipping up the trees crowding the road as they flee, she wonders if they will survive the night.

Chapter 13

Mira

I LEAP TO THE SIDE, grabbing the blade, and surge up with it held in my fist. The creature shrieks then sniffs the air, eyes darting back and forth.

'Where are you?' it says, voice like the hideous grating of claws on granite. 'Where have you gone?'

Is it . . . blind? Can this creature not see me? I wave my arm, keeping the blade poised for attack, but the creature crouches, still sniffing the air. Its joints are all turned inwards, like an inverted spider with an almost human face, yet it seems bleached of sunlight, as though it lives in the depths of the sea. I rake my memories for any mention of a being such as this and only find one answer.

Mermaid.

Not quite fish, not quite phantom squid, and not quite siren either. A creature that dwells in the deepest parts of the ocean, where even the light fails to filter down. It doesn't need sight because its other senses –

It snaps its head to me. '*Found you.*'

– are excellent.

Vaulting over the table, it misses me by inches, cursing and scrambling like a spider over the floor. I scoop up the treasure box and turn just as the creature barrels into me, jaws gnashing. I fend it off with the blade, swiping at its chest, and it shrieks, cowering back. Breathing deeply, panic blooming inside me, I look to see if I can make it to the door. I hear a thump outside, more footsteps in the corridor, then a gasp of horror before another creature shrieks in glee. There is more than one mermaid aboard and, from the sound of the footsteps, at least two other contenders are seeking treasure elsewhere on the ship. I have to escape while I can.

'Evil human, nasty, all of you,' the creature says, drawing my focus to it as its pale eyes rake back and forth. Black blood clots across its chest where I swiped out with my blade, but it doesn't seem to have slowed the creature down. In fact, the wound has already clotted.

I don't dare talk, barely dare to breathe, as it sniffs the air, searching again for me. Carefully, one tread at a time, I wend my way back to the door, blade outstretched in my shaking fist. I need to time this right, when I cannot hear the others in the narrow corridor outside. When I can safely make a dash for it.

'You think there aren't more out there, waiting?' the mermaid taunts. 'They brought us all to the arena, lured us with meat and blood . . . but you're fresher; I can smell it. Human, and yet . . . not entirely.'

'What you can scent in my blood will be the death of you if you cross me again,' I hiss, reaching the door.

The mermaid lunges, but I'm faster. When it's a handbreadth away, when I can smell its foul breath, I strike. My blade crunches past rows of teeth, through bone and blood and flesh, lodging in the back of its skull with a dull thud. It twitches horribly, its dark blood oozing down my arm as I lower it to the ground and pull its carcass loose from the blade.

Tremors racking my limbs, I blink quickly, gathering myself, and wipe the blade down my thigh. The creature's blood still clings to my arm and I suppress a shudder, opening the door. I leave it alone, dead and hungry, and rush back through the ship on nimble feet. I hear others still onboard, but manage to avoid them. If there are more of those creatures in the water, I need to return to Kell. He is without a weapon, a perfect target.

At the side of the ship, I find Sember and Heath panting, covered in blood. Sember wipes a hand over her forehead and I see two mermaids floating behind her in the water. Dead. 'You found treasure?'

'I did,' I say, quickly opening the treasure chest tucked under my arm. Releasing the clasp, I find a string of pearls and a brooch, glittering with gems. I toss the treasure box to her with the brooch inside and she catches it deftly, tucking it under her own arm. Then I wind the pearls round my wrist, tying them off securely. 'Just creature or human as well?'

'Creature blood,' she breathes as Heath ducks, an arrow flying to embed itself in the wood behind his head. 'I smell like a fish market.'

'But the other contenders are *not* going to like losing,' Heath adds. 'We need to leave. Carefully.'

I stride forward, ducking down beside the entrance, and try not to look too closely at the two dead mermaids floating on the eddying waves. The contenders from the Spines are nocking arrows, crouched on a rock, waiting for us to escape. And the others . . . they're either engaged in their own battles or searching for treasure in the bowels of the ship. I bite my lip, searching swiftly for Kell, and relief floods me as I catch sight of him still clinging to the rocks on the opposite wall of the arena. Somehow, he hasn't been hunted. Yet.

'Fey and Soturi are close by, there are more creatures in the water and at least three of the others fighting,' I rattle off quickly, turning to Sember and Heath. 'I'll cover you both. You get back to your circle.'

They glance at each other. 'And what about you?' Sember asks.

I pinch my lips together, then smile. 'I keep my word; I save myself. Get to your circle and claim your victory. I'll get to my circle just after you. You can't liberate Agnes if you're dead now, can you?'

Without waiting for their answer, I bolt over the side of the ship and dive into the waiting water. Beneath the surface, there are eyes everywhere. Pale, glowing, waiting. I catch a glint of scales, of a huge, yawning maw, before the waves churn and I lose sight of it. But in that moment, in that glimpse, I piece together what it is, what they have dragged here from the sea for the crowd's entertainment.

The morgawr.

Sea serpent, hunter of humans. It is the cursed creature on every sailor's tongue. They whisper of this monster with haunted eyes, this creature of the Southern Ocean, where no ship dares sail any more. I grit my teeth, cursing the ruling council for their arrogance, their stupidity in bringing it into the heart of Arnhem. The morgawr is death.

All it wants is to feast.

Those pale eyes reappear, rearranged like a scatter of dice, like points of reference on an ever-changing map. It's hungry, but I'm too fast to be caught. Darting like a fish, like the siren I am, I pierce the water like a needle, finding the rock I seek. Emerging, I grip an ankle, raking it towards me with a hissing breath. Soturi, the male contender from the Spines yells out, but my blade is already at his throat.

'You've already lost out on first place. Lower the bows and get back to your circle or you'll be food for the morgawr.'

Fey blinks down at us, calculating their odds if she doesn't do as I say, then carefully drops her bow. I catch a flash at her throat and see she has found a piece of treasure, a necklace. She must have been trying to pick a few of us off to better their odds in the future

Trials instead of claiming just this one as a victory. 'The morgawr? You're certain? They brought *that* here?'

I glance up at her, then back at Soturi before jerking my chin. 'Leave now, don't shoot the Skylan contenders and I'll swim with you. Deal?'

Fey spits on the ground in frustration but says, 'Deal.'

I cover them, swimming with my gaze locked on those scattered eyes, searching for the flash of scales, for the telltale sign of the true monster and its jaws. They reach the rocky side of the arena and I don't wait for them to pull themselves up. Scanning the waves, I see Sember and Heath, just a short length from their circle. But my relief is short-lived as the sea grows still around them. I haul in a breath, ready to scream a warning, when the morgawr crashes to the surface, revealing a dark, fanged mouth, slitted eyes, onyx scales, a huge and towering body. It eyes its prey. But Sember merely turns, as Heath hauls himself out of the water, and stares down the monster as though it is nothing to her.

And smiles.

Between blinks, the spear she holds is a pole and she thrusts it up as the creature's jaw snaps down to meet her, wedging its mouth open.

I blink again, knowing I must have imagined how the spear of silver seemed to grow and twist in her hand . . . but she's already reached the rock, tossed the ornate box into Heath's waiting hands and now she's scaling the side of the arena, hand over fist, to stand beside him in their circle. Victorious.

The morgawr thrashes back and forth, knocking against the sides of the arena and I'm dimly aware of the crowd's roar, of the churn of the water, as the monster's tail bucks and smacks the waves. I take advantage of the chaos and dive, length after length, sliding through the water, heart on fire in my chest. I reach out with my fingertips as I streak past all those pale, watchful eyes, making for the circle.

Then the water sucks me back, a giant crack vibrating through my bones, and I realise the morgawr has snapped that silver pole in two, freeing its jaw, and, worse, its teeth. I swim towards the surface, heart thundering in my chest. Turning back, I find only death.

'Mira!' Kell cries, holding out his hand to me, already waiting in our circle, terror limning his features. I throw myself forward, soaring through the water, and find the rock, the rough surface, then Kell's hand gripping mine as he heaves me up and out of the water.

I fall, dripping wet, into the circle as fangs snap above our heads, stopped by some mighty force protecting the circle, before they can close round us.

'Oh shit,' I hiss, scrambling to my feet. Above us, the morgawr's jaws drip with blood. It unleashes a ferocious roar, then slithers under the surface of the water. I sink back down and press my hands into the solid rock beneath me, closing my eyes until my crashing pulse begins to calm. I was just seconds away from being its next meal.

'Did you find any treasure? Are we through?' Kell asks, crouching beside me.

I nod, holding out my wrist, the pearls clustered in a glowing ring. 'We're through. The Skylan contenders won the Trial. We kept our end of the deal with them. And we are *alive*,' I breathe, finally looking up at the crowd, hearing their shouts and screams, the pummelling of voices assaulting my senses. 'That's all that matters.'

Chapter 14

Brielle

BRIELLE WAITS UNTIL THE VERY last second to turn the horses on to the hidden mountain path. Travelling deeper into the foothills, she knows the diversion may cost her if they realise she has strayed from the known roads. Or they may realise too late and not take the turning. She murmurs the witch word to disguise the opening in the trees, creating an illusion of leaves, branches and driving rain. She wishes Lowri were here with her, her sister, more accomplished in illusion spells than even the high witches of their old coven. She would wince at the paltry attempt. Brielle glances behind them, a huff of laughter escaping her as she pictures her sister tutting.

They've missed the turning, Nova says, suddenly appearing beside her on the rain-slicked bench. *Well done, Hunter.*

'Inesh and Dreska—'

Are not afraid of what lies behind them, or before them, Nova says. *They are ready to fight if needed.*

'Good.' Brielle nods, guiding the horses. She hears a

noise at their backs and swears, cursing the skies. 'Stay with them. I may have a need . . . It seems our pursuers are more canny than I thought.'

Nova hisses, hopping on to the roof of the coach. *One made the turning. They're gaining, Brielle. The other coach has corrected its course as well, just behind them . . .*

Brielle curses again, knowing the pass is too far. Even if she sets the horses to canter, they won't make it. 'Remind our witches of the words I taught them. I left two blades under the seats. If we are attacked, they must defend themselves.'

Nova yowls and vanishes, leaving Brielle to navigate a path through the ditches and stones. As she rounds a corner, the track opens out, long and exposed, the trees falling away on either side. Something prickles in her veins, something akin to fear. Not for herself, but for the young witches inside the coach. She grits her teeth and clicks to the horses, speaking a command.

They break into a canter.

Brielle braces herself as they shoot forward, the coach wheels bumping off every stone in the track. Heart racing, she glances over her shoulder as the other coach rounds the corner. Then the other one just behind. Through the driving rain, she tries to discern a face, even a feature, but all she can see are two figures at the reins, guiding the coach closest to them and horses built for speed. She swallows, turning back to the track and her blood stills.

'They can't possibly . . .'

The other coach is gaining on them, somehow overtaking the first despite missing the turning, flying over rough ground to the left, and the horses . . . Brielle swears. Not horses at all, she realises. The coach is pulled by grindlewolves. Two huge beasts, as tall as horses, with snapping jaws. Their pale fur flashes in the waning light, rain sluicing down their sides. The witches sit huddled on the bench, gripping the reins lashed to the monsters. As Brielle watches, one turns its head, snapping its jaw at her, and she shudders. A howl snags her attention and she whips to the right, finding two more grindlewolves breaking from the trees. Her fingers tremble as she grips the reins tighter. Grindlewolves are used on hunts. Not to capture . . . but to kill. With one coach just behind them on the left, and one further back on this road, and now two grindlewolves on their right . . . they are being herded, she realises. No doubt there are more grindlewolves, possibly a whole pack, keeping pace in the shadows.

One of the coach windows flies open and Inesh sticks out her head. 'They'll feast on our bones, Brielle! Grindlewolves took three from Ichbarrow last year! They hunt in packs. There'll be—'

Another howl splits the sound of hammering rain and Brielle eyes two more huge hulking shapes, leaping beside the coach on her left. Surrounding them, just as she feared.

'. . . more,' Inesh says faintly. 'I need a weapon, a bow and arrows, anything . . .'

'Two blades, under your seat!' Brielle calls back. 'Can you throw?'

'Grew up with an axe in my hand, Hunter!'

Brielle's breath leaves her in a whoosh of relief. At least one of them can fight. That's something. She growls at the horses, snapping the reins as she senses their fear. They know they are hunted too. The other window opens, Dreska appearing, and Brielle falters as she sees what she plans. 'No, Dreska! You could fall beneath the wheels!'

But Dreska only frowns, shimmying out of the window, clinging to the side of the coach before flinging her body on the bench beside Brielle. She breathes heavily then holds out her hands. 'Give me the reins. I can guide the horses, but I can't throw a blade.'

Brielle nods, calculating quickly, picturing the pass, still some distance away. They'll be attacked long before that with a grindlewolf pack closing in.

'All right,' she says, thrusting them at Dreska. 'Keep straight as an arrow, only veer when we're reaching the turns in the track up ahead, and give yourself plenty of—'

'Leave this to me,' Dreska says firmly, clicking to the horses, issuing a firm command.

Brielle nods, steeling herself, and clambers to the top of the coach, crouching as she pulls the first blade from her sash. A grindlewolf leaps, claws extended, aiming for the coach.

Before Brielle can aim, a blade whips from the window beneath her, finding the creature's throat. It falls, tumbling behind them, and several howls rise around them in the gathering dark.

'Good aim!' Brielle calls, fire pumping through her veins. But before Inesh can move to the other side of the coach another grindlewolf leaps. A blade is buried in its eye within a heartbeat, claws scratching down the side of the coach, Brielle's fingers still extended in the throw as she watches it tumble away down the track.

There's an angry shout from one of the hunters in the coach behind them and Brielle laughs breathlessly as it swerves, avoiding the slain grindlewolf, heading off the track in a shower of loose stones and rain. It nearly topples over as the grindlewolves pulling the coach are dragged back on course, the hunters cursing as the creatures howl and strain on their reins. But they won't move, won't do as those hunters command. That only leaves . . . the coach on their left.

One down, one to go.

'Brielle, watch out!'

She flattens herself against the roof of the coach just as a blade soars over her head, a witch curse shrieking past her, hitting a grindlewolf keeping pace with them in its chest. The creature yelps, slamming to the ground, convulsing in the rain and mud. Brielle whips round, seeing the hunter that aimed for her, their coach now level with hers. Brielle hisses, loosening another blade from her sash, pinching it between her fingertips. She can't see the rest of the grindlewolf pack. They've either spooked and left for easier prey or else . . . they have another plan.

She aims a blade at the hunter holding the reins, piercing the fists that hold the leather. The witch cries out, dropping the leather reins, losing control for a moment and the other hunter scrambles for them, cursing Brielle.

That's when she catches the flash of grindlewolf fur and teeth.

Leaping up from ahead, straight for the horses.

Dreska cries out, throwing a hand towards them, a witch word sharp on her lips. Brielle watches on in disbelief as the spell holds true, hitting the grindlewolf square in the gut.

It levitates, up into the air, claws extended, teeth gnashing . . . and lands on the ground as they thunder past.

But there's no time for Brielle to marvel at the young witch as Dreska takes a sharp turn off the long straight track and the pass finally comes into view. Bordered on each side by huge mountains, a river streams through it and the bridge . . . is gone.

'Skies,' Brielle whispers, narrowing her gaze. The river has swelled its banks, the melt running off the mountaintops as spring warms the frozen caps. It's impossible now for the horses to cross . . . without a little help.

She swivels. The hunters and their coach are just behind them, grindlewolves almost snapping at their wheels. If she has enough magic, if she says the right spell . . .

It's a risk, a huge one.

If they can cross the river, then they can shake off these hunters. But if Brielle miscalculates, if the horses bolt . . .

Then they're dead.

'Inesh, Nova!'

Inesh sticks her head out of the window. 'Yes?'

'I need you both on the bench beside Dreska. Hurry. We don't have long.'

Dreska gasps, glancing over her shoulder at Brielle, eyes wild as Inesh climbs through the window, swings round the side of the coach and sinks down beside her. Nova shelters between them, hiding from the now torrential rain. 'You're going to try to cross? We'll never make it!'

'Not without some encouragement,' Brielle agrees softly. She shoves back a hank of hair plastered to her face by the rain and reaches inside her jacket for a tiny, stoppered bottle. The last of the wyvern blood she drained and kept from the creatures that killed her mother. 'Don't fail me now,' she says, then with a final glance at the swollen river she downs it.

The blood hits her heart like a fist, magic blazing through every inch of her.

She feels more alive than ever before, like a roaring inferno, an exploding star. She stays crouched, whispering witch words to the horses, lending them more strength, speed, giving them the magic pumping through her. And, as the spells weave over them, taking hold, they crash forward, racing for the bank and the river beyond.

There's a cry behind her, the howl of the whole grindlewolf pack, but she doesn't turn. Doesn't blink. Not as she plants her palms on the roof of the coach and roars a single word.

Volatus.

The wheels judder, the horses gallop for the river and, as they reach the bank . . .

They fly.

Soaring up and over, they leap in an arc, vaulting the river, the rushing roar of it drowning out all else. Brielle grits her teeth, the spell alive, cast free as her heart flies to her throat, as the water rises to meet them.

And the horses touch down on the opposite bank, the wheels of the coach smacking into the ground a moment later. Brielle is pitched from the coach, falling into the mud of the bank and she rolls quickly, coming up with a blade in her fist. The horses calm, slowing, then finally stop, Dreska and Inesh still clinging on with blood-drained faces. Across the river, the hunters screech to a halt. The grindlewolves paw at the bank, the coach at a standstill.

Brielle smiles, staring at them as they glare back furiously. And she catches a flash of ice-blue, piercing eyes.

Do you recognise them? Nova says, slinking round the coach to sit beside her, licking her paws.

Brielle replaces the blade in her sash, straightening to stand. 'They are no friends of ours – that's all I know. We must continue on our way, as swiftly as we can to Ennor. Whoever sent them does not want me to return.'

Chapter 15

Mira

THE HORN BLASTS THROUGH THE arena and I sag in relief. The first Trial is over. We survived.

Skylan is declared victorious, and we shuffle round the edge of the rock face, avoiding getting too close to the edge as we're escorted back to the court by the guards. I crane my neck, searching the faces of the contenders surrounding us, seeing who survived. A thin wail pierces the close air of the tunnel, and I have my answer. Sapira, from the Valstran region of Stanvard, stumbles at the back, face in her hands. I glance around, pulse quickening, and count two from the Spines, two from Leicena, two from Skylan, but the Middenwilds . . . I swallow. There is only Pascha. Tall and staring straight ahead, a gash dripping blood down his bicep as he takes the long walk through the tunnel alone.

'Two dead,' I murmur to Kell disbelievingly. All those pale orb eyes in the water, the morgawr circling, the weapons scattered like jewels over the rocks . . . For the first time, it truly sinks in. I'm not just separated from my home, and it isn't only Agnes under threat. This is not a game. I cannot simply strike a deal with a stranger who will make a plan to save me, however enigmatic they appear.

I could truly die.

'They can still carry on without their partners, if they wish to,' Kell says quietly as a guard jabs him in the back, telling him he's dragging his feet. 'Although from the looks of them both . . .'

'Would you?' I ask, looking at him.

He shrugs. 'I didn't even do anything in this one. But it's not as if I can leave like they can, is it?'

'Depends why they're both here, I guess,' I say as we exit the tunnel, stepping out into stark sunlight. I cringe, holding my hand up to shield my eyes from the glare, and realise I'm shivering. The cold and wet is clinging to my skin, rattling my bones. But it occurs to me that Kell is right. 'I have a thought.'

Kell glances at me, raising his eyebrows. 'Does it involve more deals?'

'More like making friends,' I say, subtly indicating the other contenders as we're shuffled into carriages to carry us through the streets of Highborn. I'm done with trusting others to get me out of a situation, it's true, but I don't see this as putting my trust in someone else. If Kell and I can find allies, we'll increase our chances of survival *and* escape. 'We need to know what makes them tick. What the stakes are for them. Why they're here.' We're seated with our guards, so I don't say any more, but I catch Kell's eye, and see the wheels whirring in his mind, just as they are in mine.

The following morning, we're all led to a brunch in the gardens. Members of every court across the continent are in attendance, and again we contenders wear our country or territory's colours. Kell and I split up. He takes the contender from the Middenwilds, Pascha, who is standing at the edge of the garden, arms crossed, glowering at everyone. I make for the contenders from the Spines, Fey and Soturi, who arrived by drakeback. As I approach, they both nod. It's the warmest I've seen them greet anyone. Usually, they bare their teeth and hiss.

'We owe you our lives, Mira,' Fey says, threading her arms across her chest. Her white-blonde hair is tied back in a series of intricate knots, dark kohl shaping her eyes to narrowed points at the edges. 'Name your cost.'

I wave my hand, stopping a few feet away. 'You owe me nothing. It was a deal and the Trial is over. I have no interest in watching anyone become a meal.'

'Then perhaps we can offer you a truce,' Soturi says quietly. 'We don't come after you in the next Trial; you don't come after us.'

I tilt my head, then nod. 'Seems fair.'

'You're an islander, aren't you?' Fey says suddenly. 'Your watch and ruling council, they do not treat you well.'

'They'll get what's coming to them,' I say fiercely. 'Just because I'm an islander, does not make me – or my people – any less. It does not mean we deserve to suffer under their rule.'

'You misunderstand,' Fey says, taking a step closer. 'In the Spines, we overthrew our rulers. We are from the most northern town of the Spines, and they did not treat us well either. They despised how rural we are, how we value community over profiteering. They called us backwards. Now we fight in the Trials to honour our people, out of choice, not under duress. We fight to show all those who sided with our past rulers that we are stronger without them. That our way of life matters more than greed and power. If you need an ally beyond the Trials, if you and your people choose to fight for your islands, look to the Spines. We *chose* new rulers to represent us. Now we vote and interrogate every new law that is passed. We chose rulers who outlawed the hunting of our drakes.'

A slow smile spreads across my features, even as my throat thickens at the thought of my friends, my people, still sheltering on Ennor, with Rosevear destroyed. With each day that passes, my fear grows for their safety. With Eli and Lowri in another world, Agnes and I trapped here, and who knows where the rest of the crew of the *Phantom* are now, they're more vulnerable, weak – even with the ruling council's focus here on the Trials. But I can't show it at a brunch surrounded by delegates and contenders from other territories, where enemies could be hiding in plain sight. Not if I want to save Agnes and myself. And to hear that they did it, that the Spines overthrew rulers just like our ruling council, gives me hope when I need it most. 'We will call on you if you will stand with us. You have my word.'

There's a shift among the crowd and as I glance around me I notice a few men being led out of the garden, and through a side door back into the court. The door snicks closed behind them, and I bite my lip. Gazing over the crowd, I feel a pair of eyes on me and find Sember, champagne flute in hand, sipping slowly as she raises her eyebrows. So she saw them leave too. I raise one eyebrow back in silent challenge and she nods before beginning to stroll around the crowd, pausing to admire a flowering plant. I move idly past the buffet table, rounding a group of grinning Leicenans discussing the first Trial with their contenders. A shudder eddies down my spine. It's a game to them, a diversion. The Leicenan court, I've heard, is very fond of games and intrigue, and their relationship with Arnhem serves them well, for now. A stab of envy pierces my heart. If only my life was a series of diversions. How different everything would have been.

Sidling up to the door, I furtively check no one is watching us as Sember draws a coin from the pocket of her dress. I blink, and it's suddenly slender and key-shaped. I frown, wondering if I imagined the coin in her hand completely. She winks at me as she turns the handle, the lock clicking. Then she pushes me through first, whisking the door closed in our wake. I hear voices further along the dimly lit corridor and hold a finger up to my mouth. Sember pinches her lips and we slink towards the voices, stopping short outside what must be a servant's entrance into a main palace reception room. In a crack between door and frame, I spy a group of merchants with jowls and bulging waistcoats, and a man I know all too well: Otho, one of the ruling council. The man who sat in the watch's keep at Penscalo, toasting a victory with Captain Spencer Leggan before I was taken.

'I must say, Otho, you did promise us more of a show. There wasn't a cloud in the sky.'

'I agree entirely,' another merchant says, helping himself to a handful of grapes. 'What is she going to do that'll make the Straits so impassable? Really, it's hard to believe.'

'I concur,' the jowliest merchant of all says, before tipping a glass of blackcurrant-coloured wine between his fleshy lips. 'Didn't kill that morgawr either, did she? It snapped that metal bar in its mouth like a toothpick. We need proof.'

'Proof? Was it not enough to see her in the arena? I'm a man of my word and so are my brothers. The Straits will be impassable.'

'When?' another merchant asks. I'm sure I recognise him from the trip I took with Eli to Hail Harbour. He's one of the men we overheard talking when we took tea. Eli's features, the memory of his calm reassurance, is suddenly with me. And I wish, more than anything, that he was here now, listening too. He would know exactly who these merchants are, what they deal in, if they own mines in Valstra and why the ruling council want them on their side. But he's not here. And I must gather the information that could turn everything round for us, for his sake, for Ennor and Rosevear. Even if, at times like this, I feel his absence more than ever.

'If you're asking us to sign up to a trade route that has been impassable for decades, and to break our contracts with Skylan,' the man continues, 'we need to know when.'

Sember stiffens and I glance at her. I wonder, not for the first time, what her role back in Skylan really is. And why she was chosen to accompany Heath in the Trials.

'Soon,' Otho replies, leaning back to sprawl in the armchair he's sitting in. 'Soon, my friends. When the Trials are over, when you've seen what our little champion is capable of, you will want to be the first to place your assets on the ships embarking from Lorva. Space will be limited and if you want the most competitive prices . . .'

'Show us what this storm bringer can do, Otho. Then we'll talk.'

I step away, avoiding Sember's gaze, and tiptoe back to the brunch. But, as Otho's words sink in, everything clicks into place. The ruling council haven't brought me here, forced me to compete, as a general show of might. It's a calculated move to elevate Arnhem.

They want to use me to destroy the Straits.

Perhaps they never intended to allow Agnes to leave. Maybe they'll hold her life over me for the rest of our days. Back outside, I pick up a flute of bubbling orange juice and gulp it down, my mind on fire. I'll be used for every voyage to ensure the Southern Ocean is safe. I'll have to bring storms so fearsome that they'll kill everyone and everything up and down the Straits.

My blood turns to ice as I realise the full extent of their plans. They don't just want Arnhem to be great. They want to control the entire continent.

Hira is waiting for us in the disused hall the next day, arms crossed, an uncharacteristic smile on her face. 'You both survived the first Trial – well done.'

I shrug, as if it was nothing, as if I haven't been awake all night, discarding plan after plan, trying to find a way out of what the ruling council is going to force me to do. 'You delivered our messages?'

'I did. And my Malefant was pleased to hear word of this law before any other coven.'

Trying to hide my relief, I catch Kell's eye and find he's doing the same. 'So, they know we are here?'

She nods. 'And now we must prepare for the second Trial. I know now what your limitations and your strengths are.' She points to Kell. 'I know you're not a coward, so why did you linger at the edge of the arena? Can't you swim?'

He grimaces and shrugs. 'Never learned. Is it likely to be flooded again like that?'

'No,' she says, beckoning us to a table where she's placed her research of past Trials, underlining all those with a flooded arena, which have been few throughout the past decades. 'There has never been more than one water-based arena in each set of Trials. They don't like to repeat any. It would show weakness or at least a lack of creativity and ingenuity. And, as you know, these Trials are political and Arnhem cannot be viewed as a weak host. So, unless they have come up with something entirely new, we can narrow down what type of Trial might be next.'

'Can we rule out sky-based?' I ask, poring over the list.

Hira wrinkles her nose. 'Not entirely . . . but if you're talking about drakes or wyvern, the spectators would still have to be able to see the action. And so the covens would need to safeguard those in the stands with wards. And remember what I said about capture the drake egg? They won't want all of you to die before they can crown a victor.'

'How generous of them.'

'A land-based Trial seems most likely,' Kell says, tapping his finger on the parchment before looking at me. 'Which means we can work together on this one.'

I bite my lip, considering Kell's strange flame magic and my own ability to lure a storm. Neither of us have full control, although Kell seems to have a better grasp on his ability than I do on mine. And although we have made allies, we don't want to show our hand too soon, and for it to backfire. If the ruling council's dealings hinge on my and Kell's performance, we have to walk a tightrope: survive, place just high enough so that Agnes is not threatened due to our lack of victory, but not appear so strong as to win the ruling council any favours. We cannot show how formidable we can be. 'We need to focus on agility and working as one.'

'And beat Skylan this time,' Hira says, getting up. 'The ruling council wants to see a win.'

I stay quiet, not mentioning the deal we've struck with Sember and Heath. Hira needs us to win for her own ends; if we win she'll secure the favour of the ruling council for her coven. If the Skylan contenders stay true to their word, then we don't need to win. We just need to stay in the game. And if they don't come through for us . . . I just need to stay alive long enough to find Agnes and get us both out of here – before I become a wielded weapon so vile, so vicious, that the entire continent falls into the clutches of the ruling council, and changes everything for the Fortunate Isles. Forever.

Chapter 16

Lowri

LATE THAT NIGHT, LOWRI FINDS Eli in the topmost room of the house, his father's study. In the light of a lone lamp, Eli is digging through the drawers of a desk, a heap of old correspondence, books and newspaper clippings strewn all around him. Lowri watches from the doorway as Eli frowns, as he casts aside a letter before slumping back in the desk chair.

'It's hopeless, Lor,' he says. 'I'd need a year to sift through all this. But if my father was here, if we had only left for Fallow a little earlier—'

'Don't think like that,' Lowri interrupts softly. 'It'll drive you mad. We can't change the past.'

Eli looks up at the ceiling, then back at the desk, as though gathering himself together. 'I feel like I'm chasing a ghost. I'm mourning someone I never got the chance to meet.'

'You can still mourn,' Lowri says, moving further into the room. She picks up a paperweight, a snow globe: a depiction of the city of Fallow encased within. 'Even if you can't get a firm grasp of who he was, you can still grieve the loss of him.'

Eli flashes her a small, grateful smile. 'You know you are actually my favourite cousin?'

'Don't let Caden hear you say that,' she says, grinning. 'Or Ethlet.'

Lowri raises her eyebrows. 'Yes. Skies. Another cousin.' She shakes the snow globe and watches as the pale, glittering flakes whirl around crooked little houses. 'You may not have found your father as you hoped, but you've found her.'

'That's true,' he says after a moment. 'Very true. It's not nothing.'

'And maybe the Society will give you more of a sense of him. Maybe he'll seem like less of a ghost.'

Lowri shakes out the umbrella, craning her neck to stare up at the Society headquarters. Set just off centre and not quite in the heart of Fallow, it's tall and round in the middle, with two storeys shooting out on either side and a sense of grandeur about it. The walls are pale stone, the windows framed in black and just beyond the glass she spies silhouettes shifting.

They ascend the steps to the glossy black double front doors, stepping into a monochrome hallway of chequered flagstones. A huge grey chandelier dominates the ceiling, casting floating shadows over the white walls. Lowri finds her vision still dips and sways at times, her veins still faintly ink-ridden. And when she's tried a spell, a whispered witch word, shadow wreaths her fingertips like smoke, the spell having less potency, less impact than usual. She is drinking less and less of the Fallow Fog brews, not wanting to tip over and consume too much shadow. It's now a waiting game, hoping her light magic will heal and expand to fill her veins once more.

Ethlet steps forward to greet a woman with spiked auburn hair wearing a grey checked skirt suit and lurid yellow heels. Lowri places her umbrella in a stand by the door as Eli's gaze sharpens, lured to the painted portraits on the walls. Ethlet shakes the woman's hand, and she disappears through a door at the back.

'Isaiah's portrait is upstairs,' Ethlet says, following Eli's gaze. 'I'll show you before we're announced.'

The woman with auburn hair walks back in, gesturing to the staircase. 'They're ready for you, the full complement after your message sparrow arrived . . . We're all very intrigued.'

'Message sparrow?' Lowri asks Ethlet quietly.

'We attach a message to the leg of a sparrow, feed it a little fog and away it flies,' she explains as they walk up the staircase. 'Sometimes they get distracted by crumbs, but they're usually mostly reliable. We started using them in the war, when the Rexilium brothers' forces were bearing down on Fallow and no one could leave. But a small sparrow? Very nippy. The brothers didn't bother detaining them.'

Eli stalks quietly ahead as they reach the top of

the staircase, scanning every portrait until, finally, they're left in an antechamber before a huge set of doors. Beyond, they can hear the murmur of voices, occasionally peppered with a bark of laughter.

'This one,' Ethlet says, indicating a portrait on the left wall. Eli moves to stand next to her, eyes hungry as they rake over the painting of his father. Lowri's heart squeezes, watching him. She's never thought much about who her father might be, but for Eli it's a question left unanswered. A man who appeared to be a hero, a scholar or a coward, depending on who spoke of him. And now, so close to his life in this place, Lowri can feel Eli's need for answers.

'He has your eyes. Or, rather, you have *his* eyes.'

'Do you think so?' he asks quickly.

'The shape.' She nods, throat suddenly thick. 'Hard to tell on the colour, with it being greyscale.'

'But there's a definite likeness,' Ethlet adds. 'You walk like him too. And he was quiet like you, always thinking things through, always following many pathways before speaking his mind. A strategist. Prone to brooding if left too long to his own devices.'

Eli looks at her and blinks. 'Thank you. That's – I needed to hear that.'

Just then, the doors are thrown open, voices and warmth spilling out. 'Ah, they're ready for us.'

Ethlet takes the lead, and when Lowri and Eli stride in, side by side, they are met with a vast, round hall. A chandelier winks overhead with a thousand colours captured in prisms. They create darting sparkles of light that dance over the white-washed walls, another small use of light magic in a grey world. And before them is an array of round tables. Seated at them are people of all ages, dressed in black and grey: old men with grey, spiked beards, young people with thick spectacles and obvious curiosity, middle-aged people with keen eyes and the most remarkable footwear, and all of them with tiny glass bells set before them. Silence falls like a blanket over the gathering of what must be around a hundred people, and Ethlet clears her throat, apparently suddenly nervous.

'Esteemed members of the Society of Fallow, I present Elijah Tresillian – son of the recently deceased Isaiah Kellinick – and his cousin Lowri Tresillian. They have recently crossed over . . . from another world.'

There's a murmuring and the gentle tinkling of several of the glass bells. They wink prettily, the light from the prisms above glittering over them, creating a strange, hypnotic kaleidoscope of colour. After the last few days of grey, Lowri finds it quite dazzling and wonders if this display of small light magic is rather like a display of wealth in this world. She notices a person close to her, a woman with short-bobbed hair, who holds her glass bell aloft, ringing it gently.

Ethlet holds up both hands. 'There will soon be time for questions, but first we put forward a request. Lowri and Eli are from the world that the Rexilium brothers fled to. They bring news that the brothers have set themselves up as rulers and have now turned their sights on the rest of their world. War is possibly inevitable, and Isaiah's son would like to take any knowledge back that he can use to arm his allies against their schemes. Will a historian on the Shadow War take the time to supply them with information?'

The tinkling of the bells ceases as they all look to each other. Then one man rises, a man with a spiked beard and a long, pointy chin, who is wearing a waistcoat. 'I will be your historian. Then they must submit to the Society's questions.'

'Of course,' Eli says, inclining his head. 'Many thanks for assisting us. We will answer what we can.'

The historian invites the three of them to sit at his table as drinks are brought in and a series of debates begins, speakers standing to talk, all punctuated by the ringing of the bells as the members take their turn to air their knowledge or opinion. In deference, it seems, to the speaker, no one talks in private conversations, instead ringing their glass bells in agreement or to indicate they would like to address the gathering. A hot drink is placed before Lowri, pale grey with an unfurling flower in the centre of the cup. She sips it and tastes springtime, the delicate floral notes perfuming the air around them. She wonders what colour it would have been before the Shadow War leached it of light.

Eli raises his eyebrows and she notes how he drums his fingers on the table. He's restless, she realises. The matters being discussed around them are not what he has come all this way to hear about. As a young woman stands to give a report on the state of the fog above her hometown, Holloway, some distance north of the city of Fallow, Lowri files away the information that this fog has spread over every settlement, it seems. Anywhere that magic has permeated the world, a fog hangs above. The historian looks at them as the young woman finishes her report and the meeting seems to adjourn, with conversations breaking out on individual tables. More drinks are brought in on trays and, finally, the historian can speak.

'I'm Hellius, keeper of the history of the Shadow War,' he says, smiling at Eli. 'I was a good friend of your father. My condolences.'

'Thank you,' Eli says.

'You're a witch?' Hellius asks, turning to Lowri. 'Ethlet says you are like Eli's mother. Isaiah spoke of her.'

'She was my aunt,' Lowri replies, 'although I never knew her. But, yes, I'm a witch, rather than human.'

'Interesting,' Hellius murmurs, eyes boring into hers. 'And your coven is against the Rexilium brothers?'

'Well . . .' Lowri begins. 'It doesn't quite work like that in our world. Covens stay out of politics; they do not question the ruling council, which is what the Rexilium brothers call themselves in our world.'

'Here, they called themselves the Imperium,' Hellius says softly.

A shiver runs down Lowri's spine. 'Meaning all powerful?'

He nods. 'They swept through three territories before we beat them back here in Fallow, ending the war. But, as you have seen, the scars of that time remain. Shadow looms over every town and city. They bled the light magic from the world. And then they worked out how to open a portal and moved on to yours.'

'Could you tell us how their magic works?' Eli asks.

'It works much like yours or mine,' Hellius says with a crooked smile. 'But amplify that by three. They somehow found a way to combine their shadow magic and to consume light magic, making everything they do much more powerful. It took all of us to defeat them. At the height of their power, they could blot out a sky, create portals within our world, travel vast distances with a finger snap. And their shadows had substance. They were working on creating a shadow army before we won and forced them from our world.'

'A shadow army?' Lowri asks faintly.

He nods. 'A whole body of creatures, created by them, that they could direct at will. Almost unstoppable.'

'Skies,' Lowri utters. 'And how long ago did they cross over to our world?'

'Over a hundred years ago.'

Eli frowns. 'Surely they would be dead by now?'

Hellius wags his finger. 'Not with the light magic they consumed. Left alone, they could live several lifetimes. I'm afraid that if you don't deal with them soon your world could end up like ours. You may not have long.'

'What do you mean?' Lowri asks.

'Well, think of the fog like a sponge. It absorbs any light magic, but never enough for it to dissipate completely. You're a walking source of light. But to create a portal—'

'I need light as well as shadow,' Eli says quietly. 'Is that why my father . . . why he never came back?'

'He tried. For many years. But in the end he exhausted himself trying to create a portal to get back to you and your mother. It took him to an early grave.'

Eli sits back, staring down at his hands, and Lowri senses the brooding disquiet clouding his mind.

'A witch can command light and shadow magic, or so Isaiah believed,' Hellius says, accepting a drink as he avoids their eyes. 'Would you say that's true?'

'I wouldn't know,' Lowri says with a tight smile, thoughts lingering on her cousin and what he has just learned. How it will torment him, if he allows it to do so. She leans close to Ethlet and murmurs, 'As soon as we've answered their questions, I think it's time to leave.'

'Talk to me,' Lowri murmurs as they step out of the Society building, the sound of those tinkling bells ringing in her ears. The Society had so many questions for her and Eli about their world. About the geography, creatures and about witches. Lowri found herself answering more and more, while Eli slumped in his seat, shrinking in on himself.

Eli sighs, gesturing to the Society building. 'They have such a grasp of the science of magic in this world, the individual strands of light and dark, the research . . . Think of the advancements we could make if I could *just* have more time here. But if what Hellius says of light magic is true . . .'

'Then we have to leave right away,' Lowri says.

'Or we may be stuck here like my father,' Eli agrees as Ethlet leads them through the streets of Fallow. 'I want a couple of hours in my father's study in case he made any notes, in case Hellius did not have the full information, but be ready.'

They leave Fallow after dinner, heading for the graveyard. Ethlet chatters in a ceaseless stream to fill the heavy silence. Eli has several of his father's journals stashed in his jacket, and that will have to be enough. They're not sure if he'll be able to step between worlds with any more of them, in case they too are suffused with shadow, soaking up light magic like the fog above, or simply too heavy a weight to carry between worlds, like an anchor, dragging them back. Travelling between worlds is so new to him and, as Lowri points out, if it works, then perhaps he will be able to return for the rest of them in time. When they reach the graveyard, he places a hand on his father's gravestone, turning his face from them. Lowri's heart twists as Eli says a quiet goodbye to the man he never had the chance to meet. Then he steps away, eyes leaden, and takes Lowri's hand.

Ethlet hangs back after they say their goodbyes. Then Eli murmurs quietly and a doorway appears. Lowri sighs in relief as somewhere else begins to take form beyond, a place other than the graveyard coming into focus. A room becomes visible on the other side of the doorway.

'Strange,' says Eli. 'I thought of Mira, focused on walking to her, but that doesn't look like her room in Ennor Castle. Nor anywhere else on Ennor.'

Lowri steps closer, examining the space: a sparsely furnished room with a small window looking out on to blue sky. Then Mira appears. Exhaustion marks her features, her hair is tied back in a messy plait, fighting leathers encasing her body. Lowri holds her breath as Eli reaches out for Mira and she looks up, her eyes flaring wide. She forms his name with her lips, leaping across the room . . . only to slam into the doorway.

'No . . . what?' Eli says, placing his hands on the doorway, muttering curses as he tries to push his way through. But it's as though there is a physical barrier between them and Mira. Lowri covers her mouth with her hands as Mira places her palms against Eli's, crying now in earnest. Eli grows frantic, banging on the doorway, calling her name. But they can't hear Mira. And it slowly dawns on Lowri that Mira can't hear Eli either. Eli stills, placing a palm flat on the barrier between them as Mira places hers on her side, aligned with his. They stare at each other, desperation and longing so keen, so raw, it nearly rips Lowri's heart out.

Then guards flood Mira's room.

Wearing scarlet jackets, just like the watch, they grab Mira's arms, pulling her away. She opens her mouth wide in a roar, tackling one to the ground, kicking away another, straining to get back to the doorway Eli created. But more take hold of her, trying to yank her away. Eli slams into the portal, over and over, bellowing, shouting . . .

'Mira! Mira, fight them! You have to fight back!'

But smoke and shadow coils, blotting the room out completely as the doorway fades, leaving only her eyes, full of fear, her mouth shaping the words, *I love you*, before she disappears completely.

Eli tries summoning a portal again. Then again. He pulls the books, his father's notebooks from his pockets, throwing them on the ground that focuses once more. Lowri watches, heart in her mouth as he braces his fists against the swirl of smoke, the only thing he can conjure. Eventually he stops trying, his shoulders shaking as he stares at the space where the portal was. 'Mira's in danger. They've captured her. And I can't do anything. I couldn't help her. I . . . This has never happened before. I don't understand. I don't . . .'

Fear grips Lowri in an unyielding fist as Eli turns slowly towards her. 'I can't form a portal, Lowri. I can't get us back.'

Chapter 17

Mira

MY SOBS RATTLE IN MY chest as I'm dragged away by the guards, panic bleating in my ears. All I can think is that Eli can't get back. He and Lowri can't get back from his father's world. They are trapped there. And there's nothing I can do about it.

I find a hand gripping mine as we're escorted to the arena for the second Trial, ten days after the first, and I cling to it. It is the only anchor in a sea of what is fast becoming hopeless. All I can see is Eli's face as he stood on the other side of that portal, trying to break through, his panic, the growing realisation that he could not step between worlds and come back. And Lowri, standing behind him, fingers covering her mouth, tears streaming down her cheeks... Are they hurt? I couldn't tell. I could only see them, and the trees surrounding them. The place Eli showed me the night before he left our world entirely. What I can't figure out is why. Why can't he step back? Is it something holding him there? Or worse... Is his magic no longer strong enough?

Kell murmurs quietly the whole way to the arena, trying to calm me, trying to wrench me from my own mind, from the swift spiralling descent of my thoughts, and into the present. But as we reach the tunnel, the guards prodding us forward, I'm still shaking. I have to forget Eli's face, his panic, or I will be distracted. And I will not survive the second Trial. There is a part of me that's been waiting for Eli to rescue me, to return and make everything all right. But seeing him trapped there, beyond my reach, I realise he cannot save me now. Not this time.

It's time for me to save myself.

Sember and Heath walk out into the arena first to the roar of an almighty crowd. We walk out in ranking order of the first Trial, with Sapira, the lone contender from Stanvard at the back, chin held high. Soturi and Fey are just ahead of Kell and I, representing the Spines, with the Leicenan contenders, Elséne and Oliette, behind us. I've found them to be very quiet, keeping largely to themselves at the events and parties thrown at court to show us all off. Pascha, the remaining contender from the Middenwilds is notably absent. He must have dropped out, forfeiting any possible victory, or maybe he never found a piece of treasure himself and was eliminated. I wish now that I'd asked, but I was too focused on making allies and trying to escape this place. And now all I've been thinking of is Eli's arms surrounding me again, of setting Agnes free. My stomach twists, remembering Pascha's face after the first Trial. His devastation.

We walk out to the spatter of spring rain. I tilt my face upwards. The clouds are a dome over the arena, squat and sluggish. There is no wind, no movement in the sky, and I lick my lips, assessing the terrain. It could become slippery, and my footwear is not designed to grip. All my scheming, all I have learned about the ruling council's plans beyond the Trials, has left my head. I can only think about Eli. I'm desperate to be with him, but what if he can never get back to our world? What if it's permanent? What if he'll never be able to return to me?

I shake myself, gripping my hands into fists, and remember that I'm no good to him dead. I'm no good to myself, or to Agnes, or my islands, or anyone, if I die today. There is no way out of this, no one coming to rescue me. The only way out, as ever, is through.

I need to focus.

'Look,' Kell says, leaning across to me. 'The arena floor.'

Sweeping my gaze over it, I gasp. We are in the same arena as the first Trial, but it's no longer a flooded space. Now it is fully exposed, a large oval stretching off to the distant stands of spectators. And all over the ground, walls and doors form a complex labyrinth . . . but then I notice the movement.

'The walls are shifting,' I say, whipping to meet Kell's gaze. His eyes widen. The maze-like arena below has doors that close and walls that move, creating an impossible Trial. One that has no discernible pattern. They're at least twice our height and sheer, unclimbable, seeming to be made of a bronze type of metal. It's a mechanical labyrinth with no roof, open so that the spectators can see everything that transpires beneath them. 'We could be trapped in there. We could be lost for days . . .'

We all watch as a section in the wall of the arena opens on the furthest side, below the rows of people watching from above. And several creatures, a pack, move out into the arena, stalking between the walls of the labyrinth. My heart leaps to my throat as I watch them move, see their jaws open wide, catch the glint in their ravenous eyes. Five monsters that will hunt us.

Five wither beasts.

The ruling council has gathered another creature of nightmare. I've heard stories spoken by merchants in Port Trenn, relayed to us on Rosevear round hearths and at meets. I begin to shake in earnest as the guards prod us all forward. I catch Sapira's soft whimper at the back before she exhales a deep breath. Turning to look over my shoulder, I meet her steely gaze and nod. She nods back, pressing her lips together. She must have heard the same stories growing up. But we will not tremble. Not out here, not in front of the crowd. Not in front of the ruling council, or the rulers of our opponents' territories. We will not show fear. In these Trials that seem on the surface to divide us, pitting territories against each other to gain power in the continent, we are united in wanting to stay alive. And, after the first Trial, none of us wishes to see anyone else die.

I wonder if this happens in every set of Trials, that the contenders form an odd bond. Even if they signed up for these Trials, volunteered and trained and wanted to be here . . . there is surely a tipping point when you're actually here. Perhaps it's seeing the monsters in the first Trial, knowing what you face and realising you could really die. And the glory, the victory, is meaningless in death.

A guard steps between me and Kell, pushing him to the left as I am shoved to the right. Separating us. I don't have time to reassure him before the commentator begins, their voice blasting over the arena, drowning out all other sound. But we both know what it is that we must do.

'A glorious day for the second Trial!' the voice booms, and the crowd cries out in agreement. The rain plasters my hair to my neck as I glance up, trying to pick out individual faces. But it's just a sea of open mouths, of narrowed gazes, of pumping fists. As though *they* are the monster here to consume me.

'But maybe not such a glorious day for our contenders . . .' There's a wave of laughter and my blood runs hot. How dare these people, this mindless mob, *laugh*. A growl tears from my throat as I realise I am a spectacle. We are *all* a spectacle, entertainment, seen as nothing more than creatures in a trap. I am a distraction, a prize the ruling council means to display, to use to coerce the merchants into using an alternative trade route. To pay into their coffers. And dismantle, piece by piece, the power that Skylan holds over the continent.

One of the wither beasts calls to another, a beating sound vibrating in its throat that I can feel echoing through my bones more than I can hear, and they all pause, sniffing the air. Then one snaps its jaws and they continue stalking. But, as I watch, one gets trapped, a door closing on it, and it's stuck in a closed corridor. That wither beast begins moving back and forth in agitation. I swallow, watching it, trying to mark where it is, so I can at least avoid that area.

'Each contender will need to cross the maze and find their way to the exit at the opposite side. They must pass through a tunnel out of the arena in order to complete the Trial. But with a few twists and turns, and even a few treasures along the way, it's all to play for.' My eyes dart to the maze again, scanning for these supposed treasures. But nothing stands out . . . Perhaps I need to be in there, searching on the ground, before it becomes apparent.

'The contenders from Skylan will get a head start for winning the first Trial, and then each territory will follow in the order they placed. We are splitting you up to make it that bit more interesting . . . What a challenge this will be!' A wither beast bellows, joined by another, then another, and a shudder runs down my spine. They sound restless, ready to hunt, and with all of us working alone we're easy targets for a pack that can communicate with their bellowing roars. Will they herd us? I wish I knew more about these monsters.

'Wait for the horn, contenders, and may you bring honour to your country!'

The crowd shrieks as the horn blasts, signalling the beginning of the second Trial. I lock eyes with Kell across the arena and point to one side, hoping he takes the hint. When it's our turn, I take a huge breath, trying to calm the drumming of my heart, and sit on the edge, looking down into the labyrinth of walls and doors below. It's a drop of ten feet, easy to twist an ankle if you land badly. Another test. I lower myself over the edge and down into the maze.

I fall and roll, coming up in a crouch. Blinking quickly, I take in my surroundings, placing a hand on the nearest wall. It's tall and smooth, just as it seemed from above, cool to touch as though it is indeed forged metal sheets and, as I feared, twice my height. Without a grappling hook and rope, there is no way I could climb up and over them. I begin to walk, keeping my hand on the wall, taking the turns that will lead me towards Kell. But, as I'm nearing his side of the arena, there's a creak and a click at my back. I whip round, finding a doorway has closed. I hear the crowd roar, but I can't see what they can see. Hastening my footsteps, desperate to reach Kell, or to find a weapon, anything I can defend myself with, I round a corner and stutter to a halt.

Blocking my way is a wither beast.

I freeze, stilling every muscle in my body, hoping it only tracks movement, that I may still be able to escape . . . but then it snorts, eyes locking with mine. And I know it's too late.

It has me in its sights.

Chapter 18

Lowri

Eli's words hit her like stone.

I can't form a portal, Lowri.

I can't get us back.

He tries to open another portal, thrusting out his hands, shadow wreathing his arms. But all that emerges is a shimmer in the air before him, like a pool with a pebble cast into it. He drops his hands to his sides, then tries again. And again, growling in frustration, agitation marking every movement. The distorted shape of other worlds ripples suddenly on the fifth attempt, and Lowri holds her breath. But then it fades back to the trees before them, the gravestones, the grey tones of this world. And Eli sinks to his knees.

'I've left it too long to return,' he murmurs. 'It must be the fog. It must have soaked up any light magic I had . . . I should have known they'd retaliate, that they wouldn't suffer a defeat in the isles . . . and now they've got Mira.' His voice cracks on her name and he turns to Lowri, despair dragging him down. They've been in the graveyard for hours. Twilight is sweeping in, claiming the world and sending chills over Lowri's skin. She looks at the looming fog above Fallow, just a few minutes' walk away, and swallows down her own bitterness, her own despair. Lowri doesn't want to think of what this means for them, that they could be trapped here, trapped in this world of shadow, away from their own world, their own lives . . . forever.

She takes a deep breath, pushing her own feelings aside, and steps towards Eli, placing a hand on his arm. 'We're not getting anywhere here. Let's go back and make a plan.'

'Isaiah's notes – maybe there's something there, some more knowledge we have yet to uncover,' Ethlet begins, her voice fading along with her hope for them. It's clear to all three that the magic they used to get here, Eli's abundance of power formed and grown over many years in his world, is blocked in this one. It won't work for the return journey. But none of them say it, none of them acknowledge the enormity of what it means. That they could be trapped here.

Lowri walks ahead this time, with Ethlet and Eli trailing behind her. Ethlet talks in a non-stop monologue about Isaiah's research, his books of notes, his experiments with the fog – anything to try to get Eli to open up. To talk back.

When they reach the townhouse in Fallow, Eli strides up the narrow staircase, straight to his father's study, and when Lowri tries to follow him in she finds the door locked. For a moment, her fingertips hover over the handle, a witch word on the tip of her tongue to unlock it. It's always been his weakness, this tendency to brood, to carry the weight of the world on his shoulders, to never let anyone past the charming veneer he presents. From what she has seen, only Mira has truly broken through. But she's not here. And, worse, she's in danger. Only Lowri is here, and she doesn't know how to reach him.

With a soft sigh, she leaves him to stew in the tangle of his father's notes and research, returning downstairs to form a plan.

'Gracious, can you sense if I am more restored than before?' Lowri asks as she enters the lounge, finding the grimalkin sprawled before the fireplace. 'Is my magic at all balanced yet?'

Mostly. You are still rather short on light magic, and, as a witch, you should have more. But there is enough for you to cast a little.

Something he says catches her attention. 'When you say, as a witch . . . Do you mean that creatures and humans hold different levels of shadow and light to be in balance?'

Yes. Your cousin wields shadow magic, and for him to be in balance he needs far less light magic than you. But – Gracious swipes his tail back and forth *– he is not in balance. Even less so than you. The little light magic he needs has been drained from him and in this world he cannot create more. Just like the others in the Society, just like his father.*

Lowri blinks, falling back into the sofa. This changes everything. Everything she thought she knew about magic, everything the coven taught her. The fundamental basis of magic and burnout and balance – it's not just based on magic in one form. It's all to do with the two twisting strands of light and shadow. 'Is the balance of magic between just shadow and light? Are there more strands?'

'Isaiah's research with the Society pointed to more,' Ethlet says quietly, walking in to flop on the sofa beside her. 'He was seeking other forms, other strands, that might bring a new kind of balance to help banish the fog. And so that he could form a portal and return to Eli. His mother, your aunt, did she ever speak of Isaiah?'

'I wouldn't know,' Lowri says. 'I never met her. She died in childbirth, before Eli could even form a memory of her.'

Ethlet's hand flies to her mouth. 'Oh, I'm so sorry. So he truly knows nothing of his father. Not even her memories of him.'

'It's why he's so cut up. He's forever chasing past ghosts.'

Ethlet nods, her features troubled as Gracious watches them quietly. 'We have to go back to the Society. Isaiah's research and notes might be here in his office, but they're uncatalogued, scattered. He had his own way of organising things, and now I need to bring some order to his work. But at the Society someone might have answers. They might even be able to help.'

* * *

A message is sent to the Society, and Lowri waits anxiously as they assemble their members. Ethlet tempts Eli out with the invitation to speak to the members and he leaves his father's study seeming haunted. This time, in that great round hall, Eli addresses the gathering and the tinkle of those bells falls eerily silent. He speaks of the portal between worlds that his father had taken half a lifetime to try recreating. And he talks of how he is now having the same troubles, and that he and Lowri cannot return home. Lowri's heart cracks as he tells the Society what he saw through the portal, of Mira, his love, in danger. His anchor to our world. The person to whom he could not cross over and reach.

'She was being held by the ruling council's guards. The Rexilium brothers have her. I implore all of you to dig into your memories, your knowledge, and perhaps I can piece together a solution. Anything you can tell me might help us. Please . . .' Eli says, swallowing. 'She's in danger and this is only the beginning for us.'

After some conferring, a woman with a lined face and grey eyes stands, silence falling once more like a spell. 'Your light magic is being sucked into the fog, as you are aware. It's like a sponge, wringing our world dry. Isaiah found this too. The longer he stayed, divided from your world, the more difficult it was for him to be able to return.'

'But you must have a solution,' Eli says desperately. 'Some way to restore the light magic.'

'I'm afraid not.'

Eli grips the chair back, schooling his features as he speaks smoothly, carefully. 'Isaiah was working on another theory, though. Of light and shadow not being the only strands of magic, that there could be more. Other ways to bring balance to Fallow and the rest of this world. Did he share this research with anyone? Anyone here today?'

Many pairs of eyes blink in puzzlement, whispered conversations breaking out over the room.

'Anyone?' Eli asks a second time. But he's once again met with silence. Not a single handheld bell rings out.

'The Society cannot help you,' the woman eventually says pityingly. 'This shadow, this curse of fog, is beyond all of us.'

'A complete waste of time,' Eli mutters darkly as they descend the wide staircase, back into the entrance hall. 'All we've done here is wasted time.'

Lowri hesitates, catching something in the corner of her eye. A message sparrow, swooping into the entrance hall below. It pecks at something on the ground then flies up, landing on the banister beside Eli. Lowri extends a finger, murmuring a witch word to call it to her. It looks up, beady eye regarding her, before it flutters over, landing on her finger.

'What have you got there, Lor?' Eli asks softly, meeting her eyes with a smile.

Lowri whispers another word, the message turning to ash in her fingers. The message sparrow squawks and leaves her finger, flapping for the open door and narrowly missing Ethlet's left ear. 'An appointment we cannot miss.'

It takes Ethlet half an hour to lead them across Fallow, all of them clutching umbrellas. 'You're still too conspicuous,' Ethlet hisses at Eli. 'If you'd only worn those yellow shoes . . .'

'Nothing says "I'm not up to anything; don't bother following me" than a pair of bright yellow shoes – you're right,' Eli says as they step round a gaggle of schoolchildren wearing red shoes. 'Which street did it say again, Lowri?'

'Gallow's End.'

'Cheery,' Eli remarks.

Ethlet sighs. 'I liked you both more when you were despairing.'

Lowri snorts, covering it with a cough as they turn on to the street. Aptly named, it seems even more gloomy than the rest of Fallow, as though the shadows are deeper here, darker. They reach a door and Lowri raises her knuckles to knock, but it opens before she can. And framed in the doorway is the historian they met at the Society – Hellius.

'We need to talk,' he says. 'Come in.'

Chapter 19

Mira

HUGE AND FANGED, THE WITHER beast locks on to me immediately and growls. The sound reverberates through every inch of me, a cold sweat breaking out on my skin. It's twice my height, taking up every inch of space, eyes narrowed and vicious. Without a weapon, with only the clothes on my back, I have nothing with which to defend myself. I don't wait for it to come at me. As a door opens in the wall on my left, I run.

Skidding round corners, heart slamming into my ribs, I race in total panic, calling for Kell or anyone who might hear me. Distantly, I'm aware of the crowd, but my terror overtakes everything, to the point where all I am is a fast-moving feast. A door begins to close before me and I push back and slip through, my skin scraping against the narrow opening, and force it closed behind me. But the wither beast thumps into it on the other side, cracking it open. I cry out, bones barking as I push against it, digging my feet into the ground and shoving with everything I have.

'Kell!' I cry on a desperate exhale. 'Anyone!'

I can't die like this. Not before a baying crowd, a wither beast mauling me, the glimmer of freedom a distant dream.

I gasp as another body shoves all their weight against the door as well, and the door closes, leaving the wither beast shut away on the other side. I double over, bracing my hands on my thighs and look up to find Soturi, one of the contenders from the Spines. He's got a bow and arrow slung across his back, steel in his eyes, and when he looks at me, a small smile lifts his lips.

'You will not die here, girl from the islands,' he says. 'Not today.'

'Why are you helping me?' I manage, standing to face him.

'Because you were born for more than this. You have not come this far to die for the entertainment of a crowd, or your rulers' pleasure.'

'Thank you,' I say, clasping his fist in mine.

He eyes me carefully and I can only just hear him over the sounds of the crowd. 'Sember Lockswift spoke to Fey and me. We see what your rulers are, what they are capable of. We will stand with you against tyranny. But we must be careful. If it seems as though we are helping you, this may affect your friend . . .'

I blow out a breath and nod. So Sember is gathering allies. 'Thank you. Truly. Just help me find Kell. We can split up, draw less attention. Help us to stay alive so that—'

But my words are snatched away by an almighty crack as the wither beast breaks through the door behind us. Soturi whips out an arrow, firing it faster than I can see, but it's not enough. The wither beast rakes at the ground, releasing a deafening roar, and Soturi presses the handle of a blade into my hand. 'Fight with me.'

I don't need asking twice. With a weapon in my fist, I circle as far to the left as the space allows, as Soturi distracts the wither beast, firing arrows into its flank. As it readies to charge, blood dribbling down its sides, I leap for it. The beast is still focused on Soturi and his arrows as I scramble up its side. It starts to buck as it realises what I've done, but I don't give it time to throw me off. Angling the blade, I slam it into its skull, driving down with a roar. It bucks again and I'm afraid I've just enraged it further, fists still wrapped round the handle of the blade, embedded in its skull. But then it groans, tilting to one side, and collapses to the ground. I leap away just in time, landing awkwardly on my feet. My ankle twists painfully and I gasp, but I can't give in to it. I have to keep moving. I have to stay alive. Suddenly I'm aware of the crowd, half cheering, half disappointed that the fight between us and the creature is over.

'Soturi, it's dead,' I breathe, tugging the blade free from the wither beast's skull. But when I look down, I find Soturi on the ground beneath it. 'Soturi?'

He grunts and I slip round the wither beast's lifeless form, kneeling beside him. My heart stops when I see the blood. A gash, right along his side, bleeding freely.

Fast footfalls sound and I look up to see Kell rounding the corner. Relief spreads across his features as he sees me, then turns to horror as his gaze lands first on the wither beast, then on Soturi. 'Is he dead?'

I shake my head, then swallow. Blood trickles down to my fingertips and I look at my arm, vaguely surprised to find a cut down the length of my bicep. It's long, but shallow, and as I look at it, I feel the first thumps of pain, like a second aching pulse. 'He defended me. Saved me. He said they spoke to Sember. That they're with us.' My voice cracks on the last word and I look down at Soturi.

Kell swears, kneeling on his other side, assessing him quickly. 'Soturi, can you stand?'

'I don't . . .' He blinks quickly, features turning pallid. 'I will try.'

Kell shrugs out of his shirt, using it to bind the wound as best he can, but the blood blooms over it almost instantly. We get on each side of Soturi, pulling his legs from beneath the wither beast. He winces but stays silent, and we help him stumble up to stand. He staggers forward, features pinched and pale, and I think in that moment he's the bravest person, the calmest person I've ever met. And I don't want him to die.

'We need to find Fey,' he grunts. 'Help me . . .'

'Of course,' I say, still bracing him. We hear a distant scream and I bite my lip. 'Let's get a move on.'

Staggering through the maze of walls, we find ourselves in a larger space, many doors leading off it.

There's a click as one of the doors opens, and Kell's magic ignites in his palm, focused on what might be coming through. I grip my blade harder, ready to defend all of us.

'Oh, a welcome party,' Sember says, as the door snicks open and she walks towards us. If anything, she looks almost bored, but I don't miss how her gaze falters when it lands on Soturi's side. 'Well, hurry up. I've been looking for you.'

I frown, not believing what I'm seeing. 'How did you just open that door?'

She smiles, flicking back a strand of her hair. 'Now *that's* a bit of a secret, I'm afraid. Can you manage him? He's not looking too good.'

'I found them. I kept my word,' Soturi grates out.

Sember nods. 'And kept them alive. Well, come on, places to be and all that.'

She turns back to the door, beckoning to us to follow. When we're through, she turns back, hiding what she's doing, but the door clicks again, as though locked. Then she's off, scouting ahead, opening and closing doors as Soturi slowly gets heavier and heavier, slumping further against me and Kell. I can't figure out how she's manipulating the maze like that, but there's no time to watch closely.

When I'm sure I can't drag Soturi another step, she ushers us through a final door, and I look up, to the rows of crowd above the great door that leads through the tunnel, out of the maze. Heath is waiting there, arms crossed, staring at us. 'Took your time.'

'Apologies, Your Royal Pain-in-the-arse-ness,' Sember says, hands on hips. 'Sorry I was a bit late ensuring the survival of our *allies*.'

'It's us that owe you in this Trial,' Kell says. 'Not that I'm not grateful, but why help us? And in a Trial, in front of a whole crowd?'

'You could have taken victory easily like you wanted. You didn't need to save us . . .' I say.

'It's simple really,' Sember says, growing suddenly serious. 'The ruling council want to block the use of the Straits. They want to control the flow of merchant goods and therefore the wealth. Skylan will be crippled and Leicena could turn on us. It'll mean all-out war across the continent. None of us want that. Not even the people of the Spines.'

'But if I die they can't block the Straits,' I say quietly to her.

Sember steps towards me. 'If you die, the Straits will boil over with vengeful sirens. And the Rexilium brothers will find another, someone else who can do what you can. And they may not be as good-hearted as you. They may *want* a war.'

I shiver, seeing the truth in her gaze, what she fights for, what her alliance really means. Sember Lockswift is not just Prince Heath's keeper. Whatever she is to Skylan, though, she's playing a dangerous game.

'Soturi!' a voice cries, and I look round to find Fey running for us. Soturi collapses to his knees as she throws her arms round him, panic plain in her face. 'Hold on, just hold on.'

'It was a wither beast,' I say in anguish. 'He defended me. He fought it off.'

She takes a shuddering breath and cups his cheek. 'Of course he did. He's the best of us.'

There's a deep rumble and the sound of that great door to the tunnel opening. We all look across to find a way out of the arena. The Trial is over.

'Time for us to get out of here,' Heath says. 'Best you get moving too. But do you need a hand with him? Sember's very good in a crisis.'

'And apparently you're about as useful as pudding.' She snorts, worry furrowing her brow, despite her quip, as she looks at Soturi. 'Fey, can you carry him?'

'She can if Mira and I brace him on the other side,' Kell says, waving them off. 'You two go. We have a deal, don't we? You need to claim your victory. Thank you for helping us.'

'Our pleasure,' Sember says. Then she and Heath step through the doorway into the tunnel, and out of the arena, to defend their position as winners of the Trial.

I look out over the crowd, suddenly aware once more of their presence above us. There's no hiding the fact that we've worked together now. An entire audience has witnessed us – from three different territories –

working together. As I scan the faces, the noise of them all bleeding into one, endless din, that's when I see her.

Agnes.

Flaming red hair, mouth a full O as she screams for me. I jolt as though shot, nearly dropping Soturi. My breath comes too fast as I watch her, then I'm calling her name, tears fogging my eyes. She's alive. We lock eyes and she grins, tears filling her eyes as she reaches her arms towards me. Then I see who is beside her. Nero. His lips curl in a taunting smile, eyes filled with cold, as two guards brace their hands on Agnes's shoulders. And I have never hated someone so much in my life. Nero's gloating smile falters as I glare up at him, a frown deepening a furrow in his forehead. Then the guards pull Agnes away, and she's gone.

Fey, Kell and I drag Soturi the final few feet out of the labyrinth in the arena. He collapses as soon as we get into the tunnel. The roar of the spectators falls away as the doorway closes in our wake and I only notice it from its marked absence. The guards flood the space, taking over and hauling Soturi to the witches waiting to heal him. Kell and I are left to walk behind, and all I can see is Agnes. Her anguish. Her spirit, still fierce as fire. And then I picture Nero, the curl of his lip. And wrath consumes me.

Later that night, when my rage has turned to acid, I curl into a ball on my bed. The cry of a drake echoes across Highborn, over and over. Soturi is dead. As his drake mourns, the city falls into an unnatural hush and all I can hear is the drake crying for his rider. A silent tear tracks down my cheek, then another. So much unnecessary death. And all a show of the rulers' power, a battle played out in an arena before a crowd. I wonder if the merchants have agreed to use their route. If they are impressed. Somehow, I doubt it. Kell and I ranked second before last – the Leicenan contenders were both cornered by a wither beast and chose to forfeit and ask for help, bowing out of the Trials. And, somehow, Sapira from Stanvard came first, beating Sember and Heath to the tunnel.

I was so close to death. Again. I can still hear the wither beast's roar, smell its steaming flesh, feel the terrified thump of my heart. For the first time, I truly believe I will not make it out of these Trials alive. But, if it comes to it, if I am alone in the next Trial . . . I bunch my hands into fists and cry in earnest. Then I am unlikely to make it.

For the first time, I contemplate the very real possibility that I may never free Agnes. That I won't see Rosevear again. That I will die with Eli trapped in another world, and I may never see those I love again in this life. My spirit breaks for the first time, and in the darkest part of the night I feel the walls caving in. I am truly, utterly alone.

Chapter 20

Brielle

AFTER OUTWITTING THE HUNTERS AND their grindlewolves, Brielle leads her coven to a safehouse in a village near the Leicenan border. They hide until the following day, waiting for the cover of darkness to continue onwards, ditching the coach and securing a smaller, sleeker carriage as they reach a town just over the border. Three days and nights of relentless travel is enough to bind Inesh and Dreska into constant companions and fast friends. But for Brielle every mile is torture. Her friends, captured, taken and the possibility of those hunters finding them again at the very forefront of her mind. She taps her fingers restlessly against her leg, watching out of the carriage window as the blur of Leicenan vineyards race past outside. She should have been there, should have protected them, not left so swiftly, believing everything would be fine on the isles in her absence. She should have factored in the ruling council's relentless drive for power and the strong possibility of retaliation.

'Driver!' She raps sharply on the roof of the carriage, not for the first time. 'Faster, get us there faster!'

No ship will sail to the Fortunate Isles from the northern port town of Normé, despite flashing her purse, full of coin. So she books a passage for the three of them aboard a ship to Port Trenn and stands on deck the entire trip as Nova stays by her side, watching the sea consume the land.

There is nothing you can do.

'The first Trial, no, the first *two* Trials, will be over and done with,' she says. 'I should have been there. I could have got Mira out, Kell too.' She doesn't mention the unthinkable: what if they're already dead? What if, even now, the ruling council is surrounding the islands with their ships . . .

Hunter, focus on the next move. Caden will know more when we arrive. There is no use fretting. Think like the hunter you are. Think like the Tresillian witch you have been forged into.

'Ever the pragmatist.'

As are you usually, Brielle. This crisis is the first true test of your character. Do not fall short.

Brielle stifles an indignant snort, annoyed that Nova is right. At Coven Septern, she was never tested in this way, not since she went rogue and stalked her mother's killers. But, since Lowri's defection, and then her own, and now this . . . this *crisis*, as Nova calls it, she is indeed being tested. Her only hope is that Eli and Lowri have returned from Eli's father's world between

Caden sending the message, and now. But, somehow, she doesn't think so. She cannot feel the presence of her sister in this world. There is still a silence, a space unfilled, which troubles her more each day. The lack of stability, of grounding, leaves her shaken, wobbling to find her equilibrium. The world is changing, but she must stay steadfast. If not for herself, then for her young charges. For Lowri and for her friends.

'We were gone too long. Foolish of me. *Foolish*.' She swears, gripping the railing, and steadies her breath. 'What has it been? Two weeks now? Longer?'

Nova says nothing, merely swishing her tail.

The moment she sets foot on Ennor, she knows things are very, very wrong. And when Caden greets her, gaunt and tall, her brother cannot meet her gaze. Not fully.

'Tell me,' she says, gripping his shoulder.

He swallows. 'Mira and Agnes are still in the hands of the ruling council. Alive for now, that's all we know. Mira is representing Arnhem in the Trials. Penscalo has been recaptured by the watch.' He blinks. 'There are more people fleeing other islands, finding their way here. We are the last stand now against the watch and ruling council. They have been swift, brutal—'

'And what of Lowri? Eli?' Brielle asks desperately, trying to find some good, some hope.

'That is the worst news of all, Bri,' Caden says quietly, eyes finally meeting hers. 'They have not returned.'

* * *

Drake cry haunts the city of Highborn. As Brielle and Pearl slink through the shadowed back alleyways in the gathering twilight, Brielle realises what the cry means. The creature is in mourning.

'Unusual for drakes to travel this far south, isn't it?' Pearl asks quietly. 'Especially to somewhere so populated by humans.'

'It is,' Brielle agrees. She doesn't want to admit it, but that ethereal cry is known as an ill omen in the Spines, where the majority of drakes reside. 'Best get off the streets and to an inn.'

'Why an inn?' Pearl asks, tilting her chin.

Brielle smiles. 'Best place to hear the gossip. And, usually, the food's better than in those fancy places. I'm hungry.'

Pearl mirrors Brielle's smile, sharp tiny teeth on display, and Brielle wonders, not for the first time, how deadly her companion truly is for Caden to insist that she accompanies Brielle. As soon as Caden had filled her in, Brielle made a quick plan with him, Kai and Merryam, trying to contain her guilt over not being there aboard *Phantom* the day they were taken. Leaving her newly formed coven under the watchful eye of Amma and Tanith, she repacked straight away, replenished her purse and set sail for the mainland of Arnhem with Pearl.

'Mira's always been brave,' Pearl says quietly. 'Aboard Renshaw's ship, when we were captured, she held her own. Never gave in, never faltered, even when Renshaw . . . well. She's a monster.'

'So this is personal for you?' Brielle asks, weaving round a group of revellers. The streets are packed with people from all over the continent descending on Highborn to witness the Trials unfold.

Pearl glances at Brielle. 'My family are Mer, Eli and the others. My home is Ennor.' A carriage trundles past and Pearl swerves to avoid one of the horses as it tosses its head. 'Mira is one of us now and that's why Caden sent me. We never leave one of our own behind.'

She's loyal, then, Brielle realises, regarding this slight girl quietly. They call her little ghost, and she has heard rumours of her talents, how she slips in and out, how she employs the use of poisons rather effectively. Loyalty is the vein that runs through the heart of Ennor, but that's not why Pearl specifically was chosen by Caden for this mission. She's sure of it.

She worries most for Kell, a seething rage burning slowly inside her at the thought of the watch ripping him from Helene and taking him to be used as a pawn in these Trials. Mira, she knows, is a fighter. She has a heart of iron, a will that cannot so easily be broken. But Kell has been hidden and protected for so long. She's not sure he will know how to survive the Trials. And then there's Agnes. Brielle has no knowledge of where she could be. She hopes that Pearl is also very useful as a spy, that *little ghost* has more than one meaning.

'Lead the way, Hunter,' Pearl says as they enter the merchant's quarter of the city in the south-east.

Far from the coven strongholds in the north of

Highborn, where the most established houses line leafy streets, the merchant's quarter is more ramshackle in nature, and far more populated. As such, it's a melting pot of poor and rich, a place to make your fortune, or die in the attempt. The inns and pubs are the best grounds to hunt for information in the city, and Brielle glances down a cobbled street still packed with revellers and street hawkers, the scent of their wares wafting over her in heady waves: baked goods, cheap bottles of lemonade and ale, pickled eels curling in pots. She looks both ways, checking they haven't been followed, before heading through the old wooden door of the Wanderer's Rest.

Inside, the air is so smoky and thick you could chew on it, the atmosphere rowdy and the beer flowing free and fast. Brielle and Pearl find a small table that wobbles near the bar, and Brielle has to duck her head as a tray of frothing drinks is scooped up and carried above her by one of the barmen.

'Watch your pockets in here,' she says to Pearl. 'And I'll order for—'

'You do know where I grew up, don't you?' Pearl interjects, placing her forearms on the table. 'If there's a better pickpocket than me in this place, I'll shake their hand and *give* them my coin.'

Brielle eyes her. 'Where *did* you grow up?'

'Finnikin's Way,' she says with a wink, neatly hooking two glasses off a tray as a barmaid is distracted, and passing one to Brielle. She sniffs it, shrugs, then takes a tiny sip of the pale green wine before looking back at Brielle. 'Caden didn't send you here with someone you'd need to coddle.'

Brielle shrugs as well, realising she may have underestimated this girl. She clinks her glass against Pearl's. 'Fair enough. I heard that community disappeared. Just upped and left without a trace. Do you miss any of them?'

Pearl laughs quietly. 'In a word, no. The day Eli rescued me from that place was the day I was born anew. Doesn't mean I don't wonder where they've hunkered down, though. They're smart – it's how they've survived so long. The ruling council and their watch would have a job catching them.' She glances around. 'So, who are you hoping to see here?'

Brielle takes a long sip, her gaze lingering on a group walking inside. 'The watch.'

Pearl splutters, wiping her chin. 'Have you lost it? *The watch?*'

'They're going to sit down at the next table, so act natural,' Brielle mutters, flagging down a passing barmaid to order some food.

Pearl's version of acting natural is to shrink further into her chair, glancing crossly at the men barging through the crowd to take seats round the table next to them. The four men are all off duty, but Brielle can tell a man of the watch from a mile away. Entitled, superior and rough round the edges. One of them grabs the arm of a barman, clicking his fingers as he orders drinks 'on the house'.

As Brielle and Pearl's food arrives, they eat their slices of pie and greens quietly, senses attuned to the men and every jewel of information they begin dropping unknowingly into their laps.

'That drake needs putting down. What a noise,' one man says, scratching at a lump on his ear.

'Along with that girl they're keeping in the tower room.'

'Weren't you minding her?'

'The redhead? No, that's Fred. Did you hear he's in the infirmary, though? The girl bit him. *Bit* him! Those islanders are feral.'

They all guffaw and Brielle bends her fork into a curve. The arrogance, the sheer *nerve* of them. But good on Agnes for fighting back. And at least now Brielle can find her. There are only three towers at court and all she needs is a set of keys. There are witch wards everywhere; they'll have to break in without witchcraft. She looks up to signal to Pearl that it's time to go, but the girl's meal is almost untouched.

That's when she notices Pearl's gone.

Brielle glances left and right, being careful not to appear like she's searching, then spies Pearl's halo of blonde hair bobbing up behind one of the men at the next table. They keep talking – discussing the 'other island girl' in the Trials, and how she's lucky to still be alive after the last Trial – as Pearl places small glasses next to each of them, which they pick up and drink without even noticing where they came from. She's back in her seat a few heartbeats later, innocently chewing a mouthful of pie.

'Delicious rabbit,' she comments, chopping up a piece of carrot.

Brielle says nothing, narrowing her gaze on Pearl, who merely smiles innocently at her, then continues chewing.

The men of the watch carry on talking, and Brielle gleans that Mira is alive, so is Kell, and Agnes is causing a lot of trouble for the watch drafted in to guard her. She also learns who is leading the Trials, and when the next one will take place. In just two days' time. She polishes off her drink just as one of the men blows out a big breath.

'Feeling a bit . . . hot in here, isn't it?' he says, fanning his face.

'Now that you mention it . . .' the man across from him says.

Their eyes all turn bulbous, and they clamp their hands over their mouths as they leap up, dashing for the bathroom. When they're gone, Pearl sniggers quietly and stands up. 'Time to move on?'

Outside, Brielle rounds on Pearl, mindful of the revellers surrounding them. 'What was in those drinks?'

'Bitter root,' she says with a shrug. 'Only a little bit. It won't kill them, if that's what you're worried about.'

Brielle shakes her head, oddly impressed. 'Remind me not to piss you off.'

'Don't side with my enemies, Hunter, and you never will.'

Brielle chuckles, turning to move on, when she spies someone across the street. 'Helene?' It couldn't be her here, could it? Surely she hasn't left Egan. Surely she wouldn't have followed Kell here. Brielle frowns, moving with swift steps towards the slight woman with the old-fashioned Leicenan hairstyle, pushing past a steady stream of revellers and hawkers. But when she reaches the spot where the woman was standing she finds Helene has shifted into an alleyway.

'Brielle, no—' Pearl says, tugging on her sleeve, but Brielle shakes her off, stalking forward.

It's not until footsteps sound behind her, until a whisper of wind snakes past her nose smelling of copper and something else, something distinctly witch, that she realises Helene is not here alone.

Helene steps forward, worry etching her features. 'I'm sorry, Brielle. They gave me no choice.'

Brielle whirls, finding two hunters blocking her path, then another, emerging from the alley behind Helene. Not the hunters that tracked her across the continent, though. No, these are hunters she knows all too well, the hunters of Coven Septern.

'Hira, Shayle. What a delight to see you both. Completely by chance, I assume?' Brielle says carefully, sizing them up. 'I'm surprised you're not at Leicenan court on assignment or keeping some merchant happy in a mine in Valstra.'

Shayle scrunches her nose. 'You always were mouthy when cornered.'

'You're not an easy witch to track down,' Hira adds, folding her arms across her chest. Then she throws out a hand, catching Pearl by the wrist. 'No, no, little ghost. Don't try anything.'

'You're coming with us,' Shayle adds, at her side. 'Both of you.'

CHAPTER 21

Lowri

'IF YOU STAY OUT THERE in the street, they'll only spot you,' Hellius says, beckoning them inside. 'You've created quite a rumble in the Society. Isaiah was very careful who he trusted his theories with and many of the members were overly cautious. They believed his research risky. Potentially dangerous.'

'And were you someone he trusted?' Eli asks pointedly.

'I was,' Hellius replies. 'And, if you come inside, I can prove it to you.'

Lowri wonders if this is a trap, if the temptation of two otherworldly visitors is too great a prize. But she is long past wariness. The desperation and longing to return to their world is almost tangible, a riddle she must solve. 'Know that if you are lying to us, I have a very good right hook.'

Hellius raises his eyebrows at that and chuckles before disappearing into the room beyond.

'Maybe I should make the threats, Lor,' Eli mutters. 'Although you do have an exceptional right hook.'

They walk into a room dominated by a large worktable, covered in the detritus of a man obsessed with magic. Jars of powders, rolled parchments riddled with inky words, cuttings from plants, flickering candles and an indisputably pungent aroma. Everything is greyscale, just like all else in Fallow, but to Lowri there seemed to be a glint of something that could *almost* be an array of colours.

Hellius stirs a small pot on a stove along the back wall. 'I mix Fallow Fog in with everything now. Would you like some soup?'

'We're here about your message, not for soup,' Lowri says, moving round the table. Her gaze catches on a book, eyes widening slightly before she looks back at Hellius. 'Tell us about yours and Isaiah's theory.'

'And why you have one of my father's notebooks,' Eli says.

Hellius holds up his hands, eyes darting to meet Eli's before settling on the notebook. Back when they'd met this historian of the Shadow War in the Society, he seemed friendly, harmless. But now the spiky beard and the close-set eyes appear a little sly to Lowri, as though he had been hiding a side of himself before. 'Ah, that. I was keeping it safe. You see, we worked on everything together. We were partners . . .'

'And now you're trying to pass his work off as your own, aren't you?' Eli says, folding his arms. 'I have read my father's theories, been through his office. My father may have had a unique filing system, but he kept meticulous records. And you were never mentioned as a partner. In fact, in a note I read this morning, he mentions you as someone who tried to discredit him. Or did that slip your mind when we first met you?'

'Merely friendly rivalry.' Hellius titters nervously. 'Would I invite you here today if I didn't have the best intentions?'

'Tell us what you want, and then it'll be clear what your intentions are,' Eli rumbles.

For a moment, Hellius maintains his false smile. Then it drops, along with his pretence. 'Fine,' he hisses, then points a finger at Lowri, the slyness in his gaze intensifying. 'I wanted her here. A witch, a creature from another world with light magic?' He shakes his head in barely concealed hunger. 'If I were to take her light magic, I could save Fallow. I could save our world. I would be lauded, rich. No one would ever question my knowledge, my authority—'

'You should have stopped at saving Fallow, Hellius,' Ethlet says quietly. 'If it were Isaiah, that would have been enough.'

'And that's why he failed,' Hellius snaps. 'His ways were too by the book. It's no wonder the Society wouldn't believe his theories. No wonder he received no funds, no resources. All theoretical. All too politely requested. Whereas I—'

'Would kidnap a creature?' Lowri says. 'That's what I am to you, isn't it? Not human, therefore someone to be controlled, drained of light magic.'

Hellius shrugs. 'Witches aren't human. Isaiah told me about your catalyst to call forth the power inside you: creature blood. You're no better, witch.'

Lowri swallows. 'That may be.'

'A trade, then,' Eli says. 'Tell us what you know, and we will give you light magic. If that's what you desire.'

'But how?' Hellius says, holding up a finger. 'That is the real question. One I have pondered on since your arrival. And that answer . . .' He laughs. 'The answer is in you. The two of you. Light and dark, together. Two strands, combined, strong enough to open a portal. Strong enough to right the balance in our world.'

'You speak in riddles,' Ethlet says impatiently, 'and it smells like cabbage in here. Get to the point.'

'You always were an insolent little—'

'The point, Hellius,' Eli says with deceptive softness.

'Isaiah had a theory,' Hellius says quickly, a grin flickering on his lips. 'A theory of how to draw light magic out of a witch, and bottle it. So that it could be consumed, or it could be contained to grow and grow, until it could be released into the fog, and the shadow would dissipate, beginning the cycle of renewal, of healing.'

Lowri narrows her eyes. 'An extraction?'

'Precisely.'

'And why was this theory not in any of his notebooks, Hellius?' Eli asks, thunder gathering in his voice. Then his eyes widen, sliding to his father's notebook that Hellius has on the table. 'Did you . . . steal that?'

Hellius frowns, all pretence dropped. 'He would have done nothing with it,' he hisses. 'And when I saw you in the Society building – a witch! A creature carrying light magic! – I asked for a private audience with the head of the Society. I pleaded with them to allow me to carry out one of your father's theories—'

'They said no?' Ethlet asks.

Hellius's mouth twists. 'They said no. You were guests of our world and the theory was unproven. But if you were to offer your blood willingly, if you gave some to me, I could prove the theory . . .'

Lowri leans her head to the side, considering. 'How much blood?'

Eli looks sidelong at her. 'No, Lor.'

'We have little choice.'

'I won't risk you.'

Lowri blows out a breath. 'We are taking great risks every hour that we stay here! You took a risk when you walked between worlds. Is it not my turn? My choice to make?' She crosses her arms, every moment of being controlled, of being told *no* at Coven Septern rearing up in her mind, her own personal monster of bitterness and frustration, and it wears her mother's, her Malefant's, face.

'The witch has a point there.'

'This does not concern you, Hellius,' Lowri snaps.

She steps towards Eli and he runs a hand down his face. 'I carried you here when you were dying.'

'And you can carry me back out if you must. We will

take Gracious with us. Isaiah's research too.' Then she adds gently, 'I am not asking your permission, cousin. Allow me to make my own choices.'

Eli sighs deeply, eyeing her. Then he nods. 'So be it.'

Lowri turns to Hellius, holding out her wrist. 'How much blood, then? Tell me and I can decide.'

'Not your blood,' Hellius says, licking his lips. 'Your magic. You must speak the witch words for giving, for offering. That's what Isaiah surmises in his notebook. You must use your witch words and offer up your light magic.' He moves to the corner, throwing a covering off a large contraption. Made of glass and silver, it gleams in the dull light, a balloon-like glass bottle with an open funnel at the top, covered in a latticework of silver. At the bottom is a stopper, like a tiny tap, and inside there is nothing.

Eli walks to it, examining it carefully. 'The silver encases the magic. The glass itself is tempered. I saw a sketch in one of his notebooks, but there was no explanation. I just flicked past . . .'

'It distils the magic within, changing it from fog, if it's shadow, to liquid,' Ethlet says in awe. 'He theorised that the light magic would act differently, that it may sink, that it may be more concentrated and therefore heavier than shadow, which floats as the fog does, overhead.' She shakes her head slowly. 'Isaiah spoke of this process, but I thought it was only theoretical. To see the apparatus he dreamed up . . .'

'The sketches that you stole, I presume?' Eli says sharply to Hellius.

'And aren't you glad of that now?' Hellius says. 'If not for me, his work would be deep in the Society archives. They wouldn't have even thought to give you his theories, his dreams . . . They never believed in him.'

'But you did, and instead of working on it with him, supporting him in his request for funds from the Society, you stole the design and created it for your own gains. He didn't know about this, did he?' Eli presses, gaze like a blade, pinned to Hellius.

'He didn't,' Hellius says, deflating for the first time. 'I'm sorry.'

Eli looks away, crossing his arms. Silence descends for a moment before Lowri makes a decision. Not for Hellius, not for his selfish gains, but for her, for Eli. For his father's world and theirs.

'So I offer up my magic, into this funnel at the top . . .' Lowri says.

'Then the device distils it. The shadow will remain in a cloud in the top of the balloon, just like the fog. The light will sink, pooling, so that it can be drained in liquid form.'

'In theory,' Eli says.

Hellius shrugs. 'As Ethlet said, that was your father's theory.'

'Well,' Lowri says, clearing her throat. 'Give me some space, all of you. Hellius, a tumbler to draw the light magic. Ethlet, watch the door. And Eli . . .'

'Yes?'

'Do not interfere. No being the hero. Not today.'

Eli chuckles darkly. 'You know me too well, Lor.'

Lowri smiles, then gestures to the funnel at the top, feeling her magic, still slightly wrong, almost syrupy as it clots in her fingertips, too little still, as though poured from a bottle, rather than a well. She calls upon a witch word, the one for the act of giving. The one for selfless love. And she allows it to pour from her lips, sweet as honey, gentle as spring rain.

Amoria.

CHAPTER 22

Brielle

BRIELLE SPINS ON THE SPOT, a witch word on her lips. But it's hopeless. With Shayle, Hira and another hunter, Grieshal, all crowding round her in the tight confines of the alley, she has no chance of escaping them.

'Release Pearl and Helene, and I'll come with you. Neither of them are witches,' Brielle says, squaring up to Shayle. If Pearl and Helene could get away, if she doesn't have to worry about them, she can try to escape.

'No, I don't think so. The little ghost is coming with us, as well as your friend from the Far Isles.' Hira jerks her chin at Pearl. 'She's got a reputation. More lethal than most of Coven Septern's hunters, that one. Nice try.'

Pearl bares her teeth and Hira takes a half step back, alarm flitting across her features. Brielle chuckles. 'Scared of a ghost now?'

'Enough,' Shayle says, looping a spelled braided rope round Pearl's wrist, tying it to her own. 'We'll draw attention.'

Brielle blows out a breath, realising they both must comply as Helene gives her a hapless shrug. They stalk through the back streets and quiet alleyways, the sound of nightly revellers drifting to silence in their wake. But, as they walk further into the streets of Highborn, Brielle realises they aren't heading towards the coven house. They're going in the opposite direction, towards a safehouse buried in a web of bland merchants' homes, one seldom used by the coven except to provide respite to weary travellers and friends of the coven from the continent.

When they arrive, they don't march in past the front door as Brielle expects, instead slinking through the gate set into the alleyway behind the property, before shifting between the shadows into the silent kitchen.

Her confusion grows as they're not taken to the Malefant, who she expects to be waiting for them, but to an empty lounge on the first floor, looking out over the leafy night-time street. In fact, the entire safehouse is deserted. The hunters ward the room so no one can leave or enter. And, most interestingly, so no one can listen in to what is spoken of inside the four walls.

Finally, Shayle releases Pearl, who bolts for a window, trying the catch. 'It's no use,' she says. 'The wards will hold you in here.'

Pearl shrugs then sits down on the window seat. 'Worth a try.'

Helene takes a seat in a high-backed armchair, scowling at the hunters, while Brielle hovers by the door, curiosity overcoming her fear. 'What's this about? You're breaking the rules by not taking us straight to the Malefant at the coven house . . .' Then her eyes widen. 'She doesn't know we're here, does she?'

Hira and Shayle exchange a shifty glance before Hira speaks. 'We need to present a compelling enough case before we bring this to our Malefant and the other high witches.'

Brielle raises an eyebrow. 'Oh, you're going to be in a whole heap of trouble for this.'

'And if you raise the alarm and get us caught, you'll be tried in a witch trial for defecting,' Shayle points out. 'So, what's it to be? We all get caught and face a witch trial, or you listen and we avoid the ultimate destruction of all covens?'

Brielle blinks quickly, realising they are deadly serious. 'That's quite an ultimatum . . .'

'It's what could happen,' Hira says.

'We're listening,' Pearl says quietly.

'Your friend Mira told me something very interesting before the first Trial,' Hira begins. 'And, before you ask, yes, I've seen her and Kell. And, yes, they're still alive. But, with the final Trial tomorrow, their future is uncertain.'

'What did she tell you?' Brielle asks, hiding her relief just as Helene can scarcely hide hers. They're alive. All is not yet lost.

'She told me something that she and Agnes overheard

about a law being passed that would give the ruling council the power to control magic.'

'And thus the power to control the covens of Arnhem,' Shayle adds.

Hira fixes her gaze on Brielle. 'I looked into it, carefully enquiring about the way laws are set, then listened in to a conversation between some of the captains of the watch at a drinks reception.'

'And you found some truth in it?' Pearl asks.

Hira nods. 'More than I would have liked. I told Shayle and Grieshal, and they agreed to help me. We have to bring it to the coven leaders, before it's too late. But if this becomes a civil war, we need the isles secured. We need the sea advantage, as well as the land.'

Brielle's smile does not reach her eyes. 'Which is where Mira comes in and those allied to her.'

'She cannot die tomorrow. Nor can she triumph. We need to free her. She must return to Ennor and ensure that the Fortunate Isles do not fall under the control of the watch. We need the storm bringer on our side. And we may need Ennor as a base for the war to come.'

'What about Kell?' asks Helene. 'Is he dispensable to you?'

'I extend this to Kell,' Hira says, glancing at Helene. 'He has an unusual gift. Magic, but in the hands of a human. The ruling council will want to control him, and others like him. This new law would not only concern witches. It should worry all of us.'

'Including the apothecaries,' says Pearl grimly. 'It even filters down into how we treat our sick and wounded. The level of control with this law would be immense. So how do you propose we help our friends escape?'

'We need a distraction during the final Trial tomorrow,' Shayle says. She hesitates, before continuing. 'It's a risk, but we can see no other way to free Mira and Kell. Perhaps with you here, with your help, it will be possible to free them. But we need a distraction, and we need their guards tied up.'

'And what of Agnes? You know Mira won't leave without her. She'll be in the crowd with the ruling council, looking on, or they'll have her stashed somewhere.'

Hira smiles. 'That particular rescue is in hand. In fact, Shayle? Our guest is outside.'

Brielle frowns as Shayle removes the ward on the threshold and a slight, rather ordinary-looking girl wanders in through the front door. With mousy brown hair, pale skin and a snub nose, she wouldn't stand out in a gathering at all. Which, Brielle realises, probably means there is far more to this girl. She eyes the metal hair pin fastened in the girl's hair. If she didn't know any better, she'd say it wasn't a hairpin at all. In fact, it seemed to be many things all at once. A coin, a key, a blade . . . She blinks quickly, eyeing the girl with increased suspicion. There is magic in that object, and yet it seems to emanate from her. But she is not a witch. Nor does Brielle sense that she is a creature.

'Ah, you found the hunter,' the girl says, nodding to Brielle. 'And a couple more friends. Excellent. I'm Sember, by the way, a friend of Mira's.' She laces her fingers before her, raising her eyebrows. 'Shall we go over the plan?'

Chapter 23

Mira

ONLY SIX OF US CONTENDERS remain. As I walk through the tunnel, Kell by my side, all I can hear is the slow thundering of my own heart. I see the arena in blinks, taking in the sun gilding the crowd, the wide bowl of pale blue sky, then the ground beneath us. Green and lush, with gentle rolling hills and bushes. For this, the last Trial, they have allowed us a weapon of our choice, anything except rifles. A blade is strapped at my hip, a bow and arrow strapped across Kell's back. But, even though we all now have weapons, somehow, I know they are not meant for us to turn on each other. Kell and I speculated what this Trial would be, after a sea with a listing ship and a labyrinth. We continued to train, even with Hira absent, the guards giving us no news of her whereabouts. Was she investigating the new law the ruling council planned to pass? Or had she been reassigned by her Malefant and the ruling council, our fates left to ourselves to figure out after we failed to win the first two Trials?

I kick a stone at the edge of the tunnel, watching as it tumbles down to thud into the grass below. Will it be another land-based Trial? Now I gaze at those rolling hills, it seems certain that it is. But who or what enemy we must fight is unclear. Soturi's death has haunted me this past week, his drake crying out over and over across Highborn. I curled up in a ball and picked at my food for two days and nights. Mourning the loss of my freedom, my old way of life, the people I loved who are gone.

But then I rose. And I reminded myself that it's not over. I'm still alive. Kell is still alive and so is Agnes. Our hearts still beat in their cage of a palace and the ruling council has not broken us yet. I must stare down death one final time.

The ruling council has a last trick to test us – that's clear from the serene scene of the arena. To see who will triumph, who will fall, and decide on the narrative they will write to suit their own ends. If I succeed, I will be their champion, proving the strength of the ruling council. If I fail, I will be dead, symbolising the fall of the isles and how they have brought us all to heel. They will use me like the pawn I am to them, to suit their own ends. But we have our own plans. Our own allies in this Trial.

We're led down to the arena, the guards escorting us as a group to the very middle. I look around, ignoring the crowd, taking in the terrain. There are very few places to hide. We're mostly exposed. Wind whistles through the space, stirring my hair, and I bend low, placing my hand on the grass. All real. There is no spellwork here.

Sember sidles over, leaning in to murmur in my ear. 'She's in the crowd. She's watching.'

I grow still, blood beating hot through my veins. Agnes is here. They've brought her to the Trials again. 'Where?'

'East of us, ten o'clock. She's in a balcony box with the ruling council. Her bruises have faded, but she's tried escaping multiple times, so I've been told. Her guards have been rotated out; they refuse to guard her.'

'Why?' I ask, forcing myself not to look. Not to seek her out just yet.

'She bites.'

I chuckle, low in my throat. 'That's my girl.'

'We have a plan, and you have to trust us. But, first, we need to get through the Trial, to survive it.'

'To win it, you mean,' I say, side-eyeing her. After today, I'll know if she's been able to stick to her word, to our deal. That she might actually have got Agnes out of here. I've fought against trusting her, but, despite all that has happened and the betrayals I have faced, I do. I really do trust her. Perhaps I just trusted the wrong people before, like Seth. But maybe I shouldn't close the door on trusting others completely. We need her today. I need her to come through for us.

She inclines her head. 'That too. Winning is for Heath. I promise that if you'd met his father you would understand.'

'We have a deal, Sember Lockswift,' I say, turning to her. 'You're saving Agnes's, Kell's and my life today by helping us escape. That's all I need to understand. Thank you. Can you share any of your plan?'

She winces. 'If I do, and it doesn't work, then it implicates those I am working with. For now, we need them to seem loyal to the ruling council. You will learn who your true allies are soon enough.'

'All right.' I sigh softly, willing myself to just trust, as I trusted my people on Rosevear before all this. As I trusted the others in the seven I swam out with on the rope, with my life. Every time, as natural as breath.

Sember nods, ending the discussion, and turns back to the arena. 'I've heard they've saved the worst until last.'

'Predictable.'

'Indeed.'

I take a moment then to survey the crowd, gaze lingering on the eastern stands. My stomach drops when I see Agnes, everything else falling away. She's unmistakable, her wild red hair, her pale face, her eyes burning with hate. I fix her in my mind, the simmering rage, ever present, burning in my heart. They thought they could capture us and bend us to their will. They were wrong. We will never be theirs, in our hearts, in our souls.

'Contenders!' a voice projects over the arena. 'Welcome to the third and final Trial. Your objective this time is simple. Survive.'

The gong sounds, the crowd cheers, and the six of us exchange glances in confusion. We pull out our weapons, ready for what is to come. Silence stretches across the massive space. Even the crowd is growing still. What are we meant to survive?

'I don't like this,' Kell whispers, readying an arrow in his bow. 'If we all survive, what then? We all win?'

'I imagine this Trial is so awful that they're expecting to scrape what's left of most of us off this finely clipped grass. That, or watch us forfeit like cowards,' Heath remarks, drawing his sword. 'I suggest we put aside our differences. Fight the common enemy.'

'Agreed,' says Fey, also palming a sword. I haven't seen her since the last Trial, and her eyes are hollowed out and raw. My heart bleeds for her. For Soturi. For her loss. 'We can worry about victory later. I don't like the feel of this.'

A drake cry sounds from somewhere to the west and she breathes a name, which sounds something like *Javilick*. She swallows, turning to us. 'That was my drake, that was his warning cry! For—'

Then the sky shatters all around us.

I flinch as the sky, once pale blue, is now crowded with something else, something other.

Fey spits on the ground. '*Wyvern.*'

Panic engulfs me and I have to force myself to count them, to control my breathing. Five, six, seven, eight, nine. There are nine wyvern in the sky, moving swiftly towards us. In all the previous Trials Hira had listed and researched, none mentioned wyvern. I look across to the ruling council, lounging in their seats, watching on idly. Do they want a spectacle today, or a massacre?

'The stands are warded,' the commentator booms as the crowd begins to shriek and scream, some scrambling from their seats. 'The creatures will not harm you!'

'Only us,' says Sapira bitterly, blade in hand. 'I should have forfeited; I should have left . . .'

'It's too late to think of that,' Fey says, drawing herself up to her full height. 'They're pack monsters. They hunt for sport, and if we're in a tight group, we're more of a target. Spread out. Get into pairs. Sapira, come with me. Don't try to bolt and forfeit, they'll pick you off. Everyone, aim for the mouth, the eyes or the belly. The wings will burn, if you can somehow make fire.' She flicks a look over us all. 'It is my honour to fight beside you.'

Then she's gone, Sapira chasing after her. I look to Kell, then back at the wyvern, now close enough for us to see the span of batlike wings, the mean eyes, the dark scales and vicious claws. 'Sember? Heath? It's your call. We can stick with you or split up like Fey said and try to draw some off.'

'I can't see how you'd have any control over drawing them away,' Sember says. 'We're all pretty much done for.'

Kell opens his palm and pale flame ignites, curling upwards. 'Surprise.'

Sember is quiet for a moment then laughs, a breathless, delighted sound. Then she pulls a coin from her pocket, flips it up, and into her hand lands a silver blade. She winks at him, holding two blades now, narrowed to deathly points. 'Surprise, yourself.'

'Nice,' I say, nodding. And all those moments click into place. When Sember led us through that door in the side of the palace, she unlocked it as though by . . . magic. And it was. Her magic. The walls of the maze, the bronze sheer sheets of them, all metal. Of course she could open and close each door at will. She can manipulate metals. I smile, hope igniting in my chest, and jerk my chin at the twin blades she now holds. 'Know how to use those?'

Heath rolls his shoulders, then twirls his sword in one hand, as if it weighs nothing. 'In Skylan, we train from birth. Sember and I met in the military.' He flashes me a wicked grin and I realise this prince has been holding out on us. He's not affected or weak at all, as they both led us to believe. His eyes settle into a deadly stare and I know I've grossly underestimated them both. 'First kill wins.'

I grin back, raising a hand to the sky. 'You're on, prince.'

Then as the first wave of three wyvern bear down on us, I dig deep inside myself. I don't consider control, or how much it will take from me. I mould all I am, all the fury, the love, the burning need to live, to be free . . . and I call a storm towards me.

I call it down upon us all.

Thunder booms in the distance, answering my call.

And Sember's eyes widen, her head tilting towards me. 'Did you . . . Is that *you*?'

'Haven't you heard? I'm dangerous. The ruling council want me dead. Either that, or to control me. Make me their weapon to wield,' I say lightly.

'It's true, then,' Sember breathes. 'The ruling council intend to use you to make the Straits impassable. Now I understand.'

'They call me Storm Bringer, but I am no one's weapon. I intend to break them *all*.'

The sky darkens as clouds roll overhead. And as the rain begins to shower down, the first wyvern reaches the arena. Kell sets an arrow aflame, pulls it back and releases it. We hear the hideous shriek as it connects, exactly where he intended. Then the wyvern hits the ground, sprawling across the grass. One wing flutters, then falls still, an arrow sprouting from one eye.

Kell exhales softly, reaches for another arrow and nocks it against the bowstring. 'I used to hunt the rabbits on Egan. They got too clever for traps, so I had to learn to use a bow and arrow. I believe I take the win, prince.'

Heath laughs, shaking his head as the other two wyvern beat a path around us, shrieking and hawking. 'If you need a job after this, I could use a decent guard.'

'It would be my honour,' Kell says, then lights up a second arrow with pale flame from his palm, and lets it fly. It finds its mark, burying into a wyvern's throat. The wyvern drops to the ground, already dead before it hits a small hill.

Heath doesn't have time to reply as the third dives suddenly, claws reaching for him.

He ducks and rolls at the last minute, angling his sword up to nick the wyvern's belly. It roars, flying upwards as the second wave begins to descend through the rain, the rest still hovering above, as though to draw out the spectacle of our deaths. Three more, bigger than the last, all splitting up to soar in a ring round the arena.

I steel myself, reaching towards the clouds and feel the first crackle of lightning, of the power I've been too afraid to unleash as a wyvern dives straight for us.

Chapter 24

Mira

I HOLD MY NERVE AS the wyvern shoots like an arrow through the sky towards us. Kell dives to the side, crouching behind a hill as I plant my feet, staring it down. And, somehow, I know I can do this. I can unleash a storm of magic. I can bring lightning down on this creature of hate. I barely move, hardly breathe as it draws ever closer. When I can see its membranous wings, when I can smell the foul scent of its breath, I draw my hand into a fist. I call the storm to strike it.

Lightning forks from the clouds.

Piercing the wyvern.

It crashes to the ground in a wreck of smoke and crooked wings, smouldering in the spray of rain just a few feet from me. The charred scent of its wretched flesh fills my nose and I cough, breathing into my hand. Kell leaps up, awe widening his features as he releases a whoop.

I turn, victorious, the magic inside me, the side that is wholly siren fizzing in my blood. And my heart stops.

The next two wyvern are circling Sapira and Fey. And they're completely exposed.

'Fey!' I cry, already running across the arena, leaping hills and skidding across the soaking grass. They stand, shoulder to shoulder, blades in hand and the only sign of fear from either of them is the slight tremor in Sapira's arms. I close the distance, barrelling towards them as the first wyvern dives.

A flame arrow streaks past me, released from Kell's bow, but it doesn't hit its mark. The wyvern extends its claws, reaching for Sapira as Fey throws her blade, straight into its wide, fanged mouth. Sapira rolls at the last minute, the wyvern falling between them, the blade buried in its throat, killing it instantly. I catch the glint in Fey's eye as the wyvern twists and twitches on the ground, its reeking blood hissing over the grass. She is formidable. But there's one more, readying to dive for them both.

And Fey is now weaponless.

I reach up with my fist as time seems to slow, as the wyvern dives with a feral shriek, eyes locked on Fey. Sapira staggers up, already moving towards Fey, the crowd going wild, hungry for human blood. The clouds bloom and darken, lightning streaking to the ground, once, twice . . .

But every time it misses.

I pump my legs faster, watching in helpless desperation as the wyvern's claws extend just above Fey's head . . .

Sapira jumps, both hands holding her blade aloft,

spearing it in the eye. The wyvern shrieks, crashing into Fey, and they're a tangle of limbs and claws, Sapira and Fey both lost to view for a moment. I finally reach them, clearing the rain from my eyes, and find Sapira in a heap. She blinks up at me and groans as I hold out a hand to haul her back to her feet.

'Anything broken?' I ask quickly, checking her over. She has a gash down her temple, but otherwise she seems all right. She's survived.

'I'm . . . I'll be fine,' she says and swallows. 'But Fey . . .'

We both move towards the wyvern carcass, finding Fey trapped beneath. Her breath is shallow, and I hear the cry of alarm from her drake in the distance. Then I see it. A claw, wedged over her middle, restricting her breathing. She must have cracked ribs and if one of them has punctured a lung . . . I blink quickly, pushing the blare of panicked thoughts away. All I can do is try to get her free. One step at a time. Sapira falls to her knees, feeling for Fey's hand, gripping it tightly and Fey's eyes are unfocused as she turns to her. 'Dying defending someone from a wyvern is an honour,' she manages.

Sapira sobs as I move to take Fey's other hand. 'Fey, look at me. Fey!'

She huffs softly, but turns her head towards my voice. 'Siren. Storm bringer.'

'You will not die today. Do you hear me?' I say, throwing all my will into my words. 'You. Will. Not. Die.

Today.' Then I turn to Kell as he reaches us, dropping to his knees beside me. 'Kell, we are going to shove. Sapira, you are going to grip Fey under the shoulders, dig your heels in and pull. Hard. Are you with me?'

'We're with you,' says Sapira.

Kell nods, moving to my side as Sapira wipes at her face, then levers her hands under Fey's shoulder blades. 'Ready?' I say. 'Count of three. One, two, *three*.'

And I shove.

Kell puts his shoulders into it, Fey releasing a strangled moan as the monster shifts . . . and Sapira drags her clear.

The rain pours down in a torrent around us and I brace my hands on my thighs, pulling in a breath. When I turn to Fey, Sapira is speaking to her quickly, testing her bones, wincing when Fey cries out. She looks at me and Kell. 'Three fractured ribs, I believe. And a sprained wrist. But I don't think there's internal damage. Her lungs and her heart are intact.'

'What you mean is lucky to be alive,' Fey grates out, eyes turning skyward. 'I'm fresh meat for them to pick at when they tire of chasing you. Leave me. Guard yourselves.'

So much death. So much suffering. And all so that men in power can take more and more. I stand, staring straight at the balcony where the ruling council hold Agnes. I see her, blanched features, tears streaming from her eyes. So afraid. So full of bitter rage. Then I look past her, to the three men who sit, delighting in this spectacle, in the show of power over this warrior from the Spines.

And I roar.

As more wyvern circle above us, more than those nine I first spotted arriving, as the storm smothers us all in its heady wrath, I release all my hate, all my anguish, and in my heart, I promise retribution. I promise revenge. This is more than Renshaw, more than the watch. It's always been them, behind every decision, every move to swipe at our lives on the isles. They are the puppet masters and we have all been controlled by their wants, their desire for power, for control. But no more.

I am not powerless.

Breathing heavily, I turn to Sapira, who looks up with shining determination. Then she strips the killing blade from the wyvern, extracting it from its eye. When she rises, I see only fire and a will to fight. I see . . . myself.

'In Valstra, the merchants take everything. They leave us with nothing but hard lives in their mines. And now I see them, all around this arena. That they will keep taking, unless we stand up to them,' she says, her voice a soft, vicious hiss. 'I thought it was an honour, fighting for Stanvard in these Trials. But now I see it is just another way for them to control us. It's just a huge game to them, with the continent as a playing board. They play with our lives. For *profit*.'

'But together . . .'

'Together, we can stand against them,' she says, then looks past me, to the sky. 'I will guard Fey until we can get her out. You focus on the wyvern horde, keep them from us.'

Looking around, I find Kell has joined Sember and Heath and they have downed another wyvern, with the last swooping up to join another wave. I gasp, staring upwards, through the driving rain.

At a skyful of wyvern.

I go to join them as they stop to wipe the rain from their eyes, drawing the wyverns' ire from Sapira and Fey. We are ready to face the final assault.

'Do we have a plan?' asks Sember.

'Kill every one of them, and try not to die?' Kell replies.

I stand tall with my blade, counting them. Ten wyvern now and only four of us. The crowd grows strangely quiet, and I glance up at the stands. They're all watching us, horror on their faces. Perhaps this is too much death even for them. Perhaps the ruling council, in their need for blood sport to unite the people and entertain them, have taken it too far. I seek out Agnes's eyes and touch my heart with my fingers, then hold my hand out to her. She does the same and I know in this moment it could be goodbye. The only goodbye we'll be able to make.

I blow out a breath and look at the others: fierce, proud, clutching weapons, not ready yet to break. The council pitted us against each other, yet we've banded together. I'm not ready to die yet. Not here, not today. Not with my people so far away, not with so much at stake. And not with Eli a world away. The thought of him leaves me raw, and all I want to do is cry out for him, for all we have lost. The pain of wanting him is suddenly so deep, so sharp and searing. I murmur to him, as though he is here with me.

I whisper, *I love you*, into the storm. Then I gather myself, pushing him gently away in my mind. Perhaps it's my final goodbye to him too.

'Kell, pick off the outliers if you can,' I say, my voice hardening. 'Sember, Heath, you spread out, but stay close enough so that you can support one another.'

'And you?' Sember asks.

'It's time I find out what the ruling council were so afraid of. What they seek to control, to use for their own gain,' I say with a smile. 'It's time they learn what a storm bringer can *really* do.'

I take a step forward and then say over my shoulder, 'Kell, add your flame at the right moment. You'll know when.'

Then I set off, striking out alone across the vast arena, as the wyvern soar ever closer, like winged death against the thunderous sky.

Chapter 25

Mira

I BEGIN TO RUN. THE ten wyvern in the sky above me swoop closer. Heart pounding, focus narrowing, all I can feel is the twist inside my veins. The fire and sea, lightning and thunder, all wanting to break free. Gathering everything inside myself, I push my will up into the clouds, and thunder booms loudly over the arena. The crowd begins to panic, a fresh torrent of rain hitting them as the wind picks up. I'm soaked to the skin, but I don't stop. I feel it all, the wild pulse of the storm, the friction as the cold air meets warmth, the electric fizz as the lightning forms. I am the storm and the thunder.

I am a reckoning.

The first wyvern of the horde overhead draws its wings in, shrieking as it spears the air. I throw out my hand, the wind whipping my plait around my head, and lightning forks from that storm cloud to the ground, frying the diving wyvern in its path.

Killing it instantly.

It thuds to the grass, but already two more are taking

its place, preparing to dive. And the real fight truly begins. I hear the shouts of Sember and Heath as they engage their first wyvern. The two that have me in their sights hover above me, trying a different tactic, rotating quickly so there is always one at my back where I can't see it as I turn, heart thundering like the swirling storm. Then they both dive as one, claws extended. I grit my teeth, drawing my fist to my chest, and close my eyes. I sense them, the rush of wings, the narrowed hate and call on the storm. I call for lightning.

Then I open my eyes.

Lightning crackles from the sky and in a flash of searing light they're both fried. I stumble at the impact as both bodies hit the ground on either side of me.

When I look around, I'm surrounded by charred wings and the stench of their death. Breathing heavily through my mouth, I feel for the first time the toll it's taking to use this side of myself, the magic in my veins. But the shouts of Kell and the others sharpen me, and I whip round.

Drawing together all my strength, I get to my feet and walk towards them. Lightning forks from the sky, thunder crashing overhead, and as I hold a hand up to the thunderous clouds a cone of wind spins down, hitting the ground beside me. I realise, I am no longer a girl.

I am storm and lightning and rage.

I am the bringer of their destruction.

Two wyvern fall twitching to the ground, five circling

and diving, harrying my friends into a tight group. My pulse thuds in my ears and I know it's time. This is the moment. I call to Kell.

'Kell, now!'

Kell looks over, terror lacing his features as he throws both his hands towards me, releasing a plume of pale flame. I guide my fist towards that flame, the spinning tornado gleefully consuming it, thickening and whirling . . .

And I unleash it.

Straight at the five remaining wyvern.

Two cannot escape fast enough, and with harsh cries are consumed by the pillar of moving flame. The final three try to fly, beating their wings in desperation, clawing at the air, even as they're pulled back, the tornado reaching for them as well.

With a burst of fire, they're all incinerated in the whirling vortex of death. Heath collapses to the ground, panting, as his sword clatters at his side. Sapira begins to cry in relief, burying her face in Kell's shoulder, as they stand tall above Fey. And Sember merely nods to me, a smile flickering on her face. I bend my will round the tornado, asking it to cease, to calm. And, with a wrench, it begins to still. The bodies of the wyvern crash, one by one, smoking and still burning. The scent is overpowering and I cough, tears streaming from my eyes as I make my way to the others. The rain begins to patter and I realise . . . I have control. For the *first time*. I did not lose control of this storm.

And the wyvern sent to kill us are all dead.

The final Trial is over.

I walk over to the others on trembling legs, waiting for the commentator to declare the victor. But the crowd is whispering, a wave of murmurings all around us, and when I look to the ruling council I see they are arguing with the other representatives.

'They can't agree,' I say in disgust. 'None of them will concede.'

'Does that mean it's not over?' Sapira says, staring with barely concealed terror up at the stands, then the sky.

'Oh, it's over,' I say with a grin, spotting someone in one of the stands. A friend, a face that brings hope as a blaze. She waves, angling a mirror at the emerging sun, the flash winking over the arena. There's another flash in response on the other side in the crowd and I realise our allies are assembling. A signal. Sember's plan is in motion. 'Be ready. This is about to get interesting.'

Sember catches one of the flashes of light and sighs in relief. 'Right on schedule. Actually, you know, they've been a little slow . . .'

'Who?' Kell asks as I look back up to where Agnes was seated. But, of course, now she's vanished.

I draw my blade, feeling the welcome weight of it in my fist. Then a firework erupts from the stands: red stars, like blood, exploding across the arena. Another is set off in a far corner, then another, and chaos explodes like a bomb. The crowd begins to leave, a great wave of people, all pushing the guards away, stopping them from coming for us. That's when I see her. The wave of dark red hair, the narrowed, spiteful gaze . . . the woman who killed my mother.

Captain Renshaw.

My heart jolts. Has she been watching the Trials, hoping I'd fail? I haven't laid eyes on her since that day Mer injured her, blood blooming across her shirt . . . when she admitted she killed my mother. I lock eyes with her, and I tremble. Not with fear, but pure hatred. She took my mother. She gloated over the binding spell that took all the memories of my father. And she would have gladly killed me too. She's in the stands, far from the ruling council, but she's not fleeing to escape like the rest of the crowd. In fact, she's smiling. I snarl, narrowing my eyes, and wish she was closer so I could finally end her. But as she regards me, standing here, full of hate for her, I find her smile widens in apparent glee. Then she's hidden from my view by the jostling crowd.

I release a breath. If she's here now, she still wants to capture me. What did she call us that day of the sea battle? Her *haul*. I'm a creature to her, nothing more. She'll come after me again – I'm sure of it. I have to get back to Ennor. We need to prepare for the attack I'm certain is coming. There's no use in hiding. The watch would overturn the isles to seek me out. They would destroy everything just to watch us burn. Seth, her son, was murdered by the watch right before my eyes. Does she even care? Or was he really as expendable to her as he always claimed?

A shiver runs over me as I remember Seth. I know he will haunt me – our connection, his betrayal and his terrible death – to the end of my days. Was there more that I could have done? Would he have redeemed himself, if only he'd had the chance?

Sember, with Heath at her side, tugs on my hand, drawing my attention to her, and says, 'Come on. Time for you to leave.'

I go to move, but Kell doesn't. 'Kell?' I say, looking back.

But he shakes his head, standing by Heath. 'I've a new job. Protecting this one. An offer I couldn't refuse. Always wanted to see the world, travel to new places . . .'

I grin at him and reach out to clasp his fist. 'I wish you well, my friend.'

'If you see Helene, the woman who looked after me on Egan . . .'

'I will tell her where you are and that you're safe,' I say. Then I look to Sapira. 'Can you return home?'

She swallows. 'Prince Heath has assured me he'll see me safely home to Valstra. He'll ensure Fey reaches her drake too, so she can make it back to the Spines. I have . . . things I must do. These Trials have opened my eyes.'

I nod, hugging her tightly, then look to Sember as the first guard finds his way on to the arena. 'Time to go.'

We disappear quickly between the still smoking carcasses of wyvern, Sember reaching a door in the wall enclosing the arena. It's hidden below the seating for the spectators, so well concealed that I did not even realise it existed. She flips that coin I've seen her use many times up in the air, and in her palm lands a key. She places it in the lock, gives it a shove and sweeps her hand out. 'There you are. Your escape route. I discovered how the guards get in and out after the labyrinth Trial. They're *very* chatty after a few drinks and the clink of more coin in their pocket.'

She smiles at me, mischief glinting in her eyes, as I say, 'You'd better go and claim your victory.'

'I had,' she agrees. 'Or His Royalness will get bored and complain that it's all taking too long. You'll find Agnes just outside, courtesy of some interesting allies I scooped up . . . friends of yours, I believe. Our deal is complete.'

'Thank you. For saving us, for rescuing Agnes. For . . . sticking to your word,' I say, taking her hands in mine, then pulling her into a hug.

'A pleasure working with you,' she says, hugging me then pulling away. She dusts herself off, flips back her hair and gives me a wink. 'Well, I'd better round up my stray prince.'

I watch for a moment as she wanders back to the others, seemingly oblivious to the reeking, dead wyvern surrounding her, the chaos in the stands and the ruby red fireworks crackling in the air. Then I walk through the door, closing it behind myself, closing it on the Trials for good, and step into a narrow tunnel. I can hear the muffled voice of the commentator in the arena, scrambling to hold the crowd's attention as he proclaims Skylan the victor. I huff a small, humourless laugh, shaking my head. The ruling council will be vicious in their revenge. But I believe the damage to our world would have been far greater if I had won and stayed their captive to manipulate. Now, there will be no violent storms throughout the Straits. Their plans to dominate the sea route, to control the flow of goods and wealth around the continent has failed. Tomorrow I will pay the price. But today, *I* am victorious.

I step out of the tunnel leading to the outer arena walls, into the fields surrounding Highborn. And standing there are Brielle, Pearl and Agnes. I *did* see Brielle in the stands. Sember chose excellent accomplices indeed for our rescue.

I choke on a sob as Agnes covers her mouth before we run to each other. I hold her so tight and don't ever want to let go as I cry into her hair and she cries into mine. There were moments over the past weeks when I didn't know if we'd escape. If I'd ever be able to free her. And that day in the throne room eclipses my vision. Hastily, I push it away, suppressing a shudder and remind myself that she's here. We're both free. My sister in all but blood is in my arms, heart still beating. I wrench her away from me, checking over every inch of her as she does the same to me.

'I didn't know if you were still alive, if you'd been killed in the Trials—'

'I can't believe we got out. I thought—'

We both laugh and hug again as Brielle clears her throat. I look up and smile at her, my former hunter, now my friend. I walk to her and Pearl, hugging them both. 'Thank you,' I say, throat scratchy and thick from unshed tears. 'For saving Agnes. For saving me.'

'We found a little help in an unlikely place. Well, more than one, actually,' Brielle says, lifting her chin as she looks over my shoulder. I turn to find a man standing there, someone who looks all too similar to the men of the ruling council. 'This is Rue. An ambassador for the ruling council.'

He crosses his arms, watching me. 'That was quite the display.'

'No thanks to the people you work for,' I reply. 'Why are you helping us?'

His smile is soft as he glances at Brielle, then back at me. 'Let's just say I've seen the whole picture now.'

In a flurry of motion two witches appear a few feet away, and I grip my blade, ready in a heartbeat to fight. The one on the left is Hira, but I don't let down my guard. The other one has to be another witch from her coven, and their Malefant is no friend of mine.

'Stand down, fierce one,' Hira says with a sigh. 'Shayle and I helped Brielle get you out.'

'So that's what you've been doing, instead of preparing me and Kell?' I ask. 'Or was there another reason for your absence?'

Her mouth twists. 'I apologise. We needed to confirm

what you'd told me and when we realised the repercussions of the ruling council holding you . . .'

'They knew they had to act. Possibly against the wishes of the Malefant,' Brielle says. 'I don't expect you to trust them, truly, Mira. I just ask that you trust me and Pearl.' She turns back to Hira as I nod. 'What of the wards around Highborn?'

'Down for the moment,' Shayle says at Hira's side. 'But where is Kell?'

'Prince Heath of Skylan has engaged his services,' I say.

'Well,' Shayle says and whistles, 'I had better inform Helene.'

'It was his choice,' I say with a shrug. 'I wouldn't have let him go otherwise.'

There's a rumble of shouts from inside the arena, as though the guards are entering the tunnel running underneath where I've just exited. Rue turns to look before fixing his gaze on Brielle. 'It's time.'

She hesitates for a moment, before striding up to him. They whisper together and her eyes widen as he smiles, her hand brushing against his. A faint blush colours her cheeks. Then she blinks rapidly, turning away from him to face the hunters of her old coven. 'Hira, Shayle. Thank you.'

They both utter a witch word and vanish. Then Brielle comes over to the three of us, ensures we're all holding her hand or arm, and with the witch word, *Traversa*, the ground falls away from beneath me.

We land in a heap in the hallway of Ennor Castle, Amma there instantly to greet us. Kai barrels for Agnes, scooping her into his arms, and I have to look away when they kiss.

'Finally! I thought that would never happen,' Pearl mutters to me, and I smile. Then Pearl's face lights up as Merryam runs in, kissing her on the lips and holding her close before turning to embrace me.

'I knew they'd get you out, but I'm sorry it took so long, my friend,' she says into my hair, her hold on me tightening. 'If they hurt you . . .'

'They didn't,' I murmur, relaxing into her hug, her friendship. 'Only my pride and a few bruises. But I have to ask you, is he . . . did he?' I swallow. 'Did he make it back?'

Merryam pulls away slightly, looking at me, her features falling. 'Mira . . .'

'They'll think twice before taking on an islander now!' Kai says, clapping me on the shoulder.

I glance up at him, releasing Merryam, finding a grin brighter than the June sun on his face and I nod to him. 'That they will. Those mainlanders don't know a *thing*.'

He grips my shoulder and bends low to whisper. 'Thank you. For not giving up. For bringing Agnes back. I am your brother, always, Mira. Always.'

My throat thickens, tears stinging my eyes just as Caden thunders in, relief on his features as he picks me up in a bear hug. 'Thank skies.'

Tanith and Joby appear and I start crying again,

hugging them too, so utterly grateful that I'm here, that they're all here. That we're all alive.

Then I look over their heads, expecting to see Lowri. And him. But when they don't appear, even when Maggie bounds up, licking my face and nudging her great shaggy head at my chest, I turn to Caden in confusion. And when I find his face falling into lines of worry, just as Merryam's has, panic seizes every inch of me.

'Where are they, Caden?' I ask, dread cracking open my chest. 'Where's Eli?'

Caden opens his mouth, then closes it again, shaking his head. Everyone around us stills.

'They haven't returned, Mira,' Tanith says quietly. 'I'm so sorry. We believe they may be lost to us, trapped in another world.'

Chapter 26

Lowri

AMORIA.

A spell not often used, an act of giving that depletes a witch's very self. Lowri pours her light, her shadow, her hopes and dreams and fears for Eli and herself into the instrument, feeling her bones grow heavy, her thoughts as formless as the fog covering Fallow. She doesn't hear when Eli says *enough*. She doesn't sense her knees buckle, her cousin catching her before she falls. It's only when Gracious finds them, breaks into the room and bellows in her mind that she stops. Darkness threatens, stars speckling her vision. She breathes in and out, refuses to give in.

When her eyes flutter open, she looks straight at the instrument. And smiles, finding it contains not only shadow magic in a foggy cloud.

But light.

Light magic, distilled and shimmering, a shade she's never seen before, perhaps a new colour entirely, one pale as the moon, bright as sunlight, gleaming like pearls. She brushes her fingertips against the glass and her magic gathers on the other side of the glass, as though wishing to be reabsorbed, wanting to be used. Even as she watches, the light grows stronger, glowing softly, as though the magic itself is a sentient thing.

'I've never seen anything so beautiful,' Ethlet breathes, transfixed.

Eli lowers Lowri into a chair, kneeling beside her. 'Are you all right? Did you give too much?'

'I'm fine,' Lowri says, fighting a wave of tiredness. 'I understand it now. Burnout, replenishment, the balance of my magic. When I gave it away, when it left my veins . . . I could sense it. The light and the shadow. And more colours in between, a whole spectrum, like the tiniest jewels.'

'The components of a witch's magic,' Hellius says in awe, writing it all down. 'Each creature, each human, has a formula, a cocktail of every strand in different quantities.'

'And mine is mostly light magic,' Lowri says in hushed wonder, watching as it expands and ripples. Then she turns to Eli. 'Your father was a genius. To create this instrument, to find a means of studying magic in this way. To distil magic, to transform it and be able to use it. Remarkable.'

Eli smiles sadly. 'His legacy.'

'But without a creature like you, a witch, he was never able to use it, to see it in action.' Hellius blinks quickly. 'You realise what this means?'

'We can break the fog,' Ethlet whispers.

They all stare at the instrument for a moment, Lowri contemplating Isaiah's legacy and what this means for Ethlet's future. 'If he had been able to walk through worlds, to traverse back to your mother, Eli . . . He could have brought her here. He could have saved this place long ago.'

Eli runs a hand down his face. 'Five days, Lor. I would give anything for those five days.'

Lowri cannot find the words to comfort him, cannot offer him anything. Death is beyond her, beyond all of them. She places her hand on his shoulder and murmurs, 'You may not have been able to save him, but you can save his world. By bringing me here, you've done what he could not. That will be *your* legacy.'

'And this,' Hellius says. With a guilty look, he offers a notebook to Eli: a dark-grey battered thing that seems to bulge with many words. 'The notebook your father left in my safe keep, that I should have given you when we first met. I was wrong to keep it. I'm sorry. It's what he would have taken to your world if he'd had the chance. It contains details about what you've seen here today, about burnout and theories on the complexities of a witch's magic, writings on how he could save your mother, if she struggled with birthing you.'

Eli's fingers tremble as he takes the notebook. Lowri watches as his face clears, as his shoulders drop, as though he has released a burden, carried for far too long. 'He . . . he really meant to return to save her, didn't he? He meant to all along. I . . . thank you. Thank you, Hellius.'

Hellius nods. 'Now, drink the light magic. Drink and restore your magic, so that you can traverse home. And you too, witch. The instrument allows it to expand quickly. Drink and restore balance to your blood.'

They assemble in the graveyard, as before. Ethlet hovers a few steps away, watching anxiously, Gracious at her heels.

If you return, witch, you may not recognise me. I may look like any ordinary cat.

'I'll always know what's really beneath that fur, Gracious,' Lowri says with a grin. 'Light magic or no, you fool no one. You should speak to Ethlet, though. You belong to each other now. I might have taken you with me, had I not found balance. But you're needed here. *She* needs you.'

Gracious twitches his tail and rolls his eyes in a way that is definitely *not* catlike. *As you wish, Lowri Tresillian. She has much to learn. A world to save, it seems.*

'Ethlet,' Eli says, moving towards her, 'I want you to have this.' He pulls out an envelope, addressed to her. 'The deeds to my father's house. I found them in his study and sent a message sparrow to a lawmaker to ensure it was transferred into your name. It's yours now. Your home.'

Ethlet takes the envelope and presses a hand to her mouth. Then she rushes at Eli, hugging him, and he pats her on the back through a stream of unintelligible words.

'Good luck with the fog and the light magic. With time and that instrument, you should be able to draw off enough light magic to begin the process.'

Ethlet swallows. 'The Society may not accept me . . .'

Eli levels his gaze on hers. 'Convince them. Show them. You are Isaiah's niece and you have more inside you than you know. Thank you for helping us.'

'Thank *you*.' Ethlet steps back, wiping her eyes. 'You really are Isaiah's son.'

Eli bows his head and beckons to Lowri, clasping her hand in his own. Then, with a final glance at his father's gravestone, grief pinches his features. It is so hard to shape into something he can understand and heal from, when all his father has ever been is a hollow absence, and even now there are questions unanswered. Lowri grieves for him, for herself, for the love of a parent neither of them have ever truly felt, as he tears his eyes away and focuses on the space before him. Now, the ripples of time and space are almost instant, strong and assured as Eli's magic flows from him.

A doorway.

A threshold.

Eli looks to Ethlet and Gracious, then past them to Fallow and the looming fog. Regret and sorrow crowd his gaze, but Lowri shakes her head gently. 'No sadness, Eli. You will find your way back here one day.'

'And I'll be waiting,' Ethlet agrees, eyes shining. 'We all will.'

Eli nods. 'Thank you for welcoming us, Ethlet.'

She rubs her eyes with her sleeve and gestures at the doorway. 'You need to go, before it closes.'

With one last look, laden with so much loss and love, Eli walks through the doorway, pulling Lowri with him.

Together they step across other worlds, other places, different from before. A dark city with bright lights and hungry stares; then the edge of a tidal island, the sea slopping over their feet as it rushes over a walkway, a high gate before them with a K twisted into it. Then they step again, away into a town, a broomstick cracked in half on the ground beside them, a great cliff rising up on one side with what seems to be a huge city perched at the top of it. Then they step again, finding a path of night and stars. Eli grips Lowri's hand tightly, pulling her sideways, and the world settles before them into somewhere familiar. Somewhere they both love. Somewhere that calls to their very souls.

Home.

Lowri looks at Eli and finds he's staring towards Ennor Castle, hunger pinching his eyes, and hope. Someone opens the door. Then Eli drops Lowri's hand, his breath hitching and he's running, just as Mira chokes, running too, and they're in each other's arms. Tears stream down Lowri's cheeks as she watches them both, her heart swelling in her chest.

They are *home*.

He walked to Ennor, but he also walked to her. Mira Boscawen. The girl made of two halves, with a foot in each world. Just like him.

A meow that is not quite a meow echoes around her and she looks down to find Nova pouncing for her, clawing up her chest to settle round her shoulders. The warmth spills into her skin as a silent tear shivers down her cheekbone. 'Nova.'

Never again, witch. It's been too long. And what do I scent on you . . .? Did you meet a grimalkin?

Lowri laughs shakily, running her fingers through Nova's fur. 'He wasn't a patch on you.'

'Lor!' a voice calls, and she looks up as Caden appears, then Brielle, both running for her. Nova jumps down, landing gracefully by her side as she opens her arms to Brielle, then Caden. She hugs them both, crying quietly, and knows she made it, at last. To her people, her family. Her true home.

Chapter 27

Mira

SOMEHOW, I JUST KNOW.

There was an absence in our world, a space where he used to be. Perhaps it's in my heart, maybe it's the ghost of the boy who moves through shadow, but, when the world shifts, I gasp. Pressing my hand into my heart, I feel the pull of him, like the moon lures the tide, like the ebb and flow of the waves rushing over shell and sand.

Eli has returned.

He's found his way back to me.

I rush from my room, running through corridors, flying down the staircase, and when I step out of the front door, he's there. I sob, tears already filling my vision, his smile swimming before me like sunshine, like my first breath of air in weeks. I run to him. I run to his arms and feel his own wrap round me. I'm home. At last, with his heart beating beside my own, I'm home. I reach up to his face and his lips meet mine, his touch sending trails of honeyed light through my veins. Everything that's happened, everything we've been through, dissolves in this moment with his lips touching my own.

'You found a way,' I say, smiling through my tears.

'And I brought you back what you asked for,' he says, holding something out to me. A snow globe, perfectly formed, of a town with a dark cloud hanging above it. 'The city of Fallow, a piece of another world.'

'Your father's world,' I say in wonder.

'Yes.' He closes my fingers round it, then leans down, kissing me softly. I close my eyes, drinking him in. It's home, it's us, it's me and him. We break apart and he takes my hand, tugging me gently into a pool of shadows. When we step out, we're together on his favourite beach on the other side of Ennor, the waves lapping over shells, his hands at my waist, bracing me. He runs his palms down my sides, tracing my form, as though still not believing I'm real. That he has returned.

'When I saw you in that doorway,' he says shakily, 'when those guards pulled you away . . .'

'I know,' I say, reaching up to run my fingers through his hair, to press my body to his. 'But I'm all right. I escaped. Our friends, they helped me get out of there.'

'I should have been there for you, rescued you. I should have got back sooner.'

I smile at him. 'I do not need you to rescue me, Elijah Tresillian. I rescued myself. I fought for myself. I just need *you*. To be alive, and whole, and returned to me.'

We kiss again, wrapped in each other, our souls cleaved as one, once more. But we both know it's borrowed time, that this perfect moment, this reunion, can only be a temporary, fleeting thing. The ruling council will come for us and their revenge will be brutal. We must prepare to fight.

He doesn't know everything that's happened here. And, as much as I want to live and breathe in this slip of space and time, I have to tell him. He knows I was captured, but he doesn't know the full story, or where it leaves us and his people. He doesn't know that, even now, our enemies will be amassing their forces to wipe us out forever. That they intend to control magic and that they have their sights set on a bigger prize. The entire continent.

'Eli, we have to talk.'

His happiness dims for a moment as he searches my eyes. He pulls me down to the sand, his arm draped round my shoulders, his gaze locked with mine, as if I'm the most precious thing in the world. 'Tell me everything.'

I swallow, blinking up at him, and figure out where to begin. 'As soon as you and Brielle left, a rival coven descended on *Phantom* . . .'

Our discussion continues as we traverse back to Ennor Castle, where Amma provides bread and butter and cold slices of pie, fluttering around Eli, who speaks to her quietly. I've brought him up to date as much as I can, but I still know little of his time away. More people gather, some from Rosevear staying within the castle walls, some from the town of Ennor, needing to see with their own eyes that Lord Tresillian has returned.

'It seems we have much to discuss,' Eli says at my side as we enter the formal dining room where everyone has gathered. 'I'm very glad to see you all.'

We take our seats round the table. Our inner circle of thirteen: Brielle, Caden, Lowri and Eli, then Agnes, Kai and I, Tanith, Joby, Merryam and Pearl, and finally Bryn and Feock. We gathered right here not so very long ago, all with a stake in the isles' future. But now it appears that for the ruling council controlling the Far Isles and the Fortunate Isles is only the beginning of a bigger, more ambitious campaign. It began with their plan to bring us all to heel and for the watch to rule over us with a fist of iron. It may end with all-out war.

'The ruling council mean to go to war if they do not get their way,' Brielle says, spreading her hands wide. 'The law controlling magic is only the start. Once they control the use of magic, they own the covens and apothecaries. And with the factories in the north, and what they are manufacturing,' she pauses, 'they will unleash forces with weapons of magic upon the continent and create an empire.'

'And you learned this from the hunters of Coven Septern?' Bryn says through a puff of pipe smoke.

Brielle nods. 'The coven set in motion the rescue of Mira and Agnes from the Trials, and they had help from a young woman called Sember Lockswift of Skylan. She has an obvious interest in not allowing Arnhem to gain the upper hand on the continent, but I trust her,' she says. 'And, as for the rest of the coven, I'm told that Lessifur herself – head hunter of Coven Septern – went with a band of hunters to scout the wild north. She wanted proof to take back to her Malefant. She returned with a first-hand report of the factories, showing merchants delivering metals mined in Valstra.'

'Which is one of the reasons they want to control the shipping route and scupper the use of the Straits,' I say.

'Exactly,' Brielle says with another nod. 'The ruling council want to control what is mined, how it's delivered to Arnhem and the distribution of weaponry galvanised with magic. It's war they want, and conquering the isles may only be the beginning.'

'Is Lessifur going to Mother with this information?' Caden asks.

'Yes,' Brielle says. 'Well, she'll already know by now.'

'And yet she hasn't tried to contact anyone? She hasn't offered the coven's support, or anything?' Lowri asks.

Brielle smiles sadly and shakes her head.

'Who is galvanising the weaponry with magic?' Eli asks, leaning forward. 'Did the hunters say?'

'A rival coven,' Brielle replies.

Agnes leans round Kai to look at me. 'Perhaps the same coven that took us from *Phantom*.'

'Could well be,' I agree.

'Perhaps the same one that sent their hunters after me and the two fledgling witches I found on the continent,' Brielle says. 'We had quite the journey returning here after we found out *Phantom* had been ambushed.'

'This is building a worrying picture,' says Feock, deep in thought. 'Magic is power, and power can be intoxicating.'

We all fall into silence, contemplating the power the ruling council is gaining. The fact that they want me as their storm bringer, to wreck the Straits, to intimidate the other rulers and representatives from across the continent witnessing those Trials . . . they are not only interested in wiping us out. They want full control.

'We learned more about the ruling council in the city of Fallow, where Eli and I traversed to,' Lowri begins, looking to Eli.

Eli holds his hand out to me. 'May I show them your gift?'

I nod, placing the snow globe in his hand.

He holds it aloft, and everyone cranes forward to look. 'This is Fallow, where my father lived. And above it is this dark cloud that they call the fog. It drips down over the city of Fallow, leaching all the light magic from it. It means the world is now almost entirely black and white, with no colour apart from some little twists of light magic remaining. It's a remnant of shadow magic, magic like mine, from a Shadow War that the Rexilium brothers started. We learned that magic is made of strands, mainly light and shadow, and if they are not in balance –' he shakes the snow globe and dark glittering flecks rain down over Fallow – 'the aftermath can be devastating.'

'In this world, the Rexilium brothers are known as the ruling council,' Lowri says softly.

I lean back in stunned silence, remembering what happened in the throne room, the shadow that they held round Agnes's throat, constricting her airway until she couldn't breathe . . . They really are just like Eli. Not only that, they're from his father's world. They traversed here. 'And did they win the war they started?'

'No, they lost,' Eli says, placing the globe on the table. 'And they were driven out of Fallow. They formed a portal, left their world and stumbled into ours. They are far older than they appear. The coup that formed the ruling council was, in fact, those same brothers, some hundred years ago.'

'So these Rexilium brothers, the ruling council, they are repeating what they did before?' Feock asks, folding his arms. 'This is bad news indeed.'

'The question is, will they first pursue Mira here to Ennor and return to establish their hold on the isles? Will they seek to recapture their Storm Bringer? Or turn to greater conquests?' Tanith muses.

'They are full of pride,' Agnes says, throwing back her hair. 'They cannot bear to be slighted. And after Mira's escape from the final Trial, in front of everyone . . .'

'Then it seems likely they'll return here first,' Kai says. 'And finish what they started.'

Eli nods in agreement. 'We need to be ready.'

'My concern is the rival coven assisting them,' says Brielle. 'Those witches, the magic in their weaponry. It's enough to bring us to our knees. If they came to Ennor, we'd have no hope.'

Eli leans back in his chair, thoughtful. 'Then what do we need? What kind of allies should we seek?'

'Witches. Magic wielders,' Lowri says. 'Brielle, our fledgling coven, it's too small, not yet established.'

'And we cannot trust Coven Septern,' Brielle adds. 'The Malefant and high witches could be debating this issue for weeks. They may decide to sit it out completely, not choosing to support either side, despite their hunters assisting us.'

'Cowards if they do,' Caden says.

'What we need are witches from outside Arnhem. Allies that would not want to see the ruling council win here, then turn their gaze on other territories.'

I bite my lip, considering Brielle's words. And Fey floats to the front of my mind. 'The Spines,' I say, and Brielle's eyes meet mine. 'Go to the Spines and seek a woman called Fey. She's a drake rider. We can seek witches, find allies there.'

'This feels like a good moment to chime in,' a voice says from the doorway. We all turn to see a young woman leaning against the door, a glint of silver in one hand: a large, rather ornate key. As I watch, it reforms, changing into a coin, which she pockets. I grin as Sember Lockswift winks at me. 'I'm afraid I let myself in. Hope you don't mind. What an interesting gathering. Did you really think I'd miss out on all the fun?'

CHAPTER 28

Brielle

LOWRI OPENS HER BEDROOM DOOR that night to see Brielle hovering on the threshold.

'You're wearing your travel leathers and your sash of blades.'

Brielle shrugs. 'Can't waste even an hour, Lor. We need allies. I've spoken to Eli and Mira and they agree with me. I can't stay here and wait, not with that threat hanging over us. We need more witches. We need allies outside Arnhem, who would want the ruling council taken down too.'

'Where are you thinking of going?' Lowri asks, twisting her hair round her finger. 'Skylan? Sember seems very genuine, but she made it clear the king will not send aid until the ruling council actually makes a move against them. Which may well be too late for us.'

'The Spines,' Brielle says, tapping a finger on her sash. 'Mira told me that the two contenders at the Trials spoke of overthrowing their own rulers. They said that if Mira ever needed help, the Spines would answer. I intend to find out if the covens there would make good on that promise, if I can find Mira's friend, Fey.'

'It's risky,' Lowri says. 'If the ruling council hear of what you're doing, if they realise we are building our side against them—'

'Let them hear,' Brielle says. 'They mean to break us either way. Let them know we won't be so easily broken. It's just a question of when at this point, not *if*. And Lor, I want to take Dreska and Inesh with me. To see what it is to be a hunter and go on assignment, just as I was taught at their age.'

'You think they're both hunters?'

'Inesh, certainly,' Brielle says with a nod. 'Not sure about Dreska just yet. She certainly has the fire for it, but she may be more inclined to spellwork. They haven't been exposed to the ways of a coven as we were. It hasn't moulded them in the same way. It might be that they are both hunters, but that they still practise spellwork with you. We can tailor their learning, so they are adept at both.' She tilts her head. 'Our coven might be the first of its kind in more ways than one.'

'An interesting proposal.' Lowri's smile grows. 'Take them and train them in your way. And when you return, I will see if they take to spellwork.'

Brielle's returning smile is a whisper in the dark. 'Thank you.' Then she reaches out, hugging Lowri fiercely. 'I'll be home again soon.'

Brielle leaves her sister, striding down the corridor,

but as she reaches the staircase she's aware of a presence at her side. 'Spying are we, little monster?'

Always, Nova says, licking a paw. *You know, I could come with you. There may be more wraiths in the Spines.*

'And ample opportunities to feast?'

You wound me, Nova says with a flick of her tail. *Perhaps I've grown fond of you and do not want to see you harmed.*

Brielle bends low, eyeing the familiar. 'Stay with Lowri. Your place is here, and I need you to watch over her. She'll be working on the wards, no doubt. I need you to ensure she doesn't burn out again.'

As you say, Hunter. I will look after my witch. And, Brielle?

'Yes?'

Watch over our fledglings. I believe I've become rather fond of them too.

With the sea route patrolled far more rigorously by the watch than ever before, Brielle opts for the land route. Bumped along stony roads in stuffy carriages smelling of horse hair, she, Dreska and Inesh play rounds of cards and practise the forming of witch words on the tongue.

'*Lucerne,*' Dreska whispers and the candle she's cupping in her palm begins to glow. The wick ignites in a spurt of flame and she smiles, satisfied.

'Now, Inesh, you put it out,' Brielle says, crossing her arms. They've been through this exercise every day, the words for *candlelight* and *extinguish* in witch now inked into their veins, just as all the witch words she and Lowri know have been.

Inesh bends towards the flame and says, '*Tace.*'

The candle snuffs out, a thin trail of smoke threading its way upwards before disappearing entirely.

Brielle is more aware than ever of the murmurings on the road, of the sidelong looks in taverns and inns, the additional guards surrounding merchants and their wares. The continent is on edge and she would bet coin on it being the ripple effect of what was discussed at court during the Trials, and the events of the final Trial itself, where a girl called a storm to bring lightning down on a pack of wyvern.

They practise like this as the terrain becomes mountainous across Skylan, whiling away the hours, before the road begins to level out as they reach the port of Hafenged. Brielle leads them between tightly packed buildings, past heaps of huge luggage cases and runners carrying messages and orders up the narrow, stepped streets that weave like veins down to the cold waters of the Straits. Everywhere, she senses eyes on them. But it's more than the press of curiosity. This feels personal.

It's not until they secure passage aboard a fishing vessel, slippery with the scars of scales despite being scrubbed, that Brielle finally allows her shoulders to drop. As the sea swallows up Hafenged, she finds herself fully occupied with the crossing. And the rolling stomachs of Dreska and Inesh, who have never endured a crossing in their lives.

'It's eight hours, isn't it?' Dreska says drowsily as Inesh clings to a bowl, turning greener by the minute.

'Less now, I promise,' Brielle says before turning away and whispering a feverish witch word. She senses the drain on her magic instantly – weather spellwork is taxing, especially on a solo witch. But she needs the sails to fill with more than a flutter of wind – she needs her fledglings in the Spines safe and well. Brielle clings to the railings, spots crowding her vision. She blinks thickly through them, knowing that she's used too much, too quickly. She thumps down beside Dreska and Inesh on the deck as the sails fill with the wind she called, giving the vessel a brief surge of strength in the chop.

Her efforts shave off three hours and when they reach a quay with stony buildings rising up behind she hurries Inesh and Dreska off as quickly as possible, the growing dusk casting a flinty chill over the small town in which they've docked. The fishermen tie up. With their wares sold in Hafenged, they have their partners and children to return to now and a warm welcome awaiting them.

Meanwhile, Brielle guides her fledglings to an inn she knows a little, remembering the first time she was here. It was midwinter, the cold like a razor, ice packing the streets, a sharp chill to the air that turned her nose pink, sending shivers dancing along her ribs. And dark. Almost constant, sunless dark. She remembers there were torches everywhere, lit and spitting with fat, the warmth gliding over her cheekbones as she knocked the snow off her boots and entered the inn.

Now, she looks at the swinging sign of the inn, remembering it all as if it was yesterday. Her quest for vengeance, to slay the wyvern horde that killed her birth mother further north. She sighs, her breath hanging as fog before her eyes. The Drage Inn is looking substantially less shabby than on her last visit. As though, since then, coin had rolled into the pockets of the owner, splashing over every corner.

'They overthrew their rulers,' she murmurs, reaching for the door handle.

'What did you say?' Dreska asks, teeth still clacking from the voyage.

Brielle looks her over, then eyes Inesh. 'We'll find a warm welcome here, I'll wager. Your stomachs will settle with a little food and drink.'

She pushes open the door, stepping into the bar beyond. And finds three witches, all with bows drawn, arrows pointing straight at her chest. She stills, assessing them quickly, positioning herself smoothly in front of Dreska and Inesh. The witch in the middle smiles humourlessly.

'A hunter from Arnhem and two fledgling witches,' the one on the right says calmly. 'The fisherfolk were right. Give us one good reason why we shouldn't kill you all where you stand.'

Chapter 29

Mira

THE SEA CALLS MY NAME that night. I walk down to the shore at first light, give in and sink beneath the waves. The sea is calm, but not content. As I pull myself through the water, running my fingers through seaweed and over the grit of the seabed, I detect a coiling, a tenseness. But I cannot sense anything lurking, or any boats or ships other than our own nearby. As I leave the waves, emerging on to the rocks below the castle to stretch out my limbs in the early sunlight, I give the inky waves a final glance. I wish I could stay longer and float, adrift for a while. But I know that if I stop, if I take even a breath, all this might not be here on my return. Tomorrow is for the sea.

Today is for the isles.

Eli has already risen, gone to meet with Joby and Mer to discuss the state of their ships. When I get down to the kitchen, I find the remnants of his breakfast, and Amma busy around the huge wooden table, replenishing breakfast loaves and butter, passing out cooked eggs and sliced apples. There are people from Rosevear here, and some of them are helping Amma. They smile in greeting and I sit among them, eating breakfast, drinking a mug of milky tea. Agnes walks in, sits down beside me and bumps my shoulder. This small moment, this gesture, means everything. For the space of a breath, I forget why we're here, what's happened to us, that we're a whole people displaced. We could almost be at her home, drinking tea in her room of finds and treasures, her cheeks dusted with flour after a morning spent at her father's bakery, helping to knead the bread for the day's baking.

Then it all rushes in.

'Are you ready to train?' I ask her.

'Define train,' she says, reaching for a hunk of bread and the salted butter, scraping it on before smearing some bramble jam on top.

'We need to inspire them,' I murmur, ducking my head close to hers. 'So many women fought for their lives that night on Rosevear, but it was in desperation and fear. We need to be better prepared. We've never had the chance to learn, and we have to now. All of us. I want them to feel ready for it not just to be terror that spurs them on, but hope.'

Agnes nods as she finishes chewing. 'Leave it with me.'

When I step out into the practice yard, shielding my eyes from the sunlight, I bump into Caden, standing with his arms folded. He smiles and my heart thumps hard in my chest. For a moment, it overwhelms me. In the bleakest moments during the Trials, I wondered if I'd ever be back here again. Somehow, this time in the training yard stayed with me, a place I wanted to return to. To become stronger, more resilient.

To become a weapon I alone choose to wield, on both land and sea.

Caden nods towards the rack of wooden practice swords and I smile back at him. 'Admit it, you missed this,' I tease.

His smile widens further, face splitting into a grin. 'All right. I missed this. I missed beating you.'

I laugh, reaching for a practice sword and we begin a series of drills, warming up our muscles with blocks, thrusts and jabs. Agnes wanders in, reaching for her own practice sword, and copies the series of steps, and then Merryam and Pearl join us. I notice a few women and girls gathered in the doorway, watching us. Agnes beckons to them, but they shy away. I wonder if this is too much, too soon, after the events of that night on Rosevear, if the trauma of that night is still too raw, if I'm expecting too much of them.

But then Grier, a girl who is now one of the seven on Rosevear, strides from the doorway, determination in her features as she grabs a practice sword from the rack. She watches Agnes closely, mimicking her footwork. She stumbles a couple of times, but keeps trying. And Caden pretends not to notice her presence, focusing on my footwork, my jabs and thrusts, but I notice the slight flush in his cheeks, the smile ghosting on his lips that he can't shift. He *wants* to train them. He wants us all to be strong.

A lump forms in my throat as the first woman steps forward, reaching for a practice sword and moving to the edge of the courtyard. Then more join us, gradually at first, until, an hour later, we're a full courtyard of women and girls. Some from Ennor, many from Rosevear and Penrith, all prepared to fight for our isles, our home. I blink quickly, willing tears of pride not to leak from my eyes as I move through the steps, staring straight ahead. One of the women of Penrith begins a work song – she starts the words and we repeat them in a call back to her. My chest tightens as I sing with everyone, our voices steady and sure, just as they are when we mend the nets on Rosevear, when we clean a catch, when we rake over the slender fields.

Caden wanders among us all as we train, fifty or so of us: fisherfolk, bakers, farmers, mothers, daughters. He occasionally adjusts someone's stance, corrects a move, or footwork, sowing encouragement among us. And under the spring sun we prepare the only way we know how, with a song in our throats and a will in our hearts.

This is who we are. Survivors. A people that faces every disaster head on and gets back up to begin again. I catch the eye of a woman from Rosevear, the mother who had the cottage next to my father's. The woman whose child we rescued that terrible night when the watch first torched our homes. She winks at me and I feel the tears spill over, tracking down my cheeks. I've never felt so fiercely proud of my people, so sure of my place in this world as one of them. There's an ache in my chest, my fractured heart mending.

I may be siren, I may be my mother's daughter, but I'm also my father's.

I'm a daughter of Rosevear.

Eli waits for me in the kitchen at lunchtime, arms crossed, leaning against the wall as Amma chats to him. She's a flitting bird, first at the hearth, then the larder, then at the table, and I barely catch her movements between blinks.

'Are you up for a little spying, Mira?'

I grin at him, reach up and press my lips to his. Sparks warm my veins as he brushes a stray thread of hair behind my left ear, and that small gesture fills me with sunlight.

'What did you have in mind?'

'A trip to the mainland,' he says, leaning in closer so I can see the flecks of starlight in his eyes. I want nothing more than to kiss him properly, to align my body with his and feel his arms round me, but then more people pile in, laughing and talking, and I clear my throat, hiding the flare of colour in my cheeks.

'You want to know what they're up to, don't you?'

He shrugs. 'Since you escaped the Trials, there's been nothing. No sign of the watch, no retribution. I know they're gathering their forces, but Joby and Mer have found no vessels in the water surrounding Ennor. And unless you have sensed something in the sea . . .'

'Nothing,' I say. 'It's eerily quiet.'

He nods, as though that's made his decision. 'We'll leave at dawn for Port Graine.'

CHAPTER 30

Brielle

BRIELLE PRESSES HER LIPS TOGETHER, taking in the three witches, the fletch of their arrows, the wyvern hide of their boots and vests, and the way the other patrons regard them, their eyes shining with nothing but respect. And she makes an educated guess. 'You know who I am.'

'Brielle Tresillian of Coven Septern.' The words are a guttural snarl from the witch on the left. 'One of the covens that works with your ruling council.'

Brielle's shoulders drop almost imperceptibly. 'I *am* Brielle Tresillian. I am hunter, witch, but not of that coven. The first time I was here, I defeated a horde of wyvern. Killed them for murdering my mother for sport, further up north. The last time was ridding frost sprites from a village, where a child had been taken. I found the child and reunited him with his family. This is Dreska and Inesh. Tell them what coven you belong to, witches.'

'Coven Ennor,' Dreska says, and Brielle glances over to see her chin raised, staring down these three fierce witches of the Spines like she could take them *all.* Brielle's heart swells with fierce pride. 'Brielle and Lowri Tresillian's coven.'

The witch in the middle blinks, then says a word that Brielle doesn't catch. The three of them lower their bows, but do not put away their arrows. 'And you plan to hunt here?'

'I'm looking for a woman who my friend, Mira Boscawen, made an alliance with in the Trials. Who made her a promise of aid, if it was sought. She goes by the name of Fey, a drake rider.'

The witch on the right smiles, the ice in her eyes melting into a soothing blue. 'We know Fey. And we have heard tales of your friend Mira, girl of the islands. Storm bringer and siren. Defier of the ruling council.'

Brielle loosens a taut breath. 'That is she.'

The witch on the right smiles then, finally, they put away their arrows, their bows, and the witch in the middle calls the barkeep over. 'Three chillvain brews, if you will. My friends here have had a long journey.'

The patrons around them turn back to their gossip and their drinks as Brielle steps forward to a table the witches commandeer by the fireside. Inesh and Dreska stay huddled in their travel cloaks, not yet thawed from the voyage. But Brielle tips her chin, throws back her cloak and eyes the nearest witch. 'And what of your coven? You hunt wyvern too?'

'As you see,' the witch says, propping her booted feet up on the fire grate. 'We all ride drakes too. Fey is one of our hunters.'

Brielle raises her eyebrows. 'So she's witch? You sent a witch as your champion in the Trials?'

'There's no rule against it. Fey didn't use her magic in the Trials. She was careful. Discreet,' the witch says, as the barkeep hurries over with a tray of steaming mugs. 'Thank you. Creatures will only allow creatures to ride them. Never a human. If you were from the Spines, you'd know that. Soturi was not witch . . . but he did have witch blood in his veins, through his mother, a fearsome hunter in her time. Enough that his drake bonded with and claimed him.'

'Huh,' Brielle says. If Mira's account of their arrival is anything to go by, the contenders from the Spines made it pretty obvious. 'And I suppose if any of the territories on the continent were paying attention to more than their own squabbles over trade routes and profit, they would have known that too.'

'Exactly,' says another witch, striding over to them from the front door. Dreska and Inesh reach for their mugs, taking in this new witch through the steam as they sip from them. But Brielle stands, sensing the power immediately, sensing the presence of a master hunter. The witch stops before Brielle, holding out her hand. 'I'm Fey, friend of Mira's. Is she with you?'

Brielle takes Fey's hand in her firm grip and shakes it. Her magic pulses under her fingers. It's more potent than she realised. 'Afraid not. She's stayed on Ennor. We're readying for war.'

'So I imagined,' Fey says, a faint smile tracing her

lips. 'You see this?' She indicates a fresh pink scar, still healing, stretching across her skin. 'If it weren't for Mira, this would mark the skin of a dead hunter. My brother, Soturi, was killed in the Trials. And still the other rulers see us as little more than drake riders and a potential threat. But we – we see them. We see all of them for what they truly are, especially now.'

'It was a truth-finding endeavour for you?' Brielle asks.

Fey nods, sliding into a chair. 'The ruling council is a threat to all of us – that much we gleaned. If your isles fall, like the Far Isles, then it won't just be a symbolic move of power. They will have an unbreakable stronghold. If you lose, if the isles fall entirely, it sends a message to every territory on the continent. It'll rip it apart, or they'll all bow before them. Either way, it does not suit us.'

'And you offered Mira your help because of this?' Brielle says, taking a sip of the chillvain brew and instantly warming. She taps her finger against the mug. 'I've never known an apothecary brew to be served in an inn before.'

Fey smiles. 'We view magic differently here: it is life, it is warmth, it is all. It is not hoarded or used to establish power and greed like in your Arnhem covens. Here, magic is shared. Which brings me to your fledglings . . .'

Brielle glances at Inesh and Dreska. 'What of them?'

'They need to train, to prove themselves, to learn the ways of a coven?'

'Yes.'

Fey claps her hands once. 'Then you will stay at the coven house tonight and we will go out tomorrow.'

Brielle frowns. 'Go where?'

'To the ice. So you can learn the ways of our coven,' she says, nodding. 'Tomorrow we ride drakeback and hunt wyvern. Prove yourselves worthy of riding drakeback and I will know how much aid I can send to your isles. A drake senses honour and the good in a creature's heart. If your intentions are true, we will support your plans.'

They assemble well after the sun has graced the cold land the next day. Dreska and Inesh whisper about the brevity of night here at this time of year, discussing the eye masks they wore so they could sleep. Brielle, remembering her last visit, only smiles. This is the nature of a hunter's life, adapting to the changing landscape, the weather, the shape of the day in each new place. To her, this ever-changing pattern, life on the road, is home, far more than Coven Septern ever was. Now she has a new home on Ennor, she doubts it will be any different. The call to travel, to hunt, is in her blood. And now is the time for Dreska and Inesh to discover it is in theirs too.

'A fine day for it,' Fey says as she holds out three sets of gloves and spelled goggles to the witches. 'Wear these. They'll help you see. Keep a grip on the reins, so you don't fall mid-flight. The drakes are kindly, but if they're harried they'll protect the rest of their bloom, the other drakes in their pack, before considering their rider's comfort. And if you mistreat them, or if they sense ill intent, they will refuse to carry you.'

'Consider us warned,' Brielle says as Dreska and Inesh take the goggles and gloves and put them on.

'Do we actually get to ride one?' asks Dreska, wide-eyed, as she stares at Fey's drake, steam snorting from its nostrils.

'You will sit behind my witches for now. No flying solo today, fledgling.'

'It's Dreska,' Dreska says, moving her dark hair from her eyes to meet Fey's. 'And Inesh.'

Something sparks in Fey's gaze and she nods. 'Of course, Dreska. You'll ride with Figgi. And Inesh? You're with Nairis. Brielle, with me.'

Brielle turns for Fey's drake without looking at Dreska or Inesh. They have to learn to move through the world without a coven at their backs. If they are hunters, they will often hunt alone. They must learn to rely only on themselves.

The cool ridges of the drake's back do not dig into her flesh as much as she thought they would. Instead, she finds herself seated comfortably, able to grip a secondary rein behind Fey, her boots in stirrups, holding her in place. Fey looks back only once, her goggles hiding her expression. Then with a sharp whistle, the entire bloom of drakes rise into the sky. The beating of wings as the drake climbs the air drifts is almost too much for Brielle at first. But as the drakes form a pattern, spearing in formation over the icy caps of the mountains surrounding the town, she releases a breath. The wind whips over her stinging cheeks, thighs chafing as she clings tightly to the drake's back, but she's enjoying it. She's not traversing, this is not the result of an uttered witch word moving her through space. She's actually . . . flying.

Glancing left then right, she sees Dreska and Inesh on the back of the two other drakes, Figgi and Nairis in front of them. Then Figgi emits a whistle that could almost be mistaken for the wind and Brielle notices the horde of wyvern. They are snaking over a plain on an air current below, harrying a group of creatures on the ice that look almost like wither beast, but with pale, iridescent fur.

'Hellicorn,' Fey shouts over her shoulder to Brielle. The word catches on the wind, whipping into her mind. She's heard of them, but never seen the elusive creature, let alone half a dozen in one place . . . 'They're sacred. Legend goes that if a hellicorn greets you and allows you to approach, you and your descendants will be blessed. Here, you take my reins.'

Brielle scrambles for them as Fey lets go, swinging her bow, secured to her back over her shoulder, an arrow already nocked. Brielle grins, finding the other witches have done the same. Except . . . Inesh and Dreska both hold bows as well.

'You've armed them,' Brielle says, too stunned

to object that they may fall, that they may lose concentration, that they do not know how to traverse to the ground safely should they slip.

'This is the way of our coven, Hunter,' Fey says before pulling back on the bow, unleashing an arrow. The feral cry of a wyvern is the only sign that it has hit its mark. 'We'll know soon enough if either of them are truly hunter-born.'

Just as Fey says this, Brielle glimpses another arrow unleashed. But this time it's from the right. She whips round, seeing Dreska's grin of triumph, and the empty bow in her hands. Fey laughs then fires another. Figgi and Nairis do the same. The drakes roar into the wind, scattering their prey far below, and the hellicorn take off into the ice, hidden once more from the wyvern.

In moments, the drakes spiral downwards, alighting on the plain. Brielle leaps to the ground, landing next to a wyvern carcass. The arrow Dreska shot is buried in its skull. She turns to her as Inesh shimmies off the drake's back, whereas Dreska leaps as Brielle did, landing on her feet and striding over. She bends to inspect the wyvern and nods, satisfied. 'Father would call it a clean kill.'

'This one over here is still alive!' Nairis calls and they all stalk towards her. The wyvern twitches on the ice with a hiss of pain and fury. 'Who will claim the kill?'

Brielle nods to her fledglings. 'Well?'

Inesh glances at Dreska then steps forward. Fey hands her a blade, one piercing and silver, engraved with swirls. Inesh's gaze lands on Brielle and Brielle sees all those thorns, that wildness that she first glimpsed after saving her from existence as a wraith. Brielle nods, encouraging her. Inesh nods back, stepping forward, and when the blade is against the wyvern's throat she doesn't hesitate. With a sharp cut, Inesh ends the wyvern's life and Figgi catches the blood spraying out beneath in a wide bottle.

'First blood,' Fey says, approval saturating her tone. 'I believe, Brielle, that Inesh here is a hunter. In fact . . . judging by the flight of that arrow, I would say Dreska is as well.'

Nairis takes a small vial of wyvern blood, offering one first to Dreska, then to Inesh and Brielle. Inesh holds it up to the light, eyeing it curiously. 'Each has different properties, do they not?'

Brielle grins. 'That's right. You can learn about that and more from Lowri. I believe . . . well. You may be the first ever fledglings to be both hunter *and* witch.'

Fey nods and turns to Brielle. 'Not once did you or your fledglings baulk. You accepted our ways; you rode drakeback. We will aid you. We will fight with you. And . . . all three of you will leave here on the back of a drake. You must train, and quickly. We will leave for the isles together when you have mastered flight.'

Chapter 31

Mira

PORT GRAINE IS MORE WATCHFUL than Port Trenn. I hide my hair and face under the brim of a wide hat, tucking the tendrils under. My shirt and breeches conceal my shape well enough and with Eli opting for a wool jumper rather than the black jacket, which usually means he cuts such a striking figure, we blend into the poorest and quietest of the ports in Arnhem. Leicenan accents slice apart Arnhemian words until sometimes they lose the meaning entirely. But with a gruff word or two we pass among the fisherfolk, the crews and the merchants undetected, all under the eyes of the ever-present watch.

'The Wayfarer is our best bet,' Eli says quietly as we pass a crew just arrived on a trade ship from Morgana. They've all got the lean look of scarecrows, of sleepless, wind-tousled nights, and half, or even quarter rations, to see out a long journey. As we turn the corner on to the next street, a brawl breaks out and the watch are on them in moments, hauling the one throwing punches away. Eli moves to grab my hand, but stops himself. We have to look and act like them: two members of a crew stopping off at this port.

The Wayfarer Inn is tucked away near the road that leads to Highborn, to the north of the port. Offering room and lodgings above, and rough fare in the pub below, it's a crossroads, a meeting place, where travellers gather and trade in whispers, to which we intend to listen. If any ships are getting ready to sail for the isles, there may well be information imparted by loose tongues here. In Port Trenn, Merryam reasons, the ruling council wouldn't be able to conceal their intentions easily – Hail Harbour is not a port for warships – but in Port Graine, they have long stationed ships of their armada here. It's an open secret between merchants that if you want to pick up a hand or two for the trade route to Morgana there will be people hanging around in Port Graine, hoping to earn a few coin. The watch captains know this too. It's where they may find strays to man a warship.

As I duck beneath the lintel, the scent of smoke and damp wool mingled with cooking smells and hops hits me. There is no cheer, only the grumbles of those who have stuck like barnacles to this port town, who see life pass them by and yet still spend their days fastened to a bar stool. There is a group of the watch, scarlet jackets slung over the backs of their chairs in one corner by the window, and I turn up my collar, noting in the same moment the wanted posters plastered on the walls. It's not hard to find my own likeness staring back at me. Or Eli's. We are wanted, and the reward for our capture is enough coin to set up any man or woman for a life of plenty.

We order a round of hard bread and chunks of pale, tangy cheese and tankards of rough beer, and find a rickety table within earshot of both the watch and a few young men who have the look of crew: salt-stained clothes, skin aged to leather by the elements and sharp chips for eyes, full of hunger. One of them, tall and lanky, holds a clay pipe, chugging on it like Old Jonie, his keen eyes assessing us before losing interest and sweeping back to the creased hand of cards he holds. He and his companions take it in turns to place cards in the middle of their table, betting with a few coppers and cheap tin pieces.

The watch, however, are ordering rounds of drinks, rowdy in the way that those who believe themselves superior generally do. I cringe away, but Eli just breaks off pieces of the bread, unfazed, his features hidden in shadow. I nibble at a chunk of cheese, willing my heart to stop thumping so hard in my chest. We're chancing our luck far too much for my liking, sitting here.

In the end, it's not the watch that divulge too much. It's the crew, playing cards at the next table, who eventually spill the information we're looking for.

'Merchants getting slack with their wages, are they, Todd?' one says to the tall, lanky one. 'Or is it another one of your excuses?'

'You lose, you cough up. Them's the rules,' the other one says, voice pouring out thick and slow, like oil. 'Merchant wages or no. Them's the bloody rules.'

Todd tamps down his pipe. 'Did I say I wouldn't pay? Mayhap I have a new position. A better one than aboard that creaky old scrapheap you two call a ship.'

'Trade ships are honest work,' the first one spits. 'More honest than the likes of you.'

'What work you talking about, Todd?' the other says, eyes narrowing. 'Another one of your fancies?'

'Like that girl he was soft on,' the other says, creasing up into wheezing laughter. 'What was she called, Eliza, or Lisbet . . .'

'Lilibeth,' Todd says, lighting his pipe. 'And this ain't no fancy. 'Tis truth. I'm off there now, in fact. Learning the ropes, so to speak. Beautiful ship, a beauty. New crew, well paid, well fed.'

'No such thing,' the first says, dismissing Todd with a wave of his hand. 'You pay up by tomorrow, or I'll sell your debt to the Pentecosts. You won't want them rattling your door.'

I shudder involuntarily. The Pentecosts are a band of racketeers, smugglers, that even the watch won't bother with. Bryn always stayed clear of their haunts in Port Trenn when he visited to glean information for us. I've heard that they're more than trouble. If they mark you, or if you cross them, you're dead.

'No need,' Todd says, proudly drawing out a silver coin and tossing it to his companions before rising. 'You two fight over that. You'll see no more of me.'

Eli marks his progress to the door with watchful eyes that he then slides to meet mine. He raises his eyebrows and we get up too, careful to avoid the gazes of the watch. They've grown quieter, I noticed, since Todd began his boasting, too keenly aware of all of us sitting nearby. I want to leave this place, to return home to Ennor. But we need to know who's employing Todd, and who is handing out silver in exchange for work.

We follow him at a distance, tracing his steps to the edge of Port Graine, to the end of the port where the ship builders have their yards, far from the merchant vessels docked and ready for their next shipment.

Todd disappears from view, ducking inside one of the offices skirting the dock. But we no longer need to follow him. He's led us right to the heart of what we feared.

'There are so many,' I breathe, counting the tall ships, all gleaming and new. Men are in the rigging, fitting new sails; others in the offices, swarming around the sides. All shouting to one another, calling orders . . . and, everywhere, the watch. A sea of scarlet. 'Even if they don't intend to use this fleet to surround the isles . . .'

'They are preparing for war,' Eli says quietly in agreement. 'This isn't a defensive fleet. Perhaps we will be their first conquest, but there can be no doubt. They're preparing to invade the continent.'

Chapter 32

Lowri

Eli calls together another meet of the thirteen, or at least all of us currently on Ennor, and he and Mira tell us about what they discovered in Port Graine. The fleet, no, *armada* of warships preparing to set sail.

'They'll be ready in a matter of days,' Eli says with deceptive calm. 'It's my hope that the ruling council wouldn't direct them *all* to our shores.'

'The warships may be planning to capture key ports along the Straits and secure the sea route,' Caden says, 'thinking strategically, given what we know of the Rexilium brothers, their goals and their past . . .'

'Agreed,' Eli says. 'But in case we are one such location to "secure", we must be ready. Let us assume they plan to divide the armada between multiple locations, relying on the strength of their weaponry and new vessels.'

'You mean, let us assume they are arrogant enough to believe they can secure multiple key ports and isles all at once?' Mira says with a smile.

'We cannot underestimate them, but yes.'

With Brielle gone and Merryam and Joby somewhere aboard *Phantom*, scouting the waters surrounding the ports, it does not take long to make decisions on next steps. Messages are sent to call everyone back to Ennor, to ready themselves for those warships, in case the ruling council intend to send them here first before moving on to the continent. And a message is sent to Sember, calling in her promise of help, even if it is not a full Skylan offensive on the horizon. The promise of her help alone could be enough to stave off an attack. Ennor Castle is quieter than usual, more sombre in the week that follows the meeting. But, Lowri reasons, all she can do is prepare as best she can for these warships that may be sent to Ennor's shores.

'It's been some time since a Tresillian witch graced this library,' a voice says from the shadows as Lowri crosses the threshold.

She smiles, running her fingertips along the books on the shelf nearest her, watching Tanith as she walks down the spiral staircase. 'It's been some time since I've met a drake in their human form,' she replies.

Tanith blinks quickly as she reaches the bottom of the staircase, facing Lowri. 'You've met another like me?'

'One other,' Lowri says. 'She visited Coven Septern some years ago. I was twelve or so, and Mother wouldn't let me speak, only listen. But she, the drake I mean, was there to discuss relations between creatures and witches with members of a coven of the Spines. They wanted to set up continent-wide laws on hunting, and a list of creatures prohibited from being hunted.'

'And was the drake successful in her endeavour?'

Lowri scrunches her nose. 'Sadly not at our coven. Mother wouldn't lend her support. She distanced herself, as she always does. Claimed a list like that would be political and so she would not lend her voice, or that of Coven Septern.'

Tanith sighs, her scales catching the light from the windows that face out to sea. To anyone human, it would be hard to discern, but Lowri, being witch, can recognise it instantly. The shifting scales; the timeless beauty; her scent, all amber and wild, dusting her skin.

'But you say a drake in their human form, as if the forms are interchangeable?' Tanith says. 'As if we can shrug off skin and don scales instead?'

'Well, from my studies of drakes in the wild north, it does seem that way.'

'I . . .' Tanith swallows. 'This knowledge. I've been searching for answers for so long. I have always lived alone before coming here. I was captured, trapped in the Spines. I've had very little interaction with my own kind.'

Lowri frowns. 'But the research is all kept at Coven Septern. Is it not duplicated and kept here?' Then realisation dawns. 'Of course not. Mother will have removed anything remotely interesting from this library when Caden and Eli were brought here. She will have had a keen eye on Eli, even then, given who his father was. Knowledge is power.'

'And power in the hands of anyone but a Tresillian witch residing at Coven Septern, benefiting the coven . . . I see,' Tanith says, trailing off into a whisper. 'When this is all over, when we are safe, perhaps you would be able to discuss what you have learned with me. Anything you might remember reading. I always thought that if I gave up my human form I might forget everything. I might forget . . . someone.'

'It would be my pleasure to help you,' Lowri says warmly, 'but I'm assuming you didn't summon me for this?'

Tanith shakes her head and indicates two chairs near the windows, and they both sit down. 'We need to talk about the wards on Ennor Castle and how they work. Who they're tied to.'

'They've always felt strange to me, the wards here. Like none I've ever sensed before.'

'That's because the wards *are* Amma.' Tanith smiles, taking in Lowri's confusion. 'I know, not something I've come across anywhere else before either. Certainly not something that seems possible, from my research in this library. But Amma protects more than the walls of Ennor Castle. She was created by Elena, Elijah's mother, to protect the Tresillian line within its walls, especially her son. So, when Eli was sent here, she became more than a spell. She became a guardian, a protector. A tangible presence that took the form and voice of Elena herself.

Amma raised Eli and Caden, kept them safe and well, and Elena's greatest spell, the final one she cast, means that she lives on here for as long as the wards are not breached or broken.'

Lowri sits back, contemplating this. 'But Amma's influence, the wards, extend only to cover the castle. What of the island, the town?'

'There are other wards on the town, but none as strong. Hillary Tresillian did try to destabilise Amma in revenge for what was taken from the coven, but I was able to nurse her back, thanks to the knowledge in the grimoires, left behind here in the library. Perhaps they were not interesting enough for your mother to remove.'

Lowri smiles sadly, looking around. 'I will work to strengthen the wards on the town. All those people . . .'

'If there's time,' Tanith agrees. 'Otherwise, we will be facing a siege, if they have to retreat to within the walls. But that's not what I needed to discuss with you. We need to talk about if Amma fails.'

'If she dies?'

Tanith nods. 'As the Tresillian witch bound most closely with Ennor and House Tresillian – even more so than the Malefant, given her loyalty to Coven Septern – it is for *you* to carry the load if Amma should fall. If the wards on Ennor Castle fail, you will need to embody them, to be the life force, the source of magic that creates the wards until we can separate you from the wards created by Elena and forge something . . . new.

Amma has spoken at length about this, especially after the blow your mother dealt to her. And now you are here and whole and well.'

Lowri blows out a breath at the thought of the risk, not only to her magic, but to that of everyone around her should she fail to be strong enough. This goes beyond Amma's death. If she is to carry the wards in Amma's absence, her own life would be forfeit if the wards are breached – if they should fail, if *she* should fail. For a moment, the responsibility, the enormity of it, overwhelms her. She is only just past becoming a full witch, but spellwork takes a lifetime to master. Magic potent enough to be worthy of becoming a Malefant takes decades to command. Is she even worthy of this? Is it more than she is capable of?

'Will you guide me?' she blurts, her gaze meeting Tanith's. 'If it comes to it, will you stay by my side?'

'I will guide you as best I can,' Tanith says. 'I am bound to House Tresillian out of choice, but you should know that if Amma dies, if the wards fracture, I will lose my human form. I will become drake once more and I may not remember you. I may not remember any of this. Unless of course . . .' She blinks. 'Unless there is another way, as you have spoken of. A way I have not come across in my lifetime or in any of my studies.'

Lowri leans forward, gently taking her hand. 'We'll get there. We just have to—'

'What's that?' Tanith says suddenly, eyes spearing a point on the horizon, through the windows looking out over the ocean. She rises quickly, gaze fixed on that point, stepping closer to the window, and Lowri follows, narrowing her eyes. There. Movement, a shimmer of dots moving then disappearing, then emerging again in the distance. Many of them, so many they're scattered along the breadth of the window frame. Lowri's heart leaps to her throat. Eli miscalculated. The ruling council haven't divided the armada.

'We're out of time,' Lowri whispers, horror sweeping through her. 'They're already here.'

Tanith stumbles back, then rushes from the library to raise the alarm. Lowri leans forward, pressing her hand against the window, focusing all her senses on the armada on the horizon. Ships, hundreds of them, and she realises with sinking dread what this means. The ruling council no longer intend to bring the Fortunate Isles under their absolute control. It's not about securing a key location. They mean to wipe them out, every islander.

This has to be the full complement of ships Eli and Mira saw in Port Graine, readying to sail. The ships built for war.

Here to destroy Ennor.

Chapter 33

Mira

THE SOUND OF THE WARNING bell echoes across the Isle of Ennor. I freeze in the practice yard, scanning the faces around me as everyone else pauses. Silence envelops us as the clang of the bell rings on, the only noise discernible in the eerie absence of sound as gaze meets gaze, as confusion widens into understanding . . . then plummets into fear. Eli emerges from a pocket of shadow at my side, features grim, as Caden stalks over towards us.

'It's time,' Eli says. 'They're here.'

My breath stutters. 'How many?' I ask urgently.

Eli's gaze lands on me, full of flint and storms. 'All of them. The entire armada.'

Caden swears under his breath, a momentary flash of terror gripping his features before he collects himself. As I watch, he squares his shoulders, raises his chin and settles his features into calm strength. Then he turns to the yard, surveying the women and girls who have kept returning every day, practising until the sun sits proudly in the sky. 'Secure your young, your children and the elderly within the walls of the castle, then come to the armoury,' he says. 'Now is your moment. Now is the time to fight for your home, for your people. This is the moment you've all prepared for. The ruling council's forces have arrived.'

A flurry of emotions pass over every face – sheer panic, terror, acceptance. Then determination. A woman, older than most in this courtyard, brings her practice sword to her chest and bows her head. In a wave, every person in the courtyard copies the gesture, a silent thanks for our training, for the hope Caden has sparked within all of us. Then, quietly, everyone places their practice swords back on the rack before they leave, streaming out through the doorway to secure their families. To prepare for what will come next. I place my own practice sword on the rack, fear and flame igniting in my chest. Eli's words are like a blow. All of them. All those warships . . . all sent here.

'Joby and Merryam are readying the crews,' Eli says to us, 'but the ruling council have sent every warship Mira and I saw in Port Graine. They've sent them all, and it appears that a few merchant ships have joined them too.'

My heart beats faster, the clattering bell still ringing in my ears. 'Well, haven't they been busy . . .'

'How many?' Caden asks.

'At least two hundred. The warships and commandeered merchant vessels mainly. Some appear to be Renshaw's. The watch are manning many of them, and some of the ruling council's personal guard. It suggests . . .'

'They're united against us. The Rexilium brothers have rallied the merchants . . . They've come to secure their sea route,' I say. Blood beats hot through my veins as the numbers, the sheer size of their forces, sinks in. There's not a chance we can defeat them completely. Not on our own, not with our crews and islanders, who are scarcely trained in combat. And if I bring a storm, if I seek to sink them all, will I be able to turn it from the isles at the last moment? Or will the people of Ennor suffer? I think of my mother, what she did . . . no. I cannot think of that now. I take Eli's hand. 'I need to ask the sirens for help. You know that they will only see hearts, though, so if any of our own people should fall into the sea . . .'

Eli nods quickly. 'I'll warn Mer and Joby to spread the word among the crews and fisherfolk.'

'I will begin assembling our people on land,' Caden says, already moving to the doorway. 'Eli?'

'Yes?'

Caden hesitates, then strides to his cousin, clasping his arm. 'Don't die. I'd have no one to beat in the practice yard.' He flashes us both a grin, masking his worry for Eli, for all of us, then disappears.

I take Eli's hand and he dips his forehead to mine. 'We haven't had long enough.'

'No,' I agree, closing my eyes. 'Not nearly long enough.'

'Until the end, Mira?'

I tip back my head and kiss him, knowing what this kiss could mean. A goodbye. A final parting. When I draw back, his eyes are on mine. 'I will love you until the end.'

He smiles. 'I will love you too. Until I am nothing but pieces of starlight and sky.'

A single tear falls down my cheek as I whisper back. 'And I will find you there, in that starlight. But not today,' I add fiercely, gripping both his hands tightly in mine. 'I have given up too much. I have lost too many. I cannot bear to lose anyone else I love, and I will not lose you now.'

Eli nods once, saying nothing, then releases my hands. 'Go, seek the sirens. I love you.'

Then he's gone and I'm left in the empty practice yard. I shape my hands into fists and turn, stalking through the doorway. Already, my senses are alight, seeking out the storms on the horizon, twining my will around cloud and sky. If the ruling council are bringing war to our shores, then they will get their wish. I will bring them a storm. I rush through the castle, push back the front doors and find the fickle sea, which only this morning was still and calm with slumber, now churning and watchful. Ready to roar.

I smile.

Far away, thunder booms.

*

As I leave the castle, walking down the hill to the sea, people stream back and forth, calling between each other, rallying, readying. Children are carried past me to the castle, elders are helped up the hill, or pushed on carts. I focus on what I can control, what I alone can do. I want to guide every elder, carry each and every child. But there is only one of me, only one storm bringer, one girl with a siren lurking inside her. Now that the armada is on the horizon, it's as though a veil has been removed, and I can sense every vessel in the sea. The siren map – stitched into my veins, my mind – awakens. I see them all. Every cursed ship here to destroy us. And when I get to the quay, pressing my hand to Kai's shoulder, hugging Agnes one final time, I expel a breath, wrenching myself away from these people I love – my home, my heart – and dive off the end of the quay into the waiting tide.

At once, my blood ignites in a blaze of fire and the sky darkens overhead, as though it has ignited too. I look up as clouds bloom, bruising the skin of the sky in shades of charcoal, and the rain slaps the surface of the sea. Soaring through the underwater world, like an inverted sky, I see the hulls of ships and other vessels, still far off, but closing in, all too rapidly. This is a fight for our lives.

It's time to call on everything my mother left waiting for me in my blood. The rolling fields of raging clouds, the echoes of past storms in their wake. The crackle of lightning, the fire in the sky. And the thread that connects me to all that fierce wild.

I reach out with my senses bound to the ocean, allowing my mind to rush and leap through the eddying currents, far away to where my siren sisters reside. That side of me, the side that is all siren, grasps the knot of their minds. And pulls. As one, I feel them respond to my beckoning call, knowing what this is, what it means. The answering cry is sharp and hungry, all claws and teeth and thoughts of bleeding hearts. But they are coming. The sirens have answered my call. They are ready to fight my enemies and to feed.

There is little need to wonder why I did not sense this armada gathering. The ruling council have enlisted a coven to their cause, witches that, even now, might be setting traps for me and my kind. I swim towards those shadowy shapes, sitting on the lip of the waves, counting the battleships, the cannons, the weaponry. It's not until I turn back for the shore, ready to deliver the information I've gleaned from the sea to Eli and Caden, that I sense something else in the deep, a dark, looming presence. A creature I have not encountered before. I can sense its ancient hunger eclipsing my siren sisters' own hunger by far. And I know this battle is not only meant for the land. It's also meant for beneath the waves.

Like an arrow, I streak round the hulls, pressing myself into the barnacle-clad wood. My heart picks up, even as I try to calm its panicked beat. The ruling council has lured more than one sea monster today to our isles. Then I hear my siren sisters.

Mira, daughter of Lowenva.

We sense kraken and morgawr and something else . . .

There are eyes in the sea.

Terrifying, ancient, ravenous . . .

A monster, ready to be unleashed, I realise, listening to them. I swim to Ennor, back to the shore, and sense the first of the sirens darting fast and true to swim alongside me. We emerge on the shoreline at the same moment, just as Lowri's form shimmers and becomes flesh beside us.

Gallena the siren leader nods to me and Lowri, then turns, assessing the armada and the sea beneath. 'You humans and your own witch magic are no match for this.'

'We have to be. *I* have to be,' says Lowri, and swallows. 'Too many will die. There will be no one left to stand against the ruling council.'

Gallena murmurs to the other sirens, all arriving now, and they turn to the skies. I look as well and locate what they have sensed. Wyvern. A whole horde, hovering as a pack, just beyond the armada. Awaiting the signal to hunt. Perhaps a coven aboard one of the ships down there is controlling them too.

'I cannot be in the sea *and* the sky. If I bring too great a storm, if I lose control . . .'

'You could kill us all,' Gallena finishes. 'History repeated.'

My breath stills in my chest. My mother, Lowenva, was the last storm bringer. She brought a storm and couldn't control it, killing her sisters, taking too many lives. I inhale sharply and shake my head. 'No, Gallena. History will not repeat. Not today.' I look to Lowri, aware of the burden on her. Our only witch. 'Have you heard from Brielle? Can Tanith survive?'

She grimaces. 'I haven't heard from Brielle since she left for the Spines with Inesh and Dreska. And we do not know if Tanith will remember anything, even who she is loyal to, if she takes her drake form. I cannot be sure I can haul her back, help her remember. Her attention may be scattered. She may panic and bolt, or worse . . .'

Lowri doesn't finish her sentence, she doesn't need to. A disorientated, panicked drake without a sense of who they are, or who they have been, is a volatile resource at best. At worst, a death sentence for all of us. I rub a hand down my face, calculating, assessing. Without a way to stop the wyvern, the people on Ennor are sitting targets. They'll be hunted for sport, picked off one by one before the ships even reach our shore.

'Lowri, stay on Ennor and bolster the wards,' I say. 'Speak to Tanith . . . and tell her I'm sorry. If she will fight for us, then we need her now, more than ever, but she will have to be sure that in her drake form she will not turn on a friend.'

Lowri nods and I think of Joby. I think of how this will break his heart, if she resumes her drake form and she cannot remember him. 'You fight in the sea, Mira. I will defend Ennor on land. And Tanith . . . Tanith will defend the skies.'

'And find Eli for me. Tell him . . .' I begin, taking a breath. 'Tell him I will meet him in the stars.'

Then I nod to my siren sisters, and we dive beneath the waves.

Chapter 34

Mira

THE MONSTERS LURED FROM THE deep are awaiting us. My siren sisters are all claws and sharp teeth, almost translucent, designed for the hunt. For the kill. But my nails aren't sharp, my bones and blood are human, and the weapons I rely on are my blade and my wits. A storm cannot reach us down here under the layers of the ocean. A storm bringer cannot upend the sea. But in the siren sight I inherited from my mother, I sense the ancient forms of the enemy. Kraken. Morgawr. And dwarfing them both . . . I gasp. It can't be . . .

Leviathan.

As I gape at the ancient, sprawling form, I remember the moment this tapestry of the ocean was bound into me by Coven Septern. And what I had to sacrifice for my siren sight to awaken. My memories of my father, all knowledge of his voice, his arms round me when I was a child, his soul . . . gone. All I know is that once I *had* a father. And now, faced with this monstrosity, as the siren side of me overwhelms my human side, I realise that the sacrifice I made may save us all.

My siren sisters shrink away, a ripple of thoughts flowing through my mind from theirs.

Our enemy . . .

. . . thought it was dead.

It comes to hunt us, not the humans . . .

Who lured it here? Who drew it from the south?

Witches, enemy witches, evil sorceresses.

They want our blood and bone for their spellwork.

They lured it.

They . . .

Them.

The map of the ocean I can sense around me ripples, reforming, as though a net has been shaken. The armada is revealed in all its sprawling, terrible glory in my mind, rows upon rows of vessels, most likely cloaked before from my sight and that of my siren sisters by some clever witch spellwork, but now we can sense them. Perhaps the spell no longer has a hold on us. And below us the leviathan is a colossal monster, part serpent, part whale, with a huge, gaping maw, fang-like teeth and glowing yellow eyes. It coils low in the murk of the seabed, awaiting a feast of sirens, waiting for my sisters to begin their own hunt for hearts, to pick them off as they grapple with their prey.

Bodies and debris begin hitting the water, our own ships and boats exchanging cannon fire above. Flames dance on the surface, painting this world of the sea in a myriad burning colours. It's as though the sea is aflame, orange and gold and yellow, and between there is shadow and the hulls that promise death. As these flashes of flame bloom on the roof of the ocean, my siren sisters gather. For highlighted by those flares of flame is the morgawr, slinking along an undercurrent, a sly coil of hunger. As I watch the shimmer of siren scales, I sense two more monsters, a kind I have fought before. Kraken, vast and ravenous, their tentacles tasting the sea's currents, one already rolling towards the feast aboard our fleet.

I turn to Gallena and find her features more angular here than in her home of the siren graveyard, sharpened by her senses. She wants the human hearts peppering the water. She wants to hunt and feast. But there is a greater part of her looking to protect her sisters, determined to rid the ocean of the dark monsters that would hunt and torment them, now or in the future.

Split into your clusters, my sisters. Beshenya, Karenza, take the morgawr. Niardema, lure the kraken to the opposing armada. My cluster and Mira, we take the leviathan to his final grave.

A battle cry rises in my mind, the sirens gripping blades carved of bone and spines, like my mother's weapon, wielding them as axes. In a flurry of translucent limbs and teeth, the morgawr is quickly beset by Beshenya and Karenza's cluster. One thrash of the monster's huge tail sees three sirens batted in the middles and I freeze, heart in my throat. But they rally, rejoining their sisters, and the hunt begins in earnest.

I dart alongside Gallena, past the cluster luring the kraken away, clearing our path for the king of all sea monsters. As we find the creature, he snaps his jaw, then unleashes a roar that jars my very bones. My siren sisters falter, their instinct to flee from their natural predator almost overwhelming them.

I'll get in close, I say to Gallena. *It may not mark me the same as you.*

She nods and I'm off, weaving over and under a current, flying between the shadows cast by the hulls of the vessels overhead. The leviathan extends, uncoiling, its yellow gaze captured by a siren near Gallena. In a movement that belies its huge, bloated form, it lashes out, gripping her with its fangs, tossing her body down its throat to swallow her whole. A siren wail crescendos in my mind and I shudder, feeling every inch of my sisters' horror. But as the leviathan feeds I take the chance and come up behind. As quiet as a whisper, I get into position.

Ready to be the distraction.

The lure.

My heart thumps against the cage of my ribs and I remind myself I'm doing this for all of us. The leviathan will devour our fleet. We will never be able to enter the waters surrounding Ennor again if it stays. We'll be land-trapped, desperate. Now it's found a rich hunting ground, it will linger, like the old stories say, for generation after generation until the land is bled dry. As I grip my blade, fighting off my fear, I am ready to swim faster than ever before.

But there's an almost invisible shimmer over the leviathan's scales as the water undulates around it and, suddenly, the ocean tastes metallic. I freeze, my gaze shifting over the leviathan as it turns on Gallena and the other sirens. Then I realise. The metallic taste is spellwork. It's the same scent and taste pluming like perfume in the halls of Coven Septern. There is a witch influencing the leviathan, probably more than one. The creature is being guided, controlled, just as the witches controlled my senses and that of my sisters by cloaking the armada.

I swim forward, stabbing my blade into the leviathan's tail, blood gushing in a deep purple cloud around me. But it doesn't turn, doesn't even flinch. In desperation, I cry out to my siren sisters.

Gallena, flee! A witch controls the monster!

She tries to bolt, but she's not fast enough, the leviathan has already set its sights on her. It lunges and the sirens surrounding her scatter, screaming, as its fangs clamp down on her leg.

Chapter 35

Lowri

LOWRI WATCHES AS MIRA DISAPPEARS with the sirens into the sea. Then she whispers a witch word, eyes on the horizon, on the armada that's come to devour her home. She lands in the entrance hall of Ennor Castle and the ground shudders beneath her. Lowri gasps, throwing out a hand to grip a side table as the walls seem to strain inwards. She blinks quickly, feeling the strange tang of another coven's magic invading the castle.

'We're out of time,' she murmurs to herself, sensing the press against the wards, against the very bindings of Elena's protection.

She hurries through the castle, corridors pinching and shuddering, checking rooms and halls, the kitchens and infirmary, as she searches with increasing urgency. Then she whisks up the back stairs, knowing where to find her. Lowri heads straight for the library and finds Tanith kneeling before Amma, who is sitting in an armchair, flitting in and out of focus as she groans, reeling with each whip and crack of magic against the wards binding her together.

Tanith glances at Lowri, relief on her face. 'Come, Lowri. The wards are buckling. You must sense it. Amma is weakening too fast. She can't last much longer against this assault of spellwork. She won't be able to stop them.'

Lowri hides her panic, rushing to Amma's side. 'If she dies . . .'

'Then the wards will have fallen, yes,' Tanith confirms. She straightens, drawing a vial from a dress pocket. 'This is my blood, witch. Imbibe it. You need a strong catalyst to delve deep into your magic. You and your fledglings and Brielle, should they make it back to us in time, need it *now*.'

Amma stutters in and out again and Lowri pushes back her fear over Brielle's long silence, over what has transpired on her assignment to find aid in the Spines. 'You would share your blood with me . . . with us?'

Tanith nods. 'I would. The blood of a drake. The richest, most powerful creature blood in this world.'

Lowri's fingers tremble, but she takes the vial, determined to show Tanith the respect she deserves. This gift is fabled, rare. For a moment, she is overcome by the gesture, for a drake to trust a witch, a natural enemy in many parts of the continent, including here. For *her* to be the one who is trusted.

'Why?'

She smiles sadly. 'Because I believe in a better world. And because now I entrust this castle to your protection. My battle is elsewhere. Within myself, and without, in the skies,' Tanith says softly. Then she turns for the window, the sunlight catching on iridescent scales where her skin is exposed. She walks forward, stepping up to the cushioned seat and thrusts back one of the windows. A stream of air, laced with brine and granite, rushes in.

Knowing what she is about to do, Lowri takes a half step towards her. 'How do you know you won't turn on your friends, your family?'

Tanith sighs as more scales glisten along her cheekbones. 'I must trust that my head is stronger than my panic. I must believe in my mind, in myself. Tell him . . .' She swallows. 'Tell Joby I wish we'd had more time. Tell him I'm sorry I failed to find a way, that if I remember him, if somehow my soul remembers my human existence, I will find him again. We will begin as we should have done before, with hope.'

Then she faces the wind and sky, the wyvern in the distance . . . and leaps.

Lowri gasps, rushing for the window, gripping the ledge as she leans out. She searches for Tanith, scanning the sky, fearing her broken on the rocks below.

But then she hears an almighty rumble. And a bronze drake, fierce and beautiful, soars up and away into the clouds. Tanith roars with the force of a tempest and Lowri covers her ears, the depth of the drake's bellow rattling through her entire being. Tears smart in Lowri's eyes as she realises the sacrifice Tanith has just made for Ennor. For them all. Her human life sacrificed to transform back into her drake form, to battle their enemies and save them all. As she watches, the wyvern streak straight for Tanith, changing course as they dash towards her bronze flanks. She whistles low over the waves, striking the masts of three ships with her tail, before darting upwards, leading the batlike wyvern towards the eye of the sun.

And in that moment Lowri's heart thuds with renewed hope. For there, far away, are more shapes moving closer. Drakes, flying towards Tanith. Drakes with riders on their backs.

'Brielle,' she breathes, tears spilling on to her cheeks. She grins, her heart filling with hope in her chest. 'It *has* to be you. You found a coven in the Spines to help us. You've – you've returned.'

Another crack rocks the castle, throwing her back on to the window seat, the vial of Tanith's blood dropping to the floor and rolling towards Amma. She rights herself quickly, sensing the wards fraying dangerously. Holes forming, the threads of Tresillian magic, Elena's old magic, straining. She reaches for the vial, uncorks it and readies herself to imbibe the most potent catalyst she has ever taken.

She allows it to splash down her throat before stoppering it, in the hope that she can hand it to Dreska, Inesh and Brielle as well. 'A small swallow, yes,' she whispers to herself. 'Not too much, the effects will be—' She chokes suddenly, dropping to her knees, palms slamming the floor.

Lowri feels *everything*.

The wooden floorboards creaking beneath her fingertips, the trees they once were, the bite of the axe that shaped them. The movement of people two floors below, the strain of an ankle of one of them – an old injury that twists each footfall. Then the whispered prayer to an old god on a woman's tongue, the waves far below as they froth against the rocks, the sun in the sky as it warms the granite walls, the clang of a bell, the flat cadence of it as a rope is pulled, hitting always in the same place, it clatters and clatters . . .

Lowri feels the blood pumping in her veins, rich and full and powerful. She can barely contain it. Doesn't *want* to contain it. She wants to pull apart the world, weave it as she wills it, pull down the sky, flood the land, rake the earth with her desires, *burn it all down* . . .

'Steady there, witch,' Amma murmurs. 'Remember who you are.'

Lowri looks down at her fists, finding the lines of her veins inky and bulging, viscous and brimming with glorious magic. She looks at her reflection in the windows, onyx eyes peering back at her, a vicious smile pulling apart her lips. 'I must control it,' she rasps, forcing her lips into a thinner line, suppressing the wicked fickleness freckling her mind with pure possibility.

She goes to Amma and stands over her, taking her hands in hers. Amma places her translucent, barely-there fingers in Lowri's, and all Lowri senses is the gentle burn of magic, of Elena Tresillian's last protection of Elijah, and Ennor, the physical embodiment of the wards. She closes her eyes and allows her senses to guide her, to find the wards round the castle that are Amma, that are witch. She must reweave the tears . . . and then push the wards out, to encircle the town below as well. Rebuild them bigger than before, even as the other coven out there in the armada pushes and pulls them apart as she works.

Another shudder rocks the castle and Lowri feels her true self uncoiling, her magic awakening, the power of a Tresillian witch flowing through her like a river of ink. She's aware now of the coven on those ships, the enemy witches, trying to smash the wards. Amma is dying before her, the wards stitched to her slowly unravelling. Lowri feeds them, coaxing the magic, reshaping and reforming the wards, allowing Amma to relinquish control to her through their joined hands. Then, as the tears are mended, she binds the wards to herself, as they were once bound to Elena. And she begins to push them out, inch by inch, desperate to save as many people in the town below as she can.

As Lowri feeds the wards, she senses more beings beyond them. The monsters Mira faces below the waves, and the ones Brielle and Tanith engage in the sky. With grim determination, she hopes that it will be enough.

That, combined, they can save Ennor.

Chapter 36

Brielle

THE DRAKE BANKS LEFT, SOARING in formation with its bloom as Brielle clings to the reins. The isles emerge below them like green jewels, a storm of clouds whipping up around them.

'This is Mira's work. A storm is coming,' she calls to the others as she strains her eyes through the spelled goggles, assessing the terrain below. The armada are all dark shapes and blots, the Ennor fleet engaging them far fewer in number. The ruling-council forces have not yet breached the wards and landed upon the isle's shores. She releases a ragged breath. She is not too late.

It seemed to take an age for them to train, to learn to ride drakeback. Even now, Dreska and Inesh ride behind two trueborn riders from the Spines. In truth, Brielle found herself not wanting to leave. For her, Lowri is family and Ennor is home, but in the Spines she found another home, somewhere to which she would want to return, again and again. A piece of her heart is now held somewhere in the ice and thick furs and wooden walls of the coven house.

But the coven had deemed them ready, and together they answered the call from the Fortunate Isles. They flew in formation, ready to defend a people ruled by leaders who want to control, not protect – just as they'd been, the peoples of the Spines, before they rebelled, before new rulers were elected.

A sharp whistle from the witch on her right, Skanni, signals the bloom to loosen formation and Brielle looks around, feeling the unease in the drake she rides. Wyvern. A swarm of them, their batlike bodies hovering on the air currents flowing over the armada, poised to strike. An air current most likely created by a witch. She glances at the vessels below, sweeping her gaze over the ships, and discerns a faint shimmer, then a matching one in the sea. A rival coven, then, doing the ruling council's bidding. Here to help wipe out an island and bring the Fortunate Isles to heel.

She grimaces, the thought of her own kind turning on humans like this leaves bile coating the back of her throat. There is one person she is sure will be part of this armada: Captain Spencer Leggan. If she sees him, if they're on opposing sides today, it will not end well for him – at her hand, or at an islander's. He is on the list of those long past redemption, along with the ruling council themselves, and Captain Renshaw.

The drake beneath suddenly releases a low-pitched call and the bloom to either side of Brielle takes it up. She frowns, first checking on Dreska and Inesh, on drakes with other witches behind her, then she sees a creature soaring up from Ennor. Another drake. With no rider.

Brielle gasps in awe as the drake answers the call, bronze scales glinting, her body almost feline, sleek in the way that the male drakes are not. She slinks up into the clouds, opening her wings wide and sunlight glances off them, casting a web of rainbows out over the land and sea.

'What a beauty . . .' Brielle breathes. Then realisation hits her. It's Tanith. The librarian of Ennor, giving up her human form, all her human memories, to fight the wyvern. To save Ennor. A lump forms in Brielle's throat as she pats her drake's side. Such sacrifice, such majesty. She narrows her gaze on the wyvern moving in to harry Tanith, and crouches low over her drake's back. She won't allow these wyvern to kill another she cares about.

A shrill whistle pierces the air and Brielle's heart thumps with the roar of her drake. Then her drake beats its wings, lifting them out of the air current and into a smooth, practised dive, straight for the swarm of wyvern. Brielle leans into the drake's scales, gripping the reins in one fist, freeing a blade with the other. The other drakes dive all around her, the air whistling against their scales and she eyes a wyvern with claws stretched for Tanith's side, readying to rake her beautiful bronze scales. Whispering a witch word to guide her hand, with a practised motion she flips the blade and throws it, striking the eye of the wyvern. It shrieks, claws retracted, batting back and forth into other wyvern, sowing chaos and panic in its swarm, before falling for the hungry sea.

Brielle smirks in satisfaction as her drake veers round the swarm and she flicks blade after blade, drawing them from her sash, piercing the tightknit horde. Tanith herself roars, the fierce bellow of a female finding her voice. She extends her claws, gripping a wyvern and tossing it into another, blood painting the clouds. She wickers as another dives for her, but with one flick of her long, scaled tail, the wyvern is beaten from the sky, falling in a daze into the sea beneath. Soon they are scattered, allowing Tanith to soar upwards. Brielle's drake rises to greet her. Tanith inclines her head, gaze sweeping to meet the drake—

But with a shriek a wyvern swoops in, claws digging into her side. Tanith's cry of pain shakes the skies as more wyvern latch on to her, moving in for the kill.

'No!' Brielle cries, but it's too late. The swarm tear into Tanith, shredding her wings before swooping free. She beats the ruined remains of her wings once, twice, trying to gain height before the horde fly in for the kill. But she can no longer fly. Brielle watches, heart in her throat as her drake unleashes a mournful call. Tanith calls back, a bleat of desperation and of fear. She tries once more to beat her wings against the air, to gain purchase on the air currents, but to no avail. She spirals down in a freefall.

Right over the Isle of Ennor.

CHAPTER 37

Mira

MY HEART LURCHES IN MY chest as Gallena screams. The leviathan shakes her, yellow eyes swivelling, frenzied and wild, and she just manages to stab his jaw with her jagged blade. He roars, releasing her, and her siren sisters dart forward to drag her back.

I hear Gallena's cries in my mind, *End the witches' thrall over this monster! You alone may make it, if they believe you are among their allies.*

I nod fiercely, gaze fixed on the surface, on the ship gliding nearby as the sirens scatter. If the sirens swim up, the witches may sense them, particularly if there is a hunter on board. But they may not sense me with my human heart. It's a risk, going alone, but one I have to take.

Keep him distracted, I say before swimming upwards, aiming for the hull of the enemy ship. I linger underwater, inching my way for the surface, then find a length of rigging draped down the starboard side. Quickly scaling it, I drop on to the deck and roll, hiding behind a huge coil of rope. The wind smells of storm and, when I look up, I smile. The storm I called has answered, hanging low over the armada, awaiting its moment to unleash. But that time is not just yet. Not with the drakes overhead fighting the wyvern. Not with our own small fleet engaging the first wave of the enemy's ships. Let it hang there for a while as a threat to our enemies.

Two men steal my attention, sailors speaking with a Leicenan lilt, and I realise I've clambered aboard a merchant ship. For a moment, I wonder if Eli is on a ship such as this, sabotaging their vessels before dissolving into shadow. I shift round the coil of rope, finding a jacket drying over a barrel, and take it. I stuff my hair beneath the collar, hiding the dripping wet tendrils, and on silent feet, blade in hand, I move behind the barrel where the jacket lay discarded, eyeing this section of the deck. The sailors finish their conversation, moving off, and that's when I see them. Three witches, standing at the bow of the ship, hands linked, staring down into the inky depths of the ocean.

The witches controlling the leviathan.

There are thuds behind me, and I move back into the shadow of the coiled rope, grimacing at the imprints of my wet feet on the wooden boards of the deck. I bite my lip. I don't have much time. A sailor walks past, shouting an order behind him to the crew, and I take my chance. Slinking between shadows, before more sailors come up on deck, I move closer to the witches and I can hear their murmuring. It's a familiar sound, and it takes me back to the day I gave up something precious in Coven Septern –

the irreplaceable memories of my father – in exchange for the siren map, for the knowledge of my siren ancestors to be stitched into my blood and bones and mind. Witches, it seems, are more powerful when they work a spell as a trio. And to keep a monster such as the leviathan under their thrall is a powerful spell indeed.

Perhaps the time is now for a distraction. I look to the skies and imagine the storm clouds darkening, growing heavy and full above us. I force my will upwards, into the heart of those clouds, to create the rattle and shake of thunder. Then I tighten my fist round my blade and wait. Thunder cracks overhead, lightning cutting a swift path to a ship just to the starboard side. The three witches falter, their concentration broken as they whip back and forth, before one of them calls the other two to attention, to focus on the leviathan. I smile grimly as thunder booms again, then the rain begins to descend. Within seconds, it slicks the deck, sailors calling to one another, securing the mainsail. They're distracted too, focused on the impending storm, and now I know which of the witches is leading this spellwork, keeping the leviathan in their thrall. The witch on the left. And when she turns again, casting her critical gaze over the ship as the sailors quickly work the ropes, my breath stills in my throat. Blue eyes. Piercing blue, a blue I have seen before.

She's the witch who burned my mind aboard *Phantom*.

The witch who captured me and took me to the ruling council. It all began with those eyes of ice, that spell she burned into my mind with a witch word . . .

inferna. If it hadn't been for her and her coven, Agnes and I would not have been captured. I would not have had to take part in the deadly Trials.

Now, it's personal.

This witch will not survive me.

Not today.

A flame of rage burns bright in my chest, but I wait for her to turn back to the bow before I move. Then, just before she's once more clasped the hand of the witch next to her, I hurl myself across the deck. Careening straight into her middle, I slash at her hand with a feral cry, so she does not have time to grab hold of something and to steady herself.

'Remember me, witch?' I hiss with guttural fury in her ear.

Then I pull us both over the railings, into the jaws of the waiting sea. The witch only has time to gasp in shock before we plunge into the waves. I dig my blade into her side and she thrashes against me, mouth opening in horror, bubbles streaming out. But I'm not done. I drag her down, deeper and deeper, to where the leviathan waits. My siren sisters are playing a dangerous game, and my blood burns hot when I find their numbers are decimated. But the leviathan seems to have paused, blinking slowly, as though unsure where it is, unsure of its purpose here. The spell of the three witches combined has been severed.

Is this the witch? Gallena asks, her voice in my mind a thread of notes. She's in pain, and it angers me further that this witch, this coven, saw fit to hurt us. To side with the ruling council whose only wish is to destroy and conquer. They may have sought favour by siding with them, but it was at the expense of every other magical being in our world. I cannot condone it. Nor can I suffer her to live.

It is, I reply, pulling my blade from her side. *About time she meets the monster she turned on us.*

Then I kick the blue-eyed witch towards the leviathan and look on as she attempts to flee. The leviathan blinks slowly, fangs exposed in its giant maw as the witch forms witch words, holding her bleeding side. But its already too late for her. She traverses five lengths above us, trying to reach the surface, but the leviathan growls, the rumble rising up through its body sending a shiver of current over me. It narrows its yellow gaze and lunges. Its jaws grasp the witch and before she's even had the chance to scream she's swallowed whole.

The sirens raise a cry of victory as the leviathan ambles away, snapping for the bodies plunging into the water, flinching as burning debris plunges from above. It changes course, whipping its vast tail, and retreats deeper into the ocean. I hold my breath, sensing where it moves and realise it's no longer interested in the hunt here. Hunger sated, it drifts on a current and I feel the collective relief of my siren sisters.

Turning to survey the rest of the armada, to sense the other sirens and their battles with the kraken and morgawr, we learn the morgawr has been defeated, and one kraken is latched to an enemy ship, slowly crumbling it in its tight grip as the bodies of sailors plunge into the cold waters. The other kraken is already gone, lured away by the sirens to its death. Gallena falters in her sister's arms and I swim to her, taking her hand.

Your fight is over, I say. *Take our sisters and feast on enemy hearts. Then return home and heal.*

She nods, exposing her sharp little teeth. Then, in my mind, I hear her call. She beckons her sisters. She looks at me and, with her other hand, scrapes her palm gently down my cheek, leaving the sting of rasping scales. *After we have hunted the leviathan. We cannot risk such a monster prowling this close to our home – it would come back and feast at its leisure. Your mother would have been proud of you, fierce heart. Go now and end them on the land. Bring the storm the world needs to right itself.*

Storm bringer.

There was never any other way for this to end but in a tumbling tempest.

I will, I say. *Thank you for being the sisters I needed.*

Then with a call to hunt, the sirens vanish in a flash of claw and scales, leaving me with the storm in my heart and above, in my world. Leaving me with the knowledge that I alone must end this.

That I am the storm that rights the world.

Chapter 38

Brielle

BRIELLE WATCHES, POWERLESS TO STOP Tanith's fall from the sky. Her own drake streaks after Tanith, Brielle clinging on as the force of the dive loosens her from the drake's back, snatching her breath away. She grips the reins, each inevitable thump of her heart charting Tanith's end. Tanith collides with the earth north of the main town, flattening a deserted field. The air whomps in her ears as Brielle's drake slows her descent, wings braced and pumping the air as she hovers, readying to set down beside her. Brielle leaps off as soon as the ground is close enough, rolling to spring to her feet, already running before her drake lands.

The battle of the sea, the storm localised over the armada, slips away as Brielle takes in the bleeding mass of Tanith's flank. She stutters at the horror wrought by the wyverns' raking claws and . . . worse . . . she's still alive. Feeling every moment of this agony.

'No . . .' Brielle breathes, sinking to her knees beside Tanith's jaws. Tanith's eyes roll back as she huffs steam through her nose, then they close. The drake that carried Brielle moves closer, inspecting the length of her body, huffing, before a mournful rumble emanates from her throat. She hunkers down beside Tanith, and Brielle wipes a tear from her eye. The mournful cry from her drake sounds melodious, as though her drake is singing a death song.

A shadow ripples across the field and Nova streaks over the grass then Eli steps out of it, Joby releasing his hand as soon as they're through. He runs for Tanith, sprinting across the field as Eli strides forward, trailing shadow in his wake. Brielle looks at them both, assessing them quickly. Injured from the skirmishes on the sea, but still in fighting shape. Not yet defeated. But this . . . this could end Joby. Brielle can see it in his eyes. The terror of loss, the shock of a love ripped away too soon, before they've had a real chance to explore it. She shifts back, moving to stand and give him space as Eli stops beside her.

'Her wounds . . .' he says quietly.

'Too extensive to heal,' Brielle replies. 'In her drake form. She does not have long.'

Eli pulls in a haggard breath, running a bloodied hand down his face. 'A great loss.'

Joby moves closer, placing a hand on the corner of Tanith's jaw, bowing his head over her. Brielle's heart breaks for him as his shoulders begin to shake. Two more drakes set down behind her and she turns, finding Dreska being lowered to the ground, bow still gripped in her fist, then Inesh, refusing help, leaping down from the drake's back as Brielle did, hair unbound and wild all around her.

A hunter born, that one.

Brielle looks down to see Nova at her feet. 'Indeed. If she sees the end of this battle, if I do, I will train her. Dreska as well – she has the same fierce spirit.'

It's not like you to consider failure, Brielle, Nova says. *I'm here to collect them. Lowri needs them both. She needs three to complete her work on the wards.*

'Take them,' Brielle says. 'Lor is well?'

Nova blinks. *She has the blood of Tanith as her catalyst. My witch is power incarnate.*

Brielle releases a steady breath. 'Good. I've – I've missed her.'

And she you. Survive to see each other in the flesh, Hunter.

Then Nova stalks to Inesh and Dreska, whipping round their ankles. Brielle nods to them, whispering the witch words to send them to the castle, and they all vanish in pockets of light.

'Is there any hope for Tanith?' Eli asks, turning solemnly to Brielle.

She regards him, the clear signs of battle, the worry pinching his features, his eyes, troubled and deep, too old for such a young face. The weight of this too, this moment, this death . . . Is there a way to save Tanith? If only Tanith was in her human form, then perhaps, just maybe.

'Can Joby coax her to become human, as he once did before?' she asks. 'There are still tales among the drake riders of what he did, how she transformed for him. Their story has become legend in the Spines. If she can transform again, despite not remembering him, despite her wounds, then there could be a chance for her. I can traverse with her to the castle and work on healing her.'

Eli is quiet for a moment, contemplative. 'Sometimes, it is not the memories that bind us together. It is when two souls call to one another across time and space, across lifetimes. It is beyond memory, beyond our understanding. It's when two souls are cleaved into one.'

Brielle's breath catches and she nods. 'Let us hope you are right.'

Eli goes to Joby, placing a hand on his shoulder, and speaks quietly to him. Joby's shoulders relax and he grasps Eli's arm before Eli steps away, allowing him the space.

'He's going to try,' Eli says as he comes back and stands next to Brielle. 'He's going to talk to her as he did when they first met, when he freed her. He's going to lead her back. To see if there's a way they can find that bond again.'

Joby sits by Tanith's side, turned towards her, and begins talking to her, weaving the tale of the first time they met, in the Spines. Brielle dashes another tear from the corner of her eye and looks to the sky, then the sea. The drakes are still chasing the wyvern, witches firing arrows and crossbows at their eyes. But there are so many in this swarm, and already the drakes are weakening from their constant harrying. A wyvern is hit, falling from the clouds, and lands in the sea, slopping a wave that topples a small merchant vessel in the enemy's fleet. Brielle shapes a fist, but the victory is short-lived. Five wyvern form a dive formation then swoop for one of Eli's ships, their claws raking at the deck, bodies falling into the water. Eli stiffens, the shadows around him intensifying.

'Hunter, I must go. My fleet, my crews . . .'

Brielle nods. 'Leave this with me.'

Eli turns to her. 'The Tresillian witches have never been as strong as now. May your magic stay true.'

Then, with a tortured glance towards Joby and Tanith, he's gone, stepping backwards into shadow. When Brielle looks over to the fleet and the armada, she sees a swirl of shadow appearing then reforming, over and over, as people from his crew are dropped back on the ship from the gaping maw of the ocean. Of course. He chooses to save his people over fighting the enemy. He chooses individual lives over a bloody victory. A true leader. She blows out a breath. And now he's left two of his inner circle in her hands, entrusted her with their precious lives. She cannot fail him, cannot fail *them*.

Looking to the skies, she sees Skanni take down another wyvern, slowly gaining the advantage. One drake takes out three with a plume of flame, their smoking carcasses descending to crash into an enemy ship. But it's not enough. There are still too many. They cannot come to Brielle's aid. It's all down to her.

She looks back at Joby, his hand on Tanith's scales, a pool of dark blood growing under her. She's breathing out steam, her eyes fluttering closed, and she knows that even if Joby does coax Tanith into her human form she may not survive. Her wounds may be too great. Brielle needs to buy them both time.

She strides forward, crouching beside Joby. Tanith doesn't even flinch at a hunter, a witch, so close to her. A worrisome sign. 'I'm going to work on her here, Joby. You keep talking to her, keep her calm.'

He nods, barely looking at her and continues telling a story in his soft burr. She rises, moving round him to Tanith's flank, assessing the deepest wounds. She is no healer. But she knows the basics of the witch magic from her training . . . Maybe it'll be enough. It has to be.

She leans down, placing a hand on Tanith's glistening bronze scales, and closes her eyes. She forms the witch words she knows for healing, for life and mending and hope. She pours her magic in, sensing the flow and pull of her blood, pumped by her heart, the slow trickle of her life waning. She imagines stitching, weaving. Binding Tanith back together, pulling her raked flesh back together.

Tanith chuffs, claws pawing the ground and Brielle remembers the burning sensation of having a deep wound sewn up. So she channels cool, a breeze of winter chill, the first frost of the season, and Tanith huffs in what sounds like relief. Brielle pulls back her hand, opens her eyes and sees the wounds have stopped bleeding.

Then Joby chokes out a gasp and Tanith begins to transform. Her drake flanks shrink, her whole being growing smaller and smaller, until her scales seem to disintegrate entirely. And there, in its place, is a young woman. Slightly different from how Tanith first appeared as a human, now with shorter bronze hair, scales still glistening more obviously over her skin. She curls on her side and Joby gently lifts her into his arms. She says quietly, 'I remember you . . . from before. We know each other, don't we?'

Joby releases a shuddering breath, blinking down at her. 'We do, Tanith. We do.'

Just then, there is a roar from the sky, a drake cry echoing across the isle. Brielle's breath catches in her throat. The drakes and their witches are victorious. The few wyvern left are fleeing into the thunderous clouds, shrieking with rage as they fly. But, below, she finds the armada regrouping, breaking through Eli's fleet to reach the shores of Ennor. Soon it'll be a battle for the land. Brielle has to get Tanith back to the castle, and soon.

She moves towards Joby and holds out her own arms. 'May I?'

Joby turns to her, features drawn in lines of fear, and Brielle knows he doesn't want to hand Tanith over. But he relents, pouring her slender frame gently into Brielle's arms. 'I will meet you at the castle. After . . . If . . .'

'Go and fight,' Brielle says firmly. 'Trust me now with her. Fight for the time I'll need to heal her.'

Neither of them say it, but if that armada reaches the land invasion is inevitable. They do not have the forces to resist them. Now it is about fortifying the castle, drawing everyone vulnerable back, and just hoping that Lowri and their fledglings can succeed with reforming the wards.

'Hunter, I owe you a life debt,' Joby rumbles softly, grasping her shoulder. 'If I do not see you again, safe travels in this life and the next.'

Brielle fractures slightly, but holds it all inside as she nods, then whispers the witch word and traverses.

The last thing she sees is Joby's face, hope lifting his features, before he's crossing back towards the town, to the final battle that could end them all.

Chapter 39

Lowri

INESH AND DRESKA APPEAR IN a swirl of magic. Lowri inhales, looking down at Amma, and finds their fingers interlaced. The cracks in the wards have been repaired, for now. But she cannot push them out to encompass the town of Ennor without help. Only the power of three will do.

Dreska bites her lip as Inesh raises her chin, and it strikes Lowri how very like the two sides of Brielle they are: one hesitant, no doubt calculating quickly, each scenario playing out in her head; the other is grounded in courage, methodical and unwavering. Her heart twists for them, for what she is about to ask of them.

'I know you've both had a long journey from the Spines. I know you will be tired and frightened. But I need you. We must bolster the wards, the three of us, together. If these islanders are to stand a chance of survival, we must give Eli, Mer, Pearl, Joby and Caden a chance of defeating as many vessels on the waves as possible before they reach our shores.'

'There are still wyvern out there, riding the air currents,' Dreska says quietly. 'I sense half a dozen left.'

'You sense . . .' Lowri takes a breath, eyeing her appraisingly. 'Do you sense any other creatures?'

'Below the waves, I can sense sirens, but they are moving further away and . . . others. Huge predators.' Dreska licks her lips. 'They are hungry. One feasts on human hearts.'

Lowri blinks quickly, not showing her fear at what Mira now faces. Not knowing if she is still there with her siren sisters, if she's still alive. 'When we survive this, you will become a hunter, Dreska,' she says quietly. 'The first of our new coven.'

'And I?' Inesh asks, clasping her fingers before her.

'You are a hunter too, from what Brielle has told me.' Lowri smiles. 'But you both also have an aptitude for spellwork. I will train you both too, when this is over. Now come. We do not have long.'

She hands the vial of Tanith's drake blood first to Dreska then Inesh, their eyes flaring wide as their veins darken.

'Oh!' Dreska says as Inesh giggles, a high chattering sound, more creature than witch.

'Settle, fledglings,' Lowri says. 'Take my hands and follow my lead.'

What could be mere moments, or hours later, Lowri stumbles, eyes flying wide as the walls shudder again. She is so deep in her work, so focused on the weaving, and now the wards are moved further out, almost covering the town below. Her fledglings are both lost still, consumed by the spellwork, as Nova brushes up against Lowri's ankles, purring in her monster-like way. Lowri senses for the first time how Nova soothes her, taking away the sharp edge of her magic. They look at each other and Nova blinks before leaping up to curl beside Amma on the armchair.

'Lowri . . .' Amma says. 'Lowri, it's time.'

Lowri reels, her senses spinning as she comes back to the library and her own form. When she looks down at Amma with her own eyes, she finds her translucent, flickering in and out of focus, losing whatever form Elena created with her dying will. Lowri sinks to her knees beside her, letting go of Inesh and Dreska's hands. They blink slowly, as though they too were both far away, veins limned in inky magic, and step towards the window.

'I'm here,' Lowri says, taking both Amma's hands, which feel at once like a whisper, like silk, like fog on an autumn morning.

'Release me,' Amma gasps softly, smiling at the witch. 'Only a Tresillian witch can do so. And I have done what Elena intended: I have safeguarded Ennor for her boy. But now there is you, and you are ready to take up the mantle. I feel it. I see it.'

'She's right,' a voice says from near the door, and Lowri straightens, not turning round. She would recognise that voice anywhere. 'You are the truest Tresillian witch since Elena's passing. Truer than me.

You are the rightful heir to the Tresillian magic and grimoires. The next guardian of Ennor.'

'Mother,' Lowri murmurs, heart twisting, despite herself. 'You're late.'

'I am sorry.'

Lowri's heart skips a beat and she turns round then, taking in the Malefant. Regal as ever, neat and seemingly unremarkable. But Lowri knows that looks can be deceptive and Hillary Tresillian, the leader of Coven Septern, the strongest witch she's ever known, is like steel. A melding of metals. Unbreakable. Unbendable.

'Sorry for what?' she asks. 'Being late to the party? Or not pledging your help sooner?'

The Malefant's features soften. 'Sorry for not being the mother that you, Caden and Brielle needed. Or wanted. Sorry for being a Malefant first, even before –' she swallows – 'even before being a good sister to Elena.'

Lowri regards her for a moment. There is much she could say, accusations she could hurl. She could even walk away or ask her to leave. But in the end, she realises, the bitterness would set in. Sorrow over not having the mother she wanted or needed hardening and souring. She doesn't want that for herself. The best thing is to accept her mother for who she is and know to expect nothing more. That path would only lead to disappointment. And, right now, Lowri needs to be strong. She needs the Malefant of Coven Septern to stand beside her. 'Thank you,' she breathes. 'Now tell me you're here to help and not hinder.'

'I've brought my best witches and hunters. We stand with House Tresillian as it has always been.'

'Against the ruling council?'

Hillary's mouth twists. 'Against the usurpers, yes.'

Before Lowri can ask her what she means, there's a clap as magic displaces the air in the room and Brielle comes in with a bleeding form in her arms. Tanith.

Brielle's gaze snaps to Hillary, then Amma, before finally resting on Lowri. 'She needs to be healed. She fought in her drake form so valiantly. She's wounded. I've done my best.'

'We will help her,' Hillary says firmly, summoning two witches into the library with a commanding witch word. She nods to them. 'Get that table. Bring it into the light. The drake needs to be healed.'

The table is shifted next to Amma, and Brielle lays Tanith's broken body on to it. She's a mass of wounds still and Lowri holds in her shock as Brielle steps back beside her. For the first time since they were little, Brielle reaches out a hand and Lowri squeezes her fingers, comforting her sister as the Septern witches begin their work. Brielle is always the strong one, her emotions in check, her decisions built of stone. But now Lowri feels the tremble in her fingers, senses the way in which she's keeping it all inside. She draws her other hand round their clasped ones, wanting Brielle to know she is here.

The walls shake again, dust shivering from the ceiling, and Lowri senses something hard slamming into the wards. She glances to the window, finding the sea a churn of flotsam, flame and bodies. The armada has thinned, several vessels limping away from the isles, but Eli's fleet has suffered far greater losses. The few still holding back the might of the armada are smoking or surrounded. Her heart creeps up her throat, and all she can do is feed more of herself into the wards, thickening them like a second skin.

Amma reaches out a hand to Tanith, wrapping her feeble grip round Tanith's fingers. She is almost nothing, a wisp, a cloud, a memory. 'You saved me. And now it is my joy to save you. Live long, love longer.' And, with that, the last of Amma, the final piece of Elena Tresillian, flows into the drake and she dies.

Lowri stifles a sob as her mother sucks in a breath, a single tear tracking down her cheek. Where Amma lay, there is nothing. And Lowri senses a shift, a reweaving of the wards as the role of guardian, of the last of the line of Tresillian witches, passes fully to her.

Then Tanith draws in a breath. Brielle stiffens as Tanith's eyes open. The two healer witches pause as the drake regards them, then her gaze travels to Brielle and Lowri. She smiles, and it's oddly reminiscent of the creature wrapped inside her. 'It seems I was mistaken,' she says in her melodious voice. 'Perhaps I have nine lives, like a familiar.'

There's a sudden boom like thunder, then the entire wall of windows shatters. Lowri throws up her hands, crying the witch word for shield, as glass scatters across the floor. Hillary waves a hand, forming another word, and the glass reforms, intact once more.

They all stride to the windows and Brielle hisses. 'The wards have been breached. An enemy ship approaches the isle . . .'

'It's Coven Mereen,' Hillary says. 'The wily serpents.'

'Inesh, Dreska,' Lowri says, looking to them, trembling with fury that her work, all her careful work of extending the wards, has already been cracked by this rival coven. 'Stay with Tanith and guard this library. It holds too much to fall into enemy hands. Nova?'

I will guard the grimoires and the fledglings.

Lowri nods and turns to Brielle and Hillary, who nod in return. 'Please stay and work on the librarian,' Hillary says to the fledglings. 'This drake is precious.'

The three of them traverse down to the town.

When they land on the quay, Caden greets them, eyes flaring wide when he sees his mother. 'Decided to do the right thing, have you?' he says, frowning. 'Or come to argue a point and insist your coven stays outside any politics while my people die?'

'The former,' Hillary says briskly. 'Now direct my coven, Caden. Where should we focus our efforts?'

Caden opens then closes his mouth, as his frown partially disappears. 'Two ships have snuck in past the wards. They hold the witches. Eli could only traverse in with Pearl.'

There's a sudden shriek from the ship to the far left, which has breached the wards. Then bodies begin hitting the water: half a dozen witches, abandoning ship, leaping into the waves. Lowri looks up at the deck and sees a girl leaning against the railings. A slight girl with pale blonde hair and a wicked grin.

'Little ghost works swiftly,' Caden says with a chuckle. 'Looks like your efforts will be needed on the remaining ship carrying witches to our shores.'

'Coven Septern, with me,' Hillary commands, and they all vanish.

More ships from the armada begin pushing against the wards in the surrounding waters and Lowri feels every single one. She begins reeling the wards back in like a net, so they are not shredded by Coven Mereen's magic, further and further until eventually, they only protect the castle and its surroundings once more. Looking down at her hands, she sees her veins drip black, and she senses the crisp edges of burnout.

'Caden,' she calls, searching for him as he rallies the people. There's a boom of cannon fire, an enemy ship testing the wards, and it lands far too close to the shoreline, raising a gasp from the people of Ennor. 'Caden! Anyone who cannot fight must get to the castle. Everyone else . . . needs to be ready.'

Caden searches her features and nods, speaking quick commands to a group of runners. Lowri watches as they weave through the people, dispersing the news. 'There is no more preparation we can do,' he says, placing a hand on her shoulder. 'You should retreat to the castle as well, keep the wards strong.'

'I will fight by your side, brother,' she says softly.

More ships sail closer, then Lowri sees *Phantom* go up in flames. Caden takes a step forward, tracing his gaze over the waters around it. 'Eli was on there! He was—'

'I'm here,' Eli says from behind them, gravel in his throat as he coughs. Two sailors stumble away from his grasp and he runs a dirty hand down his face. 'I must rescue our crew still aboard the last ships of our fleet. Stand tall, Caden. Never falter.'

Eli takes a shuddering breath and traverses again. Lowri bites her lip, scanning the last of their limping fleet. He's closer to burnout than she is. Closer to the edge of his power.

The crowd on the shore, including the fierce women and girls trained by Caden – from Rosevear, Ennor and Penrith – grip their weapons as the enemy ships approach the shore and the quay. A strange quiet hangs in the air, broken only by the occasional muffled sob. A melancholy sweeps over them all, silence shivering and cloaking them. It is as though they are already ghosts.

But then . . .

A voice.

One older, cracked voice parts the silence. A woman with grey hair, clutching a sword to her chest. She begins to hum. Another picks up the tune, then another, and Lowri's heart swells. Other voices join in, stumbling over the notes at first, then singing in synchronicity. A chorus of many singing a folk song, one they know well on the isles. A song about braving the wildest of storms. The gathered begin singing in rounds, beating their boots on the ground. Caden hauls in a breath and joins them, his deep voice weaving under the higher notes. It's more powerful than a war song. Steadier than a sea shanty. It's hope, its home, it's the layers of their ancestors' voices, all joined as one.

As the melody weaves around her, tears trace down Lowri's cheeks. She feels every Tresillian witch standing beside her. Generation after generation, staring down the enemy. And her heart is a fist, formed of iron. She opens her hands, magic dusting her fingertips, opens her heart, her mind, her soul.

Ready to unleash her power and save her true home.

CHAPTER 40

Mira

I SWOOP UNDER THE ENEMY ships, reaching the quay before the first one lands. There are four lined up in the harbour, smaller boats being launched over the sides, full of men of the watch in their scarlet coats. I hurry up the quay steps, cursing the high tide. If it had been low, their biggest ships would not have been able to creep so close to our shore. We could have picked off more of them as they tried to land on the rocks outside the town.

'Eli!' I cry as he traverses through a shadow beside me. He stumbles, releasing the hands of two of his crew, Merryam and another, before collapsing to one knee. I wrap my sodden arms round his neck and bury my face in his shoulder.

'Mira . . .' he breathes, then coughs, steadying himself before pulling me into his arms. 'You're still alive.'

'It seems we will not be meeting in the stars just yet,' I say, relief bubbling up from deep inside me. 'How many have we lost?'

'Too many,' he says, releasing me. He's covered in ash and soot, his sleeve singed as though he's pushed burning wood aside, the flesh of his arm scorched and bloody.

We both look to the boats, the men rowing towards our shore. 'I must find Caden, ensure he has assembled our best archers.'

Just then, a shout cuts across the quay, Caden's voice a booming command. We watch as a group of archers that he's assembled sweep their bows high, then release. A slew of arrows barrel overhead . . .

And find their targets in the men of the watch. Men fall from the boats trying to reach the quay and a cheer goes up from the shore, before Caden shouts again, signalling another volley. Eli moves through his people, stopping to nod at some, clasp the hands of others, and I follow.

Caden, Lowri and Brielle are standing ready. Merryam flits through the crowd, greeting us, then Joby appears. I embrace them all hurriedly, the relief that they're still alive a painful throb in my chest.

Then another girl appears, a tall boy beside her, and I gasp. 'Sember? Heath? You can't be here! If you should die—'

'Then my father might actually pay attention. No doubt they will continue on to every port along the Straits after this if they are not defeated today,' Heath says with a laboured huff. 'We are at your service.'

'Did I not promise to come to your aid?' Sember says with a wink, brandishing a sewing needle that, in a blink, extends into a swish of a thin, sharp sword the length of her forearm. 'You forget, even pampered princes learn where the pointy end is supposed to go.'

I hug them both, gratitude overwhelming me, as another volley of arrows launches over our heads in a whoosh. 'Attach yourself to a crew. Caden's organised everyone in groups. I will see you on the other side.'

Sember squeezes my shoulder, Heath nods solemnly and they're off, rushing for the quay where they soon join a group ready to pick off the first men of the watch that reach the quay steps.

'Mira!' Agnes cries, and I look just in time before she flings herself at me.

I hug her back, sniffing and stifling a sob. Thank skies, thank the old gods, thank everything that she's still in one piece. 'You should be at the castle, Agnes. Our people, the wounded . . .'

She stands back from me, shaking her head fiercely, then pats her mother's blade, strapped at her waist. 'I was built for this, same as you. Same as all of us. Only the infirm and young are up there. Only the badly wounded. Rosevear is ready. *I* am ready.'

I stare past her, seeing the many women in the streets, women from all the isles, clutching weapons, ready for the fight of their lives. Pride flares inside me, pride for them, for where I come from, for these people. *My* people. Then I see Agnes's father, a huge, gentle man, a baker, nodding to me, axe in his fists. Then more, my father's set, the fisherfolk, mothers, grandmothers. We are all here. We stand as one.

Then I see Kai, their leader, their hope, and I draw in a deep, trembling breath. 'Whatever happens next, know we are one,' I say to them all. 'One people. Proud of all we are. All we could still become. The watch is here to take our futures. We will not let them. We stand together.'

'Together,' Kai repeats.

'Together,' Eli says, smiling.

'*Together!*' everyone shouts, a single word filled with flame and thunder.

'Together,' I whisper, turning to the ships now flooding the harbour, the men disembarking to land.

Caden moves through the crowd, reminding everyone of their formations, their groups and crews, some drawing back to the streets and squares behind for the second and third wave. He rallies archers to fire more arrows as the witches' cries of victory echo across the harbour, Hillary and her coven traversing in to stand on the quay. Pearl arrives with them, and she comes straight to Merryam, kissing her quickly before shifting on silent feet, like the ghost she is, ready to strike.

'They won't see her coming,' Mer says, grinning.

'They never do,' Eli agrees.

The first of the watch reaches the shore and are cut down by islanders with blades in their fists and fire in their chests. I catch sight of Sember and Heath making fast work of three men, their bodies tumbling back into the sea. Hillary rallies Coven Septern and they form into threes, casting witch words over the ships in the harbour, fire instantly spreading over the decks. Then I tip my chin back to the sky. The clouds are a mottled patchwork of purple and deepest blue, spilling rain in thin sheets. Ready to be unleashed.

I was born for this.

To rake thunder from the clouds.

To be the storm that rights our world.

For a reckoning.

I throw my will into the swollen clouds, calling for lightning, for the sharp sting of retribution. And with a final look at the waiting ships, at my people's faces shining with fierce hope, at the men of the watch aiming their rifles, shooting at the first wave of Eli's crews . . . I know I can control it. I will direct the will of the storm with all my rage, but also my love.

I unleash.

Lightning cracks open the sky, casting Ennor in darkness and flashes. It strikes, hitting ship after ship, thunder booming and rolling, an ever-constant battle drum. I shove everything into it. Every piece of my pain, my heart, my soul and wish for the very world to tip over. I will it to be born anew. Then as the rain falls in a swift torrent, flooding the streets, flowing out in a river, forcing back the invaders, I breathe, leaving the storm to rumble on. To wipe the slate clean. I pull out my blade, bare my teeth and, with a cry of war, join Agnes in the fray.

The watch reaches the quay and Caden roars, surging forward, swinging with double swords at the very front. For a breathless heartbeat, I watch him in his truest form, a dancer with twin blades, effortlessly perfect in his execution. I realise how much he's been holding back in my training. Then I catch a rifle aimed at Agnes and rush for it and the man aiming and firing, thrusting up my blade so he shoots at the sky. He swears viciously and I feint left but sweep my foot out. He stumbles over it, cracking his boot against my ankle and I hiss in pain before slipping my blade under his ribs. His breath leaves him in a gurgle as his rifle drops, blood already pooling on his tongue as he looks up at me. I pull out the blade, wipe it on his jacket and kick him over, already moving for the next.

A few get past, but Caden takes down more than the rest of us, those twin blades flying in a ceaseless arc. Then I look up, and find a rifle aimed at my chest. Time slows as the gunpowder bursts in a cloud, as a bullet leaps from the barrel. But there's a flash of movement. Sember, with a wave of her hand, seems to . . . catch it. She grins at me, opening her fist and the bullet is a glittering, smoking coin. For a heartbeat I stare in wonder at the young woman before me. I realise then what she is – not a bodyguard for a spare heir, but a weapon. Skylan's weapon.

Then she turns, her thin whip of a sword cutting across another man of the watch. His eyes bulge in surprise as blood pours from his throat, before he slumps to the ground. Dead.

Sember blows me a kiss, then vanishes back into the fight and I see her again beside Heath, further along the quay, fighting as though they are one blade, one person. Military training, indeed. They're formidable.

I catch Eli out of the corner of my eye, pulling two men of the watch into shadow, their mouths open in a desperate howl. But I don't see where the shadow spits them back out. I'm already swiping at a shoulder of another man of the watch, the sudden slash of pain snagging his focus before Agnes finishes him.

'How many more?' Agnes says, breathing fast as she pulls me close, rifle fire cracking past my cheekbone.

'Too many to halt,' I reply, this time pulling Agnes towards me as more rifle fire crackles around us. 'They look like . . .'

'Renshaw's crew,' Agnes hisses, features darkening with hate. 'Her thugs.'

I grin at her, nodding to a pair of them climbing the steps for the quay. She returns my grin and we pounce. I drag them both back to the water's edge, back into the sea, and we topple over the brink. Lightning forks from the sky, showing the fear in their eyes in a flash, and I roar at them, more siren than girl. I cling to them both, forcing their heads below the waves. Then as Agnes guards the steps, kicking back their desperate, clawing hands, I pull them down further, deep into my world. My mother's world. The place that was stolen from her when Renshaw and her crew murdered her.

They cease their fighting, lungs spent, and I push them away, their bodies floating underwater. Then, with grim satisfaction, I dart back up to the surface, back to

Agnes and her waiting hand. Grasping it, she lifts me up and squeezes my arm in bitter understanding. Nothing will bring either of our mothers back. Not ever. But vengeance certainly soothes the bitter burn of what Renshaw did to mine.

There's a bellowing shriek, almost snatched by the driving rain, and a flash of red hair I know all too well. Renshaw. She's on a ship in the harbour, leaning over the railings, face puce as she calls for her crews to return. I watch her, blood heating in my veins, the call of revenge as sweet as a siren song, and I calculate the distance I would need to swim, the side of the ship I'd need to climb to reach her.

'You'll be shot down before you even get close,' Agnes says in my ear. 'Her crews are already retreating. They're leaving. And the watch, look.'

We hug the steps as men and women, the enemy, turn tail, running for their boats, for the sea, abandoning the isle as they're chased off it. I watch as women of the isles pick up the rifles of the fallen, screaming their rage, firing at their retreating backs.

Then I look up, finding Eli murmuring in Merryam's ear, her teeth bared in a snarl of hate. He nods once and she grips her blade as they step into a waiting shadow. I gasp, swivelling to look back at Renshaw's ship, and see the shadows move. They have gone to do what I could not.

Merryam steps out, right beside Renshaw. She grabs her shoulder and thrusts the blade upwards, deep beneath her ribs. Merryam locks eyes with Renshaw as her aunt blinks her shock, as she staggers. I see Merryam's lips move, and I know what she's saying. *You deserve this. This is for Seth. For me. For a life that should have been, after my mother died. For Mira and her mother. For the pain you have inflicted.* Renshaw kneels on the deck and all I can see is her red, coiling hair before Eli pulls Merryam back, and they vanish again.

I clutch Agnes's arm as my storm swirls viciously above us, lightning striking over and over, the wind lifting to a howl. It depletes me, but it also fuels me. Cools me. The fire in my heart, burning for so long, is finally smouldering. Too long have I waited for this, for a reckoning. Renshaw is dead and all the hate in her soul has gone. I expel a long-held breath, picturing my mother. Her kind, clever eyes. Her stories, her songs, her love of the sea. And I know she is with me now. She is with all of us in this moment.

Her death is avenged and the world is righted.

Those who have made it away from Ennor begin setting sail, limping from the harbour, joining the rest of the fleeing ships. But as those few straggling ships rejoin the decimated armada, further out, I realise which enemies did not come to shore, which of them were waiting until they could seize the victory the watch would have won for them.

The ruling council of three. The Rexilium brothers, safe out there aboard their ornate warship. Now they sail for Penscalo, for the safe harbour they do not deserve to claim.

A cry goes up from Ennor, a victory and a mourning, and it catches in my chest, tears rising up my throat in a gasp.

'Have we – have we won?' I ask Agnes as more of the enemy stream past us, desperate to escape the islanders and our wrath. We venture up the steps, on to the quay strewn with bodies, and Caden is standing there, drenched in enemy blood. He smiles at us, flicking red in an arc from his swords. Then he draws in a breath, beginning a chant.

'Together! Together!'

The answering cry rises across Ennor, and Agnes sobs as we cling to one another. Kai appears, cradling a broken, bloodied arm, then an exhausted Eli, Mer propping him up on one side. I rush to Eli's side, taking Mer's place. I squeeze her shoulder, tipping my forehead to rest against hers in silent thanks. The kind that cannot be shared with mere words. Then I draw Eli into my arms as the rain continues to fall, holding him close, not wanting to let him go.

I close my eyes, feeding my senses out into the storm, sending it after those stray ships. Sending it to harry and taunt them.

'You are spectacular,' he says against my lips. 'The storm, your rage . . . I'm in awe of you. I love you, Mira Boscawen.'

I look up into those star-flecked eyes. His uninjured

arm rests round my lower back, pulling me in closer, and I brush my lips against his. 'And I am completely in love with you, Elijah Tresillian.'

He smiles, kissing me hard, and I laugh, kissing him back. We survived this storm. We will not meet in the stars just yet. I pull back enough to brace his side, grinning up at him through salt-tangled hair as all around us the cheers continue.

We walk through the smoking streets, not believing at first that it's real. That we've done it. That we drove them away from Ennor, that we saved so many of our people.

Victory belongs to us.

Chapter 41

Mira

'WE MUST GET TO THE castle,' Kai says. 'Take the wounded to the healers. Call a meet.'

Eli nods his agreement then winces. 'Kai, your arm...'

Kai laughs humourlessly, then bites his lip. 'It can be set.'

'I'm sorry, my friend. I'm too drained to traverse with you to find a healer,' Eli says, swallowing. Caden moves to prop him up on his other side as he sags suddenly. I stagger before Caden and I find our balance and he takes the weight.

'I'll take him up the hill, Mira,' Caden says, looking down at me, flecks of enemy blood dotted like freckles over his cheeks and forehead. 'Let me be his strength.'

I nod gratefully, relinquishing Eli's weight to Caden. 'You're burned out,' I say quietly, worry gnawing at me as Eli's eyes close. 'Please tell me you're not wounded as well.'

Eli shakes his head. 'Not wounded.'

We limp up the hill. Merryam begins passing the message among the people in the streets, to bring the wounded that can move inside the castle, to stabilise those who cannot and send a runner. The rain lessens and I tilt my face to the thunderous clouds still lingering, wishing it to calm. To disperse. To leave us completely and trail the enemy ships.

The storm does my bidding and I walk up the hill with Pearl and Agnes, tired and spent, spots cluttering my vision as I sway slightly, but with victory printed on my heart. Yet in my mind the greatest threat still lingers. The Rexilium brothers, the ruling council of three. The men with the same strange magic as Eli, who have controlled us and divided us for too long. Who would still yet sweep over the continent, claiming each territory for themselves.

Someone begins singing our song again. The one we sang as the storm of ships came to wipe us out. I sniff, tears spilling from my eyes as the sunlight breaks through the clouds, and the rain ceases. All around, the melodious voices of home, of my islands, of my people join together. An old folk song of withstanding, of hope. A song that unites us as we join arms and march up the hill to Ennor Castle.

In the formal dining hall we gather, the thirteen of us, along with a few others. Those representing Penrith, Ennor, Rosevear are now joined by Hillary and her head hunter, Lessifer, from Coven Septern, as well as Sember and Heath from Skylan. Skanni and Fey, Brielle informs me, left on the back of their drakes, harrying the last few wyvern before them as they flew back to the Spines and their coven. We owe them a great debt. Just the thought of proud Fey, here in our skies, leaves a lump in my throat. I vow to travel to the Spines when I can, when this is all over, to thank her in person.

Gathered round this table are humans, witches, creatures. Tanith is present, although washed out and unfocused still, despite the healer witches' best efforts. She needs rest, but we need her presence, her wisdom. Her voice. Now, more than ever, we need *every* voice.

'We've driven them back, but it can only be temporary,' Kai says, fidgeting with the bandage bracing his broken arm against his chest as he speaks. 'And the damage, the losses . . .'

'Caden and Merryam's crews have begun the count,' Eli says, holding a bandage to his arm as well, but soaked in apothecarist-made ointment to heal the scorching of his skin. 'The apothecary in town is leading the healing along with the Malefant's best healers. I have sent for Howden, to ask if he will travel from Port Trenn. As many as possible will be saved and healed.'

'We must discuss the power vacuum,' Hillary says, rapping her knuckles on the table, her face a portrait of harsh lines and angles, ruthless and domineering as ever, without having to raise her voice. 'If we intend to do something about making this victory more than temporary, then there needs to be a redistribution of power.'

'Is that all you're interested in?' Lowri says softly.

Hillary's gaze narrows sharply. 'It's simply following a coup through to its natural conclusion. It can be bloody and drawn out, or it can be quick and relatively painless. As soon as the ruling council is dispatched, their watch and guard will be leaderless. Lawless.'

I shudder, picturing more of these arguments for control as would-be rulers of Arnhem and the isles fight over the prize of leadership. I picture my people suffering in the meantime, and perhaps forever, if we are unsuccessful. I raise my chin. The watch, the ruling council, the whole lot of them do not deserve to rule us. We need fairness. We need a voice.

'What about the merchants?' Eli says. 'We know they will support whoever treats them the most favourably. And they bring wealth to our shores, both from exports and imports. Without them, Arnhem will fester. We would be at the mercy of our neighbours, most likely Leicena or potentially Skylan.'

All eyes turn on Prince Heath and he shrugs. 'Lord Tresillian has a point. My father would see this territory as a prize indeed. Best not give him any reason to send his ships as well. He'll be in a foul enough mood when he learns of the campaign the ruling council launched here, most likely to continue along the Straits if they hadn't been beaten back.'

'He speaks honest and true,' Bryn agrees, nodding. 'We would be a prize for the taking, a strategic piece of Arnhem that others may covet. The ruling council must go – that's a certainty. The watch must be leashed. Laws must be passed that protect the interests of all and that protect the isles. But will that mean a new ruling council? A new set of three?'

Silence stretches, then everyone talks at once. I don't open my mouth to create more noise. Instead, all I can think about is the sea. Rosevear. The life that Eli showed me is possible here on Ennor, with investment, with choices. He offered a chance of a future unburdened by hunger, by worry. Where every islander could rebuild and live in peace. Where we could be who we were always meant to be. Where I could swim in the ocean and be free. I take a breath, looking up to see that Eli is watching me with a smile. As the others discuss power and the aftermath, all I see is home. All I see is him. I smile back at him, and sink into my chair. I do not want power. I want the freedom to carve my own path, same as I've always wanted.

And now I've found that path, right where I began.

The conversation dies down, and there is one voice that holds sway above the rest. One with a vision for a different kind of world.

'You speak of power and rules and laws, but you forget that's where you started,' Tanith says, her voice like smoke, and everyone strains to listen. 'I have seen your lives from above. I have seen the way humans exist like a candle – you burn so brilliantly, then you are gone. Witches, you seek gain for yourselves. Do not try to argue otherwise; it is not in your nature. Well, maybe not all of you . . .' She smiles at Brielle and Lowri. 'Around this table we are making history. This moment is unlike anything known before. Humans, witches, creatures, all here together, ready to talk. Keep your ruling council so the merchants and the other territories and all the others with their weapons and their small minds do not swoop in to claim the isles. But create a new ruling council, one that reflects what we see here today. One that respects all beings that exist here.'

'Human, creature, witch . . .' Brielle says quietly, folding her arms. Awed silence settles over the room as everyone sits back, contemplating this. 'A new trio. Every being represented. Laws created fairly that don't seek to damage or curtail anyone, but to maintain equilibrium. And peace. All in favour?'

Every hand is raised. And, just like that, Arnhem has the potential for a new future.

Two days later, after the worst of our wounds have been healed by the witches and the apothecaries, we assemble the people we have. As I search the faces of those that travel with us, I realise it may not be enough. Not if Hillary's high witches cannot convince the other covens in Highborn to join us in creating a new ruling council. The Malefant of Coven Septern has stayed with us while her witches traverse back to rally the other established covens. All except Coven Mereen, of which she murmurs of retribution, of torching until even the stone is scorched and raw. We will ensure Highborn bends to new rulers. Fairer ones. People who are not interested in conquest and expansion.

The rest of us move in for the final blow. The strike that will end the ruling council for good. We pile on to the boats that are left, sailing for Penscalo. Lowri stands beside me, Brielle and all of Eli's inner circle. Tanith has remained behind with Joby to raise the alarm if a sudden ambush occurs. Even Nova sits without a twitch at Lowri's side, staring at the horizon. It's a journey of hope and, when we land, word has already gone out. There are people there to greet us. To join us. Even a few scattered merchants are there to trade with the islanders. It seems the last of the watch have holed up in the prison, guarding it like a fort.

'Not everyone fares well under the watch's rule,' a merchant with a mining interest in Valstra says, puffing on a long pipe, the collar of his jacket pulled up to hide his features as he walks alongside us through the town. 'The metals I supply for their weapon factories in the north no longer carry the same value. They pit us against one another for a better price. And that's after having to pay the toll to Skylan to cross through the Straits.'

'Then you would welcome negotiations with a new ruling council?' Eli asks.

'One under which we prosper, yes.' He nods, a puff of smoke pouring from between his lips. 'I shall discuss with my fellows.'

As the looming prison comes into view, all I can think of is the Trials. My fellow competitors who fell. The people cheering in the crowds. I set my jaw, keeping my blade close. So many deaths. A distraction to please a crowd, while they robbed us of our freedom. I can still hear it echoing in my ears. Still feel the thud of each heartbeat as I fought the morgawr for their sport. And, before that, the hangings. The day my father and Bryn were led out to the gallows. How powerless I felt, how small, in the face of such a mighty force as them.

And all my fury ignites once more. I remember how the watch captured my father on the beach that day, which now feels like a lifetime ago. How they captured me, threatened Agnes's life. I wish I could remember my father's features, his voice. I wish that he wasn't just a shadow moving through that day in my memory. The most vivid part is the scarlet coats of the watch, pouring like blood over the beach as they arrived to take him away. I shudder. I owe them something, I realise. My vengeance.

So long ago, it feels now, I bound myself to Eli with a bargain mark, agreeing to protect Rosevear, to seek revenge on those that murdered my father. We have had our revenge on Captain Renshaw. And Seth is dead – Renshaw used him for her own gain just as she used my mother. Now is the time to pull the watch out at the very root of their power here in the Fortunate Isles.

Now is the time for that promise to Rosevear to finally be fulfilled.

We surge through the streets unchallenged, reaching the prison, and with Brielle and Caden leading the charge, the few guards left defending it are cut down, or turn and run. We walk in, triumph echoing in every footfall as we sweep into the courtyard. The Rexilium brothers are standing on the platform, where once my father stood with a noose looped round his throat. And, as though history repeats, Captain Spencer Leggan, the captain of the watch in the Fortunate Isles, who first took my father and Bryn from the beach on Rosevear and sentenced them to hang, stands before them.

CHAPTER 42

Mira

'HOW CONVENIENT,' BRIELLE HISSES AT my side. 'Four enemies all gathered in one place.'

Captain Leggan's lip curls as he regards her. 'You always were delusional. What have they told you? That they'll create a better world? Grow up, Bri. Look around you. No one wants something better – everyone is out for themselves.'

'You would think that,' I cut in. 'Always been out for yourself, haven't you?'

'I just despise islander vermin.' He sniffs. 'A better world is an orderly world. Magic must be controlled, contained, and your islanders were stopping trade with your unlawful activities. The ruling council want Arnhem to be great, to be *mighty*, but you just want chaos. Well, look around. That's what you've got.' He looks again at Brielle, spreading his arms wide. 'You think as a witch, a *hunter*, that the creatures of this world will accept you? That humans will allow you to live with the power you have, unfettered? They're afraid of power.'

'In the wrong hands, yes,' Eli says. 'Power in your hands has sown much fear.'

'Indeed,' Tiberius Rexilium interjects with an indulgent smile. 'But now you're all gathered here in one place. It is convenient, I agree, Hunter. Excellent choice of phrase. You needn't fear us; we are benevolent rulers. If you follow our laws, we will care for you all.'

'Even now, you believe you have the upper hand,' Hillary Tresillian says with a small shake of her head. 'You believe you can best us? That Arnhem would still bow to you?'

Tiberius's gaze narrows. 'Cut off the source of *your* power, and what do you have, witch? Nothing. You are nothing without magic, without monsters.'

'Control.' Hillary smiles coldly. 'It's always been about control, hasn't it?'

'And expansion,' a voice says from the side of the courtyard. Every head swivels, gazes raking the shadows as Rue steps forward, arms crossed. 'But at what cost, brothers?'

'Brothers?' Brielle breathes, eyes widening. 'Rue, you're related to them?'

He nods his head. 'Ambassador and half-brother. Not worthy of sitting on a throne, but always useful.'

'How did I not see it before . . .?' Brielle says, looking between him and the other Rexilium brothers, surprise giving way to something akin to sadness.

Rue takes a step towards her. 'I should have told you. I nearly did, that night in the forest in Lorva. I nearly told you everything.'

Brielle shakes her head, opening and closing her mouth, as though unsure what to say.

'Useful until now, it seems. Traitor,' Otho hisses from the right side of Tiberius, knuckles turning white where he grips his hands into tight fists.

'He may still wish to redeem himself,' Tiberius says calmly. 'Rue? Bind them.'

Nothing happens. I glance over at Rue, who continues to stare at his brothers, arms crossed. When I look back at the platform, all three brothers are staring at him, aghast. Someone chuckles quietly and I can't help the smile spreading across my face.

'Shame. I really believed you were worthy of the Rexilium name,' Tiberius says. 'Did we not bring you with us here, to this new land? No matter . . .'

A coil of shadow springs from his palm, splitting and darting towards us. I brace myself for that deep darkness to thread round me, to claw for my throat, to squeeze the air from my lungs, when a creature leaps in front of us.

Nova.

But not just Nova. Several familiars, all black fur and hungry eyes and claws. And where shadow hits them, it simply dissipates.

'Do not absorb too much, any of you!' Lowri cries, stepping forward. I grin as the Rexilium brothers recoil, aghast. The witches of Coven Septern may have returned to Arnhem, but their familiars remained with us. And once Lowri convinced them of the plan . . . they agreed to feed. To stand before the men with shadow magic and absorb what they could.

Between us all, we are hungry enough for shadow alone, Nova says, and I feel her purr of delight reverberate through my bones. I know Lowri and Brielle can hear her too, and Hillary. *We will not become grimalkin. Do not worry. We will not become what these brothers created in their world from their greed.*

'So grimalkin *were* like you, before they became . . . them,' Lowri says quietly to herself, and I almost don't catch it. She turns to Eli, murmuring, and his eyes widen.

Then Tiberius is on his feet, Otho and Nero rising to stand beside him. 'Enough of this! You are undeserving. You cannot take—'

Oh, but we can . . .

Nova vaults for Otho as the other familiars leap for his brothers and the men's stifled shrieks ring out as a tempest of shadow and magic forms on the platform, enveloping them. Lowri and Brielle look on, stony-faced, as the familiars feed. I gasp in awe and horror as the tempest subsides, leaving the familiars with smoky sheens surrounding them, and the Rexilium brothers pale as parchment, scored with deep wrinkles and old, weeping eyes.

Rue steps forward and Captain Leggan, eyes darting between the platform, us and Rue, scurries backwards and dives through a door that leads into the prison. Caden sighs, signalling for Mer and Pearl to follow, and I turn to Rue as he opens his arms to address us. 'With your leave, I will take my brothers back to our world to face judgment. Long have they escaped the repercussions of their actions there.'

'And what will your fate be? Will you be punished as well?' Eli asks. 'I have seen what they did in your world. My father's world. The shadow they cast over the city of Fallow. The fog.'

Rue's smile is pained. 'I will accept whatever fate the Society in Fallow deems appropriate. I may not have aided them directly, but I did not stand in their way. Until now.' He turns to Brielle and she steps towards him, their eyes locked. 'If nothing else, I regret not getting to know you, Brielle Tresillian. I wish we'd had more moments together, if I had been lucky, maybe even a lifetime. But I will have to remember you as you are, here, in this world. And I in mine.'

Brielle reaches up, brushing her knuckles across his cheekbone, eyes never leaving his. 'If there's a way, I will find it. I won't forget you.'

Rue breathes deeply, leaning his head into her touch before she drops her hand and he walks towards the Rexilium brothers. 'A final portal, it seems. A fitting end.' Then, as I reach for Eli's hand, gripping it, Rue sketches out a portal, a doorway into another world. Their world. I see a glimpse of a city, of a cloud of darkness, slowly dripping over bent and crooked buildings.

Then Rue flicks his wrist towards his three brothers, smoke and shadow wrapping round their wrists, attached to him like a rope. They gasp, trying to resist, but Rue pulls them forward and, with a final longing look at Brielle, he removes the Rexilium brothers from our world.

The portal closes, leaving us in silence. Then Hillary claps her hands, the sound like a bell. 'It is time for us to form a new ruling council,' she says, eyes blazing as she searches our faces. 'A new age is upon us. One of witch, creature and human. Who will be the chosen three?'

Chapter 43

Lowri

'DID YOU ONLY SIDE WITH us so you could gain power for yourself?' Lowri says, not hiding her disgust as the truth dawns on her. 'You stayed on the isles to ensure a place on the new ruling council, didn't you? For a moment, I thought you might have changed, that you might have grown a heart, that you came here to protect us, that you *remembered* you have three children of your own.'

'You think I don't consider you, Caden and Brielle in this arrangement?' the Malefant hisses, narrowing her eyes. 'You really and truly believe I would work against you in these times? I ally with you for the good of all witches, and for the good of House Tresillian. That *includes* the three of you.'

'Spoken like a true Malefant,' Lowri says, shaking her head. 'Not a mother.'

She spins on her heel, needing to get out of the oppressive walls of the watch's prison. Her heart fractures inside her chest, even as she tells herself she doesn't care. She has her own coven now, her own home. She *does not care*. Even if her mother only stayed to ensure her own interests were secure, even if she doesn't love as a mother ought to love.

'Lowri, stop!' her mother calls after her, rushing to catch up. Lowri ducks through a doorway, pulling the door closed in her wake, stepping back into the entrance courtyard of the prison.

Hillary utters a witch word, the door flying open on its hinges as she marches through it. Lowri turns to look but doesn't stop. 'I don't need a lecture about how the coven doesn't involve itself,' she calls over her shoulder, barely breaking pace. 'By not interfering, by standing back because it suits you and the coven, you were *complicit*! You have blood on your hands, same as them.'

'I know,' her mother says, and Lowri hears her sigh before she says again, quietly, 'I know.'

Lowri pauses in the courtyard, whirling on her, pulse throbbing in her ears. 'And now you're only here to further the interests of the coven and yourself. You choose to side against the ruling council *now*, when your own interests could be compromised by this vacuum of power, as you call it. You tried to kill Amma! The only protection Eli and Caden ever had!'

Hillary's lip trembles, but she stands firm. 'I was wrong. I can see that now. When you left, then Brielle . . .' She looks at the floor, as though trying to find the words. 'One moment, I was so sure of my path, of my role as Malefant. But when you both defected, when you stole from the coven so blatantly, I began questioning everything.'

'So this isn't just about what Lessifur discovered in those factories in the north? Or about the law the ruling council were planning to put in place?' Brielle asks from behind her, coming into the courtyard. She folds her arms across her chest, staring Hillary down, Caden standing beside her.

'Or about you making a play for power if we successfully opposed them? If we won?' he adds. 'As clearly now we have done . . .'

Hillary looks at all three of her children and throws her hands in the air. 'That you believe I would be so short-sighted, so devious—'

'I believe you would dress it up in your mind as doing it for the good of the coven,' Lowri says. 'Like you always have. As you always will.'

Hillary says nothing for a moment, pinching the bridge of her nose. 'I owe you all an apology. Sincerely. I have put the coven before everything, before all of you. And I've lost too much, sacrificed everything. And for what?'

Caden glances at Lowri and raises his eyebrows. 'Do you expect us to be a happy family now? To believe you've suddenly changed?'

'No,' she says with a small smile. 'But I offered up my coven to protect Ennor, and all of you, in the aftermath. I stood with you against the tyranny of the ruling council, as I should have done all along. And I ask that I have a seat on the new ruling council to ensure that witches are represented. So that our kind are never at risk again.'

'What about Eli?' Lowri says. 'What about *his* apology?'

Hillary raises one precise eyebrow. 'What exactly do I have to apologise to my nephew for? Have I not kept him safe, clothed and fed with the contracts I offer him and his crews?'

'His mother, your *sister*, died,' Brielle says quietly. 'You offer less to him than you do to me. And he's blood.'

Hillary tightens her fists at her sides. 'That is untrue, Brielle. You are witch, and adopting you was the honourable choice, the *right* choice.'

'I know it wasn't out of love. I don't need to hear your reasons,' Brielle cuts in. 'But you should reflect on your relationship with your sister's son. And how you kept him from walking through worlds to find his father by withholding the very pendant he needed to find his way there.'

'Another thing I did for his own good.'

'I'm afraid none of us view it that way,' Caden says stonily.

Hillary shrugs. 'I can see my journey here may have been wasted, but we will be here. Coven Septern will stand beside you. And, Brielle?'

'Yes?'

'Lowri has made her choice clear. But if you ever wish to return to the coven, you would be welcomed back. Lowri, the door is always open to you as well.'

'Thank you, but we have formed our own coven.

Coven Ennor. One based on trust, and integrity,' Brielle says, staring down at the woman who adopted her, not out of love, but out of a recognition of potential. In that moment, Lowri is so proud of her sister, the young woman she has become, that her heart strains against the cage of her ribs. 'But I thank you for the offer.'

'Fine,' Hillary says, voice clipped and devoid of emotion. 'Then all that is left here is to form the new ruling council. I will speak with your leaders, and we will convene. But, mark me, there will be a seat for a witch on the ruling council of Arnhem. And it will be mine.'

CHAPTER 44

Brielle

'DO YOU TRUST HER?' LOWRI asks later, after they've returned to Ennor. 'Our mother, I mean.'

Brielle considers, leaning on the ramparts at the very top of Ennor Castle, looking out to sea. 'In the wider sense, or as one of the future rulers of Arnhem?'

'The latter,' Lowri says with a small chuckle, leaning her elbows next to Brielle. 'I think we can both agree on the answer to the former.'

'I . . .' Brielle sighs, running a hand over her face. The past five days since they left Penscalo has been a lot: from ensuring that Dreska and Inesh rested, a little too close to burnout from their efforts in ensuring the wards held, to helping Caden organise new crews to patrol the waters in case any enemy fleets decided to take advantage of their weakened state, to just absorbing it all. She feels the edges of her own strength wane. And yet she's still standing tall, continuing to be the pillar that is needed, for every one of them. 'I believe she will be fair and advocate well for all witches. But she must be tempered with two other strong leaders – those who represent creatures and humans – or we will find a different kind of imbalance in Arnhem. One that favours witches.' She eyes Lowri. 'I do not like the idea of a group that holds so much power in their veins also holding a territory in their hands.'

'Agreed,' Lowri says with a nod. 'Well, it'd be just like the Rexilium brothers.'

'Exactly. But who would be a match for Hillary Tresillian?'

Lowri places her cheek on the back of her hand, turning to her sister. 'That feels rhetorical.'

'Perhaps it is.'

'What will you do now, Brielle?'

Brielle bites her lip, then smiles at her sister.

'You want to get back on the road? Find your next assignment?'

'I can't help it. It's my whole life. From when my birth mother died to now, all I've known is training and assignments. Being a hunter. It's what I know; it's who I am. It's my bones and flesh and breath.'

Lowri is quiet for a moment, contemplating. 'What if we, as coven leaders, set you an assignment, then? Something for the good of the coven, but also for you. Something that will help you now. To get over that man . . . Rue.'

Rue. His name pierces the tender place between her ribs, sliding in like an uninvited guest. Perhaps if she'd had the chance to get to know him, she wouldn't have found much to like. He was a Rexilium brother, after all, even though he was a half-brother. But, if she's honest with herself, if she listens to that whispered voice in the back of her mind, she knows that wouldn't be the case. His gaze held meaning, his words landed true and, of all the people she has met in this world, he is the only one to whom she would have given her heart.

But now he is in Eli's father's world and she is here, in hers. And Brielle Tresillian is many things: hunter, witch, explorer. She has never lingered in one place for too long or dwelled on a life that could have been.

'What I need is purpose,' she says decisively. 'A plan, and coin for the road.'

'Yes?' Lowri says, straightening out as Brielle does, as her tone shifts. 'What is your plan, Hunter?'

Brielle sets her sights on the horizon, running her fingertips over the blade handles in the sash across her chest. Hunter, yes. She's a hunter. And she has fledglings now, hunters who must be trained. 'I will travel to Skylan with Sember and Heath, taking Dreska and Inesh with me,' she says with a nod. 'I will check on Kell. Then, if the court has no need of our services, we will head north. To the Spines. I have a feeling the fledglings and I still have much to learn there. The knowledge of the drake-riding covens is different from ours. And we will listen for murmurings of wraiths. After saving Inesh and Dreska, I know that is the right path. And we must build our coven.'

'Form an alliance with the witches of the Spines,' Lowri agrees with a nod. 'Bring back wyvern blood for my spellwork. And witches for me to train.'

'And you, Lor?' Brielle asks. 'What will you do now?'

Lowri grins. 'I'm going to stay here on Ennor. I will instruct Inesh and Dreska when you return with them from the Spines and, in the meantime, research the ways of drakes. Tanith will be needed in the days and months ahead, but I want to find a way for her to exist both as drake and in her human form. I wish for her to experience the joy of flight, but keep her memories for when she transforms back.'

'You wish to give her freedom,' Brielle says softly.

Lowri nods. 'I know what it is to live with clipped wings. It's a worthy aim for the first spellworking of our coven. Well, that, and helping Eli return to his father's world. The instrument that Eli's father, Isaiah, created there was quite something. Just think of the possibilities, Bri, the research I could conduct! A coven with links to the magic and spellwork of another world.'

Brielle meets Sember and Heath in the kitchens, where Sember has taken charge of the cooking. Amassing a small number of willing hands, they stand in a line, kneading bread, chattering and laughing as she swoops among them like a bird, full of encouragements. Heath, she has relegated to washing-up duty, where he complains loudly to all who will listen, but still continues.

Brielle notices the small smile he holds just for Sember when she admonishes him, their bickering flying back and forth across the vast room.

When Sember notices the hunter leaning against the doorway, she claps her hands, summoning a tray to be made with bread and cheese and a strong mug of tea. She ushers Brielle to the table, where Sember has also placed other slightly bewildered guests of the castle, and takes a seat beside her.

'Now, Hunter, I know you will be inundated with requests for your services—'

'But Sember here is going to bat them all away as soon as they get within five feet of you,' Heath says from the sink, arms in a bowl of bubbles.

Sember's jaw drops in false shock. 'You make it seem as if I'm such a difficult elbows-out sort of person!'

'You? Never,' he says. 'You wouldn't put a prince to pot-washing duty, no, no, not you . . .'

'Ignore him, Brielle. He's only grumpy because he stained his favourite shirt.'

'My only *clean* shirt!'

'You see what I have to put up with?' Sember rolls her eyes. 'Anyway, I formally offer you an assignment, Brielle Tresillian. We have need of your services in the Skylan court. Although it is a *little* different from what you are used to dealing with.'

'I accept,' Brielle says, breaking apart a piece of bread. 'I was hoping to travel there and see Kell before moving on.'

'Excellent,' Sember says with a firm nod. 'You see, Heath? Not so hard.'

'Just wait until you tell her what the assignment really is,' Heath murmurs. 'And then see if she bolts like the rest of the witches you've tried unsuccessfully to hire.'

Brielle sits back, takes a swig of tea and fixes Sember with an appraising look. 'What's the nature of the assignment?'

'Well, Hunter, it concerns an ambassador, another court and an unexpected disappearance . . .'

Chapter 45

Mira

A WEEK LATER, WHEN ELI'S magic is replenished, he, Tanith and I traverse to Highborn. The witches are everywhere, the watch are few and, as we enter the palace, I realise how vital it is that a ruling council is swiftly established. There are merchants lurking outside the court, their own personal guard surrounding them. Without the power of the witches from multiple Arnhem covens to keep them in check, I'm sure some of them would have tried to form a new ruling council themselves.

After four hours of debate, where merchants speak, where the witches send their Malefants, and Tanith and I represent the interest of creatures, the new ruling council of three is chosen. Hillary Tresillian will represent witches and the covens. Tanith will represent the interests of creatures. And a merchant called Gorran Lisk, a man with an interest in the stability of Arnhem, will represent humans. His gruff acceptance of the role (without pomp or ego) and his promise to be a caretaker of the isles and help us prosper if we agree to no longer harry the merchant vessels wins my vote. I thank him with a solemn handshake afterwards, and he bows over my hand, muttering his humble thanks. I look to the three of them – witch, creature, human – and hope we have done the right thing. Only time will tell.

I return to Rosevear the next day with Eli by my side. Kai is ready to take up his place once more as our leader, our strength. And I know now, deep in the marrow of my bones, where I belong. Where I want to be.

Rosevear.

The isle I love, my home, my heart. Cut me and I still bleed all the colours of Rosevear, the navy blue of the surrounding sea, the bright yellow of the gorse flower, the gentle mauve of the heather. And now also the shades of ruin, of charcoal and burning and smoulder. As my people and I land back on the beach and wander through the ransacked village, it is no more than rubble. No more than a collection of past terrors.

A tear traces the shape of my left cheekbone, sorrow cracking open my heart afresh, but Eli's hand remains in mine the whole time. 'No one can take this from you now, Mira. And I'm by your side.'

I nod, turning to him, and he dips his head for an unhurried kiss. 'Thank you. I needed to hear that.'

'My strength is yours, whenever you have a need.'

'And mine yours,' I say, leaning into him briefly,

before we continue up the hill to see how the meeting house has fared.

There is so much to do, but we begin to rebuild. All through the spring and the summer, all the way into autumn, we rebuild and we rally. The fisherfolk go out, landing their catch. I help mend the nets and Eli sends builders and craftsfolk to aid us. There are supplies sent from Highborn – Gorran Lisk's signature on each shipment of pearly glass sheets for our windows – fabric for our backs and sails, even musical instruments so we may begin to enjoy our free time and find some peace and healing.

I visit Penrith and discover the same there, the people slowly turning the tide on their ill fortune. We get together as we used to, celebrating the harvest scratched from our fields, lighting a bonfire and singing folk songs late into the night. This time, the people of Ennor and Penscalo join us, and I swear they could hear our voices in Port Trenn, all joined as one. The Fortunate Isles.

In months, we have habitable homes. Built one at a time. The meeting house is salvaged, the stores replenished for the long winter months. All because of the bargain I made. All because I followed my heart and trusted, even after I had been betrayed by another.

Captain Leggan eludes us still. Gone to ground somewhere, possibly rallying support for a comeback. Let him burn in his self-righteous bitterness. I am one of the seven still, my people around me. The watch didn't break us. We are home.

Each evening, as the sun wanes, I wander up to my father's grave marker. I sit by and look out at the sea, sometimes calm and temperate, sometimes frothing and vicious. Always fickle. The sea has a heart that is never entirely at rest, just like the heart that beats inside my own chest. I wait until shadows begin to rake the cliff, until Eli steps out from one. He comes to share the sunset with me, as he does every day. It has become the time I look forward to the most, when my soul is whole again, as the dusk dances across the sky.

He hunkers down to sit beside me, brushing a kiss across my temple before I turn my head, his lips finding mine. I lean into the kiss, his scent enveloping me as his arms gather me in. I trace his jawline with my fingertips, lingering in this moment. When we part, I stay in his arms, warmth spreading as a glow from my chest. I have never felt more grounded, more loved and whole than with him. 'How did it go today?'

I smile. Always the same question, the same kiss. Our new routine. And, today, I hand him a bun studded with apple pieces. 'Agnes's first batch of apple buns, from her new bakery. Her father is enjoying the building work still. Says he's found his calling.'

Eli laughs softly, accepting the bun, then breaking it in half to pass back to me. We eat in silence for a few minutes, watching a gull swoop out to sea. 'There are ripples and murmurings across the continent. Unrest. Brielle remains with Dreska and Inesh; they will not be returning to Ennor just yet.'

'Will it come here?' I ask, turning to him.

He shrugs. 'Perhaps. The Malefant is aware. Lowri is keeping her in check, reminding her that she speaks for all. Not just her coven.'

'Magic, then.'

'Yes,' he says. 'Magic is showing up everywhere in humans. A gift and a curse in equal measure.'

'Power to be controlled . . .'

'Or contained. Or, if it was up to some, exploited.'

I sigh and lean into him. 'All I want is peace now. For Rosevear and my people. For all of us to be safe.'

He draws his arm round me. 'And you have it. I am keeping a careful watch. What happened before will not happen again in Arnhem.'

'But on the continent?'

He hesitates. 'You know as well as I the hearts of man and witch. Which brings me to something . . . Lowri has been researching. Hillary granted her access to the coven libraries in Highborn and she believes she may have found a counter spell. For the binding placed on your memories.'

My heart stops in my chest. 'My . . . my father?'

'Yes,' Eli breathes. 'She needs to research a little longer, but there might be a way to restore your memories of him.'

I choke, turning to meet his gaze. 'I haven't dared to dream, dared to hope . . .'

'Too much was taken from you. We cannot bring back those we love, but, if she can find a way, we will restore this one thing.'

'Thank you,' I whisper, sinking once more into his arms. Hope flickers suddenly in my heart, the embers of a dying fire I had believed were long since lost.

We watch as the sun sets, a rosy haze drifting over the sea, and I burrow deeper into his warmth. Whatever comes next, I realise, I have this. Him. Us. Two souls created from the same imperfect whole. Someone to hold my hand amid the night and stars, someone to return to. My anchor in a storm. We will face it all together.

They say we are reckless,

That we fought and plundered and killed.

And yes, it's true, what they say.

But I ask you to search deeper.

To uncover the tale beneath.

And when you search the horizon, when the salt breeze keens, when your heart fills with calm and hope for tomorrow, know what it is.

That you've found what we fought for.

Freedom.

Acknowledgements

Completing this series has been so full of joy. A whole fantasy series, written, published and in the hands of readers! This has always been my dream and there are so many people that have supported me in making this a reality. Firstly, to you, the reader. Thank you for following Mira, Brielle and Lowri's journey over the course of these books. Receiving your messages and meeting readers in person remains one of the best things about publishing my stories.

To the librarians, booksellers, bloggers, influencers and social media darlings, thank you for pressing my books into readers' hands. Thank you for championing them and caring so very much about the world of books and reading. Without you, none of this would be possible, you keep the literary world spinning.

To my wonderful Mads, thank you. Your enthusiasm, care, you-ness is infectious, I am so incredibly proud to have you as my agent. I was so nervous all those years ago, pitching this series to you, but you didn't hesitate.

You've been my greatest champion and advocate from day one and never wavered. I wish every author had a Mads in their corner. And to my team at DHA, you're all the very best. Thank you for your time, your diligence, your patience.

To Megan Reid, editor extraordinaire, thank you for being my creative partner. For instantly loving this series and fighting for it, again and again. To the team at Harper Fire, what a brilliant journey it's been. From influencer boxes with items sourced from local creators on the Isles of Scilly, to events bursting with enthusiastic readers, it's been a dream experience publishing these books with you. Particular thanks go to Cally Poplak, Nick Lake, Charlotte Winstone, Rosie Catcheside, Aisling O'Mahony, Iona Richards, Matthew Kelly and to Nico Delort for another stunning cover illustration.

To my US publishing team at HarperCollins, thank you for bringing this series to readers on the other side of the Atlantic. Particular thanks go to; Karen Chaplin for swooping in and ensuring this series was published with such fanfare, Rosemary Brosnan, Lisa Calcasola, Anna Ravenelle, Tim Smith, Shona McCarthy, Erin DeSalvatore, Allison Wientraub, Andrea Vandergrift and David Curtis. You're all integral and I cannot thank you enough.

Thanks go to my translation publishers for picking up this series and publishing it with such passion and dedication. Seeing this series translated in different languages has been a real highlight.

And last but certainly never the least, to my family. Rosie and Izzy, this whole series is for you. And to Joe for always being the very best partner in every way, I love you all so completely. And to my wider family and friends, for supporting us, for your love and enthusiasm for my books, I am so incredibly lucky and thankful. What a dream team.